PHIL RICKMAN

NIGHT AFTER NIGHT

Corvus

An imprint of Atlantic Books Ltd

Ormond House

26-27 Boswell Street

London

WC1N 3JZ

www.corvus-books.co.uk

CORVUS

First published in hardback in Great Britain in 2014 by Corvus,
an imprint of Atlantic Books Ltd.

This paperback edition published in Great Britain in 2015 by Corvus,
an imprint of Atlantic Books Ltd.

10 9 8 7 6 5 4 3 2 1

A CIP catalogue record for this book is available from the British Library.

Paperback ISBN: 978 0 85789 872 2
E-book ISBN: 978 0 85789 871 5

Printed and bound by CPI Group (UK) Ltd, Croydon, CR0 4YY

NIGHT AFTER NIGHT

Phil Rickman lives on the Welsh border where he writes and presents the book programme *Phil the Shelf* on BBC Radio Wales. He is the acclaimed author of *The Heresy of Dr Dee*, *The Bones of Avalon* and the Merrily Watkins series. Visit his website at: www.philrickman.co.uk

Also by Phil Rickman

THE MERRILY WATKINS SERIES

The Wine of Angels
Midwinter of the Spirit
A Crown of Lights
The Cure of Souls
The Lamp of the Wicked
The Prayer of the Night Shepherd
The Smile of a Ghost
The Remains of an Altar
The Fabric of Sin
To Dream of the Dead
The Secrets of Pain
The Magus of Hay

THE JOHN DEE PAPERS

The Bones of Avalon
The Heresy of Dr Dee

OTHER TITLES

Candlenight
Curfew
The Man in the Moss
December
The Chalice
Night After Night
The Cold Calling
Mean Spirit

PART ONE

At the fading of day

It is important to be aware that every ghost story… depends on the honesty of those telling it, the accuracy of their memory and the reliability of their interpretation of the circumstances.

Ian Wilson
In Search of Ghosts (1995)

A fine late afternoon in
January and...

He wonders what this means, as he moves from dark room to even darker room, in the dust of discarded centuries. What *is* a haunted house?

Not an easy question. A case, there is, for saying that all houses are haunted and that this is rarely harmful. Everyone's home holds the residue of sickness, physical and mental. Every house stores memories of pain and pleasure. Few walls have not absorbed howls of anger, purrs of passion – and not all of it normal.

But sickness is rarely infectious after five hundred years or more. Not all memories are active.

And how many of us are normal? He plucks a strand of cobweb from his tweed skirt.

Certainly not him.

The closing hour of a lovely day for the time of year. Outside, the walls of the house are still sun-baked. This is the beauty of Cotswold stone, it seems to store the sun, so that villages look from a distance like uncovered beehives.

A lovely day, a lovely old house – from the outside, at least – and a lovely woman.

She stands beside him on the steps. She's wearing a heavy cloak of dark blue wool, ankle-length. The kind of cloak that women must have worn here when the house was young and held fewer memories, active or otherwise. From a distance, in certain lights, you might think she herself was a ghost.

'Knap Hall was derelict for decades at a time,' she says. 'Eventually – and we're talking in the 1970s, I think – it was divided up into rented apartments before it became a pub again. With a restaurant, this time. A gastropub – in the newer part, not here. Too costly to convert the older rooms, too many restrictions. So the rooms at this end, which are sixteenth century or earlier, have been mainly left alone. Which is good. For us, anyway.'

'How did they get the people out?' he wonders.

'I'm sorry?'

'Presumably some of the flats were still tenanted when it was sold for a gastropub.'

She shakes her head, doesn't know. Perhaps they didn't have to try too hard, he thinks. Perhaps people couldn't wait to get out.

'And what happened with the pub?'

Trinity shrugs.

'Lot of pubs just close overnight these days, don't they? And it was a bit isolated. And the smoking ban, of course.' She smiles her helpless smile. 'Actually, I don't really know.'

He nods. He's more interested in her mention a few minutes ago, of the house once being a home for maladjusted boys. A lot of anger there, you imagine, and torrenting sexuality.

'It needs to be cared for,' she says. 'Don't you think?'

He stares out across gardens that became fields again and are now being retamed.

'Yes,' he says. 'I'm quite sure there are a number of things here that need some care.'

He turns, looks beyond the house, to what rises above it, crowned by a stand of Scots pine.

'What's that hill called? Is *that* the Knap?'

A wooden kissing gate lets them into a footway, partly stepped, leading steeply up behind the house, overlooking a walled garden, its bottom wall tight to the hill. In one corner, there's a small stone building with a cross at the apex of its roof.

'Domestic chapel?'

'Used to be. The pub used it as a storeroom. Harry's bought some old pews from one of those reclamation places and we're having them installed. Do you think that's a good idea?'

'And perhaps you should have it blessed. A local priest will probably do it. Perhaps you could find out when it was consecrated. Not as old as the house, I would imagine, from the stonework.'

'Can't you do it?'

He smiles.

'Not exactly my tradition, lovely.'

When they're approaching the summit of the hill, he turns to take in the vast view, the setting sun spreading a deep watercolour wash over pastel fields and smoky woodland.

'What's that village over to the left?'

'That's Winchcombe,' she says. 'I never know whether it's a village or a town.'

'Ah, yes, so it is.' He knows it well enough, drove close to its perimeter to get here today. 'A large village these days with the heart of a town.'

A town in the old sense, a sturdy, working town, untypical of the modern Cotswolds. It has a strange history of growing tobacco.

'All very old round here,' she says. 'And nothing barbarically new to spoil it. Not for miles and miles.'

'Only the barbarically old. If barbaric is the word.'

'I'm sorry?'

'Belas Knap. If this little hill isn't known as the Knap, it probably suggests the name of the house links with the Neolithic longbarrow.'

'I suppose. It's somewhere over there.' She points vaguely at a wood behind the hill. 'Only been once. A longer walk than I imagined. It's just like an odd little hill. As if it's erupted from the corner of the field. Or it's landed from somewhere. Doesn't look five thousand years old with all that new stonework.'

'Probably a matter of health and safety.'

'There used to be dead people in there. I think they took away dozens of skeletons. I'm quite glad you can't see it from here.'

'I should take a look.'

'You wouldn't get there before dark. It's quite steep and treacherous. The ground.'

Fingers moving inside her cloak, holding it closed at the front.

'Perhaps not, then,' he says. 'Perhaps when I return.'

'I hope you're going to.'

'You know me, lovely. Be with you, I will, at the merest beckoning of a finger. Now we're in touch again. Now I know where you are.'

She smiles. A hand emerges from the cloak and she squeezes his arm affectionately as he raises it to point to something two or three miles away which lies like a chunky copper bangle in an open jewel case of green baize.

'Sudeley Castle?'

'Yessss.' Her hair's thrown back, and he sees her face is shiny with… pride? For someone else's luxuriously appointed castle?

'You know it, Cindy?'

'I know a little of its history.' He's done some reading. 'And its ghosts, of course.'

'Oh,' she says. 'Is there more than one?'

Back inside the house, she shows him a leaflet for Sudeley, displaying an aerial view of the castle with its velvety gardens. *Walk in the footsteps of Kings and Queens*, it says on the front.

There's a cut-out figure over the castle: a tall, slender woman, from a painting, her waist forming the point of a V, in a sumptuous red dress. She has delicate, composed features and her multi-ringed fingers are spread over her abdomen. Red stones in the rings, the necklace and the choker.

He rather likes her. She has, for the period, an unusually kind, intelligent face. The sixth wife of Henry VIII, herself four times married. One of the survivors.

Trinity, of course, played her in the British feature film *The King's Evening*. Not a very good film, he recalls, and Katherine

Parr does not appear until the last quarter; there's much more about the flighty Catherine Howard – wife five, beheaded for adultery. Adultery is always more cinematic. As is beheading, of course.

'You felt close to Katherine Parr?'

'More than any woman I ever played.'

'And that's why you wanted to live here?'

'She's the only Queen of England to be buried at a private house, rather than some cathedral. Did you know that?'

'I *didn't* know that.' Through the old, sour-milk panes of a mullioned window, he watches a hill beyond Sudeley Castle catching fire in the last rays of the sun. 'Didn't survive Henry for long, mind, poor dab.'

Falling rapidly into the arms of Thomas Seymour, brother of Jane, wife three, and then…

'What complicated times those must have been, Trinity.'

'And so close,' she says. 'When you're here.'

She's standing near enough for him to sense the tremor under the cloak. It's cold in here, colder than outside, though there are signs of a recent fire in the vast ingle. The room, unfurnished except for a window seat with a cushion, has uneven oak panelling on two walls and another is a dense wooden screen. The room's been cleaned out and stripped back quite recently. She insists everything will be finished in time for the summer, but the smog of dark history is not so easily dispelled.

Outside there are ladders and scaffolding. It's Saturday tomorrow but the renovation work will apparently be continuing. No expense spared to make the place habitable… and more, much more.

She's told him she didn't want a house someone else had restored. She wanted somewhere neglected, unwanted, misused. Well, he supposes a gastropub qualifies as misuse. Nothing left of that now. He suspects it had all gone before the builders and carpenters moved in. Starting their operations here, at the core of the house, and working outwards, drawing in the newer sections, opening up the stairs, rediscovering bedrooms – of which there might be as many as twenty. Like most houses with land, it's been added to over the years, and not always sympathetically.

'Trinity, was this house – when it was much smaller – *connected* with Sudeley? One of the castle farms, perhaps?'

'I certainly *feel* it was,' she says protectively. And then opens her arms. 'I can't wait. Can't wait to fill it with people. Harry isn't sure it's going to work, but… I just think it will.' Her arms drop. 'Cindy, love, you've been awfully quiet. Is there something you're not telling me?'

He doesn't react quickly enough and knows she's seen his expression. Feels terrible, he does, knowing how much this place means to her. But there are better houses than this, if you have the money, which surely they do.

But they've bought it now, see, that's the problem. No going back. Seems she tried to find him months ago, when he'd changed his mobile phone number, and his email address to something confusing. Eventually, she employed an inquiry agent to track him to West Wales.

He only wishes he felt more worthy of her faith in his instincts.

'I won't lie to you, lovely,' he says. 'I suspect that it's had its moments, this house.'

And he thinks she feels that, too, but doesn't want to tell him something, in the hope that she's wrong.

'Is that so unusual, a place this old?'

He forces a shrug.

'Just me, it is, probably.'

They've known one another for quite some years now, since the night she was the star guest on the BBC's *National Lottery Live*, which he was presenting at the time. The night she activated the big-money balls in the machine. Before her marriage, this was. They had dinner afterwards and began a period of exchanging confidences, when he learned about her yearning for the English countryside and a gentler, more gracious way of life, while at the same time recognizing the irony in her situation: that to attain her pastoral dreamworld she must struggle on for a while through the brash and frenzied carnival of popular culture.

And then she married Harry Ansell.

'You're not staying here alone?'

'No, no. I'm going back to Cheltenham. I wouldn't *mind* staying here, we have one bedroom more or less finished, but I promised Harry I wouldn't. He's in America till the middle of next week.'

'Don't,' he says. 'Don't be alone here, yet. Not being funny, see, but…'

She looks at him with dismay. The mullioned window is becoming rosy with evening. A hostile dampness will soon be forming in the gloom of the passages between rooms, like the furring of old arteries.

'It's a lonely place,' he says lamely. 'Well, that is… there are few places it's safe for a woman to be alone nowadays. Especially a… someone like yourself.'

'Oh, I'm not worried about *that*.' A small, amused light in her eyes. 'We have a security firm patrolling at night. And Katherine is…'

He looks sharply at her. Katherine Parr again.

'I don't know quite why I'm asking this, Trinity, but… has the late queen been seen… here?'

'Well… maybe.'

'By whom?'

'Different people, over the years. I'm not sure.'

'Including you?'

'Not clearly. I sometimes think I see her watching me from a doorway. Very pale. And lights. And a smell of something sweet… perfume. I don't know.'

'What kind of perfume? Roses? Herbs?'

He doesn't know much about sixteenth-century scents but suspects we would not necessarily recognize them as such. Less a precursor of Chanel No 5 than a way of masking the pervading body odours caused by extremely infrequent bathing.

'A sweet smell, anyway,' she says. 'Quite strong. Pungent.'

'And why did you think it was Katherine Parr?'

How likely was it, after all, was it that Katherine would have placed one dainty shoe on the pitted track to Knap Hall, a farmhouse full of rushes and rats?

'Little lights,' she says. 'There was a pattern of tiny red lights, like a constellation, in the... figure. I thought of rubies. Katherine wore a lot of rubies.'

'But why would she come here?'

'To get away from Thomas Seymour?'

Thomas Seymour of Sudeley – it was his castle, but after their rapid marriage she seems to have given him much of the money left to her by the King to make it splendid. Seymour is remembered not fondly by history, mainly because of his alleged attempts to have sex with the King's daughter Elizabeth – the future Elizabeth I – when she was not much more than a child. Katherine seemed to have been in love with him since long before Henry sent for her to be his queen. But to Seymour, she might still have been second best. Not so long after Katherine's death, Seymour was executed for treason.

'The Bishop who eventually gave him the last rites,' Trinity says, 'or whatever you did before an execution, said he was "wicked, covetous, ambitious" and... something else bad. On her deathbed – probably delirious – Katherine's said to have bemoaned his treachery – his attentions to Elizabeth.'

'And you think perhaps she came up here to get away sometimes from him?'

'I don't know.'

'Or meet a secret lover, maybe?'

'I never thought of that. There's also supposed to be a good-looking young man seen here. Fair-haired, wearing leather.'

'Who told you that?'

Trinity looks a little vague.

'Do you feel she's happy… Katherine, if… when she's here?'

'I'm not sure.'

Although they're inside, she draws up the capacious hood of her winter cloak, half turning so he can't see the expression on her face, muffling her response. Keeping something to herself.

'She died in childbirth?'

'After childbirth,' she says. 'Complications.'

'Not uncommon in those days.'

Something not terribly healthy here. If the only reasons for Katherine to be at Knap Hall lie in the emotional needs of a woman who once played her in a film which was not really about her…

'Trinity, would you do something for me? Would you have time to keep a little diary? Recording anything that happens, as soon after the event as you can. Would you do that?'

'OK.' She nods. 'I can try. Have to be done under cover. Harry wouldn't exactly approve. He's… not a believer.'

'Presumably he doesn't know I'm here.'

She laughs.

'He doesn't even know I know you. Poor Cindy. But I wouldn't want to talk to anyone else about all this. In my situation there are so few people you can ever really trust. Not even a vicar or anyone who might just want to… you know… get rid of her?'

Oh dear. She's being selective here. Something bad she wants removed, but something she perceives as good. A question of babies and bathwater. Not really how it works.

'Let's make it a *secret* diary, then,' he says.

'The Secret Diary of Trinity Ansell, aged thirty-four and a half.'

They both laugh.

Another woman he could have loved, if he was normal.

At the door of his car, parked on the rubble forecourt, he turns back and sees her standing outside the broken porch in the last light. A chill on the purpling air, and her face is shaded by the hood. She looks more ghostly than ever, more ephemeral, more… temporary.

Essentially she hasn't changed. Just because people have become rapidly rich doesn't mean they become bad or selfish, self-indulgent, haughty, morally lax or corrupt. And if Katherine Parr looked this good then Henry VIII was a luckier man than he deserved to be.

What he's decided is that he'll drive out of the gate, park up the lane and then find his way to the top of the hill again, alone, absorbing what he can, feeling the landscape so that it can be journeyed back to, in his meditation. He notes all the outbuildings he hasn't even entered, particularly the long stable block with its wide arched doorways and a belltower that's probably older than the one on the chapel at the rear.

How to help a woman who – dear God – wants to be haunted?

But selectively.

He watches Trinity standing by the Elizabethan porch and thinks she would actually have been quite at home in Tudor times, might even have caught the King's eye. She has a feel for history, and not in an academic way, and she senses the liminal nature of this landscape. The popular media will occasionally notice, with scornful amusement, her openness to clairvoyants, tarot-readers and… well… people like him.

As Trinity waves, he feels an entirely unexpected sting of tears, giving way to the dampening dread he so hoped he would not experience here. She wants somewhere to love and hopes she's found it. But he doesn't think this house, haunted or not, will love her back.

PART TWO

Before nightfall

Do I believe in ghosts? To which
I answer that I am prepared to
consider evidence and accept it if
it satisfies me.

M.R. James
Preface to *The Collected Ghost
Stories of M.R. James* (1931)

Another January

1

House

from: Leo Defford, Head of Production, HGTV

to: Paul Cooke, Commissioning Editor, Channel 4

Confidential update

Paul,

You'll be glad to know that we have a final – and unexpectedly accommodating – agreement with Harry Ansell for the lease of his house until the end of the year. So that's the first major hurdle out of the way. I was beginning to fear we'd never find somewhere entirely suitable.

Just to remind you, Knap Hall is an extended early-Tudor farmhouse in the hills above Winchcombe in the Northern Cotswolds. The house is set in about twenty acres of grounds, in an isolated location which, of course, suits our requirements.The word's gone out that we're developers preparing to reopen it as a hotel, so the increased traffic, installation of portacabins, etc., will arouse no suspicions locally.

Knap Hall is obviously best known through its connection with Mr Ansell's late wife, Trinity. Until her death, the Ansells had been running it as a uniquely high-end country guest house, patronized mainly by wealthy tourists in search of the authentic Elizabethan experience without the period discomforts. We don't intend to reveal the connection with Trinity Ansell, either to viewers or the inmates, until the seventh and final night, by which time her presence at Knap Hall may or may not have been proved significant.

Previously, the house has been a pub, a youth hostel and a home for antisocial boys. To my knowledge, it has never been featured on TV or radio or been included in any 'haunted Britain' guides.

We'll be assigning an experienced researcher to the task of unearthing and documenting the relevant history of the house. As we understand some of the disturbances have been quite recent, we've asked her to talk to people employed there during the period of the Ansells' occupancy who may also be useful as interviewees.The main aim, however, is to have points of reference for anything reported over the seven nights.

At present, our researcher is a journalist from a freelance news agency who knows only that it's connected with a proposed TV documentary. Now we know where we're going, we'll need to think about having someone on a perma- nent contract.

As agreed, I'll keep you fully in the picture.

best,
Leo.

PS. I've only made one short visit to Knap Hall, but I think it's fair to say that it is (rubbing hands in gleeful anticipation) *supremely* unwelcoming.

2

Fairyland

GRAYLE SEES A shoulder of near-black cloud leaning on the hill, and she flinches. For no real reason – it's probably just raining up there, or something. Only to someone a little twisted would dark weather look like a personal warning.

She's driving impatiently to the end of all that modern housing mushrooming out of once-rural villages with pretty names like Bishop's Cleeve and Woodmancote. A big, crowded suburb, now, without a city to give it identity, only the long and craggy hill beyond it.

This hill, ahead of her now, is Cleeve Hill, which forms the ramparts of the Cotswolds. She's looking for a stone farmhouse, which should be obvious and isn't.

Is this because she doesn't want to find it?

Because she doesn't want to be here at all, psyching herself up to go lie to someone who lost her job under tragic circumstances? The simple solution is to just call up the agency and quit before they fire her. Bequeath this crap to someone else. Above all, don't get interested. Don't, like, *revert*.

Grayle pulls into the side of the road, stops the car, plucks the cellphone from the dash. Go on. Do it. Might be throwing away however many weeks' wages they feel obliged to give her along with their good wishes for a better life, but what the hell? She takes a breath and…

… no signal.

No signal? *Here?*

Holding up the phone in a futile kind of way, she sees, through a side window, across the pale grey fields, two tall chimneys on top of a stone farmhouse.

It starts to rain. Grayle starts to laugh.

Tosses the phone on to the passenger seat, knowing she'd never have made that call anyway. These were just excuses; her problems are more fundamental. Like that she could be going crazy again. She leans forward to start the car, raising a hand to pull the hair out of her eyes, the way she habitually used to.

Before having most of it cut off.

Grayle peers at herself in the rear-view mirror. Jesus, she even *looks* crazy now.

The young woman's name is Lisa Muir and she's the only one of them who's agreed to talk to Grayle. The others were saying things like, *Just can't let it go, can you?* and *We had enough of you vultures at the time* and *Who told you about me, who gave you my number?*

The stone farmhouse seems secure in the middle of its land. But, as Grayle parks the Cooper on the edge of the yard, she can see, through the wintry trees, red and pink modern housing creeping up like a skin rash.

The farm belongs to Lisa's parents, who are not at home because it's market day someplace and Lisa says they like to make a day of it. She takes Grayle into a rear parlour where long, grey velvet curtains frame a misty flank of Cleeve Hill. Two chocolate labradors follow them in.

Lisa's looking apprehensive. She's about twenty-two, with neat brown hair and a baby smile. One of those slightly posh but not over-educated young women looking for a respectable but not too taxing job before marriage to someone solid. In other words, not the kind of kid who would normally take a post with the job description *scullery maid.*

'I mean, it sounded kind of hands and knees,' she says when they're sitting down with a coffee pot on a low table between them. 'Bucket? Scrubbing brush? I'm going, Oh, come *on...*'

Lisa shakes her head dizzily. Grayle smiles over her cup.

'You had to wear a uniform?'

'Kind of. Well, not the… you know, the stiff black and white Victorian stuff, thank God. Just dull clothes, really, a bit dowdy, and no jewellery.'

She's making up for that now. Pink cashmere sleeves are pushed up to show off a bunch of thin gold bangles. Judging by the velvet drapes and the quality landscape paintings in the room, her dad is probably what used to be called a Gentleman Farmer.

'The money though… that was really good. And let's be honest, even if it was crap you'd still grab their hands off to be working for Trinity Ansell. It really delivered on what you were hoping for. Like, every time a car pulls up outside, you're off to the nearest window. Who's it going to be? What film was he in? You know?'

Lisa giggles self-consciously, but her eyes are soon clouding over, both of them knowing this is a narrative that isn't going to end well. She picks up a magazine from the sofa beside her, opens it to a picture feature that Grayle has seen before, headed

A TUDOR COUNTRY HOUSE WEEKEND WITH TRINITY

The magazine is *Cotsworld*, Harry Ansell's flagship glossy. Grayle's been reading about Harry, a Londoner who made his first millions out of downmarket hobby and computer-games mags in the 1980s. How all that got sidelined to another company and left behind, along with his old name, once Harry married Trinity Ansell, the ultimate trophy wife, and became a serious country gent. Acquiring one of those traditional rural lifestyle magazines, with pictures of landowners' daughters marrying army officers, supplements on the best boarding schools and thirty pages of country houses that are never going to sell at those prices.

'You can just see me in the right-hand corner. *There…*'

Lisa's holding up a big picture, across most of two pages: guests arriving, as sunset turns to night, on the forecourt of an historic country house, its walls softly lit, Cotswold gold. The oak front door is thrown wide, and there's a tall woman in a long skirt, with her dark hair up, in a warm halo of candlelight. And, yes, Lisa, slightly out of focus, helping with some baggage.

The picture says it all. Trinity was already famous – supermodel turned actress, two Hollywood movies behind her – when her new husband gave her the magazine to play with and a pile of money. Within three years *Cotsworld* was an international bible of taste and upper-class chic. The quintessential guide to English luxury-living in a fairyland of rolling hills and golden homes where most of your neighbours are movie stars and royalty. The kind of England you can't find any more in multicultural London.

A vivid myth, Grayle thinks, as Lisa reverently lays down the magazine, still open, on the cushions beside her.

'The house… I mean they'd spent *loads* on it. I can just about remember it being a pub, and my grandfather told me it was once a school for maladjusted boys. Intensive bad-kid rehab, with these big fences? Horrible, really. Rough, you know? Took *a lot* of work.'

'But originally it was a farmhouse, right? Late medieval?'

'Tudor times, anyway. Bits got added over the centuries until it was like a mansion? From the outside, now, it looks like it's all the same period, but some of it's only about a hundred years old, maybe less. Mr Ansell had it done up so it *all* looked old, including the newer parts. Only he didn't clear it with the council, and some of these historical buildings experts were going berserk. It was in the papers, how he was going to be taken to court. But he had good lawyers and historical experts and… a lot of money. And he was doing it for her. So it all got done. One way or another.'

Grayle nods, lets Lisa talk. Smiling and nodding encouragingly, just another awed American, like all the ladies who hauled their husbands to Knap Hall. Not The Knap Hall Hotel. Obviously, it *was* a hotel, but what people were paying for was a weekend as country-house guests. *Her* guests. Trinity. Her idyll.

'There won't be anything like this again, ever.'

Lisa looking down at the luscious, twilight picture in *Cotsworld*, which enshrines her most cherished memories. She closes the magazine, Grayle wondering if she's only agreed to talk today as a way of reclaiming the golden past. She was young, she was at the centre of all that, and now it's gone and she's still young, and life stretches ahead like a dirt road.

'Why did she want to do this?' Grayle asks. 'Why did she want to open her lovely house to… paying guests?'

'Oh, they weren't just— I mean they *were* paying… a lot. Far more than a five-star hotel. As *her* guests, at *her* house. With other people they recognized from TV and movies. Except, *they* weren't paying, the celebs, they really *were* guests.'

'So *Cotsworld* magazine illustrated the fantasy, and the Knap Hall Experience made it real – at a price.'

'That was how it all started. A special offer to *Cotsworld* readers – the ones who subscribed. It didn't *say* you had to be a millionaire, but… I mean it was the next best thing to staying with Charles and Camilla at Highgrove.'

At her own mention of royalty, Lisa's eyes flicker, guarded.

'What exactly did you say this programme was?'

She wants to talk about it, maybe even appear on TV as a part of it, but she doesn't want any of it betrayed or devalued. She's glancing nervously at the digital recorder on the coffee table between them.

'It's, um, still in development, Lisa, so I'm not allowed to tell you too much. Except that it relates to the, um… the tragedy of Trinity Ansell. And some of it will be shot at the house – with Mr Ansell's permission. And you'll get a fee for talking to me and, of course, a larger one if we record an interview.'

Lisa nods, happier.

'OK.'

'What were they like, the Ansells? What was *he* like? I'm just recording this for myself – no one else will hear it.'

'Well, he… I mean, you're a woman, what would you call him? An "ex-hunk"?'

29

'At my age, maybe not quite so "ex".'

She's had Harry Ansell pointed out to her. The Three Counties office is not far from the *Cotsworld* block where he works most days. Like the building, he's stone-faced now, and you really wouldn't want to invade his space. Harry Ansell, who used to be Harry Burgess. Not too many men take their wives' names. Maybe it was about love, but it must also surely have been about business. And a kind of ownership. He was acquiring her fame.

'He kept himself pretty fit,' Lisa says. 'They had a gym in the old stable block, and they used to ride, and he went out with the hunt for a while – she didn't like that. Hunting. And yet she did in a way 'cos of the kind of people that were in it. That was the way she was, neither one thing nor the other. You remember Princess Diana? Royal but… not really. Before my time, but I've seen TV stuff. I expect you'd still be in America back in her day.'

'Trust me, Lisa. We knew more about Princess Di in America than we knew about any other English person, ever. Trinity Ansell was… like that, how?'

'Not to look at, obviously – she was dark. But sometimes she was this gracious lady, and you felt you had to curtsy if you met her on the stairs, whereas other times it was like she wanted to be your mate? Sometimes you thought she looked like… like she *needed* mates. You know? But when the house was full of titled people and celebs, you were just a servant again, and—'

'But why… what I'm trying to get at, why open up her actual home to wealthy readers? Why not just live there? I guess it wasn't about money.'

'We used to talk about it a lot, down in the staff sitting room at night. It was the nearest thing you could get to the authentic old country-house scenario. The place full of servants, making sure the house was sparkling and the fires were always stacked up with logs. And the guests… I think she almost forgot they were paying to be there. It was as if she was dispensing… what's the word…?'

'Largesse?'

'Probably. I think she saw them as like… retainers? Courtiers and ladies-in-waiting. Always kept just the right distance between her and them.'

Grayle smiles but Lisa's serious. No, it wasn't about money. This was about keeping Trinity happy. And these weekends must have paid all the staff wages twice over, which probably kept Harry Ansell happy, too. For a while.

'She was pretty smart, actually,' Lisa says. 'She was at university when she first became a model, did you know that? Doing history. She supervised all the work at Knap Hall – like, "this looks right", or "that's out of period, get rid of it". Not getting her hands dirty, obviously, don't want to break a nail, do you? She'd drive down to the castle quite a lot, see what they'd done there.'

'The castle?'

'Sudeley. They call it the most romantic castle in England. Henry VIII stayed there with Anne Boleyn. And after he died… Katherine Parr?'

'The sixth wife?'

'Who survived. And then got married to Thomas Seymour who owned Sudeley Castle. And she moved there, and she died there. So that's… two queens of England. Mrs Ansell – Trinity – she loved that. Being able to look down from the Hall, from their apartment upstairs, towards Sudeley Castle in all its lovely grounds. And after playing Katherine Parr in that film—'

'I didn't know that. Not that I get to see a lot of movies.'

'It was called *The King's Evening*. It was about Catherine Howard, the fifth wife, and Katherine Parr came in near the end, when the King had only a couple of years to live.'

'But she felt a connection? With Katherine Parr and Sudeley?'

'She went there lots. Out of opening hours, obviously, wouldn't want to be hanging out with the trippers and the pensioners' bus tours. Sometimes she took me with her, to remember things and write them down.'

'Just you?'

'Like I say, there were times when she was very friendly. The others were a bit… not jealous exactly, but you know… because I was the youngest. And just the scullery maid, and all that meant was being a bit of a gopher. Whereas the chefs and Mrs Stringer, the housekeeper…'

Mrs Stringer was the first of the former staff to put the phone down on Grayle. There was a chef, a sous-chef, part-time waitresses and cleaners and also a Mr Jeffrey Pruford, the manager and kind of a butler figure, who she hasn't yet managed to locate.

'So when there was no one staying there you'd all just look after the house – and the Ansells?'

Lisa nods, and they talk some more about the good times. Which could not have lasted more than a year. This is where it might get difficult. But this is the reason Grayle's here, to pick up stuff you can't find on the Internet.

'Lisa, when did you realize something at Knap Hall was… not right?'

'Not right how?'

'We're looking to tell the whole story, Lisa.'

'OK.'

'When did you – or anyone – first get the feeling Mrs Ansell was… I don't know… unhappy… unsettled?'

For the first time, Lisa looks a little stubborn, resistant.

'She was good to me.'

'I know.'

'I don't want to… I mean, I know what people are saying. About the house being… you know.'

'Tell me about Trinity Ansell, first.'

'I don't know much about depression…'

'*I* do,' Grayle says. 'I guess.'

3

Lights out, fires dying

OH GOD, LISA says, she's thought about this a lot, and keeps coming back to the night of the dinner.

Always a dinner on the Saturday. The full works, nine courses. Lovely big fires and candles everywhere – hundreds of candles. And Trinity wearing this exquisite dress.

'An awfully expensive Tudor kind of dress, deep ruby-red silk with gold braid. She had it on for the first time, this night, and there was like a hush when she came in? I was down in the kitchen, but you'd swear you could hear it. A real hush. I mean, all right, I know you can't actually—'

'I get what you're saying.'

One of the chocolate labradors has his head on Grayle's knee. Hard to get depressed, Grayle's thinking, with a dog around. Apparently, there were no animals at Knap Hall.

'Really something, that dress,' Lisa says. 'It was…'

Her lips tighten over the baby teeth. Evidently something here she's not too sure she should be talking about.

'I remember she had a problem sitting down at the table in it. And when she did manage to sit down she didn't really eat anything. Not that she ever ate much, anyway. I mean, back in Henry VIII's day, nobody seemed to make a connection between eating like a pig and ending up all gross. Mrs Ansell would always have these prearranged really small portions. But this night, even the small portions were coming back to the kitchen, hardly touched.'

'She was sick?'

'Not so's you'd notice. Quite the reverse. I mean, she was

always, as you know, a "hot babe", as my boyfriend would say, but this night… I mean, the men literally couldn't take their eyes off her. Nor the women, come to that. She was… electric. Glowing… What's that word…?'

'Incandescent?'

'We all thought that, even Mrs Stringer. But Mr Pruford, the manager, he said she was nervous about something. Like all her nerves were on end, all lit up. But next day…'

Lisa's looking uncomfortable, upset even, like she wishes she'd never let herself be led down this road.

'… it was like a light had gone out. It was only September, but she wouldn't leave the apartment. She was OK again after a couple of days, but…'

'How long was this before she died?'

'Not long. Weeks, maybe. I don't really remember. I don't like to think about it.'

'She… she wasn't normally – from what I've read – what you'd call a nervous person.'

'Well, no, but—'

'Socially, I mean.'

'Not at all, no. I think she actually *had* been to dinner at Highgrove, with Charles and Camilla. Or somebody. No, not nervous in that way at all. Mr Pruford… he used to say it was the house. And Mr Ansell would be away for days at a time. He was a busy man.'

'Harry Ansell wasn't there that night?'

'No, I think he was, actually. Very much in the background, though. As he would be with Trinity in that dress.'

'So, um, what about the house? Mr Pruford…?'

'Didn't like the house, never made a secret of that. Used to say it was too old and set in its ways ever to change. No matter how many rich tapestries they hung, it would still be… like a *hard* place. Underneath. He said you could always feel that late at night, with the lights out, the fires dying, all the candles out. You could feel… he just called it the hardness? And he'd know about that sort of… He was in the army. And things would…'

Grayle waits, fondling the ears of the chocolate lab.

'You didn't get this from me,' Lisa says. 'I'd never talk about this.'

'Sure.'

'Things would get messed about. Wall hangings falling down for no reason. Ash from the hearth in heaps on the furniture. Things would get dirty, very quickly – the windows. Mrs Stringer was blaming us, and then she stopped doing that and just had it cleaned up each time it happened.'

'It happened often?'

'We did a lot of cleaning. And like sometimes you'd find stuff that shouldn't really be there? Like soil… earth? Little heaps of soil on chairs and tables. Well that was just… not possible.'

'What are you saying?'

'You know what I'm saying. Only I'm not. OK?'

'What did Mr Pruford say?'

'That it— He used to say it was full of bad… bad vibes. That nobody had ever been happy there.'

'How did he know that?'

'Well, I don't suppose he did. It was just how he felt.'

'Were the Ansells told?'

'God, no. Not by us. We didn't want to— We wanted them to go on loving the place. We wanted them to stay. Like I say, it was a brilliant job. We thought Mrs Ansell was turning the place round. Just by being there. She was one of the most famous people on the planet. Well, in this country anyway. And bringing in all the other famous faces. You could see the paying guests doing like a double-take? Like, *is it really*?'

Her eyes are glassy. She's erecting barricades and scattering glitter over the darkness.

'Look, nobody talked about the other things, OK? We weren't the kind to. We only got the jobs through connections. We were trusted.'

35

'But do you think—?'

'I hated clearing the… the debris. I just brushed it on to the dustpan. We weren't allowed to use vacuum cleaners when there were guests in the house. Not in-period. I'd just brush it up quickly and empty it into a binsack and get it out of the house quickly. Once there was a dead rat…'

'In the house?'

'On a table. Like a cat might've left it, but there weren't any cats. Horrible. But you got it out of the way and didn't let it spoil your day.'

'Did anybody have any ideas what it might be? What was causing it? I suppose a hole in the roof… that wouldn't be likely after what they'd spent.'

'Is it important?' Lisa sniffs dismissively. 'I don't think it's important. Lots of old houses have something. I thought this was supposed to be about Trinity's life. Dwelling on the bad things, it just gives the wrong impression.'

'I think the producer will need to show that it wasn't all idyllic. That renovating a very old house isn't easy. That sometimes you have to fight the history you're trying to evoke.'

Lisa stares out of the bay window at the greyness of Cleeve Hill. Grayle decides it's time to move up to the next stage.

'And she was susceptible to… the otherworldy? There was some history. She was known to have consulted… not mediums… tarot-readers and like that.'

'I don't remember anybody like that coming to Knap Hall. Well, a woman once. A middle-aged woman who was looking around and had one of those… a stone or something on a string.'

'Pendulum?'

'Look, maybe you should talk to Jordan.'

'I'm sorry, who?'

'Jordan the gardener. At first I thought he was just trying to frighten me. He was like, did I know the stories about Knap Hall? Well, I didn't, but that didn't mean anything, 'cos I don't like stories like that. Not when I'm working there. He's more local than me. He said people used to think they were being followed in the passages, and they'd turn round and there'd be, like, a shadow? He said he'd had the story from his dad. Someone like that.'

'And Jordan will speak to me?'

'He might. Don't say I told you, he'd get embarrassed, but if he knows you've got Mr Ansell's permission… Jordan's kept on, part time, to stop the grounds from turning to jungle before they sell the place. Goes about once a week, I think. *I* wouldn't. It's not the same. I don't want to go near. Got more bad memories now, hasn't it? Gone darker, like the windows— why do we have to talk about this?'

'What about the windows?'

'They'd go dim, that's all. Almost so you couldn't see through them. Some of the glass was old, hundreds of years old. It'd be greasy. On the inside. And flies. Dead flies, in the grease. Probably some fungal thing… bacteria, I don't know.'

Lisa shaking her head violently, as if the flies are in her hair. Grayle nods limply, saying nothing. This is what she's looking for. But don't make that obvious. Move on.

'Were you here when the word came through, about Mrs Ansell's death?'

'No. When she went to stay with her parents, we thought it was because her mother was ill. We didn't know… anything. There was no need for a full staff, so I took my holiday, but my boyfriend couldn't get the week off so I was at home. First I knew was seeing it on the TV news. And then I got a phone call saying don't come in on Monday.'

Long silence. Lisa looks like a little girl who's fallen in the street, picked herself up and only then noticed the blood.

'All over. For ever. I was so shattered I was just like crying all day? I'm sorry… I mean, there's nothing else I can say. And I don't want to talk about any of *that* on TV, thank you. I'd just break down.'

They'd love that, Grayle's thinking. They so love it when people break down on camera.

'You'd have to film me here. I won't even drive past the end of the lane. People, you know what people are like, they're always— I'm sorry, it's sick! I *hate* them!'

'What are they saying?'

But Lisa's lips are tight and she's shaking her head. The second labrador jumps up at her and she buries her face in the dog's fur.

'Did Trinity Ansell ever say anything to you – about anything being wrong? Like when you went to Sudeley together?'

'Not really. Just about fabrics and clothes and the grounds and how she wanted a proper knot garden. She was usually quite carefree when we went to Sudeley. I think she liked being with me because I was young. Mr Ansell could be... he was a bit heavy, you know? I liked it when we went to the castle. She'd tell me the day before, so I could come in normal clothes. Mr Pruford used to say he wished Sudeley would come on the market again – not that that's ever likely to happen, the same family's been there over a century.'

'Could the Ansells actually have afforded Sudeley Castle?'

'I don't know. Probably, when the magazine was selling millions worldwide. Mr Pruford used to say he'd rather be working at Sudeley. Better class of ghost – he said that once.'

'Anne Boleyn?'

'KP. Katherine Parr. She used to put her initial after her signature. KP – kind of cool. She's buried in the chapel in the grounds, but she's supposed to haunt the castle itself. I expect the owners are quite proud of that. We went to her funeral.'

'I'm sorry...?'

'She's buried in the chapel, in the castle grounds. In a tomb. And they – they had the funeral all over again?'

'*What?*'

'It was five hundred years since she was born. So they had a public recreation of the funeral to commemorate it. I know that doesn't make total sense, but that's what they did. I expect it was because she was born somewhere else but died there, and perhaps the original funeral was, like, underplayed? Not this time. Everyone was in costume. It was beautiful.'

'And *you* were there?'

'Mr Ansell was in New York or somewhere – I think they were opening a *Cotsworld* office there. So Trinity asked me to go with her. It was all… beautiful. You don't think a funeral could be beautiful. They made a video of it for the tourists.'

'How long was this before Trinity died?'

'Few months. I suppose you want me to say I felt a deep sense of foreboding or something. But I didn't. I was just… we were both quite excited. It felt like a historical moment.'

'Why? Why a deep sense of foreboding?'

'Because she… KP was thirty-six.'

Grayle's holding on to the lab's ears.

'Same age as Trinity, right?'

'Mmm.'

'How did she die? Katherine Parr.'

Lisa looks momentarily wary then sits up.

'A fever. Puer— Puer-something. When childbirth goes wrong.'

Puerperal fever. An infection, often fatal in those days. Grayle starts to tingle. It's a familiar feeling when you know you're getting close to the story, the essence, the energy source. And when no one else has it. Is it possible no-one else has this? She's certainly not read it anywhere.

'What about the baby? Did the baby…?'

'The baby was born. It was a girl. Katherine died soon afterwards. Look, if it's going to be that kind of programme—'

'I'm sorry?'

'People saying at least Katherine went through with it?'

'Oh. Yeah, I see.' Grayle nodding vaguely, like this has only just occurred to her. 'No, I hope it won't be that kind of programme.'

39

'I hate that sort of gossip,' Lisa says.

'Did anybody at Knap Hall suspect Trinity might be pregnant?'

'No. Not at all. We thought she was just… run down. She'd put in so much work that year. We thought she was just going away to rest, spend some time alone in a… quieter place. If you see what I mean.'

'I guess.'

Not that it makes complete sense. Nobody would've expected someone with Trinity's money to hide herself away at her parents' holiday cottage in Dorset for the purposes of quietly effecting a chemical abortion with a pill.

She needs to look up the inquest reports again, and the newspaper medical features that followed. While it's uncommon for a termination drug to cause a heart attack, it *has* happened before.

What it came back to was *why?*

What it looked like was that Trinity wanted to get rid of the baby before her husband could find out she was pregnant. Maybe because it wasn't his. That was the gossip on the Internet.

Tragedy tinged with scandal. Harry Ansell's never talked about it, never given an interview. In fact, Harry Ansell may never have given an interview in his life. That was what Trinity was for.

'The dress,' Grayle says. 'That was a Katherine Parr dress, right? I don't know much about her, but in the portraits I've seen…'

'Always in a red dress, yeah. And wore rubies. She never wore it again. Not—'

Grayle waits. Lisa looks a little sick.

'I hate all that,' she says eventually. 'Hate people who speculate on the Net.'

'I can understand.'

Grayle leans over and switches off the recorder.

Time to go. If she knew why she was being asked these questions, Grayle thinks Lisa would hate her, too.

4

A soul on eBay

AROUND MIDDAY THE wind comes in from the sea and has the ageing caravan rattling like the rusting tin can it has now become.

Not a good place to have a caravan any more. One day, he's thinking – one of these days of extreme climate change – it will simply collapse in on itself, like a flatpack, and the fire brigade will be required to recover his remains.

The mobile barks, and he looks up from his book and smiles, as he always does. A phone that barks like a dog – of all the manifold manifestations of new technology, this may be the one that pleases him most. Certainly in comparison with a series of electronic bleeps arranged into a speeded-up rendering of the opening bars of the Welsh national anthem, which is what his neighbour, Ifan, the hill-farmer, has on *his* phone. This might be ironic, but probably not.

With a forefinger, he slides the answer-bar on his mobile. Embedded in a vicious gust, the caravan rocks like a tumble-drier.

'Cindy?'

The voice is coming out of his hand, the phone on speaker, to save what few brain cells remain. He draws a slow breath, made more tortured by the simultaneous creaking of the caravan's failing frame.

'Who is this?'

Well, he knows, of course. But his response conveys a faint irritability at being disturbed by so many calls. In fact it's his first in a week.

'The voice from the past,' she says.

'Be more excited, I would, if it was a voice from the future.' He takes the phone to the window, looks down the hillside at St Bride's Bay, dark and blotched. 'How are you, young Jo?'

'I'm good. Cindy, the reason I'm calling… things've changed,' she says. 'Things've moved on. Very exciting.'

'The idea of change, Jo, is an illusion.'

'And we now have a different proposition for you.'

'One moment.' He braces himself between the wall and the bed-settee, not wanting her to hear the sounds of fabrication fatigue and realize he's in the same old caravan. 'When you say *different…*'

'It certainly involves more money.'

'Now that, Jo…' Cindy straightens up, brightening his voice. '…is my very favourite kind of different.'

He remembers, with an acute sadness, his second visit to Knap Hall. The occasion on which he encountered Poppy Stringer, who worked there as housekeeper, and remembered him from the television. When Harry Ansell came home early from work, it was Poppy who smuggled Cindy into the vast kitchen and served him afternoon tea while they shared their anxieties about Trinity. How vague and hazy she was becoming. Not long afterwards, he received her first strange, short diary.

He didn't see much of Trinity that day. There was no third visit.

It was Poppy who phoned him two months later, her voice brittle as last winter's dead leaves. Leaving him shattered… bereft and heartsick at his own inadequacy, his failure to realize how vulnerable Trinity had been. His unforgiveable failure to save her from… what? Her death was neither at the house nor had anything to do with it. He can't remember what the inquest verdict was: Accidental Death or Natural Causes.

Nothing in that house could be entirely natural. He remembers a grey depression settling around him with the low cloud as, after the call from Poppy Stringer, he walked out into the rain, staring at the heartless sea, feeling that his useful life might well be over.

But apparently it was not.

Poppy again, the following November. Ringing to tell him about a television company sniffing around Knap Hall, phoning her one night, tapping her for information about Trinity's last days, asking to meet her. Did Cindy know of this HGTV? Poppy sounding unhappy. Still hadn't found another job, but should she take their money for her memories? What did he think?

Hunter-Gatherer Television sounded like one of those private production companies run by children, which might survive for as long as a year before they were reduced to shooting porn for the early hours. He hated the idea of such insects swarming over Trinity's past before her ashes were cold. Advised Poppy to say nothing at this stage. He would find out.

Digging out his tattered book of contacts, he made some calls, picking up fragments of intelligence here and there. On the Internet, his intermittent broadband told him that one of their employees was his former producer on the *National Lottery Live* show.

Cindy likes to think he played a significant part in the demise of this celebration of naked greed, only disappointed that the Lottery itself did not disappear into the same sink-hole.

Young Jo Shepherd, however, he got along with her as well as you can with a producer. In her thirties now. And a mum, for heaven's sake. Little, chaotic, curly-haired Jo – with a baby buggy and a crate of Calpol where the wine bottles used to live?

Hadn't spoken to her for a few years now, feeling that it would be quite a while before she wanted to work with him again. But now he rang her on a pretext – asking her for help in tracing the family of a studio manager on the Lottery who he'd heard had died. Thus reminding her of his continued existence and leaving her his mobile number.

She was back within a week.

Cindy, darling, how do you feel about reviving your television career?

Never called him darling before.

'So you're still busy,' Jo says now.

He answers with elliptical ease.

'Not at all, young Jo. Feet up, cocktails at sunset. Industrial dowsing as practised by Uri Geller and myself can be most remunerative.'

The thing is never to let them think you are in dire need of money, or they'll try to get you for a pittance. *Not* that money is very important here, but credibility is.

During their first meeting all he learned was that the programme would involve a debate on the paranormal taking place in a house said to be haunted. She wouldn't tell him the location because secrecy was fundamental, only that various 'experts' would gather there to discuss aspects of the unseen, and some would be sceptics.

Not exactly light entertainment, then, Jo.

It's serious television.

Then why are you talking to me? No one takes me seriously any more.

Oh, I think they do, Cindy. And those who don't will, I think, be quite surprised.

And then she was talking about money. Enough money to get a person out of his leaking caravan and into a pink-walled terraced cottage with a glimpse of Tenby harbour from an attic window.

But that's a side issue.

He knows how these programmes work. How the fees differ according to the fame level of the participants. Hears himself glibly telling Jo that unfortunately he'll be otherwise engaged for the next few weeks – another tiresome dowsing job for the minerals industry – and may not be entirely free until the autumn.

But Jo persists. When they next meet she'll have a contract with her, for his perusal. It will be for a *very* healthy six-figure sum. It's clear she's not flying solo here. Talks have taken place within HGTV, at executive level. They want him.

'Don't get me wrong, Cindy, I also know how bloody dangerous you can be. Especially working live.'

He laughs.

'Someone offends you,' Jo says, 'all normal human restraint goes out of the window.'

'Ah, Jo… the lottery show… those were exceptional circumstances.'

And so it goes on, this delicate courtship dance. The fact that she wants to show the contract to him, rather than his agent, is significant. When assembling a cast of notables for celebrity reality-TV, producers tend to go undercover. Agents are avoided – agents tend to dislike reality shows which may not display their clients in the best of lights and can destroy a career as easily as revive one. Producers will rely on their black books, those secret pages of unlisted phone numbers and private email addresses.

And a relatively junior producer, by signing someone interesting, might earn a significant bonus.

Cindy probes delicately, making careful suggestions. Wanting this job very badly, and not because of the money, so, obviously, he needs to make them think he's holding out for more of it.

'Tell me about this man Driffield,' he says.

'Defford. Vastly experienced. Been around for ever.'

'With much success?'

'Yeah, of course. Considerable success. Done well in America. Had a flat in London, nice bolthole in the Cotswolds. Key people at the networks still listen to him.'

'And yet… he sees other independent producers, half his age, without a quarter of his talent, pulling in ten times the income?'

'Cindy—'

'Getting older, I think,' Cindy says, 'our Mr Driffield.'

'*Defford*. You've been checking him out, haven't you?'

'Not much time left for the big one. Cult of youth, all that.'

'That's not what this is about. Look, what do you want me to say, Cindy? He pays my wages. Yours too, if you're up for this.'

'Jo, did you, by any chance, act on my suggestion for another person to act as researcher and consultant? Someone whose expertise in this area was… probably unparalleled?'

'Marcus Bacton? Yes, I checked him out. Certainly an expert, but… I'm sorry, Cindy. I did call him, to see what he sounded like. He sounded… a bit acerbic.'

'A *bit*. You must've caught him on a good day.'

'Leo is not used to direct confrontation. I went through the motions, saying we'd be talking to some other people. He called back within a couple of hours to ask me to remove his name from the list.'

'There's a shame.'

There's a pause before Jo comes back, tentatively.

'But he did recommend someone he thought was better qualified to handle our background research by virtue of also being an experienced journalist. Someone we could hire initially through an agency, to see if she suited us. Seemed like a good idea, so we're trying her out.'

'What?'

'Shush,' Jo says. 'I didn't tell Leo she came from a contact of yours. He's very nervous about cross-fertilization and too much getting out in advance. The ground rules stipulate that the participants know nothing about each other, which makes sense both in television terms and, I suppose, the cause of psychic research.'

He manages not to laugh. This will hardly be a cause close to the heart of anyone at HGTV.

'Who is it? Who did Marcus recommend?'

'You don't know?'

'Jo, if I knew—'

'Her name's Grayle, with a Y, Und—'

'Grayle Underhill?'

It had very much not been his intention to expose little Grayle to any of this. What's Marcus playing at?

'It might be safer,' Jo says, 'if you had no contact with Ms Underhill. We haven't told her about you, and we don't intend to at this stage. Or anyone.'

'You're saying Mr Driffield wants whatever happens in this house to be a surprise to us all, Jo?'

'Defford.'

'Of course it is.'

'And, ah… that's what I wanted to talk to you about,' Jo says.

Cindy senses a darkening momentum. He now knows what Defford is and what he's looking for.

What Jo meant about "serious television" is late-night viewing, well past the watershed, on a channel that likes to break barriers. What they're now proposing – what Jo says is "very exciting", although, having worked with him before, she clearly has her doubts – is to use the element of danger he's come to personify. The loose-cannon Cindy Mars, famous for abandoning all human restraint on live television.

But he knows – he's not naive – that this will have to be in a way they can predict and control. Or think they can. Be feeling safer, he would, if the formidable Marcus Bacton was on the other side of the wall. Grayle Underhill… very fond, he is, of little Grayle, but she's been through the mangle. Why on earth would Marcus inflict this on her?

Ending the phone call, Cindy feels himself observed. Looks up and meets the sardonic, globular gaze of Kelvyn Kite, who is ignominiously squashed into the netting of the luggage rack near the caravan ceiling.

'Am I dangerous, Kelvyn? Still? At my age?'

Kelvyn cackles sourly but makes no reply. Cindy doesn't think Kelvyn cares much for him any more. Which is understandable.

Anybody's nowadays, he is, if the money's right. A spiritual mercenary, a soul on eBay.

And yes, he'd still do this, of course he would, even if he didn't know the house selected for the project.

But of course he *does* know the house if, to his eternal regret, not yet well enough. He missed something. And now Trinity Ansell is dead.

Yesterday a parcel arrived for him, special delivery. You might describe this as serendipitous. But *serendipity* is a word used for happy accidents. And nothing about this is happy.

From the little window, he sees shiny charcoal clouds racing at him, bunched like fists.

5

Its own darkness

'IT'S FUNNY,' Jeff Pruford says. 'When there were guests in the house, they always introduced me as the steward. All part of the pastiche. I'm not even sure the term described what I did, but that didn't matter, it was near enough and olde English enough to appeal to the guests. And when you've been in the army you know how to look solemn and dignified and never laugh. You can turn it on.'

Pruford's in his forties, slim and smart-looking in a cautious kind of way, with crisp greying hair and a smoothed-out accent which Grayle thinks is Yorkshire. He was in the Royal Welsh regiment, reaching the rank of sergeant-major before losing a foot to a roadside bomb in Afghanistan.

Not that you'd know; he doesn't even have a discernible limp. On the phone she's told him the truth, that she's a professional journalist researching for a TV programme about the mysteries of Trinity Ansell and Knap Hall. And that some of his former colleagues there have spoken to her. She didn't name them and he didn't ask.

After a couple of hours, he called back and agreed to tell her what he could without breaking confidences. For which he'd accept £2,000 on the understanding she'd get no second-hand gossip from him, only what he's seen personally.

Which is evidently going to be interesting.

'The night she was in the red dress? Oh, yes. There was a very weird postscript to that. Never talked about it before, mainly because nobody's ever asked me. You talk to most blokes who've done time in the military, and they won't diss this stuff, but you don't go out of your way, not these days.'

It's mid-afternoon, in the back of an old pub close to the centre of Cirencester. Jeff Pruford's running a restaurant on the other side of town. Won't be staying here long, he's had an offer from a cruise company. Bit of travel without getting shot at, but it won't be like Knap Hall. That was… very different. Oh, yes.

'When I say "pastiche", it became quite real for all of us. Mainly because it was always real for Mrs Ansell. She thought of herself as a historian. A historian who'd let herself get diverted into modelling and then acting. A body in a frock – she said that once. With some bitterness, I think. She wanted to get back *into* history. Be a part of the past, somehow. You sensed this disillusion with the present day and the whole celebrity business. Well they all say that, don't they – "oh, I wish I wasn't famous and I could have a normal life." Then, soon as they lose a bit of fame they're clawing each other's eyes out to get back on top.'

He drinks some Guinness, wipes the froth from his lips with an actual handkerchief, remembering.

'Not her. She'd done the Hollywood film premieres and the posh parties. Now it could all come to her for a change. It was about getting herself out of London but not losing the glamour. Just a different kind of glamour. History was glamour to her. And the views are better.'

'When you say getting *back* into history…?'

'During the Elizabethan weekends, we all had to wear period costume. I had this… jerkin thing that never felt right. But when *she* was in a Tudor dress, it was like she was relaxing into it. I can't explain it better than that, Grayle.'

'Like she felt she was living in the wrong age?'

'Not any more. At Knap Hall she was in the *right* age. When there was nobody staying there, you'd still see her wandering in the woods in costume, kind of. Long dress in summer, heavy cloak in winter. Wouldn't notice you. Like she was out of it. Out of *your* world. As if she'd taken something.'

'Had she?'

'I doubt it. She didn't drink much either, and she'd given up smoking. I noticed that. When they first came here she was a smoker, but after a month or two she'd just packed in, no fuss at all. Like it didn't exist for her any more. And the music. She used to like modern folk music – Laura Marling, Seth Lakeman. And then you didn't hear that any more, only this Tudor choral music. Thomas Challis?'

'Tallis, I think.'

'Whatever. It was piped around the house, quite low. Followed you around. I could've done without it.'

'How did Harry Ansell feel about this?'

'Not sure. He didn't unload his private thoughts on the staff. Or anybody, I'd guess. Businessman, and he kept his business to himself. And *she* was his business. In all senses of the word. Whatever made Trinity happy. Putting her on a pedestal, that's an understatement. If you ever go to Knap Hall, have a glance at the chapel. I'm saying nothing, just have a look.'

'Do I get the feeling you didn't like Ansell?'

'I didn't say that. Don't you suggest I said that, Grayle, all right? I just got worried about her. The way she was becoming more and more withdrawn. Like she was fading into a tapestry. I don't think she was eating properly. I think he should've done something, that's all. To save her from herself.'

'Was she sick?'

I never thought that till afterwards. I thought it was the house. Listen, I'll tell you what I think you're looking for, Grayle, but I won't speculate about it. I think the Ansells dressed up that house to be what it wasn't. Even when it was first built, it wasn't posh. And when it got bigger it was only to accommodate… well, it was for bad lads, wasn't it?'

'I keep hearing about that.'

'It was a charitable trust, I think. Providing outward-bound holidays for young offenders. Long walks and all that. Tire them out. Not enough, apparently. One of them raped a local girl. In the grounds.'

'At Knap Hall?'

'Brought her back and kept her there all night. Quite nasty, she spent some time in hospital. Look for a happy story about Knap Hall, you'll be hard-pressed to find one.'

'So when you said it was hard, meaning the house...?'

'Who told you that? Never mind. Aye, I would've said that. Historic, but basic. But they made it into a small palace and it wasn't meant to be, and that was... it was like when you see a dead person – a corpse – all dressed up in its Sunday best with the face all made up. Sorry.'

When she offers him another drink he shakes his head. He's deciding whether or not to say something, looks down into his empty mug, begins to muse, and she notices his northern accent is more pronounced.

'Soldiers... we're funny buggers, like I say. Day I got my foot blown off, it was actually Friday the thirteenth. Didn't realize till afterwards. I remember laughing like a clown when they carried me into the hospital and there's this bloody calendar. This programme you're making... won't be taking the piss out of all that, will it? It's not that funny.'

'In all honesty, I'm not in a position to say. If it was my decision, no, it wouldn't.'

'All I can say... I'm quite susceptible to atmospheres, and I didn't take to Knap Hall. But you don't let a few misgivings about the feel of a place put you off when you're offered a brilliant job by Harry Ansell and his famous lady, do you?'

'You felt it was... unlucky?'

'I felt it was angry. Didn't like what had been done to it.'

'So, um... when she died...'

He takes a mouthful of air, breathes it out, eyelids lowered.

'I took the call – did they tell you that? From Harry Ansell's secretary in Cheltenham. I had to tell everybody. Worse, in a way, than when one of your mates is being sent home in a coffin. And the implications. I think Ansell went back there three times, four at the most, and never for very long, and never to sleep. Without Trinity… nothing. Almost a shrine when she was alive, but then… get rid. Some folks are like that.'

He talks about how quickly the house was stripped. He was kept on to oversee all that – the valuable stuff taken out quickly, furniture sold to antique dealers. And then the place was just abandoned, except for a caretaker and a gardener. Regular police patrols for a while. He looks up, smiling ruefully.

'But you want to hear about the red dress, don't you?'

She gives him a small smile.

'Aye. She loved that dress. They say she was buried in it. Or cremated, I'm not sure which – we weren't invited, though I did attend the memorial service at Gloucester Cathedral. Anyroad, night she wore the frock, there was a group of American *Cotsworld* readers staying there and, although she didn't like it, you could tell a few were taking pictures of her surreptitiously, with their phones.'

'I'm surprised she even allowed phones into the, um, sixteenth century.'

'Aye, well, that's why the woman didn't show it to her.'

'A picture?'

'On her phone. She showed it to me. An elderly lady from the Midwest or somewhere. This was the following day after breakfast. Stops me on the stairs. "Master Pruford…" – I was *Master* Pruford on the weekends – "Master Pruford, ah cain't keep this to ma sey-ulf any longer. Couldn't get a wi-unk of sleep last night."'

She smiles at his western accent and Jeff Pruford smiles at the memory, but it's fleeting. Earlier he asked Grayle if she'd be staying overnight in Cirencester and she gave him a wry no and handed over the cheque from HGTV. Although he's asked for

53

a raincheck on whether he wants to repeat the story for a TV recording, she can't see he has any reason to string her along.

'This lady… a very seen-it-all, matronly kind of woman, but she was one hell of a state. Didn't want anybody else to see it, so we went down to my office and she brings out the phone, puts it in front of me…'

He places his own phone on the pub table, reverses it so the symbols are facing Grayle.

'… and she's like this, flipping over the pictures with one finger, half looking away and then she comes to this particular one and snatches her finger back and she's looking over my head, anywhere but at the phone. So I'm looking down and at first I think it's one end of a group photo. There was Mrs Ansell standing at the door of the dining room – after a meal, she always left before the others, which was a kind of queenly thing to do. And she's standing in the doorway in that red dress, all right? Graceful, poised, a little wistful smile. I bloody wish I had it now. I asked this lady to send it to my phone, but she just said a very shuddery sort of no. I should've offered to buy the phone off her or something. What's a phone to these people?'

He puts away his own phone. The pub is old, has uneven timbers in the walls, and they're on their own in the shadows at the end furthest from the bar.

'Here's the thing,' he says. 'It was the only time while I was at Knap Hall that a real shiver went up me. Took another look, and I'm thinking double exposure? But, wait, this is digital, that doesn't happen, does it? And anyway, the other woman's…'

Pruford gives her a look that says he still isn't sure he actually saw this and can't believe he's telling her.

'I'm sorry, Jeff, which other woman we talking about?'

'Another woman in another red dress. Might've been the same, but you couldn't make out the detail. It was just like a sheen of red in the photo. Like an Impressionist painting. And her face… very pale. So pale it's like parts of it have been eaten away.'

He stops, as though he's thought of something for the first time.

'Eaten away by the background,' he says. 'By the house.' Smiles. 'Take no notice of me, Grayle, I'm daft.'

'You're saying there are two women in the picture?'

'The door's open, right? Into the next room. It's two linked rooms that were possibly the same room at one time, I'm not an expert on Tudor architecture. Doesn't matter because all you can see through that doorway is darkness – that could be the camera in the phone, only picking up the nearest lights, no depth. But I remember there were a hundred candles lit in that other room that night – literally ablaze with light. Anyway, the second woman – she's a little way behind Trinity – is in that darkness.'

'Um – I should ask – nobody in the party was wearing a similar dress than night?'

'You kidding? This was very much Trinity's show. Nobody would dare. Would *you* have?'

'I don't do dresses these days.' Grayle's feeling unexpectedly tense. This guy, this ex-soldier with one foot, he would've gotten more impact out of this if he *hadn't* admitted to being superstitious. 'So…'

'No mirrors. No double image. And you know how I know this? Because the expression's different. Couldn't be more different. The other face is very pale and not smiling. The lips seem to be parted, and the eyes are also very pale. Almost white. And they're staring from out of the darkness.'

'Staring at you? Staring at Trinity?'

'Both. That probably doesn't make any sense, but it would if you could see it. The eyes are… they're taking offence. Big time. Somebody's not welcome. That's how I saw it. Call it hindsight if you want.'

'You don't?'

'No. Stays with you, an image like that. I know it's unlikely, a faint wisp of a woman putting out all that negative emotion. But I'm just— I think I *will* have another drink, Grayle. They do proper coffee here, do you think? No, no…' Pruford's out of his chair faster than you'd imagine for a guy with one foot. 'No, I'll get them.'

'Just— Jeff, were you the only person to see this, apart from the woman who took the picture?'

He's shaking his head.

'It's worse than that, Grayle. Couldn't get that white face out of my head, and yet I was feeling very pissed off at my own… cowardice is not the word, but getting creeped out by a tiny image on a phone? I was going to have another go at that woman when she was safely away from Knap Hall, so about a fortnight later, when Trinity was not looking good, I looked up her details and called the number in the States and… she was dead.'

Grayle stares at him.

'Arrived back in the States with pneumonia. Gone within a week. And if that sounds like I've made it up to support not having any evidence for you… well, whatever you want to think.'

'So nobody else saw it.'

'Nobody I know of saw that picture, no.'

'What about what… what was *in* the picture? None of the staff ever see anything?'

'Dunno. Frankly, I'd be surprised if nobody did. But, you see, we all valued our jobs too much to want to scare Mrs Ansell. I often had my suspicions about Poppy Stringer, the house-keeper, but you wouldn't get anything out of her. Not even now. She used to work for the Marquis of Bath at Longleat – must have a stack of stories about him, but never a word.'

'Um… Lisa – the scullery maid? She indicated that after the night of the red dress, something changed. For Trinity. That night she was… the word was "incandescent". And then… maybe something soured?'

He shakes his head.

'I wasn't that close to her. Lisa was closer. She'd know.'

Grayle says nothing. Jeff Pruford's leaning on the backrest of his vacated chair.

'I wonder what she sees. If she still walks that place, what does she see? I mean, does she exist in the world she created, where Knap Hall's all aglow?'

'Different place now, I guess. Full of regrets.'

'More than that, Grayle,' Pruford says. 'If she's stuck there, God help her.'

February

6

Something touched me

FOR THE SHORTEST month, drab February can last for ever. The twenty-seventh is a silvery kind of day, and Fred Potter's taken Grayle out to lunch at the new health-food restaurant in the Rotunda, a healthy four-minute walk from the office.

Significant warning sign. Fred doesn't do health-food restaurants. Fred does burger joints and pubs, like the good old-fashioned journalist he is, despite being barely thirty.

'What would you recommend, Grayle?'

He has the menu. She ignores it, looks him full in the eyes.

'I'd recommend you get this over real quick and go grab yourself a bag of fries. *Chips.*' She slaps her own wrist. 'All these years and I still never get that right.'

She's kidding, of course; it was one of the things she got right from the very first week she was over here, on account of chips sounds so much more healthy and innocent than fries. But Fred Potter and Neil Oldham, who owns the agency, seem to like it when the Americanisms leak out.

She stares at the sepia pictures on the restaurant walls, of ladies taking the waters at Old Cheltenham Spa.

'We had another call from HGTV,' Fred says.

'Uh-huh.'

'This time, Leo Defford in person,' Fred says. 'As distinct from an assistant producer just out of assistant-producer-school.'

'You tape the call for posterity?'

Fred's scanning the menu a second time, evidently looking for the least offensive item. He's now chief reporter at the Three

Counties News Service and may one day take over from Neil Oldham as proprietor. If it survives that long.

'Defford was very encouraged by the stuff you gave them. He liked your style.' Fred lowers the menu. 'Grayle, this Quorn... does it actually taste *anything* like meat?'

'Maybe with the right sauce and a little imagination. But then I don't even remember meat. Where's this going, Fred?'

'He liked your objectivity. That you clearly weren't trying to give him what he wanted to hear. Although you did. Very much so.'

That could be because nobody thought it worth telling her *what* Defford wanted to hear. One of the reasons she didn't particularly enjoy this job. The other was that obtaining background material for a TV production company lacks what she likes to think of as the purity of journalism. Especially if you don't know how it's going to be used and really can't imagine it being anything edifying.

'And he has a proposition,' Fred says.

Grayle doesn't react beyond a wrinkle of the nose. Fred pours spring water into two glasses.

'When he was paying us to get behind the Knap Hall wall of silence... that was just a fishing trip. See if the place was what they were looking for. Now they're actually going ahead. With the programme. And the house.'

'Good for them,' Grayle says dourly. 'Whatever it's about.'

'So Defford would like you to dig deeper.'

'I'm already digging deeper. Trying to persuade the freaking gardener to talk.'

'As part of the team.'

'Team?'

'He wants you on the team. In a research capacity. Which would mean a ten-month contract. And the possibility of more work if it goes well.'

Ah. Grayle can hear the swish of curtains closing on a career, like the screening of the casket in a crematorium as the furnace gets fired up.

Fred nods at the menu.

'Whatever you're having,' she says absently. 'Nothing on there died for us.'

'Except when it was wrenched out of the soil.' Fred beckons a waitress in a vintage Laura Ashley apron, orders two Quorn risottos, sits back. 'Have you ever *heard* a radish scream? As for a dying quorn...'

Reluctantly, Grayle smiles. Fred is Gloucestershire-born, from farming stock. He can admire an Old Spot pig without wanting to keep it as a pet. But she's not going to make this easy for him.

'TV experience,' he says, 'always looks good on a CV.'

'Ten months of hack work under the direction of some emotionally retarded egomaniac looks *good*?'

Fred looks hurt.

'All right.' She sips some water. 'Bottom line: would they be paying Three Counties or me?'

'You.'

'I see.'

It's all she needs to know.

'What can I say, Grayle? I'm so sorry.'

'Well, it's, uh... a refreshingly different way of having your ass detached from the premises without having to hear the word "fired".'

Fred fishes for a smile, gives up, shakes his head. Tells her it's no reflection at all on her abilities. Simply last-in, first-out. She knows how it is. And how much better it's not going to get.

See, it's not that there isn't enough news around. News never winds down, human madness will always be a growth industry. Just that fewer people expect to pay to learn about it. Regional papers are closing down, radio stations getting their budgets minced. Blame the Internet, blame new technology. Nowadays, a journalist is any semi-literate asshole who can frame a blog, and a press photographer is someone in the right place with a smartphone.

'Neil thought it would be better coming from me,' Fred says. 'He thinks you don't trust him.'

'Heavens.'

The one incontestable truth about journalism is that it makes you cynical. And the most cynical of journalists are those working for news agencies like Three Counties, picking up regional stories to sell to newspapers and broadcast media so they can be rewritten or voiced-up by the guys who get the bylines. Or, worst of all, fed into trash TV.

But now, even TV and radio newsrooms are plucking stories for free off Twitter. Stories that aren't really stories at all. Bottom line: someone at Three Counties has to jump. She tries to convey to Fred how much she appreciates their efforts to lay a mattress on the ground for her. But there's no need. If Oldham had asked for a volunteer, she'd've been first to step up to the plate. She can get another job. Someplace.

Someplace that will almost certainly involve quitting the very convenient Cheltenham apartment and starting over, but still... even with her income flatlining, it's going to be a lot easier for her than it would be for Fred, with a wife and a new baby.

'Would at least give you time to look around, Grayle. Knowing you were OK for money.'

'I never...' Under the table, Grayle's fists have tightened. He's noticed how long she's been wearing the same outfits? 'Never figured to stay here longer than it took to prove I could work the sharp end.'

The sharp end is missing kids, street-stabbings, soap stars' extra-maritals. As distinct from crystal therapy, rebirthing, past-life regression. And a picture of a dreamy-eyed blonde holding a piece of quartz they'd made glow, on top of a weekly column in the *New York Courier* headlined *HOLY GRAYLE*.

Jesus Christ, is she ever going to live down Holy Grayle?

'You proved it,' Fred Potter says. 'You don't drink enough, but otherwise you're OK.'

'Even cut my hair.'

'Now *that* was a step too far. I liked your hair the way it was.'

'End of the day, Potter, all I need from you guys is a cash pay-off. And a reference makes me sound like Lois Lane.'

Pause. A woman at the next table is talking about all the flood damage to her holiday cottage in Cornwall, how they won't be able to sell it till it dries out, and that could be *months*.

'Listen…' Fred Potter leans back in his chair of woven cane, hissing in frustration. 'Grayle, listen to me…'

'I stopped listening?'

'He really wants you.'

'What?'

'He wants *you*.'

'He doesn't know me.'

'You know what these TV guys are like. He likes what you've done, he loves the way you linked up Trinity Ansell and Katherine Parr. He says most of the idiot researchers he's employed, it would have sailed over their heads. He wants you to go on doing it, and he's prepared to pay. For the continuity. It makes sense to him.'

'Yeah, and it makes sense to you. And Neil. Especially Neil. He gets to unload me and feel he's doing me a favour.'

'You're looking at more money than you could ever expect from Neil.'

'Yeah, for going…'

Backwards. Oh hell, how did this happen?

Weak sun fingers the art-nouveau wood nymphs painted on the windows. She still likes this place: the Rotunda, Cheltenham, the proximity of the Cotswolds which are nice in winter, pre-tourists.

'It's probably not what you're thinking,' Fred says.

'And I'm thinking *what*?'

'You're thinking one of those ghostbuster shows. Hand-held, infrared videocam. A female presenter who—'

'Who screams and goes, "Oh my God, something touched me, and it was cold!" You mean it isn't?'

65

'Grayle, I never like to pry into anyone's past—'

'*What?* Fred, you *love* to—'

'—but didn't that used to be your province? In New York?'

'OK, let's just…' She calms herself. 'Holy Grayle – I don't wanna even *talk* about that woman 'cept to say even she never sunk that low. Ghosts, that's no job for adults, it's overgrown teenagers in baseball hats. Downmarket, credulous TV. Serious people don't go there. It's discredited. That's how much things've changed, and you don't… you don't realize till you're out of it.'

Grayle examines the other people in the health-food restaurant. At one time, a good proportion of them would be New Age animals, *hippies nouveaux*, with zodiac earrings, ankhs on chains, Jesus sandals. Now both men and women here are wearing business suits and doubtless have season tickets for the gym. Health food is about health, and that's it. It's about taking care of your body to make your life last longer because this life is all you have and anyone who says otherwise is a freaking fruitcake.

She says, cautiously, 'Defford know about that? About me?'

'He might do.'

Grayle shakes her head, sighing.

They told him. They said, Grayle? Sure, Grayle is just what you're looking for.

Maybe told him how, when she first came to the UK, she was working for this subscription magazine, *The Vision*, a forum for the exchange of *anomalous experiences*, bought by the same kind of nut-jobs who used to follow Holy Grayle in the *New York Courier*. Only British and therefore more quaint.

Working for Marcus Bacton, the ex-schoolteacher who was the journal's founder, editor and proprietor. Who was serious enough to hate most of his readers.

Who, some years ago, had a minor heart attack.

Grayle kept offering to try and keep the magazine going until he was back on his feet, but Marcus was shaking his head, saying it was a mug's game. Saying this was the writing on the wall and propelling her, almost forcibly, out the door. Telling her it was time to stop casting around for a workable belief system while reconstructing other people's. Time to get back into the world. Learn a regular trade before it was too late. Or get the next plane home.

Which she couldn't do. No going back then. No going back now.

She never forgets the day Marcus told her, in his gruff, unsympathetic way, that she was on the edge of clinical depression.

Funny how you never see that one coming. Never even see it when it's fully in residence, this sinister squatter who advises you to buy more crystals until your cottage looks like some seaside fake-grotto and you don't notice.

But Marcus did, and he was right: redemption resided in the dirty world, the soiled pool of missing kids, street-stabbings, soap stars' marriages.

Almost transcendent, in its way, her two and half years at the Three Counties News Service. In that time, she's become near normal. Dating, amongst other short-term mistakes, an industrial chemist and a Ukrainian jeweller. Both good-looking, personable guys, if mostly humourless. Where was Fred Potter when he was single?

But she forgets – he's too young. She turned thirty-seven last month – how the hell did *that* happen?

Fred inspects his glass of mineral water, sees it hasn't turned to beer, puts it down without drinking.

'For what it's worth, I really don't think you're looking at mediums and infrared. Might actually be closer to a serious documentary about Trinity Ansell and her dreams of the Tudor idyll. Working-class supermodel, to glittery celeb, to gracious country lady, to... I don't know what...'

'Presence' is the term that Elsie, the kid at HGTV, kept tossing at her. Find out about 'the presence'. As if Elsie had been told not to use the G-word at this stage of the game.

Grayle looks at the long-skirted sepia ladies in the photos on the walls. Images of the dead. *Start off by talking to them about life with Trinity*, Elsie told her, *and then take it from there.* She so hates it when some stupid kid tells you what questions you need to ask.

'There'll be sceptics,' Fred says.

'Where?'

'On the programme. It isn't… you know…'

'Just fruitcakes.' She swivels back to Fred. 'But Defford still wants that house to be supposedly haunted by the ghost of Trinity Ansell, right? I was as good as told to try and stand that up.'

Fred shrugs.

'In which case, how's he squared it with the grieving widower to use the actual place?'

'Ask him. He wants to meet you next week. At the house.'

'Knap Hall?'

'His PA will text you the details.'

'Fred, you're a…' Her voice is giving out. She clears her throat, takes a drink. 'A good guy. It's just I always figured I'd maybe go back into, like, active metaphysics when I was old enough for an afterlife to have some personal significance.'

Which is not strictly true.

'Makes sense.' Fred nods, deadpan. 'Certainly explains all the Zimmer frames in church porches.'

She doesn't smile. Didn't really mean it that way. Is really not sure which way she meant it. Maybe just trying to articulate a swelling sense of trepidation, because, even if she wanted to return to the funny stuff, this is unlikely to be a good way back.

And something touched her, and it was cold.

7

Feral

GRAYLE TAKES A headache home with her. Hasn't had one in years. She swallows two paracetamol, turns out the lights and lies down on the sofa, where she has a dream about a dead person.

It's a dream she's had before. She's in the Three Counties office, working late, and becomes aware of someone watching her.

As usual, it's Ersula, her sister. The clever one.

Ersula is standing in the doorway, like a ghost should, dark-robed. Except the robe is her academic gown, with all the trimmings. Ersula has a bunch of degrees in archaeology, anthropology and comparative religion, but she is dead. Knowing this, Grayle pretends to be unaware of her presence, until there's an irregular development.

The door opens and a man walks in, a leather file under an arm, pair of reading glasses in one hand.

Their father.

Dr Erlend Underhill is an academic with even more degrees than Ersula. He still winces when she calls him dad.

He joins his cleverer daughter and the two of them stand looking down at Grayle. Looking down *on* her, on account of Grayle has no qualifications worth a damn.

Dr Underhill puts on his glasses, bends to her laptop screen and she thinks, *No, please, don't look at this…*

Still trying to figure out an intro for a story about a horse with a talent for picking National Lottery winning numbers. A story aimed at national tabloids, which, if they deign to use it, will all rewrite it anyway. Still, she has to prove she can do the UK popular-journalism thing – like how the golden hooves of Barney the shire horse are helping his owner to rein in a small fortune, that kind of stuff. Only she can't get it right. It's semi-literate shit and her father's face tells her he's seen it. She's slamming down the laptop's lid, throwing her arms around it like a kid, but Dr Underhill's laughter is already sour with derision.

I once had two daughters, he says, *and now I don't have any.*

Grayle starts to sob with rage and regret and looks up to see Ersula fading back into the doorway. Grayle's body lurches and her eyes fly open.

When she stands up, the headache has gone, but its causes remain. Did she truly think that, after a few years at Three Counties, she was going to be headhunted by one of the big, serious papers? Sending authoritative reports from some foreign war-front that people would find on the Internet and email to her father?

Barney the shire horse. Nobody took that story in the end.

In her claustrophobic kitchen, Grayle makes coffee, brings her mug back into the living room, carrying it over to the window, which overlooks a half-lit courtyard. The one-bedroom apartment is midway up a period-looking block within easy walking distance of the Three Counties News Service. The rent is just a little more than she can afford without working six, sometimes seven, days a week.

Never minded that at all. She's grown to love this work. It's so… real?

Stepping back, she sees her reflection dimly in the window. The brutally shorn hair. Getting it cut short seemed to be what you did when you turned thirty-seven. Crossing the abyss between mid-thirties and late thirties, young and middle-aged. Pushing stiffened fingers through it, she finds her open palms are in contact with what feel like tears. She only ever dreams about Ersula when she knows she's done something stupid. A dream featuring both Ersula and her father... she doesn't like to think what that might signify.

Never going to forget her father's disdain when he first saw the column head *Holy Grayle*, even though it didn't matter so much to him then because Ersula was still alive. Not much more than Christmas cards are exchanged nowadays – he never remembered her birthday anyway. It's like the savagery of the favourite daughter's passing has simply carried the lesser daughter away in its bitter slipstream.

Grayle watches a man in a wool hat and a long-haired woman crossing the courtyard, sees the teeth-glint of easy laughter when they pass a lamp on a pillar at the entrance.

To break the loneliness of last Christmas, she slept with the Ukrainian jeweller but felt no sorrow when he slipped away pre-dawn on Boxing Day, leaving a note saying he'd call her. Which he didn't. Sometimes she thinks about Bobby Maiden, a cop she'd wanted to know better but who went off with a blind woman. How can you feel jealous of a blind woman?

You don't. You just go back to work.

Grayle turns away from the window and the wool hat and the long hair. Sits down, drags over the phone and, before she can change her mind, calls up the man who maybe should have been her father.

Andy Anderson picks up. The former *Sister* Anderson, the kind the NHS doesn't employ any more in case they're infringing the young nurses' human rights.

'Funny, we were only talking about you just now,' Andy says.

Grayle says, 'You're still talking?'

Andy laughs. She sounds happy, which is weird as she's living full-time with Marcus now in a bungalow in the genteel village of Broadway, which Marcus hates.

'How is he today, Andy?'

'Disnae change. Laying intae his book most days, already makes the Bible look like a wee pamphlet. Bottom line, he's no' gonnae die yet, unless he meets Richard Dawkins in a lift and they both go out wi' hands around each other's throats. I'll fetch him.'

Grayle hangs on, picturing Marcus at his scratched and beaten desk. Dumpy old guy in glasses, an English bull terrier called Malcolm, with psychotic eyes, lying across his slippered feet as he labours on the book with the working title *In Defence of Mystery*. Bound to be an angry book, a fist in the face of the sceptical society. Like you'd expect anything else from a man fighting off the scourge called Elderly with all the rage of a dysfunctional teenager.

'*Underhill!*'

'Jesus!'

'Close enough, I suppose, give or take a few problems with the meek and the mild.'

'Marcus, look, I'm sorry if this is a bad time.'

There's a pause.

'Is it?' Marcus says. 'A bad time?'

'Well… I got fired.'

'I see.'

She told him it was probably coming the last time they spoke, three, four weeks ago, but just saying the words aloud has caused a physical reaction She covers the mouthpiece to sniff. Marcus grunts.

'Sorry to hear that, Underhill. Rather thought they might lose some other bastard instead.'

'Last in, first out.'

'Just stay off the… what was that stuff?'

'Prozac. I tried it *once*, Marcus.'

This was when the subscription magazine called *The Vision* was failing and she was blaming herself.

'Only, I can get you magic mushrooms now,' he says. 'Psilocybin. Proved to be better, safer and no bastard drug companies involved. Brew them up in a teapot.'

Grayle frowns.

'Isn't that, uh, class A illegal? And aren't we discussing this on an open phone line?'

It's living in Broadway that's done this. Andy finally quit the NHS for reflexology and allied therapies. She's good. Got offered a job at a high-end alternative clinic, in Broadway. Persuading Marcus, weakened by the heart attack, to quit his crumbling dwelling in the Black Mountains, out near Wales. Even Grayle could see he couldn't afford another year of repairs.

Now they're renting the 'bastard bungalow' behind one of the art galleries on what is arguably the Cotswolds' most tasteful shopping street.

Not Marcus's kind of place, and it's turning him feral again.

8

Shock of the cold

BACK IN THE States, there are alternative therapists as good as, maybe even better than Andy Anderson. There are folklorists and students of the anomalous even more knowledgeable than Marcus Bacton. And they certainly take themselves more seriously.

But there's still an underlying current here that you don't find back home. A fusion with the land itself and a remote, unchronicled history maintained through very ancient traditions. A quality of holistic strangeness which transcends eccentricity.

And it's in danger. Does it take an outsider to see how badly it was damaged, by all the people who bought into it, in a half-assed way? All the people with crystals in the alcoves and a tarot-pack in the drawer and a subscription to *The Vision*. The people who, when the recession bit, began to defect to what Marcus calls the limitless insanity of the Internet.

But his reaction to the approach from Hunter-Gatherer Television is surprising.

'What's your problem? Grab every penny on the bastard table.'

'You don't even know what it is.'

'Underhill, they're *all the same*. Find an allegedly haunted house, poke around at night in infrared with all their useless gizmos, follow a few… *orbs*. And, if all that fails, fetch out the bastard ouija board. Always find a convincing explanation by the end of the programme. Apply paint-stripper to the Mystery. Then go off and bugger up somewhere else.'

Grayle smiles, aware that one premise of *In Defence of Mystery* is that we should stop wasting time and money applying what we think of as scientific thought processes to what we like to call the paranormal. The unconfined spirit, Marcus says, is never going to respond to the earthbound brain. *Be aware... observe... absorb*, Marcus says, *and allow transformation to take place in its own way.*

'I...'

'What?'

'Thought you'd be disappointed in me,' Grayle says. 'It's just I—'

'Need the money. We all need the money. We all compromise ourselves to survive in the bastard material world.'

'It's more than that. I need to work.'

She doesn't need to explain. He was there when she had the near-breakdown that she failed to recognize at the time. There's two or three silent seconds, then he says,

'Actually, they contacted me some weeks ago.'

'Who?'

'Hunter-Gatherer. Appealing name, but that's where it ends. Patronizing bastards said they were looking for what they described as "opinionated enthusiasts". Lot of psycho-babble about a multi-disciplinary approach to unscrambling the paranormal. Believers and sceptics in lengthy, exhaustive and, ah, heated discussions over a period of a week. Live, apparently. Teenager who rang, to her credit, had clearly never heard of me.'

'Whoa... hold it there, Marcus, let me get this right – you're telling me you're involved in this project?'

Marcus coughs.

'*Would* have done it. Gather the money's not inconsiderable. Possibly more than I've made in the past decade.'

'So...'

'Anderson said no. Thinks I'd be in cardiac bastard arrest before the first night was out.'

'Well… I mean, she knows her stuff, Marcus.'

'Threatened to alert them to my medical history.'

'Well, I don't really think—'

'*What* medical history? It was a minor cardiac *blip*. Unlikely to recur, especially considering the way that woman restricts my diet. Virtually living off bastard cabbages now.'

'Marcus…' Grayle's picturing Sister Anderson standing in the doorway, behind an acid smile. 'You do realize they'd have you checked over by a doctor before they even drew up the contract?'

'Bastards.'

'The way it is these days.'

'So they asked me if I'd be a consultant. For their research. I declined. Book to write. Besides, the money would be some-what less if I wasn't on camera. Can't be arsed.'

There's another silence. The likely truth is he couldn't stand to be on the outside looking in. Grayle stares into her coffee where shapes are starting to coalesce. *Lengthy, exhaustive…?* The programme is clearly not shaping up to be what she figured.

'When did all this happen, Marcus? When did you talk to them?'

'Some weeks ago.'

'After I told you my job was hovering over the dumpster?'

'Possibly.'

'So, like, was this… you? You offered to put them on to someone you knew who was a professional journalist with knowledge of the… paranormal milieu?'

He kind of rumbles for a while.

'Indirectly,' he admits.

'And you didn't think to ask me first?'

'You'd probably've refused. Are you telling me you wouldn't, Underhill? Which is why I thought it might be more expedient if they got at you through your employers. Who might think of a way of handling it, out of pure self-interest. Clean break, no guilt.'

Grayle pushes away the coffee, sits up, changes ears with the phone.

'Marcus, you…' She speaks slowly. 'If I remember rightly, you were the one pushed me out of the weird stuff. Back into real life? The New Age carnival was over. You said that.'

'Meant the cheesecloth and scented candles bollocks, that was all.'

'Secular society, now, no going back. No Bible Belt buffer in the UK, so the churches are closing down faster than pubs. And you get fired for wearing religious symbolism, unless you're Islamist, in which case we kiss your ass so you won't kill us, and that just makes it worse. You said all of that, if you recall.'

'You already knew all that. It was what depressed you.'

Sure. Still in her thirties and already a walking anachronism.

'But you haven't changed,' Marcus says. 'Have you? You've just gone underground. And angry, perhaps?'

Anger. Like he could talk. But, yeah, that was an unexpected development. You get helplessly angry at being labelled a fruit-cake, screaming inside yourself at people's self-satisfied complacency, their contempt for any form of self-development, any yearning for transcendence. Like your old man, he of the New England intelligentsia, who thinks—

'What the hell are you doing to me here, Marcus?'

'Thought I was keeping you in remunerative work, Under-hill, but if you're going to throw it in my face—'

'I'm just wary, is all. Can't quite get my head around what they're planning for Knap Hall, and if—'

'Where?'

'Forget it.'

So they didn't tell him the location. Damn, damn, damn.

'Knap Hall, eh? Surely that's where the Ansell woman—'

'Marcus… I never told you that. You hear me, Marcus?'

'Of course you didn't. Interesting.' Pause. 'Is it?'

'Maybe. I don't know. Yes. OK, yes, it is. It seemed at first to be a documentary about Trinity Ansell escaping the modern age and the pressures of celebrity by buying a haunted house… and still playing the celebrity. Go figure…'

'Evidently more than that.'

'Well, yeah, now looks like they want to use her to kick off some high-powered debate on the validity of ghosts. There's apparently a long, possibly secret history of the paranormal at Knap Hall that I'm supposed to find out about. What I found was that Trinity Ansell had developed an obsession about Katherine Parr? Buried up at Sudeley Castle? Trinity played her in a movie, didn't seem to want to let go of the role. They died at the same age, both in circumstances linked to… procreation. So in my report to HGTV, I speculate that Trinity had become so locked into it all that when she found out she was pregnant she started to worry that the same thing might happen to her – that she'd die in childbirth? So she goes away without her husband, takes an abortion pill. And then has a heart attack.'

'Hope she got a better send-off than Parr,' Marcus says.

'Meaning?'

'Married a little too quickly after Henry. Not seen as terribly respectful, that. When she popped her plimsolls a year or two later, didn't exactly get a royal burial. Just put into the ground or an ordinary sort of tomb. Such a cursory job that her body turned up again. In the ruins of the chapel at Sudeley after the castle got trashed during the Civil War, century or so later. Awfully well preserved, apparently. The body.'

'Wasn't in a red dress, was it?'

'Discreetly reburied and then, in Victorian days, finally gets the fancy memorial. Underhill…' Marcus's voice has softened, become curious. 'Ansell's death happened somewhere else, didn't it?'

'At a holiday cottage owned by her parents. Never came back to Knap Hall. Memorial service in Gloucester Cathedral attended by movie stars and county gentry. You're saying no one could think she was haunting Knap Hall if she died someplace else?'

'No, not at all. In theory, it's more of a reason for her essence to be drawn back there. As I understand it, that house was the focus of all the woman's hopes and dreams and desires. That house is her.'

'Was her. It's kind of gone to seed. You read much about her?'

'Couldn't avoid her, living in the Cotswolds. Does Knap Hall have other ghosts?'

'Maybe. Nothing too significant, far as I can make out.'

'Won't matter,' Marcus says. 'All these TV bastards want is Ansell. You must realize that.'

Grayle yawns.

'I guess.'

This night, she dreams of Ersula again and wakes up suddenly in the dark.

Listening to the sporadic traffic. Thinking of when she and Ersula, on holiday with their parents in New Mexico, found their mutual love of fairy tales morphing into something more purposeful. Slipping into a sandstone cemetery at nightfall, crouching behind graves, watching shadows. When they were kids and Ersula hadn't yet discovered science and was happy to follow Grayle on a ghost hunt. Before she left Grayle behind in la-la land.

You, their father said once to the adult Grayle, almost spitting it down the phone. You with your primitive, infantile obsessions...

Breaking off, not finishing the sentence with it's your fault... you killed her.

Thus robbing the world of a superior mind.

Second time, we got it right. Dr Erlend Underhill has always left that unsaid. She tries to blank him out. But what if he's right? What if the little girl she once saw alone in the rain, near a prehistoric site called Black Knoll in the Black Mountains near Marcus's old home... the little girl in the faded cotton dress with blue flowers on it, coming towards her all the time and yet never getting any closer... what if she was just a little girl? And when she thought, later, still in shock, that she'd identified the kid from an old photograph, this was no more than the kind of corrupted déjà vu thing that occurs when you're looking for evidence that you're not crazy. What if that whole experience – her only personal ghost story – was just a product of anxiety and disorientation during the days spent searching for Ersula, maybe some part of her already knowing that Ersula was dead.

One of the more eccentric of *The Vision*'s correspondents, the cross-dressing self-styled Welsh shaman Cindy Mars-Lewis, has explained it to her according to the arcane principles of what he considers an ancient discipline but Marcus prefers to call a ridiculous conceit. She can see Cindy's placid, tilted smile, his easy shrug.

Such things happen, lovely.

But Marcus is not entirely wrong. Cindy, though kindly, is madder than a March hare on mushrooms. Cindy relishes a life on the edge, likes to smuggle the esoteric into his television persona as The Last Ventriloquist with a hand up the sinister Kelvyn Kite. So, yeah. Grayle lies on her back, listening to the swish of night traffic. Go with Marcus.

There are things we'll never know. Things we're not equipped to know. This isn't about petty science, Underhill. Not about arrogant bastards like Dawkins. This is far higher than all that, and the most we can aspire to is to live within the ambience of its mystery.

Marcus making a stand on behalf of people who don't claim to be psychic but are still convinced there has to be more. He hates humanists, mistrusts mediums who claim to be comfortable in the company of the dead, but on the validity of apparitions he's unequivocal. Grayle keeps two copies of his definitive editorial on the subject, guaranteed to reappear, in expanded form, in his book.

Ghosts... exist as momentary reminders. Accept them. Don't challenge them, never try to befriend them. Don't run towards them, waving your crucifix... back away. Instinctive, primeval fear – the shock of the cold-spot – is a necessary stiletto-thrust to mankind's inherent complacency. I've heard sceptics and atheists say, 'I don't believe in ghosts... but I'm afraid of them.' Well, exactly...

Trust terror, Marcus once said, wrinkly eyes blurred with emotion behind his spectacles. *Little else is safe.*

March

9

Until morning

WINCHCOMBE HAS AN affable air, Cindy thinks. It lies easy above the obscure River Isbourne, muddy rather than golden, and a touch hybrid – the creamy Cotswold stone giving way to the black and white timber framing you find towards Stratford and out into Herefordshire. Its shops are functional rather than twee; it still has the feel of a working town, careless of its image.

The late-medieval parish church of St Peter stands on the main road out of town, graceful, Perpendicular, unexpectedly light inside. An open, hospitable place of worship.

And then you look up and, oh dear God, here they come…

Well, now. He braces himself against the wall. Never seen anything quite like this before. At least, not in such profusion. It's as if the portals of hell have been flung wide.

Against a grey and glossy afternoon sky with its cold, baleful white sun, a demonic host is swelling from the stone: a devilish bestiary, flapping and hissing and spitting derision, beaks and claws and dragon-wings, scales and horns and poking tongues.

Forty of them, apparently, although he feels it would be unlucky to count them.

You walk around and their bulbous eyes follow you. Oh, you can laugh if you want, you can say this one looks like the death mask of Homer Simpson, but no sooner have you fled its gaze than there's another waiting on the next corner, gap-toothed and pop-eyed, ready to spring into your subconscious and out again at night, into the darkness of your bedroom.

I'm afraid it's all your fault. You advised me to get the vicar in to bless the chapel, so I came down to look for him. It didn't seem like the kind of request you should make on the phone. I'd never been to the church before, let alone looked up, but oh my God there they all were.

The famous Winchcombe Grotesques. Petrified malevolence. Cindy settles against the wall, under one that perches drunkenly like a deformed bird of prey and reminds him a little of Kelvyn Kite. He's seen many such sculpted creatures on churches before, but mostly they're gargoyles, waterspouts, serving a purpose other than to condition a visitor's nightmares.

Some accounts suggest the more humanoid images may have been caricatures of local personalities, well-known faces back in the fifteenth century. These would be the ones portrayed in states of perpetual terror, as if driven mad by the very sight of you... or, more likely, the faces on either side.

A shout from the street behind makes him turn round. An elderly yellow van putters past, plumber's insignia on its side-panel. Someone inside it raises a hand to a young woman who walks briskly behind a pram without even a glance at the church or its horror show.

Nobody remarks on them any more. Except Trinity Ansell, in the pages of her diary.

I dream about them now.

It's always when I'm alone. I dreamt about them last night. Harry was in Swindon yesterday for a meeting with WH Smith and then he had a dinner to attend so he stayed the night.

The way it used to happen, I would be walking along the street past the church, trying to remember where I'd parked the car and there would be this horrible beating noise in the air like a helicopter's rotors only made of stone, and I'd not want to look up but it came lower as if it was going to take my head off and then I had to look up, and it was one of THEM and I could see its little beak-like mouth opening and closing and then I'd see all the others coming behind it from off the church, squeaking with excitement.

I know that sounds silly, like a cartoon, but it was truly awful. Well you did ask me to keep a diary of things like this.

For the others, see, the more predatory ones, there's no simple explanation. Were these creatures carved by some individual in the throes of madness? And, if so, why did the town fathers of the fifteenth century let him loose on a place of Christian worship?

Hard to decide whether the ravages of the years have softened the savagery or made it all look more hideously organic. Maybe here on the edge of town, facing the high ground, they exist as guardians. Or as a dreadful warning, alerting townsfolk to something unspeakable, perhaps the Black Death, that voracious, indiscriminate plague that was doubtless seen as satanic.

The way he's feeling today, he wishes he was up there with them, his mouth frozen into a Munch-like silent scream, distress etched into every chiselled wrinkle, a memorial of misery as he takes out his phone and reads the rest of the photographed pages he keeps on it.

But for last night's dream I probably wouldn't have mentioned them at all. Probably just have told you about the Katherine dreams, but the things from the church are such obvious nightmare material, aren't they?

Last night it was the usual beginning sequence, which I put down to anxiety. I'm always forgetting where I left the car, which is a pretty crap situation when you have to leave it in a big car park and you're peering over the roofs of other cars and people start recognizing you and nudging one another, probably telling each other you must have forgotten which of your six cars you came in. I hate that. It makes me wish I was a Muslim woman in a veil.

But last night's dream wasn't in a car park, it was on an empty street, I think it was the one that slopes down to the river – is it Vineyard Street? Anyway, I was alone, and I was at the bottom of the street trying to get to the top where the car was parked. It was just going dark but the lights didn't come on and the top of the street seemed to be getting further away with every step I took, and I felt that I was being watched from all the windows, but nobody came out to help and I knew, the way you always know in dreams, that this was because they were afraid to come out of their houses after dark.

And then (and I knew something was coming before it appeared) I saw this little thin figure coming down the nearly dark street towards me, and when it got close enough it was one of THEM with those horrible round stone eyes with the holes in them and its tongue sticking out and I knew I had to get past it to reach my car.

Actually, when I say it was 'coming down' it was actually dancing like an old-fashioned puppet, and it had a full body, a male body, and I saw that it was naked and… you know. I knew exactly what it wanted to do to me.

And that, of course, was when I woke up, and I must have been screaming because Lisa came rushing in and we went downstairs and sat in the kitchen, in front of the stove drinking hot coffee with whisky until morning.

It terrifies me because I know it's real. It really exists. It's there on the church, you can see it.

And what happens if one night I don't wake up?

The first diary – a small but expensive page-a-day diary – arrived eighteen months ago, not long after his second visit. Only six pages were filled – six pages about the Katherine dreams, and they were disturbing enough. She said she'd started a fresh diary, would send it soon. As if she had to get rid of the first as quickly as possible, couldn't bear to read it back.

And then the call from Poppy Stringer with the worst of news. He walked seven miles that day along the Pembrokeshire coastal path, into the bitter, punishing wind.

He remembers someone – Marcus probably – sending him a copy of the *Echo*, Gloucestershire's evening paper, with a picture of Knap Hall, grimly shot against the light under the headline *HEARTBREAK HOTEL*. Obvious, but the impact was undeniable, and there was an inset pic of Trinity at her most queenly, astride a handsome chestnut horse that used to live in the stables here and has now, apparently, been sold along with Harry Ansell's hunter. Her hair was coiled under her riding hat, and she was gazing towards some invisible horizon, her lips parted as if in anticipation of a new beginning.

And now – yesterday, in fact – the second diary has arrived, like a spirit message.

The delay – all his fault. Trinity seemed to have been dissatisfied with what she'd written this time. Didn't want to take it to her parents' cottage, perhaps for superstitious reasons, so she parcelled it up, gave it to the trustworthy Poppy Stringer for safekeeping, to put away in her kitchen under lock and key. Weeks after Trinity's death, Poppy finally unwrapped the diary, finding Cindy's name on a piece of notepaper inside its cover and telephoning him. He told her he'd pick it up when he was in the area in a few weeks' time, doing a gig at a comedy club in Gloucester.

And then the club closed down, the way they do, and – unforgivably – he forgot about the diary, phoning Poppy last week in the hope she'd kept it.

Dearest Cindy,
I'm so sorry you haven't heard from me for some while. I'm doing my best but not finding this at all easy. There are some things it's so hard to share, even with you. I read some of it back and think it just reads as if I'm mentally ill. Anyway, I'm going to wrap this up because I'm going away.

There's more, but I don't feel able to write it yet,
God help me.
With love
T

He's driven across Wales to see Winchcombe church.

Now, satisfied it all exists as Trinity described, he turns away from the church and goes back to where he's left the second-hand camper van he's emptied his bank account to buy. On the way, he notes that there is indeed a Vineyard Street, just as described, dropping steeply from the town in the direction of Sudeley Castle.

He does not enter the street. The diary gives no clue to which of the macabre stone faces represents the horror that would not let dream-Trinity out of the street and put her in fear of violation.

It was his plan to go on to Knap Hall, see if he could get into the grounds and feel what might be felt there now. But there seems no point until he can make some sense of the grotesques – what they mean and in whose dark mind they were formed, all those centuries ago.

10

Hunter-Gatherer

THIS IS WRONG. Three times up and down the same hill lane, which the satnav insists is right. Three times, inching the Mini Cooper Countryman along like a ladybird on the spine of a leaf, and still she can't find the entrance, so it has to be wrong.

Grayle likes to think she knows her way around the Cotswolds, but today it's like invisible walls have formed.

It's still early – early morning and early March – and strands of white mist are snagged in the tops of distant conifers like sheep's wool in barbed wire. The pale-green fields are swelling under a sickly-pink sky, and there are various communities of trees, some bare, some evergreen, any of which might be hiding houses.

But hotels are hard to hide. They have obvious gateposts and big signs. She didn't ask Fred, who covered all the Trinity stories, thinking it was going to be obvious.

She gives up, pulls into the drystone wall and, feeling stupid and foreign, calls this Defford on her cellphone.

His London laugh is abrasive.

'Someone should've told you, Grayle – there is a sign.'

Someone should've told you. Not him, obviously. And there is no freaking sign. Be there for eight, if you can, Defford said on the phone. If you can. Jesus.

He says, 'There's a sign to a prehistoric monument called Belas Knap?'

'The burial chamber. Yeah, I saw that sign.'

And drove past it. For personal reasons, Grayle avoids prehistoric burial chambers in isolated spots.

'And about a mile after that a turning to the right?'

'I took it. I'm there.'

'And then another turning that says farm entrance?'

'Well, yeah, I saw that, too, in fact I can almost see it now, but it—'

'When a large, expensive house is left empty for long periods, its location isn't advertised.'

'Oh. Well…' Grayle nods to herself like a stupid person. 'Right. I'll be with you soon, then, Mr Defford.'

'Leo. This is television. We don't even remember last names.'

'Right.'

Television. A medium well into a second century and so much of it cheap crap now, and they still think you should be excited by it.

She can see the farm sign from here. It's quite small, on a post planted next to a metal gate in the drystone wall, where an avenue of trees steers what she took to be a rough track into bristly woodland. So the satnav was right. But it still feels wrong. A wrong thing to be doing. Something keeps saying this to her.

Yesterday, she spent ten minutes on the phone to Defford, finding out precisely nothing about the nature of his programme but a whole lot about what he'd be expecting from her.

She thought there'd be some procedure connected with switching from being employed by Three Counties to working freelance for HGTV but it just happens. Calling at a cash point this morning, to draw a couple of hundred, she found three thousand pounds had arrived in her account.

It's like Defford thinks everybody in the whole world is working for him unless they specifically opt out.

And yet, from the first, she kind of likes him. If only because she's so relieved she hasn't run him down.

The uphill drive has been tarmacked, but clearly not for some time, its surface greased with last year's leaves and overhung with the branches of spreading trees, thickening now with catkins and stuff. And then, just around the final bend, there's a wall of morning mist and this broad back, hunched in a canvas jacket, crowned by curly white hair.

Grayle, wide-eyed, lurches into the brakes, the car stalling maybe five feet from Leo Defford, who doesn't move at all. An earring twinkles. When he eventually turns it's in an entirely unhurried way, and she can see he's lowering a medium-sized video camera to his chest.

He grins, and Grayle sees Knap Hall, revealed for the first time, sprouting out of his wide shoulders like massive, misty, golden angel wings.

She gets out of the car, shaking, as Defford spreads his hands.

'No worries. Americans always drive slowly over here. Shit themselves on our roads. All these mad Brit bastards going like the clappers on the wrong side. Terrifying.'

'Um…' She holds on to the wing mirror. 'I've been living here going on eight years now, Mr Defford.'

'Blimey.' Defford's pale eyes wobble. 'I had a lucky escape, then.'

Grayle nods dumbly.

'Would've been less than auspicious, a broken hip.' Defford offers her his stubby right hand. It's warm but doesn't linger. 'So. What d'you reckon then, Grayle?'

He steps aside to uncover all of the frontage of Knap Hall in its shallow bowl, its mossy hollow below the pine-topped hill. The house, with its two distinct wings, is like heavy jewellery, made more interesting by verdigris. Its age is indeterminate, it's just old. Its windows are sunken and its stonework is the dirty blonde of Grayle's hair.

Defford looks lit up with pride.

'All ours.'

Well, lucky us. Grayle shivers in the mist. Defford's looking down into the camera, replaying some shots, nodding, evidently satisfied. She waits for him to look up.

'Um, forgive me, Mr Defford... Leo... You're saying you actually purchased Knap Hall?'

'Leased it. For ten months. Place's been on sale since last August. No interest. Not even a derisory offer. Amazing how quickly a house goes downhill when it's been abandoned.'

Certainly true of this one. You wouldn't immediately identify it as the house pictured in that copy of *Cotsworld*, where it's floodlit at night, romantic and sparkling. It looks dull and unhappy, as if it's pulling the mist around itself like a widow's veil. Some of the trees don't help. Too many larches. Nothing looks deader in winter than a deciduous conifer.

Defford says, 'Even Ansell can't afford to have a derelict pile on his hands until either the property market looks up or enough people forget about its... sorrowful history.'

He lifts the camera.

'Been collecting some moody shots while I was waiting. There could be lots of ground mist when we're all here in the autumn, but maybe not. Grab it while it's there, I always say.'

'Couldn't you... you know... simulate mist?'

'Wash your mouth out, Miss Underhill. Nothing about this production is gonna be simulated. No filters, no computer effects, no creepy music. That appeal to you?'

'Um... yeah. I guess.'

'The house itself, the exterior, we won't see that – except maybe in silhouette, a few lit windows at night – till the closing moments of the final show. Can't have it recognized. Last thing we need is crowds of teenage goths and bleedin' pentecostal Christians with placards.'

She doesn't understand, peers at him. The white hair is confusing, he could be anywhere between forty-five and sixty. His accent is the one she's come to recognize as Bloke – upper middle-class English given a faux-Cockney edge by a man who wants to get along with everybody.

'Um, is the plan that I just carry out research for you without ever finding out the nature of the project? Because if—'

'Let's go in the house.'

He turns and walks briskly back, shouldering into the mist which makes it look like he's giving off a steaming energy.

She's Googled him, of course. He used to work for the BBC in current affairs, a producer on *Newsnight*. Quitting to become the editor of a proposed Channel 5 nightly magazine programme which never actually happened. Defford emerged as a private producer, with a Channel 4 documentary deal. Wikipedia says he made a pile of money with a series of indiscreet films about the Royal Family for US cable TV, which financed his production company, HGTV.

Hunter-Gatherer. It's a term for the nomadic, foraging society in which sustenance comes from wild plants and animals, as distinct from agriculture. It suggests a chancer's life, but evidently it's paid off. According to Fred Potter, Defford and his partner have a very classy weekend cottage in several acres down towards Stow-on-the-Wold and attend the cool parties – at one of which he seems to have heard the first whispers about Knap Hall.

With the windows down, Grayle starts the motor, crawls the Mini after him, feeling ridiculous. The track forks away to the left of the house. She parks and follows Defford round the side. Close up, you can see where the original Cotswold stone, the colours of an old teddy bear, meets the much more recent roughcast. Defford's pointing out details as he walks.

'Ansell wanted to demolish this wing, replace it with something more Elizabethan. Listed Buildings guys refused outright. Seems blending the authentic with the fake is verboten. Different stages of building must be apparent. How that's interpreted is up to the individual, but some of these bastards are power-drunk.'

Grayle knows this from when she was living in a little old cottage, but she feels obliged to raise her eyebrows as they enter Knap Hall through a small side door.

'This is an early twentieth-century extension, as you can tell by the comparative neatness of the stonework. I'm told we can't touch it, how crazy is that?'

'Right.'

They're in a windowless stone passage lit by a slanting skylight bar of blue light, cold as a gun barrel. Not what she was expecting from all the lush interiors pictured in *Cotsworld*. Grayle shivers. In her haste to follow Leo Defford, she's left her coat in the car. She rubs her hands together. Left her mittens, too.

'So if someone, back before there were these regulations, had built some kind of flat-roofed, concrete extension that was like a real eyesore from outside…?'

'Then they might be forced to keep it.' Defford tilts a smile. 'Not a problem, I'd imagine, where you come from.'

Hell no, we'd just pick out the really old bits, pack them in bubble-wrap and fly them out for reassembly on the edge of the Nevada Desert.

Grayle says nothing. Why ruin your nation's reputation for irony-deficiency?

'Only the servants actually came in this way,' Defford says, 'so it didn't matter a lot.'

With the camera under an arm, he pushes open what is clearly, despite the metal studs, a fairly modern door, and they step down into a small, square hallway with one small Gothic window. Defford stops before another door, closed. This is clearly old, oak as hard as cast iron. There's an age-blurred crest on the wall above it, and the ochre stones in the wall here are no longer uniform.

'This is where it all changes, and we enter the house proper,' Defford says. 'You get the readies?'

'What?'

'If the money's in your account, means you're on the payroll and we can talk more freely.'

'Oh. Yes. Uh, thank you.'

Defford puts a hand across her to the door, drops his stubby fingers to the wooden latch.

'Good-good.' He raises the latch and steps back. 'After you.'

His woolly white hair is luminous in the dim, grey hallway. He looks impatient now, like a ram in a pen.

Grayle's expecting the dumb cliché of an eerie creak as the old door swings inwards, but it's quite noiseless. Beyond the door, there are two stone steps, down, and a musty, waxy smell. She thinks of candles and death.

Hesitantly, she descends, and it's like…

… like when you enter a church sometimes, from a busy street, and the very silence, the depth of it, is somehow active.

'Mr Defford, are you looking for an actual ghost here?'

'One way of putting it.'

'Can you say any more? What I mean is… is it, you know… is it her? Trinity Ansell? Is she what you want?'

Defford stiffens, then relaxes, shrugs.

11

The significance of holes

IT'S A BIG room, too big for a farmhouse, and parts of it are still sunk into shadow like the night's reluctant to let go. The ceiling has saggy oak beams, wrinkled and paling in places. Oak pillars show where walls have been taken out, making maybe three rooms into one. More ancient oak is ribbing the stone walls – stone made flesh by the pink light strained through mullioned windows.

Defford is weighing the air in his hands.

'Quite a dense atmosphere, yeah?'

'You could carry it out on a shovel.'

Maybe because there's no furniture in here, Grayle has the feeling of being inside the ribcage of some half-fossilized carcass. Which, for a vegetarian, is not a great sensation.

But Defford's smiling, nodding his head appreciatively. This is clearly everything he's looking for in a room, gloriously gloomy. Grayle gazes around, aware of her own heartbeat.

'So this was…?'

'A parlour. This is where the Ansells' hotel guests came to relax after dinner. Take in the lovely old vibes. Isn't there a picture in the magazine we sent you?'

Cotsworld? Grayle rocks back. This is that room…?

In the magazine picture, hazy candlelight is reflected in milky old window panes. Shivers up the velvet drapes and the wall hangings. Touches the chairs you want to sink into and the chairs just for looking at. The wall-wide tapestries, all deep reds, lions and fauns and unicorns. The portraits of Tudor ladies looking stoical and innocent, maybe with a view to keeping their heads.

In the photo, there's a mature fire in the ingle, reddened logs like open thighs. And, in front of it, half-smiling, demurely on a velvet cushion, with the flames around her out of focus like an aura… Trinity Ansell, her hair loose around her shoulders, her full lips parted.

Grayle's shocked. It's the same fireplace, dead. The same fat oak lintel, its underside smoke-blackened, greasy-looking. On the hearth below, a layer of cold wood-ash is congealed like old volcanic lava. She recalls Lisa on the frustrations of Mrs Stringer, the housekeeper: *things would get messed about… Things would get dirty, very quickly.*

Leo Defford walks across to the wall opposite the windows, which is all dark wood, thick slanting timbers like a huge wooden radiator, bleached in places to the colours of old bone. This is not panelling, too rough and must be a couple inches thick.

'Originally ships' timbers. Sixteenth century. Farmhouses were cobbled together in those days from what you could salvage. Wood from old ships, stones from abandoned castles and abbeys, that kind of thing. Now…' Defford's peering into the shadows. 'Look at this.'

An elbow comes back and he suddenly stabs a forefinger at the wall of iron-hard oak, hard enough to splinter bones. Grayle gasps as the finger vanishes, up to the third knuckle.

An unexpected sliver of sun from one of the windows finds Defford's earring and the momentary relief on his face before he hides it with a laugh. He's wiggling his finger around in the hole. This looks to Grayle to be absurdly sexual, and maybe Defford realizes this; he grins.

'Not a knothole, more like where a peg used to be. They're all over the place. Holes in the walls, gaps and old splits in the beams. Which is terrific. Drilling our own might well bring us into conflict with the Listed Buildings guys, and we don't need that kind of attention. Besides…' He taps the oak. 'Not easy drilling through this.'

'No.'

In Grayle's former cottage, you needed a jackhammer to hang a picture. But she's still trying to work this out. The significance of holes.

Defford grunts and quickly pulls out his finger, like someone has tried to grab it from the other side.

'Good-good,' he says.

Grayle sighs.

'Leo—'

'You're asking what's the programme in development? Right, then.' Slaps his hands together. 'We have a commission from Channel 4 for a series scheduled for late autumn, to run for a week. Seven or eight editions, ninety minutes, maybe, through midnight.'

'OK.'

'You might've seen a particular show where people who don't know one another are locked up together. In a place full of cameras which record all their movements, all their interaction. All their arguments and embarrassment and mutual hostility.'

He waits. For Grayle, the truth starts to dawn, and the dawn is clouded with dismay.

'The holes are for cameras?'

It's like he hasn't heard.

'These people don't have much, if anything, in common. And as the days go by they get increasingly annoyed with one another. Talk about the others behind their backs. Scabs get scratched, small disagreements escalate into bitterness, even rage. The atmosphere's thick with paranoia and insecurity, because they know that their every reaction is being judged by millions of viewers, who—'

'Mr Defford, are we talking about—?'

'—who have the power to punish them. The viewers love that. Even more when the people they're punishing have famous faces.'

Shit, shit, shit. They were all thinking *Most Haunted* and it's so much worse. It's like the walls of the big room are contracting, closing in on her like some medieval mechanism for the disposal of prisoners. Get me out of here.

12

All the reasons to be afraid

GRAYLE SHUTS HER eyes on an anguish it makes no sense to conceal. Opens them on Defford smiling, comfortably wedged in the corner by the door.

'Go on, then, Grayle. Say it.'

'*Big Brother?*'

'No.'

'What?'

'It isn't. *Big Brother*, as you might recall, started on Channel 4 and ran for several years, making celebrities out of ordinary people and real celebrities look ordinary – periodically, they'd run a series where all the *Big Brother* housemates were already famous, from the world of TV, pop music, sports, whatever.'

'*Celebrity Big Brother.*'

'Indeed. It all got dumped when it lost its cutting edge, and was picked up by the more, er, populist, Channel 5.'

'Leo, please call me precious, but I like to think I've become… well, a serious journalist, you know? And what—'

'Bear with me.'

Defford puts up his hands, tells her it's no secret that C4 have been looking for something new which would generate that same sense of mounting excitement – the tension, the unpredictability – that you got in the early days of *Big Brother*. But something deeper, more intelligent. More issue-led. If *Big Brother* was a hothouse atmosphere, imagine a coldhouse.

'I don't…' Grayle hugs herself with sweatered arms, '… really need to imagine that.'

'We'll be getting the heating reconnected, but only as background. It's no accident that the Big Brother House is always some modern module – cheap-looking, garish. Like a nursery school?'

'Because the housemates have effectively become children again. No control over their own lives.'

'It's also full of two-way mirrors and false walls hiding the cameramen. So they can walk all around the action. We're going to have to be much cleverer and subtler here, but we'll do it, somehow. And we won't be calling them housemates. Maybe settle for residents.'

Grayle thinks of the few times she's seen the *Big Brother* show on TV, all those fame-hungry exhibitionists. Bad enough in an environment that looks like a kindergarten.

'In *Big Brother*,' Defford says, 'they don't have much in common. Here, they will. They'll just have radically different attitudes to it.'

He strolls over to the window, three panes of leaded lights separated by the stone mullions. A smear of winter foliage through old glass.

'We started off with the idea of two extremes. Uri Geller, who bends spoons by stroking them and talks about cosmic forces. And Richard Dawkins, geneticist and aggressive atheist who I believed wanted to have signs on the sides of buses saying, There's no God – live with it. Or words to that effect. Obviously we were unlikely to get either Dawkins or Geller but you see where I'm coming from.'

'You're looking for people who're gonna totally abhor one another's entire world view?'

'Radical differences of opinion are and always will be at the very heart of unmissable TV.'

'People who, like, resent and despise one another?'

'I'm looking for healthy argument.'

'Living together here? Seven days, seven nights? Night after night?'

'During which one or two of them,' Defford says, 'might appear to have had… interesting experiences. Which some of the others will mercilessly scorn.'

'How do you know that? About the experiences they might… appear to have had?'

Defford smiles.

'Because we've picked the right people.'

'You already know who they are?'

'We're down to a shortlist. I'll give you a copy. Confidential. When you're sworn in.'

She looks at him. He doesn't smile.

'More binding than the Official Secrets Act. More sinister than the Freemasons. Trust me, Grayle, this is going to be the most talked-about television of the winter.'

'God,' Grayle says. 'After three, four nights, they'll be halfway to killing one another.'

And what a stupid, naive remark that was. Defford turns to her, eyebrows edging his snowy hair, lips twitching into a foxy smile.

'You really think it'll be that good? No, listen, I'm kidding.'

She knows he isn't.

'What if they just walk away?' Grayle says. 'The residents.'

'How do you mean?'

'What if they're like, the hell with this, I'm out of here…?'

Defford looks unperturbed.

'If they walk out, they don't get paid. Or don't get paid as much. And we're not talking peanuts for this, Grayle. Think six figures, and for someone big enough it can reach seven.'

'A million?'

'Trust me, however bad it gets, nobody ever walks out.'

'Shit.'

'But quality shit, Grayle. Quality shit.'

'Not what I—' Grayle starts to cough; air's full of ancient dust. 'Not what I meant, Leo. It was an exclamation of… I dunno… on one level, it's a hell of an idea.'

'But it does need very careful advance planning. On *Celebrity Big Brother*, there was always a key instruction drummed into the whole team. Stay ahead of them. Always be at least one step ahead of the overpaid bastards. If we don't always have a very strong idea of what's going to happen next, the programme can easily slip away from us. And that must never happen. That's why we need to know everything.'

'Figures.'

'We need to know… how they think… what they believe… how they're going to react to a given situation. Not too much of a problem with the sceptics, but the others…'

'The fruitcakes?'

'I never said that.'

'More than one kind of fruitcake, Leo.'

'Grayle… as you can imagine, I had you checked out. I know that way back when you were in your twenties—'

'Wasn't that far back!'

'—you worked for one of New York's smaller newspapers, where you wrote a column which dealt with what I hope I don't insult you by describing as pop spirituality.'

'Right.' Grayle nods wearily. 'You don't insult me.'

Defford tells her he was looking for an independent investigative journalist who was both sceptical and open-minded. Who didn't automatically believe in alleged paranormal phenomena, but didn't laugh at them either. She decides not to ask him if he knows Marcus Bacton. It'll all come out at some stage. If she goes through with this.

'By the time our residents arrive this autumn,' Defford says, 'this person will have learned more about them than their mothers know. More than their agents know.'

'Agents. Right. So the people in the house – the residents – this is a celebrity thing?'

'Some better known than others. But celebrity isn't the only thing we're looking for.'

All residents will be specifically chosen, he tells her, because they have a personal history of some encounter with the para-normal. Or a strongly declared belief, for or against. And if the believers claim to be experiencing something here, the programme will be looking at how their stories measure up against what's known of the house and its history.'

'So you need to know all that,' Grayle says.

'Everything. Everything about this house that's even been known or suggested or whispered about. I need the history and the legends and all the reasons to be afraid.'

'But if you know, then surely they can also—'

'No. They'll know nothing. They won't even know where in the country they are. They'll be flown from London to Cotswold Airport. Voluntarily and comfortably blindfolded. Driven here in the back of separate vans, at night, arriving at different times. Mobile homes in the grounds where they'll spend the night, before a briefing – individually – the following day. And then, at sunset, we'll take them into the house, where they'll gradually encounter one another for the first time.'

'They'll be completely disoriented.'

'Absolutely. That's essential. They won't even have seen the house from the outside. Black plastic tunnel from the mobile home to the door. They'll walk on their own from the twenty-first century to the sixteenth. The name Knap Hall will never be used. From the night they arrive, it's The House. Nobody mentions Harry Ansell, it's The Owner. The people who serve their meals and clean the place up are being brought in from London, so they won't even hear any local accents. They'll be confined to a set number of rooms, with all other doors locked against them. Access to the walled garden if they need air.'

'Is that a proviso of Ansell's? Part of the deal for letting you use the house, that it doesn't get identified?'

'No. We'll reveal all at the end. But it's why we rejected all famously haunted houses, any place that's been in one of those spooky-Britain guides or any of the TV programmes or the Internet. It would just take one of them to recognize the location and we've lost it, so you'll need to make sure none of them ever stayed here, maybe as one of Trinity's guests or a friend. It's also important they don't have any clues about the nature of the haunting.'

'When you talk about the end... what's the end gonna be? Will the viewers at home get to vote on who gets evicted from the house and in which order? At the end only one person remains, not always the most admirable. That gonna happen here?'

Defford pinches his earring.

'We're still thinking about it. We want there to be a conclusion, of course we do. And essentially that conclusion should be whether the majority of people think – from what they've seen and heard – that ghosts exist.'

'Big question.'

'And the last person left should be the one who's convinced them that there are such things as ghosts – or not. We'll try to deter them from voting for whoever they found the most entertaining, which is not the point. And we have just over six months to work out how to do that. This is a big, long-term, high-budget operation, Grayle. This programme could be – and I'll be honest here – the making or breaking of Hunter-Gatherer. A lot of competition now. Country's full of insects with degrees in media studies.'

'So what's it called?'

'What?'

'The programme. Does it have a title?'

Defford grins, drops his arms.

'I make no apology for this. We want millions of people to stay up past their bedtime.'

'Sure.'

'It's called – what would you expect?'

'I wouldn't like to guess.'

'It's called *Big Other*.'

His laughter's like a scattering of nails on the flagged floor.

'That title's our best idea so far. Come on, let's get out of here. I'll give you some interesting stuff to take home. But first – you were asking about Trinity Ansell. I want to show you one more thing.'

13
Holy Trinity

SHE GRABS HER coat from the car and they walk around to the back of the house, passing some outbuildings, most of them picturesquely old. Others are clearly quite modern, red-brick even, but these are mostly well screened by trees and bushes presumably planted by Jordan Aspenwall, the gardener who tried to frighten Lisa Muir.

Defford raises both palms against the brightening sky to describe the banks of monitors that will feed images and sounds from the house.

'What we're looking for now is a nice barn to put them in.'

'So your guys won't be in the house itself?'

'Only the residents will be in the house.'

There's a walled garden out back, which Defford says will be the residents' exercise yard, and where they go when they need to breathe. It's not very big and it doesn't have much of a view, just directly to the top of the hill, where the Scots pines frown.

Up against the wall in the left-hand corner is a distinctive outbuilding. The stones in the ivy-stubbled walls are regular and, along with the lack of a timber-frame, suggest eighteenth century, even later. An exposed bell turns on an iron bar in its little turret, below which is a small round window and, below that, the door, which is Gothic-shaped, ivy-fringed. Grayle quite likes the look of it. As much as she likes the look of anything here.

'Chapel?'

Defford nods. They're standing on a small forecourt of stone flags. He has a bunch of keys, the size of jailhouse keys or castle keys. He's tried three in the Gothic door before the one that turns and opens it into a dark cherry glow.

'After you, Grayle.'

She hesitates, suddenly recalling Jeff Pruford: *Putting her on a pedestal, that's an understatement. If you ever go to Knap Hall, have a glance at the chapel.*

'Does Harry Ansell know what kind of programme this is going to be?'

'He knows everything. Go on…'

Inside, she's transfixed by the rosy stillness. There's a narrow aisle with five pews either side, each long enough to seat maybe four people. At one time they must've faced an altar, but the altar's gone, leaving only a flaky rectangular outline on the stones. Above it, a stained glass window in three panels.

'Who built this, Leo? It's not Tudor.'

'No, it's not. Somebody at some stage must've thought Knap Hall needed religion. For one reason or another.'

The light's seeping like juice from the triple-paned window. From the centre pane, a robed figure of leaded glass faces you, offering a vessel in cupped hands. Supported by two other figures in the supporting panes, turned side-on. They stand in silence. Defford hisses impatiently and throws the bunch of keys in the air.

'Obviously –' he needs both hands to catch the keys '– there's a shitload of stuff Ansell hasn't seen fit to tell me. However, we have a lease till Christmas, which is all that matters.'

'Is it?'

'Fuck, no.' Defford breathes out slowly, looking down at his trainers. 'I'm ready to admit this is looking more complicated than I'd figured. I have a weekend cottage half an hour or so from here. We go to parties, the missus and me. We hear the goss. Tuned into the whispers, the nervous laughter. I did used to be a journalist, too, you know.'

'Whispers?'

'In your report you talked about Trinity's obsession with Katherine Parr who died at Sudeley, aged thirty-six. Same age as Trinity. And the childbirth angle. We hadn't noticed that. Inference is that something happened here to disturb her state of mind.'

'Leo, I have no evidence that Trinity was obsessed with Katherine Parr. Only that she played her in a movie that didn't do big box office, and that she liked to visit Sudeley Castle – maybe to get decor ideas.'

'All right,' Defford says. 'Harry Ansell employed a young couple – mature students – to live here, for security reasons. While the house was being cleared after the hotel closed down. Even though they were being well paid, they lasted less than a week before giving notice.'

'You've talked to them?'

'I've talked to Ansell. He didn't want to name them. But perhaps you could find out who they are.'

'Me.'

'There's plenty of time. You at all psychic, Grayle?'

'What, like I'm supposed to get my spirit guide to tell me who they are? I don't think about it. Being psychic means a whole bunch of things, and it means nothing if you accept, as I do, that we're all psychic to a degree.'

'Just asking.'

'This couple… you're saying they say they… saw Trinity?'

He considers, fingering his earring.

'I don't honestly know what they claim to have seen. I think… that there could be good reason for viewers, late at night, to wonder if there's just a possibility that something of the late Trinity Ansell remains in this house. Apart, of course, from… that.'

He's pointing at the window. The stained glass has turned his skin psychedelic. Grayle looks up, rocks back against a pew-end.

Seeing what she was missing.

'Oh my God, I was… I was thinking it was… like Mary Magdalene or somebody.'

But hell, no woman in the Bible has lips like that.

In all three glowing representations of Trinity Ansell, her eyelids are modestly lowered and she wears a semi-smile. Most of the cerise light comes from her dress. The cloak around her shoulders is a dark red wine colour. She wears a gold necklace with a ruby in it. Smaller Trinitys, side-on, are looking up at the big Trinity. The gold cup between her hands is like the holy grail.

It's like electric wires are connecting, and Grayle feels the pulse, shudders. She wasn't expecting this. Turns to Defford whose hands behind his back are jingling the keys. He's evidently satisfied with her reaction.

'It gets better. Seems the original glass had gone years ago, blown out in a storm, and the space had been boarded up. Someone seems to have told Harry Ansell what the original window had illustrated. He became… inspired would be the polite word.'

'He told you this?'

'The estate agent told me when I came to look round. Ansell hired a stained-glass artist down in Tewkesbury, then went through the whole planning process. Submitted the artwork to the Listed Buildings officials. And had it accepted for the strange reason that nobody would ever think it was old. If he'd tried to replicate the original, he'd probably've been turned down.'

'What was the original?'

'Father, Son and Holy Ghost – seen as a dove inside a halo. I suppose people might say it was a blasphemous pastiche.'

Grayle breathes in through her teeth.

'The Holy Trinity.' She looks up at the full-on face: primitive and not what you'd call pious. 'It's kind of turned this chapel into a mausoleum.'

'Except it was done while she was still alive and well.'

'Not what I'd choose to have around, if I were her.'

'But you're not her, Grayle. And it was a birthday present. His birthday.'

'This is getting…' Grayle's turning away towards the Gothic door, tightening the belt on her woollen coat, 'a tad unhealthy.'

'I just wanted you to see it before we cover it over. Which we obviously have to do because we don't want any of the residents to identify her.'

'Why not just lock the chapel?'

Defford shakes his head.

'No can do. We have specific plans for this place that are more like its original purpose. Ansell doesn't mind. He tells me he has no particular beliefs. Not in God, anyway.'

'And, like, does he know you'll be revealing all, at the end? Like whose house this is? Tossing around his wife's name and the possibility she's become some kind of sad wraith in her decaying home?'

'You know…' Defford looks wry. 'I thought that was going to be the hardest part. I thought that was the last fence and we'd fall at it. Either have to back down and promise we wouldn't reveal who the last owners were – and that wouldn't be easy. Or just find somewhere else. But he just shrugged. He really doesn't mind. In fact…'

'Weird.'

'With hindsight, I think so, too. And it gets weirder. He wants to be here, in person, while the show's transmitted.'

'In the house?'

'In the gallery,' Defford says. 'With the team.'

'Like… watching?'

'Yeah,' Defford says. 'Watching.'

'Oh.'

'Quite.'

'He tell you this personally?'

'Came through his PA. He's been unavailable since we closed the deal.'

'The PA explain why?'

'No.'

'And you don't want him in there.'

'No, I don't. Especially if I don't know what he wants.'

'He doesn't have to tell you, Leo. It's his house.'

'We have a lease. I could keep him out if I wanted to. But I'm curious.'

'You want me to talk to him?'

'I'd love it if you were to talk to him, but I'll try not to hold it against you when he refuses.'

'I'm guessing you tried to arrange a meeting.'

For the first time since she met him, Defford's displaying an uncertainty. It lasts like two seconds before he exercises his producer's prerogative and unloads it.

'You getting an idea how big your job is yet, Grayle?'

14

Watershed

GRAYLE'S TURNING IT over in her head all the way back to Cheltenham. On one level, it has to be a major turn-on for Defford. That tainted undercurrent of obsession. An atmosphere charged with... what? Sorrow? Guilt?

The fact that Ansell has never talked publicly about the circumstances of his wife's slightly sordid death.

Stay ahead of them. Always be one step ahead of the overpaid bastards.

Easier if they only exist in the monitors and you're the guy who's overpaying them. Tricky if the obsession is sitting with you in the gallery, and the obsessive is your landlord, and you don't know where the hell he's coming from or how he might react to whatever's happening in the house.

So... Defford wants her to find out, and he clearly doesn't care how she does it. What it amounts to, what is unsaid, is that he wants marital secrets. This could be worse than the lowest kind of tabloid journalism. If she could hack into Ansell's phone without him finding out, she guesses Defford would have her do it.

But, no worries, there's plenty of time, he's assured her, locking the ghosts in the house and hurrying to his vehicle – had to get to London for a meeting. Would call her tomorrow. Well, she can always resign.

She pulls into the forecourt – the apartment block's most expensive asset. Of course, she can't resign. It wouldn't be honourable or professional. Not now.

The apartment's still flushed with sunlight when she lets herself in, the opening door just clearing the nose of Anubis, the Egyptian god of the dead who sits in the boxy hallway with a gold lamé poodle collar around his neck. Her sole remaining New Age artefact, still around for sentimental reasons. She drapes her coat around Anubis and carries her shoulder bag through to the living room. Among the usual stuff, the bag contains a creamy HGTV envelope, sealed, and a CD. Given to her only after she'd nodded acceptance of the terms and she and Defford had formally shaken hands. Which in the UK is like puncturing your wrists and mingling the blood.

Grayle goes to make herself a mug of black coffee. She'll eat later. Considers calling Marcus, who got her into this. At least she can be sure that anything she tells him will stay within the yellow walls of the bastard bungalow.

Maybe she'll call him tonight. She unpacks her bag, dumps the CD and the envelope on the Shaker-style coffee table. Would Shakers drink coffee? Would the caffeine make them shake more?

She giggles insanely, stares at the envelope, picks it up with, for the first time, a small itch of curiosity. Thought about playing the CD in the car, but Defford told her the envelope contained notes on what she'd be hearing. She tears it open: photocopies.

Copy of an email? No, it's not, it just looks like one. People like Leo Defford have forgotten how to write an old-fashioned letter. Email, however, is not to be trusted with advance programme information. According to Defford, the original – like all communications connected with *Big Other* – was dispatched to the network by motorcycle courier, delivered hand to hand.

from: Leo Defford, Head of Production, HGTV
to: Paul Cooke, Commissioning Editor, Channel 4

Confidential update

Paul,

I have pleasure in enclosing our provisional list of Residents.

The following seven people would, I'm certain, achieve the

kind of balance we're looking for, although we're thinking about an eighth, which would probably need to be a woman.

Some of these know roughly what we have in mind. None of them, of course, knows the location.

I think the chemistry here is going to work, but please let me know if you have any reservations about any of the following.

best,
Leo

When she unfolds the list, for the first time, it feel like unrolling a Dead Sea scroll.

An incomplete scroll: there are only three names.

Along the bottom, Defford's scrawled,

All in good time, Grayle. Play the CD.

The next page, typed, reads:

Clip from a Hallowe'en late-night broadcast on the BBC's news and sport outlet, Radio Five Live. Presenter is Rhys Sebold.

She slips the CD into the player. Sebold? Never heard this guy on the radio, although she's fairly sure she's heard of him, in some other context. The voice from the bookshelf speakers has almost the same accent as Defford: Bloke. But it sounds younger and sometimes there's a lazy drawl – more DJ than news presenter – and sometimes he shouts.

'*OK. Kids are in bed now, full of sweets and chocolate and various other ill-gotten gains of all that trick-or-treating. Of course, the commercial side of Hallowe'en didn't really exist in the UK till America told us what we were missing. Well, THANK YOU, AMERICA!*'

[*Sound of mild studio merriment.*]

'So let's talk about what Hallowe'en means to adults. Give us a call, tell us what you think – is the night of ghosts and witches the most fatuous of festivals, something we could well do without, or does it have something to tell us about the way society's moving? With me now, through midnight, looking not terribly scared, is the comedian Ozzy Ahmed. Ozzy... GREETINGS!'

Grayle's seen Ahmed on one of those stand-up comedy TV shows. He's dry, droll and satirical rather than laugh-out-loud funny, and his ancestry means he can get away with careful jokes about Islam. The HGTV note reads:

AUSTIN 'OZZY' AHMED

Manchester-born stand-up comedian, best-known for his routines lampooning spirituality in all its forms. Ahmed, mixed-race and edgy, has recently been involved in an acrimonious divorce. His routine has made liberal use of his ex-mother-in-law, a practising witch who, Ahmed claims, has never denied subsequently laying a curse on him.

'... didn't make any of this up, that's the thing, Rhys. She was a Genuine Alexandrian Wiccan High Priestess – no, I don't know what it means either, but they lived in an old farmhouse on the moors – this is my mother-in-law and her Magical Partner, this old guy with a pointy beard – and there was this... pentagram on the front door, and a broomstick on the wall – all witches are very modest and discreet, as you—'

'Ozzy, did you KNOW she was a Wiccan High Priestess when you started going out with her daughter?'

'Restrain yourself, Rhys, I was just gonna explain about that. My first encounter with the occult was when I was twenty years old. I had this old van. And a new girlfriend, Sophie, now my ex-wife. And I pick her up one night. We're going to a pub, up in the southern Pennines – karaoke night at this country pub, about

seven miles away from my girlfriend's house. And then – sod's law – the van breaks down, about a mile from the farmhouse, six miles from the pub. Course I wasn't in the AA, couldn't afford it back then. And it's a terrible night, throwing it down. So we have to walk back, through the rain, and she's saying, in this funny little voice, "Oh, I don't think this is a good thing to do, Oz. Not tonight." I'm like What?'

'You didn't have a mattress in the van?'

'Not since the roof started to leak. So, anyway, when we get back to the house, there's all these cars in the yard, like there's a party on. But we have to go quietly in the back way, creep into the kitchen, and you could hear it right away. Eko, eko, azarak – I never forget that. Eko, eko azarak.'

'What's that mean?'

'I've no idea.'

And was this in the house, Ozzy?'

'It was coming from inside the flamin' sitting room! Oh, spirits of the west, come down. Eko, eko, azarak!'

Grayle smiles. You can hear Rhys Sebold laughing in the background.

'And here we are in the kitchen, Rhys, trying to keep a straight face – well, me, anyway. I'm going, I have got to see this. And Sophie's like, Shut up. Don't even move till it's over – they're serious about it. But, hey, come on, I've just got to. You know what it's like. My mates'd kill me.'

'You were planning to tell your mates?'

'Rhys, I was gonna tell the entire pub!'

Between little snorty giggles, Ozzy Ahmed describes how he went outside and found a step ladder in a shed and erected it outside a small round window high up in the sitting room wall. The one they couldn't curtain. Slowly he climbed up through the heavy rain.

Ahmed pauses. He's a comedian. It's all about timing.

'Rhys… you ever see something and immediately wish you hadn't?'

119

He does the build-up in a spooky voice. It's as if there's been a power cut. Candles all round the room. The chairs pushed back against the walls with black cloths over them. And…

'Rhys, I swear this has lived with me ever since. They're all… totally starkers… all these old people!'

Pause. Grayle swallows some coffee as Rhys Sebold comes back.

'Is there any particular reason, Ozzy, why old people shouldn't be naked?'

Never forget your political correctness at the BBC.

'Aw, Rhys! Not in a public place, man! All right, this wasn't a public place, but it was public enough for me, and maybe they weren't all old, but it—'

'All right, look, Ozzy, let's be serious for a moment. Wiccans, witches, whatever… what was all this about, what were they trying to do? Was it about healing – what? Did you ever talk seriously about any of this with the woman who became your mother-in-law?'

'No! Course I didn't. Do I look crazy? She'd've thought I wanted to join. I'd be getting me own presentation athame set for Christmas.'

'Your what?'

'It's a ceremonial dagger. Rhys, you're not well up on this esoteric stuff at all, are you?'

'No. And that's something I want to pursue. It could be argued that for over two thousand years a sizeable proportion of the population has been in thrall to what learned scientists like Professor Richard Dawkins are telling us is pointless superstition. But now church congregations are on the slide, Christmas is ninety per cent secular. And yet Hallowe'en, this spooky, supernatural festival, is kept going by commercial interests and people like your ex-mother-in-law who believe in spells and spirits. Yes?'

'Well, yeah, you're right. What can I say?'

'OK. Latest surveys say that, whatever they think of God, over thirty per cent of people still believe in ghosts. Why's that?'

Grayle's like, What? What the hell are you asking this guy for, he's a goddamn comedian?

'Because they're fun, Rhys. To some people. OK, it's all imagination – there are no ghosts, and witches are just people who – quite legitimately, before you accuse me of anything – like getting their kit off in the woods or, if it's raining, somebody's front room. But that's all it is. They're not healing anybody, they're not summoning spirits, because there aren't any spirits. It's all bollocks and it's always been bollocks – sorry, am I allowed to say bollocks after the watershed?'

'No, but carry on…'

'My ex-mother-in-law hates me now. Everybody knows that. I was lucky to get away without an athame sticking out of my chest. You probably remember when the tabloids went knocking on her door and asked her if she was gonna put a curse on me, and she never denied it. But, hey, I'm still here. I think.'

'You are indeed, and don't go away, because—'

'Unless having to do your show is part of the curse.'

'Don't go away, Ozzy Ahmed, because I want to bring in someone who's convinced she's actually seen a ghost – that is THE SPIRIT OF A DEAD PERSON. And not just any old dead person. This is – allegedly – the ghost of an actual witch. Let's talk to the singer, actress and sometimes TV presenter… Eloise. Eloise… greetings…'

ELOISE

Recording artist on the nu-folk scene and sometimes actress. Has appeared in several British low-budget horror films and presented a short-lived series, *Home Wizard* on Sky TV, in which various New Age methods were deployed to repair the atmosphere of unhappy dwellings, from stately homes to council flats. Eloise appears to be entirely sincere in her beliefs and, memorably, put her money where her mouth was.

Hell… Eloise? Grayle knows this woman. Not well, but well-enough to guess how the radio discussion is going to develop.

She's recalling how, a week before they finally folded *The Vision*, she opened a long letter from a woman signing herself Louise Starke. Ironically, it told the kind of story for which the magazine had come into existence.

Over the coming weeks, this story would make national papers and TV, and this woman was offering it to them first because, she said, *I trust you.* Which was kind of touching. Grayle had wanted Marcus to produce a swansong edition just to use the story, but it was too late. The printers had been paid off, *The Vision* was dead.

Hunched on the rim of the sofa as the sunset fades into evening, she listens to the sorry climax of the Hallowe'en late-night special. When it's over, she plays it all again, reading the final notes. After pouring a risky second mug of black coffee, she brings out her laptop, does some Googling on Rhys Sebold, confirming her fears.

What are Defford's people doing? This is tossing live chickens into the wolf enclosure. The coffee's making her senses feel frayed and raw as she drags the phone over and calls Marcus.

15

Burned

'OF COURSE I remember,' he says. 'But what could we do? And what difference would we have made anyway? A failed crank-journal with a circulation on the floor. By then, we were as big a joke as she was about to become.'

He's probably right, but it doesn't make Grayle feel any better. She still has a DVD collection of the first series of *The House Wizard*. It involved a lot of feng-shui and candle-burning to cleanse disturbed rooms, but it was well-intentioned and no more crazy than Holy Grayle on a bad week.

Eloise, with those big, haunted eyes and straggly black hair, became famous in the wrong way about halfway through the second series, when it became clear there wasn't going to be a third. The horror-film glamour roles had long since dried up, and she was left with a derelict cottage in the middle of a field outside a village in rural Warwickshire and no money left to repair it.

She'd bought the place with cash, no mortgage. Not that she'd've been given one for a fire-damaged hovel with a reputation darker than Knap Hall's.

'What the hell was that woman's name?' Marcus says. 'The woman who died. I should know.'

'Alison Cross. The song?'

Claiming this woman's spirit wouldn't rest until the truth comes out, Eloise rewrote and recorded the well-known north-country traditional folk song called 'Alison Gross', which goes,

> *Alison Gross, she must be*
> *The ugliest witch in the North Country*

Grayle has the album which closes with Eloise's amended version.

Alison Cross RIP
Burned in the cause of cruelty

Marcus grunts.

'That ever proved?'

'Not to my knowledge,' Grayle tells him. 'Became a cause célèbre in pagan circles for a while, but soon forgotten by the national media. Generally dismissed as a tasteless publicity stunt by the anti-bloodsport lobby.'

She keeps the cuttings: Alison Cross, aged 48, a member of the League Against Cruel Sports, a shrill voice at protest demonstrations during the period early this century when Parliament was debating whether to ban fox hunting with hounds.

Also a practising witch.

With the countryside split over the issue, Cross's coven announce they've laid down a spell to protect local wildlife against the hunt – hunt supporters finding this richly funny. Fox body-parts are nailed in the night to the doors of hunt opponents, including Alison Cross.

Nasty. But what happens next fuels hatred.

What happens next is that the Master of the Hunt has a bad fall from his hunter, sustaining a fractured femur.

Some unthinking pagan kid tells the local paper that the Goddess has spoken. Provoking a nationwide reaction from country people, most of whom are too educated ever to be accused of a witch-hunt, although fury swells the letters page of the hunt-supporting *Daily Telegraph*.

The Master of the Hunt, something of a local philanthropist, never really recovers from his injury. A few years later he's dead – prematurely, everyone says. By now, Alison Cross is widely shunned in the local community.

Before the year's end, she's dead of smoke inhalation when a fire breaks out at her roadside cottage in the early hours of the morning. Believed to have been caused by an electrical fault. Squirrels – her beloved wildlife – getting in under the eaves and chewing the wires. Coroner's verdict: Accidental Death. Community verdict: Good Riddance.

In her letter, Eloise, living in Birmingham at the time, tells *The Vision* of her personal pilgrimage, months later, to the remains of the cottage. Sending a photo of herself, dressed all in black, amongst the sooted timbers where she swears she saw the ghost of Alison Cross. In the picture, her hair is lank and there are grey circles under her eyes.

'Anybody else see it, Eloise?' Ozzy Ahmed asks gently.

This is how it starts. Gently.

'Does it matter? The message... it was for me. Even if a couple of dozen people had seen her, you still wouldn't believe it, would you?'

'Mmmm... yeah, you could be right there.'

'Broad daylight on a mild summer evening,' Eloise says wistfully. *'It was the most moving experience of my life.'*

'So you didn't just run like hell?'

'I admit I was cold and shaking when I came out, but not for the reasons you might think. And I couldn't sleep that night. Next day I went back. With a friend. I just felt I had to know what she wanted from me.'

'And did she tell you?'

'There was nothing this time. Neither of us saw anything. But we did see the local paper, and that really said everything I needed to know. There was a big spread about people wanting the cottage knocked down because it was an eyesore and the local kids were saying it was haunted. And I thought, Right, I'm going to buy it. There was no For Sale sign or anything, but we found out who the agents were who were handling it for Alison's family and we put in an offer and it was accepted the next day. So now it was mine, and all my money went into restoring it.'

'You're going to live there? Just you and the ghost?'

'That was the original intention. I just underestimated how much it would cost to repair it. The damage was more extensive than I'd thought. The family – I don't know what happened to the insurance money, but they weren't interested. They didn't exactly go along with Alison's religious beliefs. Until I came along, they were supporting the people who were campaigning to have it demolished.'

'So this was why Eloise did that radio show,' Grayle tells Marcus. 'She had no money and no prospect of any. Her TV show was over, her days as a spooky lady in the movies were over. And you don't make that kind of money playing village halls and folk clubs. She decided the only way she was going to get that cottage restored was to set up some kind of charitable trust.'

'For what purpose?'

'Museum of witchcraft, maybe. I don't think she ever really worked it out. Another idea was have it as some kind of retreat centre, where stressed out pagans could spend, like, restorative holidays. She was trying to get a trust off the ground, but even the legal fees were proving too much. She was looking to reach sympathizers, nationwide.'

'Don't suppose it was entirely successful, was it?' Marcus says.

'And all this because you convinced yourself you'd seen the ghost of a woman who died in an ACCIDENTAL FIRE?'

'Look. Obviously you don't believe that, Rhys. But I know what I—'

'You know what you think you saw.'

'So I'm having a commemorative sign made saying it's the home of Alison Cross, who—'

'Bet that'll go down well with the locals.'

'I don't care. They deserve it. They killed her, after all. That should never be forgotten.'

Silence.

'Eloise, have you even thought about what you're saying?'

'Thought about little else for months, Rhys, and it's not been the easiest time, frankly.'

'You believe that some individual was responsible for the death of Alison Cross.'

'Yes. One or maybe two. Maybe a whole bunch of them.'

'This,' Ozzy says, 'is gonna cause a lot of righteous anger in the squirrel community.'

Eloise ignores it.

'I'm not kidding myself that the murderer's ever going to be identified. Too clever, too well-connected. And fire destroys DNA, so there's never going to be—'

'Really? That's what you think?' Rhys's voice lifting in amazement. 'What do you think they actually did? Come on, let's spell this out, Eloise. Did they bribe the police and the fire brigade to destroy any evidence? Is that what you're saying? Did somebody have a coroner or two in the pocket of his hunting coat?'

'No, I'm not saying— Well, I don't know, anything's possible. Hunting controlled that village – big hunt kennels, local people employed. And a vibration starts.'

'Oh, sorry, you meant a PSYCHIC thing. Should've realized.'

'However you want to describe it. Hatred directed at Alison Cross, rumours spread about her seducing local married men, that kind of malicious gossip sets up a vibe. And some kid thinks Alison's evil and therefore fair game, so anything you do to her is OK. And that's how the vibe spreads, and that's how a fire can start... like in the mind? But when you—'

'That's pure—'

'—when you analyse it, they're still just a powerful minority. Most ordinary local people didn't support the hunt at all. Their cats were getting killed by hounds that weren't controlled properly... there was damage to farmers' fences, sheep aborting lambs because they were being terrorized by the hounds and the horses and the hunting horns. All that did much more damage than foxes.'

'Eloise, listen... listen, right? Do you have any idea how utterly ridiculous some of this makes you sound to a lot of people? I can *tell you it's not even country folk and townies any more. I live in London, right? And we're getting OVERRUN with urban foxes and some of us have grown to hate them.'*

'We come from different worlds.'

'No, no, no... YOU come from a different world, which some people might think is called Cloud Cuckoo Land. Listen, a colleague of mine was saying he'd like to have people licensed to shoot urban foxes.'

'Oh, you'd probably—'

'And I don't think that makes him a barbarian, because they're vermin. A health risk.'

'—probably shoot people like me, too, wouldn't he? Look... if we have certain principles, sometimes we're called on to stand by them, no matter what that does to our lives, our careers, our personal safety.'

Her voice has gained a quavery, preacher's strength. Sebold lets her talk, as if he knows she's digging a deep, deep grave for herself and her ill-conceived pagan-oriented charitable project.

'I believe that hunting is about violence and blood-lust. A communal blood-lust focused on one small animal. I also believe that if this same weight of violence and hatred is focused on one small woman, alone in an isolated cottage—'

'Just...' Ozzy Ahmed can't hold back. *'Just a minute, Elly. She was a witch. If she thought she was getting bad vibes directed at her, she could've raised what my ex-mother-in-law liked to call a Cone of Power. Eko, eko, azarak. She—'*

'Oh fuck off! I'm not going to just sit here and listen to you crass, metropolitan idiots demeaning everything I stand for. And don't give me that disapproving look, Rhys, you'll hear worse fucking language than that before I've fin—'

'That's—' Momentary silence, plug pulled somewhere, Rhys taking over. *'That's it. I think you have finished. I think we all know exactly where you're coming from. Eloise, THANK YOU SO MUCH.'*

16

Toast

On one of the websites, there's a close-up picture of the offending sign outside the cottage, which says,

HOME OF ALISON CROSS,
LAST WOMAN IN ENGLAND
TO BE BURNED FOR WITCHCRAFT

There's a blurry picture of white-haired, angry Alison, her face half obscured by a placard that says, FOR FOX SAKE, BAN HUNTING.

Also a recent picture of Eloise, showing how the dark-eyed beauty has given way to someone starker, more gaunt-looking, although she can't be much over thirty.

'I'm figuring that finished her,' Grayle says sadly. 'She already caught most of the backlash against the dumb witch who saw the hunt master's fall as retribution. I'm guessing she's broke these days. And desperate.'

Marcus grunts.

'Certainly desperate enough to take the Defford shilling.'

'Probably two, three hundred grand. Enough to restore this cottage.'

'If she still owns it.'

'I Googled it. It's on some pagan websites. It's all boarded up now, fenced off, but she's refusing to sell the cottage or any of the land. There's vandalism periodically, especially to the sign.'

'Well, good luck to her,' Marcus says. 'It's a chance to get her campaign before a much wider public.'

'Night after night.'

'And late at night on Channel 4, nobody's going to care how often she says fuck.'

'Yeah. Um…' Grayle unfolds the HGTV notes, finds the postscript to the radio CD, reads it again to make sure she hasn't got any of this wrong. 'Listen, about that…'

And then, abruptly, she decides not to tell Marcus what it says. This is not his problem. He has a heart condition and a book to finish. And he's right: what could they have done to make people take Louise Starke any more seriously?

'What's wrong, Underhill?'

'Um… well, you know, I now have to check her out. Find out where she's at now before they put her in front of a psychiatrist who needs to make sure she isn't gonna self-harm or something.'

'Your job to find out anything you can about her that might be used to make good television. No need to apologize for that, Underhill. Better it's you than someone who… who…'

'Who thinks she's already out of her mind? Someone who has less in common with her?'

Well, sure. She isn't about to deny that. She remembers calling Louise Starke to explain why they couldn't run the story in *The Vision*, and they had a long, amicable discussion on the phone, agreed to talk again. She was little crazy, but then so was Grayle, back then.

They never did talk again. Life intervened.

'When you think about it,' Marcus says, 'you're in a position of some power here. You get to decide what background information to put before Defford's people. And perhaps what to conceal.'

'Yeah, sure. And when they hear a nice damaging story someplace else, they just fire my ass.'

'Subtlety required, Underhill.'

'Great. Thanks.'

When she comes off the phone, part of her wants to call up Louise Starke right now, tell her the worst of it.

The worst being that she'll be sharing an allegedly haunted house for a whole week, night after night, with some people guaranteed to be well out of sympathy with everything she holds dear. Who'll be there specifically to remind millions of viewers how misguided she is, how loopy.

And who will include the comedian Austin 'Ozzy' Ahmed... and the radio presenter Rhys Sebold.

Car-crash television, or what?

Half an hour later or thereabouts, she's hunched up on the sofa, rocking with caffeine.

Radical differences of opinion are and always will be at the very heart of unmissable TV.

Get used to it or get out.

She checks the cream envelope in case she's missed a page listing the other residents, but there's only another memo.

from: Paul Cooke, Channel 4
to: Leo Defford, Head of Production, HGTV

Leo, I think we'll be happy if you confirm all these. Ahmed would certainly be a coup and negates the prevailing opinion that only losers appear on celeb reality TV.

My one reservation is that the balance between believers and sceptics, while numerically acceptable, might trans-late as rational v slightly bonkers. The addition of someone either more credible or more... shall we say savvy?... on the believers' side would strengthen the line-up, I think.

I do like the idea of the woman who claims to have seen the ghost of Diana, so try not to lose her.

Otherwise, well done – this is all looking good.

Lunch next week?

Paul.

The ghost of…?

As in the late Princess of…?

Grayle starts to laugh. Oh, Leo, you really know how to set out a stall, don't you?

In anticipation of whatever Marcus has for her, she goes back to the laptop and into the folder marked *trinity*. Already a working profile of the tragic beauty – a gangling, knock-kneed, coltish twelve-year-old when her father's stationery firm switched to a new factory in Surrey and it all started.

Trinity's mother, who apparently had never felt she should have to be northern, couldn't get the hell out of Warrington fast enough. Grayle has never been to Warrington and doesn't know too much about Surrey either, but she gets the idea: the Ansells, a sales manager married to a hairstylist, were seriously into upward-mobility. Which, at first, would've been a good deal easier for them than for Trinity who, according to the national paper obits, was not a wildly attractive pre-teen. Her northern accent was widely and cruelly imitated by the kids at her new school in Guildford.

An unhappy time. In a TV interview – Grayle found it on YouTube – a gorgeous early-thirties Trinity, enviably relaxed, tells Piers Morgan of her efforts to master southern vowels and how funny the other kids found it when she got them all mixed up. The rich-kid Piers nods sympathetically, though, Grayle figures, if he'd been been at that school he could easily have been one of her tormentors.

Watching the DVD of that interview – she's seen it twice – puts her, as an American in the UK, very much in Trinity's corner. Archetypal ugly duckling. By the time she's eighteen and reading English History at the University of Reading, the knees no longer knock, and when she drops out of college for a modelling career which turns into a movie career, she's become the swanniest swan in swanland.

She answers Piers's questions in a low, breathy voice in which every word is enunciated the way the Queen does on

Christmas Day. Periodically tweaking a strand of dark hair from her long, lovely face, she talks about her yearning for England the way it used to be, her sense of being born in the wrong era. Her growing disdain for the crass modern world of soundbites and social networking. The superficiality of it all. She tells Piers she dreams of living in a world where there's no Internet, no computer games, not even any phones ringing. Where people still listen to the silence and hear the voices from the past. She never quite explains that.

Grayle's also found some clips from *The King's Evening* and notes that Trinity had different coloured hair and a wider, more sensual mouth than KP.

Or even Princess Diana, whom Lisa Muir compared with Trinity. Must be a whole bunch of people who've claimed over the years to have seen Diana's ghost.

If it's Eloise again, she'll be toast in the house.

PART THREE

Getting dark

Ghosts... may be seen as a bridge
of lights between the past and the
present.

Peter Ackroyd
The English Ghost (2010)

Late September

17

Woohoo Hall

IT'S MID-MORNING and Grayle's in one of the porta-suites, watching, on her laptop, a recording of Ozzy Ahmed talking to the psychiatrist.

Each of the subjects has to be interviewed by a shrink – one of the old *Big Brother* rules, and you can see the point of it. Not everyone is capable of confinement. A psychiatric condition can have devastating consequences in an intense, claustrophobic situation where you're under permanent scrutiny. So here's the shrink trying to find out what experience Ozzy's had of being in a limited space with others.

'What kind of secondary school did you attend?'

'After I was expelled from Eton?'

The psychiatrist, a young, flop-haired guy, puts his head on one side, looking too wry for his years. Ozzy looks sleepy-eyed. His dark hair is longer than the last time Grayle saw him on TV. He's wearing a purple onesie that says JESUS LOVES YOU across the chest. Yeah, very funny.

'You never forget those harrowing, long nights in the dorm.' Ozzy says. *'All the competition for a bed with a wall on one side so you only had to fight off one big boy at once.'*

He's shaking his head, long-faced, a familiar, slack-eyed expression from his TV gigs. The psychiatrist nods minimally. They're in a grey-walled room at HGTV's London offices in Clerkenwell. Ozzy stretches in his leather chair. He's becoming bored.

'Thing is, you know which school I was at, cock. It's on Wikipedia. It was just a posh comp from the days before they called

them academies. My day, you couldn't pretend you was any more than a thick yob.'

Grayle notices he's put on more of a working class accent for this interview. Both she and the psychiatrist know his old man's an ophthalmologist and he grew up in Wilmslow or some other upmarket enclave in leafy Cheshire.

She's even met his mother-in-law, who still lives in that moorland farmhouse between Manchester and Sheffield and is a nice, pinked-cheeked woman, all too ready to talk, and not in a vindictive way, about the guy who held her up to ridicule for so long. Grayle's transcribed the recording.

That lazy image – very misleading, luv. Austin has a steely determination, and he'll never give up on an idea. Sophie and him – never suited. An astrological disaster, and I always hoped neither of them would get hurt when it fell apart. Never imagined I'd be the casualty. [laughter]

'As soon as it was obvious the marriage was failing, I could see it in his mind – what could he take away from it? Answer was me. I could see him studying me. And then he was reading books about Wicca and the like, devising a persona for me that would sound realistic as well as being very funny. I'm not that funny, really, though I can laugh at it as much as anybody, now. He's a very clever lad, our Austin.

The shrink – his name is Max – finally asks Ozzy some straight questions, like has he ever experienced anything he can't explain? Ozzy, predictably, says he thought he'd told Max he'd rather not talk about his mother-in-law.

Max asks Ozzy why he's agreed to do the show. It's clear he doesn't need the work.

Ozzy says he likes to meet new people.

'Do you generally get on with new people?'

'I get on with everybody, cock. Look at us now – it's like we've been big mates since we were kids.' He leans forward, peering at the shrink through his contact lenses – Grayle knows all these minor personal details. *'You gonna be there the whole time, Max?'*

'Probably. Does that bother you?'

'If it doesn't bother you, it doesn't bother me.'

Max blinks. Ozzy points a finger, smiles.

'You'll be all right, cock. Just make sure your name's far enough up the credits.'

'Thank you. Ozzy, can I go back to the question you avoided? Mothers-in-law apart, has anything ever happened to you that made you wonder if there were, shall we say, more things in heaven and earth...?'

Ahmed leans back in his chair, ponders.

'Once spent a night in a room everybody thought was haunted. Possibly because of the human remains in there.'

Silence, Max lowering his chin to his chest.

'Human remains. I see. Please continue, Mr Ahmed.'

Ozzy shakes his head.

'Can't.'

'Why not?'

'Because...' Ozzy sits up. 'I've been asked – as, I'm assuming, we all have – to tell a story, round the fire on the first night. A personal ghost story. Or a story which will illustrate why I don't believe in ghosts.'

'And which is yours going to be?'

'Not saying. Wouldn't be any suspense then, would there?'

And clams up. It wouldn't surprise Grayle to learn he's been talking to some *Big Brother* producer, learning about the always-stay-one-step-ahead rule. Determined to make *Big Other* work for him and his career.

Grayle switches off. She's watched four of these interviews with the shrink. The former Liberal Democrat MP, Roger Herridge, is the most defensive, even though there was no mention of florists (it's a long story). The psychologist, Ashley Palk, is dismissive, quite spiky about it really, as if she, as a professional, should not be subjected to this kind of indignity. Palk is the most obvious sceptic, edits a magazine for sceptics. Eloise is quiet but not in the least guarded, wearing her spirit on her sleeve.

Next to face Max – maybe this afternoon – will be Colm Driscoll, the hip-hop artist from Dublin who came off heroin into born-again Christianity. Driscoll now works with a charity helping young addicts in Liverpool and has agreed to go into the House in return for a substantial donation to his cause.

Which leaves only Sebold and…

HELEN PARRISH

Former deputy Royal Correspondent, BBC News.

After losing her job a few years ago, Parrish accused the BBC of ageism, which the Corporation strongly denied. Shortly afterwards, the *Guardian* diary column published a story, probably leaked from the BBC newsroom, to the effect that Parrish's contract had not been renewed because of fears about her state of mind after she confided to colleagues that she'd seen what she was convinced was the ghost of the late Princess Diana.

At the time, Parrish refused to discuss it and – perhaps under the impression that her journalistic career was not yet over – turned down a substantial offer for her story from the *News of the World* in its final days. Probably a mistake. I'm told that her current financial situation would make our offer hard to refuse.

Made redundant by the BBC, she's continued working, as a freelance, but it doesn't seem to have been exactly remunerative. When asked about Diana she's wryly philo-sophical but firm.

'Ghosts? I don't know. Agnostic. Go away.'

She thought for a long time that the Diana thing was going to be Eloise and is glad that it isn't. As Grayle understands it, Parrish originally agreed to do *Big Other* after an approach from an old friend who was working for Hunter-Gatherer Television as a director. Back in April, the old friend left HGTV for an unmissable offer from the States. Defford's people have stayed in intermittent contact with Parrish, who keeps assuring them that she's still up for this, but the fact remains that she's not yet signed a contract. No problem, she keeps saying, she'll get back to them.

Defford thinks she's just after more money. Word is she's effectively washed up and, as this might be her last big fee, she's pushing it to the wire. There's always money in reserve, but Defford's holding his nerve for a little longer.

Grayle goes out into the soft September morning. Personally, she'd feel happier if Parrish was all tied up. No one knows the details of the Diana story, but if it's remotely convincing, it would be a significant exclusive for *Big Other*. This is not some flimsy New Ager, this is an experienced reporter who covered wars before landing royalty. Potentially, a very solid brick in the wall against scepticism.

Outside, the fourth and biggest portacabin is being unloaded. Behind it, Knap Hall glowers from its hollow.

It's that time, just before the trees start to change colour, when the English countryside seems at its heaviest under warm, leaden skies. The trees are vividly green after a freakishly hot, dreamlike summer that started late and isn't going anywhere fast.

Metal gates have been installed a few yards inside the entrance, the posts hidden behind dark clumpy yews, centuries old. The long drive to the house is a major plus – the fact that it can't be seen from any roads. All the same, a security firm has been on site for weeks, installing new gates and fencing. Patrolling at night, originally with guard dogs, but not now.

Apparently, the dogs got restless and made too much noise. Sometimes they howled. Do trained guard dogs habitually howl? Grayle thinks not. Well they just don't, do they?

Nobody's commented on it. The HGTV people seem... well, bizarrely, they seem not interested. It's as if whatever is supposed to happen here should not be happening – is not contracted to happen – until the cameras are switched on at the end of next month. Hallowe'en, that is, the night it ends – TV is nothing if not predictable.

She's met most of Leo Defford's core production team now, and they tend to be scarily young. Have names like Emily and Jamie. Go bounding like puppies, in and out of Knap Hall. Woohoo Hall is what they've taken to calling it. Which kind of annoys Grayle. You must never let this stuff take you over, but equally you don't diss it.

Couple of the puppies have taken her to dinner at country pubs, evidently with a view to booking a room for the night, but she's resisted, pretending she thinks it's just a working dinner. They discussed the programme, she avoided talking about her background. They make her feel old, these guys, so full of ambition and ideas they clearly think are new and exciting but which sound flimsy and obvious to Grayle. Except, perhaps, for Defford himself, she's yet to encounter someone who thinks a disturbed old house is any different from a fairground ghost train.

Not that Knap Hall has done anything to suggest otherwise. Sometimes, around dusk, as she's about to leave for home, she looks down at the empty house, with its blackened, mullioned windows in its pie-crust walls, and thinks she sees movement there.

Not shapes behind old glass, more a slow shifting and reset-tling of the whole building. Like respiration.

But that's what dusk does.

18

Still there

Otherwise, Knap Hall is still being evasive, its ghosts indistinct.
We still have to bring its hidden history alive.

Defford. She doesn't see as much of him now. He sends these terse texts and emails from his phone. Hidden history. Huh. Suppose there isn't any? Does that even matter if they have the big two: Trinity and KP.

They've been shooting stuff in the house to use as insert-material. Pictures of the rooms stripped back to their basics, with rushes on the flags. People in rough clothing who will appear on the screen dulled by sepia and shadows. But who are they? They have no identities, no personalities, and time's running out. If she doesn't want to be sent in search of a reliable medium she needs to come up with something HGTV can dramatize, and fast.

From local records, libraries and the Internet, she's compiled a list of former owners and tenants of Knap Hall, going back to the early sixteenth century when it had different names – the name Knap Hall didn't appear till the eighteenth century – and was occupied by working farmers, yeoman-types, raising live-stock and big families.

Sepia is right. They were not colourful people. History – even local history – has stepped over them. She's talked to four local historians so far, not finding much to excite her. Knap Hall is still well overshadowed by the lustrously restored castle which once played host to Elizabeth I and her parents, Henry VIII and Anne Boleyn, and is now a resting place at last for Katherine Parr. All these big people, in the fast lane of history. No real surprise this place has been bypassed.

Down towards the main gate, some guys are assembling the prefabricated hotel block – yeah, really – that will house Grayle's personal suite. She'll be expected to live here during the transmission period – what Defford calls the final days. He keeps using that phrase, evidently finding it satisfyingly portentous.

Grayle walks beside the main lawn, past slender rowan trees with their blood-bright berries, thinking of Katherine Parr and Trinity Ansell, dead at a younger age than she is now. Mortality thrown in your face at every turn.

Beyond the lawn are small fields, made private by still-green hedgerows. Coming from a country of endless fences, Grayle enjoys the intimacy of hedgework. She watches Jordan Aspenwall squatting outside his shed beside his ride-on mower, tools spread out on the grass. He's now on the HGTV payroll till Christmas, apparently for more money than he was getting from Harry Ansell. He looks contented enough, a not unfriendly hand raised. All seems peaceful until a hostile fizzing on the ground directly in front of her sends Grayle backing off from a gang of wasps savaging an early-windfall apple…

… almost into the path of the white Discovery ripping up the drive far too fast. Leo Defford at the wheel, being a crazy English bastard and not even noticing her until the big SUV has gone crunching past.

The Discovery doesn't stop, but Grayle feels uncomfortable being caught just walking the grounds like she doesn't have enough work to do, even though the truth is she's barely had a day off since early April. Probably now knows more about Trinity Ansell than either of Trinity's shallow, showbiz biographers, both of whom raced to write final, unenlightening chapters for post-mortem editions. Grayle bought both these women expensive lunches, learning nothing significant. Neither ever met Trinity.

'Man in a hurry.' It's the gardener. 'You all right, Miss Underhill?'

'Grayle. I'm fine, thanks. You?'

'Lot still to do,' Jordan says. 'Just hope there's time, that's all.'

Jordan is not what she was expecting, which was either one of those private-school-educated types who write gardening columns in the posh papers, or some dark, unfriendly Mellors figure furtively fancying Trinity Ansell. Turns out to be a stocky, earnest, middle-aged local man in a plaid work shirt.

She stops at the lawn's edge. She's tried a couple of times to talk to him about the stories with which he'd tried to frighten Lisa, the scullery maid: *said people used to think they were being followed in the passages, and they'd turn round and there'd be, like, a shadow?*

Jordan said he was just having a bit of fun and, no, he'd seen nothing. He always prefers to talk about his work, particularly the Elizabethan-style knot garden he's planted in what used to be a flat paddock to the side of the house, a smaller version of the fine specimen at Sudeley. It's a complex mosaic of sculpted bushes with a gravel path around it, formerly used to reach an old barn. It's geometrically exact, Jordan says.

'So you'll be like winding down with the fall, Jordan?'

He smiles, a tad shyly.

'Anybody notice if I did?'

'I guess I would. That's not to say—'

'I seen you taking it all in. Nobody else seems to notice much.'

'I guess they're all too…'

… up their own asses.

There's a patch of quiet, the lawn dappled with shadows of trees.

'He notices.'

Jordan's nodding towards the house. Grayle says nothing. He means Knap Hall itself? Is that just how they talk around here, everything male or female, or does he see the house as some kind of sentient being?

People in overalls go in and out, guys with tools, guys with clipboards and cameras. Carpenters and electricians and plumbers and designers. The house is just another prop. Few of these people know just what's going to happen there next month, and neither does Jordan – most of the planning meetings have taken place in London or at Defford's Cotswold second home, miles from here.

'He's, um, he's resisting me,' Grayle says.

Jordan looks only slightly curious, says nothing. She decides to tell him more than she should, have one last go at bringing him out… if there's anything to come out. She'll grab anything now.

'See, my job – some of what I do here – is to find out what happened at Knap Hall before Trinity Ansell? Saw herself as restoring the house to what it had been. Only it's becoming clear she was just intent on creating some kind of small Sudeley Castle. Which history tells us really wasn't what this house had been at all. More of a working farm.'

Jordan's nodding slowly.

'And the kind of people who lived here,' Grayle says, 'were not exactly aristocracy.'

'Wouldn't be doing no knot garden them days, that's for sure.'

'I guess not.'

'Chance of a lifetime for me, look. I'm back on it, now, but for how long? He don't want it, Mr Ansell. Never really paid any of it much notice.'

'Trinity's house, Trinity's garden. You spend much time with her, Jordan?'

'Never got that close to her, to be honest. She was our boss but she never made demands.'

'What about Harry Ansell?'

'Wasn't his house. You ever talked to Mr Ansell you knew he wouldn't keep the place if… well, if she went off, folks used to say. Nobody thought…'

'Maybe it'll be sold to some Russian oligarch when we're through here. Who wants a well-made garden. Um… whoever lived here in the past, my boss, he wants to get some actors to appear as them? Only we don't really know what they were like? They're just names in the records.'

Jordan nods, expressionless.

'So I'm looking for people who might know the real history? Stuff you can't get out of books. I was wondering if you knew anybody might help.'

'Dunno who you talked to.'

'Well, nobody too local.'

Grayle lists the names of the historians she's consulted. For two of them she had to go to university faculties, in Birmingham and Bristol. And, still, most of what they knew was about Sudeley and the town of Winchcombe, one telling her at length about how tobacco was grown in the area before it was banned to protect imports.

'Tobacco Close,' Jordan says. 'That's the road where I live. Down Winchcombe.'

'But, sadly, unless Knap Hall was owned by some early tobacco baron, it's not relevant.'

Jordan considers, breathing in deeply.

'Sir Joshua Wishatt?'

'He was a tobacco baron?'

'Dunno 'bout that, but he owned Knap Farm.'

'When was this?'

Jordan shakes his head.

'En't good with dates. You talked to Mary Rutter?'

'Who is she?'

'Mary Rutter. In Winchcombe. Wrote a book. Way back. Don't think you can buy 'em now. Didn't go down too well with some folks. Went talking to the old 'uns and some folks reck-oned she was taken for a ride. All I can tell you is she wasn't wrong about all of it. When I was a kid, it was kind of, don't you go playing up near Knap Farm or you'll wind up paying Abel's

Rent. Wasn't my dad, said that, it was my… my mother's dad. So it goes back.'

'And what was Abel's Rent?'

'I don't know the details except there was a bloke called Abel and he worked for Wishatt and you didn't wanner be alone with either of them if you was female, and they used to say he was still there, kind of thing.'

'Wishatt?'

'Abel.'

'Who said he was still here?'

'I dunno. I en't never been that interested in that ole stuff. Talk to Mary Rutter, I would, but don't say it was me—'

'Your grandfather told you about it?'

Jordan shakes his head.

'I said enough. Talk to Mary Rutter. Just don't say it was me put you on to her. Always a sore point, that book. She wrote a few others, but I don't think she ever wrote about Wishatt again.'

'And she lives in Winchcombe?'

'Old cloth-weavers' cottages, opposite the church.'

'Thank you. Um… I've heard some ghost stories. About the house? I guess your grandad wouldn't be…?'

'Been dead years. He was a bugger for the old stories, if you bought him a glass or two. Me, I'm a man of science, Miss Underhill. Horticulture's a science, and science got an answer to everything we sees and thinks we understands. All this spirits of the dead stuff, I got no patience with that, look. It's just an old house. Old houses – well, be funny if there hadn't been some bad things happen there in four or five hundred years.'

'You remember the, um, holiday home for bad kids?'

'Weren't the best idea.'

'I heard about that. Nineteen sixties?'

'Before I was born, but it's never been forgotten. Wasn't properly thought out. These fellers, they think the countryside's like a desert where you can't do no harm running wild. Boys didn't even get locked up at night.'

'And one of them raped a girl. A local girl?'

'Yeah.'

'That's awful.'

'Never the same again.'

'The girl? Is she… still around?'

'Dead.'

'What… recently?'

'Year or so after it happened. Brutal. Nasty. Couldn't live with it. Took her own life.'

'Jesus.'

Another reason for local people not to be too fond of Knap Hall. Jordan's looking past her, towards the house.

'They shut the place down within a year of it, and after that it was derelict for a good while. Rooms turned into dormitories, and the extensions, so it wasn't much good for anything. After that it was a youth hostel, but I don't think that did too well. *He* don't look happy.'

'What?' Grayle turning, thinking he means the house. 'Oh.'

It's Defford, hands on hips, planted like a fire hydrant at the top of the yellow steps leading up from the house. He's staring across, maybe at Grayle, battered leather manbag over a shoulder, and, no, he doesn't look happy.

Something's happened.

She pretends she hasn't noticed Defford, thanks Jordan and heads off back to her cabin, repeating 'Mary Rutter' under her breath. 'Mary Rutter, Mary Rutter', like some combination of a mantra and a tongue-twister, until she can write it down.

Along with Abel.

And *still there*.

In the cabin the company cellphone's bleeping on her desk. She's supposed to take it everywhere, forgot.

'I've been calling you for twenty minutes, Grayle.'

Kate Lyons, Defford's formidable PA. In London today, surely, even if she does sound like she's in the same room.

'I went out without the phone, Kate, I'm sorry.'

'I think you need to call Mr Sebold. He rang here an hour ago, very unhappy. Thinks he's being spied on. People talking to his friends and former colleagues about him. You, in other words.'

'Well… yeah. But that was weeks… months ago.'

'He seems to think it's still going on.'

'Well it isn't.'

In relation to her inquiries about both Sebold and Parrish, Defford gave her numbers for the more reliably talkative of his former colleagues at the BBC. It's the part of the job she hates. Makes her feel her like a seedy private eye.

'You could have been more discreet, Grayle.'

What? Like how?

Grayle says nothing.

'Anyway, someone gave him your name. We think you should be the one to talk to him, put his mind at rest. This afternoon, not now, don't want him to think he's in control. Tell him this is something that happens to everybody going into the house. Be nice to him. He'll be reassured to hear your voice.'

Her inane, harmless babble, in other words.

'He's not going to cry off,' Kate says. 'Not in his position. But he has had a difficult time in the past year.'

'He's given a few other people a bad time.'

'Might be better not to point that out,' Kate says.

19

Little sister

'NO, NO, YOU'RE *absolutely right, I'm not a believer in ANY GOD,'* Rhys Sebold is saying. *'That's my choice.'*

Grayle's listening, through cans, to his radio interview with Colm Driscoll, the junkie rapper whose life turned around after he became a born-again Christian. On the advice, apparently, of his dead great-grandfather, a Baptist minister in Dublin.

Dead, geddit? A feature of his rehab-dreams, this ancestor, and in one manifestation was accompanied by a man with a halo.

It explains why he's on the list, but he isn't going to have a great time in the house. Rhys – this was on a different BBC radio show from his controversial session with Ozzy and Eloise – is clearly getting exasperated.

'Why do you think I should be? I think you'll find that nobody is actually expected to have a religion any more, Colm. We know a good deal more science now, and the Spanish Inquisition's long over. I'm simply expressing my amazement at your surprise that some people – not to say the majority of people – don't believe that what you were experiencing was any more than a surreal, recurrent dream.'

Grayle's learned that Rhys was unusual amongst radio presenters on a news station in that many of his questions appeared to be conditioned by his personal opinions. Isn't BBC News supposed to at least appear neutral on everything? Rhys was into making it clear to guests where he stood on some contentious issue and then generously allowing them to argue with him for a short while before he cut in and slapped them down. Then, seconds later, he'd be like they were old buddies again.

She's noticed he was often audibly hyper, talking too fast, and you'd have to wonder if he'd snorted a line of coke in the staff bathroom before going on air. Not unlikely in view of what happened later. However many noses Rhys has gotten up, you do have to feel sorry for him now.

A wide shadow falls across Grayle and she turns to see Leo Defford in the doorway. The strap of his leather manbag is diagonally across his chest, shoulder to waist, like a bandolier full of bullets. The nearer it gets to transmission, the more aggressive Defford looks.

'Well…' Grayle pulls off her headphones, ejects the CD. 'No love lost there, Leo.'

'What?'

'Sebold and Colm Driscoll. Do we have an established procedure for when two guys come to blows in the house? At what stage do we call the cops?'

Defford, face set like cement, jabs a thumb at the CD case.

'Bin it.'

'Huh?'

'Always one, Grayle. You get to this stage, and there's always one fucker who lets you down.'

Oh no…

She's on her feet, staring at him, panic setting in. Sebold already pulled out because of her invasion of his privacy? Before she can even call him? This is not going to be a good day.

Defford unslings his manbag.

'Bloke who's promised the money to a charity, you don't expect him to walk, do you?'

'Driscoll?'

Relief throws her back into her seat.

Though actually she's legitimately annoyed, having endured hours of the guy's rhythmic rants on YouTube, talked to music journalists about his angry youth. Even dipped into some of the lurid gothic literature which coloured his material before Christianity.

'One of these born-again churches,' Defford says. 'Funda-mentalist. Restrictive. His so-called minister learns about us, tells him that all spirits of the dead are from Satan. And because he's a recovering addict, Satan will see him as a target. Will delight in breaking him down in front of millions of viewers.'

'That's the kind of guy Satan is.'

'So if Driscoll doesn't want to wind up back on the smack, he needs to forget he ever heard of us. Primitive or what?'

'What you gonna do?'

'Already done it. Patted the little bastard on the back. There, there… course I understand, mate. Then bunged him ten grand for his junkies' charity.'

'You paid him ten thousand? For nothing?'

'For his silence. We don't want to be reading about this on Twitter, and we don't want any lunatic-fringe churches trying to shaft us. At least, not before we're rolling, when that kind of thing's useful for publicity. We'll get over it. Just that it leaves us seriously unbalanced, with all the weight on the sceptical side.'

Grayle wrinkles her nose.

'Seems to me, Leo, it was always that way. You don't have anybody in this line-up who's gonna outsmart guys like Ozzy Ahmed in an argument. Except maybe Helen Parrish, if she hasn't changed.'

'Parrish.' Defford leans over, grabs the Sebold/Driscoll CD and bins it himself. 'We do need Parrish in handcuffs, don't we?'

'I'm a mite worried, Leo. I've compiled an extensive biog, from her time on a local newspaper, through her period in Northern Ireland, end of the Troubles, to the Royal years, but nothing in her background hints at any interest in the super-natural. Now while that's no bad thing if her Princess Di story hangs together…'

'No, you're right, that would be a good thing. No axe to grind.'

Defford's talked personally to one of his former colleagues at *Newsnight*, learning nothing about Parrish's alleged experience other than it happened while she was shooting a documentary about the posthumous cult of Diana. As for what she actually said… well, it doesn't seem to come to much at all, and there's even a rumour she tried to backtrack, claiming all she'd said was that working on the documentary had made her feel so close to Diana it was like her ghost was walking alongside.

'We need to move on this, don't we?' Defford says soberly. 'Could be she doesn't want to tell us in case we don't think it's strong enough, and if we only learn when it's too late to get anything better…'

'That occurred to me, too.'

'I'll make a call this afternoon. To a mutual friend. Meanwhile, on the positive side, I've just been told the chapel's finished. You want to check it out?' He tries for a grin. 'Maybe we're in need of spiritual sustenance.'

'Sure.'

'Shame about Driscoll,' Defford says as they leave the cabin. 'All that lovely mutual hatred gone to waste.'

The chapel of Holy Trinity.

Not any more. God…

Harry Ansell's stained-glass window is gone. They've used ornately carved panelling to box in that whole wall, including the space where the outline of an altar was visible the last time Grayle was here. The panels have ornate foliate patterns like you find on church rood screens.

And significant holes. Always the holes.

Defford strides around, flipping switches and the now-colourless nave is lit by invisible bulbs that send sinister shadows shooting up the stonework. Shadows a lighting guy can alter at will, with more switches, according to the mood they're looking to evoke.

A dark-wood chair sits before the foliate screen. Grayle observes it from the doorway. She doesn't like this chapel any more, worries about the extreme secularization of a once-sacred space. Worries especially about what's going to be happening here in just a few weeks' time.

And her own possible role in that.

She checks out the chair. It's not the glitzy throne from *Big Brother*, more like a judge's chair from some stark, puritan courthouse.

'Welcome to the confessional,' Defford says.

He's explained this, fully. How the residents will be summoned by the tolling of the bell in its turret on the chapel roof. Come to *Big Brother*.

Although, in *BB*, it's not so sinister, usually just a small, plain room, to which the housemates can be summoned, individually. They sit in the glitzy chair, in front of the camera, to be debriefed by some unseen voice representing their controller. Nothing like a police interview room. Big Brother, a sympathetic sibling, asks how they're coping with the confinement, what they feel about their companions – which ones they get along with, which ones they hate. The housemates tend to use these sessions to unload their anxieties and put the knife into their co-habitees. While Big Brother might use them discreetly to prime some traps.

This will be the same but different. They'll sit down, alone amidst the jumping shadows, to be questioned by… not Big Brother but Little goddamn Sister.

Shit. Defford only mentioned this in passing, and the short-list for the role of interrogator included Max the shrink, and a few TV personalities known to have an interest in the unexplained. They need someone with an extensive knowledge of paranormal phenomena, faked or imagined or even arguably real. But someone sensible. Someone who knows the right questions to ask when one of the residents claims to have seen a bobbing light or felt a shock of cold air. They also need a calm, distinctive voice, unlike anyone else's.

Seems an American accent would work well enough in this context and for only a fraction of what a celeb might've walked away with. Calm is another matter. Grayle spent ten days in London, receiving expert tuition from retired BBC and ITV presenters. Means she can now more effectively grill people like Rhys Sebold and Helen Parrish, who know all the tricks.

Defford folds his arms.

'You're not going to wimp out on me, are you, Grayle? You'll have a working script for each interview. Just a question of being able to respond to the unexpected, and you're probably the only one here with the knowledge to do that. We'll do some rehearsals with one of the residents, who we'll get to be as awkward as possible for you,' Defford says.

'Uh-huh.' And then she stares at him. 'Leo, how will that be possible? You'll bring one of them in blindfold, in advance? And won't that give whoever it is an unfair advantage, knowing how it's done?'

'Normally, it would. In this case, that might not matter. We're still working on a few details.'

He means his core team, a handful of younger producers and Kate Lyons. Occasionally, Grayle's been admitted to meetings of the core team, but mostly not. Like she's not yet accepted as a television person.

'Put it this way,' Defford says. 'To expand on the Big Brother Orwellian theme, all residents will be equal... but some may have to be more equal than others.'

The set of his face tells her she's not meant to ask him what that means.

'I guess Kate told you about Sebold,' she says as they leave the chapel.

'Be sensitive to his issues, Grayle, but don't let him bully you.'

'Sensitive to his issues. Right. Um…' She waits while he locks ups, glad to be out in the warmth. 'One more thing, Leo: what's the score now with Harry Ansell?'

Ansell still isn't talking to her. She's tried the formal request, calling his office, playing it straight. She's Mr Defford's researcher and she'd like to ask Mr Ansell some questions, any of which he can refuse to answer.

He refuses to answer any of them. He doesn't even want to hear them.

Well, OK, he doesn't exactly say that. He just doesn't say anything. His secretary keeps telling Grayle he's away on business and she'll pass the message on when he returns. The evening after she received this reply for the third time, Grayle was treating herself to a vegetarian dinner in the health food restaurant at the Rotunda and there was Harry Ansell strolling past the window, a copy of *Cotsworld* under an arm of his expensive fitted overcoat. If she'd been any kind of journalist she'd've been out there, placing herself on the sidewalk directly in front of him.

Only, his face was like the steel door on a bank vault, and her ass refused to come off the chair.

'He doesn't seem to think this is anything do with him,' Defford says.

'But it is, isn't it? He still wants to watch, right? Still wants to see what happens when we go live.'

'He's said nothing to the contrary.'

'Leo, he's said nothing at all!'

'He's a very private person, but I think it's more than that. He's not seen at events… receptions.'

'Still in mourning?'

'Maybe for more than his wife,' Defford says. 'Unsurprisingly, the *Cotsworld* circulation isn't what it was. You bought a copy of the magazine, you were buying into Trinity. The magic's gone.'

'Yeah, well, and maybe that also applies to the house. See, the thing is, Leo, without Ansell… you know what I'm saying?'

'You still don't have any evidence of Trinity being a continued presence in the house.'

'You were expecting me to find something else. I failed.'

'Grayle, while I appreciate your self-flagellation, I hardly expected a DVD of Trinity doing the full Katherine Parr routine. Yes, it's a great pity this guy Pruford didn't get possession of the haunted mobile phone. And that the couple employed as caretakers vanished as fast as whatever they claimed to have seen…'

'Not that I haven't tried. But yeah, it all comes back to Ansell. Ansell's either seen something himself or has reason to believe someone else's story. Whichever, he's keeping it to himself. And even you… even you haven't told me how come you got your hands on this place so easily.'

'Haven't I?'

'Question of need to know, right? Well now I think maybe I do.'

Defford leans back against the chapel door, the ivy like a wreath around his head.

'Leo, she died killing his child. How's he feel about that? Does that in any way resonate with his reasons for renting you this place?'

He looks shocked for a moment and then sighs.

'OK. I'll tell you how that happened.'

20

Closed lips

YOU WOULD THINK, from the sign at the roadside, that it's going to be just a short hop over the stile.

But no. This is not for the disabled, and quite a challenge for the elderly.

Not that he'd consider himself in either category. Not by many years.

All right, perhaps not that many. Cindy scowls, shoulders his pink knapsack and stares into the blushing sky. Left it till late afternoon, he has, in the hope of being alone. All the same, he's never been here before and would not like to find his way back in the dark, stumbling over a tree root and breaking an ankle. No way would HGTV have him wheeled into the house.

Over the stile and into a wood. A steep, muddy footpath, spikes of light through the skeletal trees, and then he's on the edge of a wide field, sloping up, making its own horizon, all the sheep gathered in a far corner.

A sign identifies this as the Cotswold Way, though there's no obvious path here, just a grey drystone wall to follow to the ridge. He should have come here weeks ago so that all this was familiar to him at different times of day. So that he could walk it with eyes shut.

A sense of pilgrimage as he follows the wall, the land quickly falling away behind him, until he can see the spread of Winch-combe and the burnished coil of Sudeley Castle. This must be the highest you can get in the Cotswolds, and it's cold up here, even in his warmest woollen tights, and the sun's like a traffic light on amber.

At the top of the hill, there's a walkers' gate, and he waits for a prosperous-looking middle-aged couple to come down through it.

'Bit of a disappointment,' the man says. 'Just a little hump.'

'Oh, really?'

'Well, all right if you're interested in that kind of thing, I suppose.'

The woman zips up her puffy jacket.

'Well I have to say I didn't really like it. Don't think I'd come up here on my own.'

Giving Cindy a meaningful look.

'Oh dear,' he says. 'I was told it was the Stonehenge of the Cotswolds. Scout, I am, for a rambling club.'

'Somebody having you on, madam,' the man says. 'Probably worth it for the views.'

'Well, there we are.'

He watches them go before passing through the gate and down into another wood where the drystone walls are splashed with vivid moss. There is no sign to point the way. The Cotswold tourist people are doing the minimum, and he likes that. This is not really a place for tourists.

You don't even see it until you're almost there and its shadow-dome rises over a fence, and he hears Trinity's soft voice: as if it's erupted from the corner of the field or landed from somewhere.

The sky hangs heavy over the barrow. The sun has shrunk.

The first site of it, through the bare trees, thrills him in a way only such places can. Oh God, it's conscious. It knows he's coming.

Belas Knap is embedded at the highest point of the extensive Cleeve Hill, the Cotswold summit. Sunk into the soil and rock like a big, ground-nesting bird. You can walk all around it. You can, without much effort, walk over it.

Been restored, reconstructed or despoiled, depending on

your point of view, but, in essence, he feels, unchanged. It's the place that is important, the situation.

Stone Age, it is, certainly, but the stones are hidden under an overcoat of earth, and only the lintels of the entrances are visible: four of them, small accessible chambers in its sides. Bodies were found here, including the bones of children. But the term 'burial chamber' is something of a misnomer. An estimated five thousand years ago, this was a place of complex ritual worship, sited with more calculation than most cathedrals. Inside it, you can feel yourself at the centre of the world.

And you can journey. He stands on the edge of the wood, his back to the wall, fingers in the dollops of marzipan moss.

Not yet. It's his first visit. He's not ready to go in.

To show this is not about fear, he stands on top of Belas Knap. The countryside up here is bare rather than beautiful, the fields greyish. In the distance he can see pylons.

He can't, however, see Knap Hall.

Cindy shivers in the grey afternoon. Gathers his bag up under an arm, steps down from the long mound and walks round to what you would think was the main entrance at the northern end.

The end of the mound curves inwards to where two standing stones and a lintel are set into the turf. But between the stones is another and part of a wall. It was always thus, the experts think.

This is the main, ceremonial-looking, entrance. But not an entrance at all. It's impenetrable, a doorway either walled up or never a doorway at all. A false entrance, they call it, always a closed portal, and nobody knows why.

He opens his arms to it and closes his eyes.

It's like all these ritual sites. Sometimes they're bad places. You go one day, it's lurking, sinister. Another time almost welcoming, a fairy hill.

In the second diary Trinity says she came here again. Could not have been more than a month before her death. Came here with her mind in a turmoil for reasons which she doesn't really explain. Perhaps because she didn't understand herself.

Call me a coward, but I stayed behind the wall. I felt sick. I'd done a lot of reading since we last talked about it. I knew a lot more about it. But I couldn't go any closer. I thought it would help me to touch it or something, but suddenly I knew it didn't want to help me, not at all.

And then it comes.

It comes quickly. As though he's been punched in the chest by a funnelled wind. He reels away and almost falls.

Oh yes. Oh, dear God, yes.

Cindy steps back to a place of safety, up against the wall. Sinks his fingers into the marzipan moss, closes his eyes, steps away from his thoughts and the cold images come to him immediately.

There is, of course, a guardian. Maybe, considering the importance of this site, at the very summit of the Cotswolds, more than one. When he was younger, they scared the hell out of him, but now he knows that's all they're for.

All they're for. So they don't. Not any more. Old spirit, dead spirit, the deathless dead, often embittered and full of malevolence.

Cindy, barely breathing, lets it out.

When he opens his eyes, they're gazing into the false entrance, and they widen, his eyes, and he's momentarily shocked, looking between grassy thighs into the lips of an enormous stone vagina.

Well, this is not so extraordinary; a chamber like this is all about birth and rebirth.

But these are closed lips.

He shakes his head, not a little awed, tremulous with the sense of something taking shape.

21

Flawed people

MARY RUTTER IS a Google long-haul.

Or Mary Ann Rutter as it says on the book, when Grayle finally chases it up on a local history website.

Guessing Mary Ann is not exactly what you could call an academic historian. Her book, *Rogues and Roués of the Northern Cotswolds*, was published over thirty years ago and sounds like it ought to have been a steady seller in this area. But it was issued by a small regional press which seems to be long extinct and only ever seems to have made one edition. The cover is this crude watercolour of a Cotswold-looking street with shadowy guys in three-cornered hats in the moonlight.

What's odd is that Grayle's failed to track down a single copy, new or second-hand. Nothing on Amazon, nothing on AbeBooks, at any price. A book dealer in Cheltenham says she'll put out feelers.

Googling Abel's Rent, Grayle gets no closer than Abel's Car Hire in Brisbane, Australia. She finds a few Rutters in the local phone book, but only one that seems to fit Jordan's directions. She writes down the number.

All this to delay having to call Rhys Sebold.

'Grayle, hi. Greetings.'

'Mr Sebold—'

'Good of you to call me at last. Can I take it you've come to the end of your private list of my friends?'

He's told her he's in his car. On his mobile, bluetooth, hands-free.

'I know,' he says, over a throaty motor, 'it's your job. You need to make sure I'm not going to fall apart on live television. I expect you to go behind my back. But do you know what gets to me? You ONLY went behind my back. You didn't even bother to talk to me first. Do you think that's courteous, Grayle?'

She tries to explain to him that he's in line, like all of them, for an interview with Max the shrink. That it was her job to feed Max information on which he can base his questions.

'So you want to be sure I'm not psychiatrically challenged. Well, let me ask you… would it – should it – matter if I am? Is yours the kind of programme that still considers mental health something that should be hidden away?'

She doesn't reply. Feels like she's on his radio show. Feels also that Defford would be not at all unhappy if Sebold behaved like someone halfway out of his tree. The fact is, she hardly needed to talk to his friends. She got most of it from the papers and the Net. Endless stuff about the party at his apartment that was raided by the cops, the not-inconsiderable quantity of cocaine that was taken away. His court appearance, the fine, the community service, how he lost his radio show. All established fact, and he was hardly the first BBC person to find himself in the middle of this kind of minor scandal.

No, the difficult part relates to Rhys's girlfriend, Chloe. The truly awful news brought to him while he was in police custody. How damaged he'd been by this. How he might react if someone brought it up on the programme.

And the aftermath that links directly into *Big Other*: the fraught issue of the sister and the medium.

'It's not even me I'm bothered about,' he's saying. 'I get shat on all the time. I'm more concerned about Chloe's memory – I don't want that misrepresented for the titillation of insomniac viewers.'

'Mr Sebold, I don't think—'

'So, OK, let's deal with it now. Yes, I blame myself totally for what happened to Chloe. And no, I will never forgive myself.

166

I've talked about it on air, on other people's shows. I make no excuses.'

'Look, I'm sorry—'

'For my loss?'

'That's not... I was going to say, I'm sorry if you've been given the impression that the programme's in any way—'

'Don't PATRONIZE me, Grayle, I know exactly what kind of programme I'm getting into and that it's very unlikely we'll get to the end of the week without somebody mouthing off at length about the irresponsibility of recreational drug use. You want flawed people in that house, and I accept that I'm a particularly flawed person.'

His voice is louder. He's evidently pulled in someplace, killed the motor. 'But so this is not misrepresented, I want you to hear the truth. The way you would have done if you'd approached me directly instead of scraping up bits of scurilous gossip.'

Grayle closes her eyes.

'We're all of us flawed,' she says.

Last summer. A hot night. Rhys and Chloe had recently moved into a bigger flat in north London, but it wasn't a flat-warming as such, just a gathering of a dozen or so friends.

Grayle makes notes as he tells her he wasn't a big user, but he had something to celebrate: they were trying him out for the morning show during the summer, when its regular presenter took an extended break to tie in with her kids' school holidays.

He still doesn't know who called the cops, but suspects a couple of neighbours who weren't invited because they were incredibly boring people.

Chloe was a researcher on Five Live, and a good one. Never gave you a wrong name for the person you were interviewing, unlike some of them, for whom being a researcher was just the first rung on a ladder pointing skywards. Chloe had no ambitions beyond getting it right. This was what a couple of Sebold's former colleagues told Grayle, confirming that it was the cautious Chloe, neurotic about any kind of drug use, who was looking out the window when the police cars came around the corner.

Rhys Sebold in no way contradicts this.

'I remember her turning round, shouting, "*It's a raid, it's a raid!*" And we laughed. We laughed because some of the guys had been teasing her about being paranoid. We laughed, Grayle. We fucking laughed at her. We laughed because we thought she was winding us up.'

'Right.'

'In the end, I think she was so exasperated with us she just ran out, got in the lift and left the building before the police came in.'

She passed them on the steps, Grayle remembers reading. They didn't try to stop her; how would they know who she was? And got into her car and drove away – this was all in the inquest report. Found her way to the M25 and slammed into the back of a truck driven by a guy who'd been on the road too long. But at least he wasn't coked up.

'I apologize for not approaching you first,' Grayle says.

'Thank you.'

'I also…' seems as good a time as any to go the whole way, '… also talked to… Chloe's older sister. Rhiannon.'

'I know you did.'

'It seemed relevant to our theme.'

'She's a stupid, misguided woman. Please quote me.'

'I guess she was driven to what she did, like so many people, by the force of grief?'

'And was despicably exploited by these inadequate people.'

Now he's in radio-mode, like he's flipped up the overdrive switch. Grayle says nothing.

'You going to have one of them in the house, Grayle?'

'I don't think so. Leo Defford doesn't want to go down the *Most Haunted* road.'

'Pity. Because I'd just love to have a go at one of those phoney bastards on live TV.'

'Can you... tell me about that?'

'About what?'

'About the medium stuff?'

'What did Rhiannon say?'

'She told me how close they were, her and Chloe, how she was always like a second mother to Chloe and how when she died it was like a big part of her life was gone... irretrievable. She explained about the friend who persuaded her to go with her to a spiritualist church, where she was convinced she was having messages from Chloe relayed to her. And one of the messages said to... tell Chloe's partner not to blame himself. A message which she tried to pass on and... came round to see you. And she said you, like, went ballistic.'

'I've never denied that. I've never been so angry in my life. I was sickened by it. That these obsessives would try to tarnish Chloe's memory by implying she was sitting on some fucking cloud whispering to some old bat?'

'Rhiannon said you were screaming so hard at her that the neighbours called the police again.'

'Which is how it got into the tabloids. I'd still dispute the word screaming, but I'm perfectly happy to expand on that episode in the house. In fact I'm rather looking forward to it. Am I supposed not to know Ozzy Ahmed's going to be there?'

Grayle says nothing. She's thinking about what Defford said about some residents being more equal than others. It was always likely these two would learn that the other would be in the house. Defford's cool with this. Rare to reach transmission without a small amount of internal leakage. What he hopes neither of them knows about is Eloise.

'We're mates,' Sebold says. 'We have certain things in common, as you know. Not least being exposed to crazy people who happened to be related to our partners.'

'Um... was Mr Ahmed at your party? I don't recall.'

'He would've been, if he hadn't been touring Australia at the time – if I believed in something as ridiculous as astrology, I might say he'd been born under fortunate stars. And you don't have to tell either of us to express surprise when we both turn up in the house, we're not stupid.'

'That's... good. And you're, um, still working for cable TV, is that right?'

'For the present.'

He's been doing a twice-weekly two-hour talk show on a shoestring station called *Night Train* which keeps porn-TV hours. It's no secret he's looking to get back with the BBC, and the word is that he will. Meantime, how he's perceived on *Big Other* is bound to impact on that somehow and he's surely aware of this.

In the phone, she hears his car starting up. The conversation is over. He's had his say, made it clear to her that she's dealing with a guy who knows the score. She guesses that next time they talk it'll be like they're old friends.

Grayle leans back in her chair, gazing out the window. When she gets through with this, she can't see herself coming back into TV again, ever. It both amplifies and somehow nullifies reality.

The sky's turning the colours of a bruised apple. The days are shortening fast now. She walks out, away from all the HGTV buildings to the plateau of ground just above the house's hollow where Jordan's created his knot garden out of box trees. Wanders in and out of its green maze, somehow feeling the intensity with which it was designed and nurtured. The little trees are mostly knee-high now.

Jordan did all this for Trinity... or for himself? Doesn't matter; this is the only part of Knap Hall she's so far seen that seems to be, if not flourishing, at least holding its own against the entropic haze that seems to hang over the house.

She comes out the other side of the garden next to the smallest barn which, because it's too far away from the other outbuildings to be part of the Hunter-Gatherer village, is now used as storage for stalls removed from the stables and old bales of hay and straw.

Grayle wanders inside and sits down on a crumbling bale. The anger of Rhys Sebold that perhaps fronts up his inner-anguish hasn't followed her in here. It feels oddly warm, as if the very last rays of summer have found their way through the knot garden and into this little barn, which is more like a church than the chapel in the walled garden.

In the silence – a rarity at Knap Hall now – she thinks about what Defford's told her about the strange encounter with Harry Ansell that brought all this about. Wonders if Defford realizes how the house might be changing him, wearing away the boyish enthusiasm she recalls from that first day in March.

Trust me, Grayle, this is going to be the most talked-about television of the winter.

Sure, but talked about how? In what context?

Apprehension cools the sunlight. Within seconds, the phone's bleeping, and it's Defford, and she's never heard him sounding less happy.

22

Guantanamo

HE WANTS HER to go where?

'South Devon,' Defford says. 'Will you be free to do that tonight?'

His tone implies that 'Will you be free?' translates as you will be free.

He says, 'Helen Parrish lives there.'

And...?

'Where are you now, Leo?'

'I'm in the house. Finalizing some things. If you come over here in half an hour I'll put you in the picture, but, essentially, it looks as if Parrish might be about to walk away. Which is hardly what we need at this stage.'

'You said she was just holding out for more money.'

'More complicated. Her agent's in talks with ITV about her presenting a daytime holiday programme aimed at the older viewer with cash to unload. Grey pin-up stuff. Good money, free travel, lavish clothing allowance. So that's why she's been stalling.'

'You said she was washed up, hadn't worked for over a year.'

'Yes, I know exactly what I said, Grayle.' Upper middle-class roots showing as his voice tightens. 'But even I am not always right. She's apparently convinced she's lost one job because of the Diana story and won't risk losing another. And her agent, as expected, is not being supportive as regards us.'

'You talked to her?'

'Kate's talked to her, briefly, to arrange for you to talk to her.'

'But— Jeez, Leo, what am I supposed to—?'

'Image factor. Don't undervalue your guileless charm. Helen needs reassuring that she won't be considered in any way unbalanced for seeing whatever she saw.'

'Like, she's gonna look at me and realize how freaking normal she is?'

This is not what she's being paid for. Not even what she's good at.

'Drive down to her place in Devon. Tonight, because she's going on holiday at the weekend – she says. Take her to dinner somewhere. Talk her round, talk about her experience—'

'We don't really know what that was, do we?'

'We know that she was very much affected by it at the time, and still in a state of shock when she talked to colleagues in the restaurant. You'll be both sympathetic and knowledgeable.'

Grayle stares out the window. It's already gone five p.m., which means she'd be driving down there in the dark. She does not want to do this.

'What's wrong with one of the producers?'

'At the risk of offending you, Grayle, they're all too bleedin' young.'

'Thanks.'

'And she's a journalist, and you're a journalist. And also, you can offer her another hundred K.'

'Oh, I see...'

'It's delicate,' Defford says, 'but she hasn't yet said no. Kate's drawing up a new contract, which you can take with you.'

'I just show up?'

'She's expecting you, and she is prepared to talk about it.'

It's like he's setting her up as the person who'll carry the can if this woman pulls out. Well, no way.

Makes her want to join Parrish and Driscoll under the exit sign.

When she gets to the house, the whole sky's salmon-slicked, sunless but shiny. She's come early. If she doesn't have this out with the bastard now, things will only get worse as pre-transmission tension sets in.

The front door's still kept locked inside its shallow stone porch. You still have to go round the back, through the more modern part, which she doesn't like, and then – she hasn't been in here for… must be months – the old part starts playing tricks with your head.

The big room, the chamber, is not so big any more, and its whole shape has altered. A false wall has gone up: distressed panelling, with two mirrors in dark frames. Two-way mirrors, behind which cameramen will prowl, soft-shoed voyeurs. Upstairs, they've removed some oak boards for another camera which will show most of the room from above, like the roof's been taken off a period doll's house.

It's like being in a fish tank full of dark water. And now voices are rising, although the room's empty. She's startled for a moment before realizing what she'd missed before: the inglenook fireplace is also two-way, one wide stone hearth serving two adjacent rooms. Must always have been like that. Saves on logs.

The other room is reached by a discreet gothic doorway in a corner near the wooden screen. It's a little brighter and has a long, refectory-type table, where the residents will eat. Two guys are here with Defford: a young carpenter, measuring up, and a grizzled lighting man whom Defford clearly annoys by calling him a sparks. Also his PA, Kate Lyons, a bulky, middle-aged woman with dark red hair in a loose bun. She's carrying a small stills-camera.

'…think it'll probably work, Leo.' Her voice is ice-pick patrician. 'If we're giving them the freedom of the rear hall – which we'll have to, because of the stairs – then, by leaving just one door unlocked, they'll also be able to access the walled garden and the chapel without being able to get into the main building. So we'll need just one more stout door to keep them confined.'

It's like they're planning a new Guantanamo Bay. Grayle hovers in the doorway. Nobody acknowledges her.

'OK, organize it.' Defford turns to the grizzled sparks. 'What?'

The sparks is unhappy. He talks about technical stuff, and Defford hears him out.

'But can you light it like we said?'

'Leo, that room absorbs light. All I'm saying is we might just need—'

'No screens, no reflectors!' Defford smacks two fingers of one hand into the open palm of the other, twice. 'Off-putting. Screams television. I didn't say can you light it beautifully, Peter, I said can you fucking light it?'

The sparks looks sullen.

'As I keep saying and will continue to say,' Defford tells him, 'I don't want to have to use infrared at any stage. I'd rather have candlelight, even if we have to fake some of it. Infrared's become a cliché.'

'You said.'

'Mainly because of two words I don't ever want to hear in this house.'

The sparks sighs.

'*Most* and *Haunted*.'

'Well-remembered.' Defford beckons the carpenter to follow him through the Gothic doorway into the main chamber, where he shows him the holes in the wall of ship's timber. 'What d'you reckon?'

'No big problem,' the carpenter says. 'We'll just pack it around with wood-filler, paint the filler the colour of the oak, and as long as Peter keeps it in shadow…'

'He will. And can we conceal those bloody smoke alarms? And make them less… functional?'

This gets him some wary looks. Grayle can't believe how hands-on practical he suddenly is. She thought all this would've been delegated, way back, but maybe it's all down to programme security, need-to-know. If Hunter-Gatherer doesn't employ its own tradesmen, has to contract out, he needs to leave as little time as possible for details to leak. He's also allowed the word 'fake' to creep into his working vocabulary. As time gets short, principles are the first to go.

He notices her at last.

'Grayle, give me ten. We're organizing a full rehearsal next week – our people assuming the roles of the residents. Which, hopefully, should show up any flaws in the planning. Ten minutes, OK?'

'Sure.'

She nods, unsmiling, gets out of his way but not out of the doorway. She's just realized this must be the doorway where, according to Jeff Pruford, Trinity Ansell was standing in the picture taken by the woman from the Midwest. And behind her, behind where Grayle's standing right now, was a woman whose eyes – according to Jeff Pruford – were full of white hatred.

She resists the urge to move, and inspects the big chamber. The false wall makes the window look bigger, but nobody seems to have cleaned it recently. Flies have died in the greasy film on some panes, reminding her of Lisa Muir: *Probably some fungal thing... bacteria...*

Defford's evidently sticking to his determination not to recreate Trinity's Knap Hall. The *Cotsworld* picture was a lovely dream, this is the drab reality of Tudor farmhouse living. Defford has talked about starkness and a level of discomfort; how far will he take this? Will there be dry rushes on the stone flags? She notices the electric light fittings have all gone. Is it really going to be lit by sick-smelling tallow candles?

Grayle walks determinedly out of the haunted doorway, goes out into the passage, turns a corner and finds the stone back stairs facing her. Some of the residents will be sleeping up there – on modern mattresses... or something filled with straw so they won't get much sleep, inducing headaches and foul moods? What a goddamn scam this could all turn out to be.

The stairs, almost certainly the original farmhouse stairs, are a half-spiral, the stone steps forming a slow curve. Flicking at the wall switches, she walks, for the first time, upstairs, to what remains of the Ansells' apartment. This could be the nearest she'll ever get to that marriage.

23

The bed

AT THE TOP of the half-spiral, a windowless passage is lit by electric sconce-type lamps, the bulbs so old and low-powered you can see the filaments, like rings of thin children holding hands.

She has three options. A narrow wooden staircase, evidently a replacement, continues darkly to a third floor. A right turn takes you to some of the former hotel rooms, where most of the residents will sleep, but there's a tape across the passage. At the other end, Grayle's guessing, doors will be fitted to cut off access to the main stairs. One way in, one way out: no exploring. But with TV cameras running and monitored 24/7, Defford's probably right not to worry about fire spreading in the night.

A fire door to the left has a sign with PRIVATE on it in polite gilt lettering. This has to be the Ansells' own apartment. The door's ajar, raw early-evening light flaking out like old plaster.

Outside Trinity's sanctuary, Grayle hesitates a moment then shrugs.

On the other side of the door, there's a short landing then a few steps to an open door exposing this large, square, empty room where the panelling is too perfect to be all original. Two Gothic windows overlook bushes at the side of the house and the path to the knot garden. A partly conifered wood obscures the longer view.

The Ansells' bedroom, sitting room? A TV antenna cable snakes across wide, bare boards. No furniture, all the wood is in the walls: light oak panelling with a door inset, closed. The air is of desolation. If she felt apprehensive about intruding on the remains of a marriage, she isn't. With the stripping of the room, something's been vacuum pumped out of here. She imagines the stone-faced Ansell she's seen in Cheltenham striding around, pointing at this, pointing at that: out, out, all of it.

And then turning it over to Defford, who told Grayle outside the chapel about his early encounters with Trinity Ansell at parties and Cheltenham Races. How, when Trinity first began to show up in the Cotswolds it was with her old lover William Fraser, the actor. It was the later stage of that relationship, lots of moodies and fall-outs. Then Defford went to America, and the next time he saw Trinity it was with Harry Burgess, in those heady, summery, early days of *Cotsworld*.

By then, Defford had produced *Living with the Royals* for CBS, now showing in the UK on Channel 5. They'd shot some stuff around Tetbury, close to Prince Charles's place, Highgrove, and *Cotsworld* ran an editorial criticizing them for being invasive. Defford was furious. He cornered Ansell at a party, asked him what his beef was.

The answer put their relationship on to a whole new level, laid the foundations for what was happening here now.

'He didn't have one.'

Defford springing off the chapel wall, grinning, admiring Ansell's editorial instincts.

'Didn't have a problem with us at all. He just knew his readership – the way local people liked to feel protective about the Royals. Like Charles and Camilla and Anne were their valued neighbours. A kind of snobbery – Harry loved that about Cotswold society. Played up to it. I wouldn't say we became mates that night, but I think we got to know how we could be useful to each other.'

Defford was to encounter Harry Ansell several times in the next couple of years, before attending the celebrity memorial service for Trinity, at Gloucester Cathedral.

And then, months later, at one of those black-tie dinner parties at a peeling manor house near Stroud, the host a now-wealthy Labour peer who used to be in TV and once worked alongside Defford on the BBC *Newsnight* programme. Defford speculating to Grayle that this was the first time since losing his wife that Ansell had been persuaded to appear at any kind of social gathering not connected with his business. Defford remembering how everybody was walking on eggshells. Only a dozen guests, and four of them singles so Ansell wouldn't feel out on the edge.

Over dinner, a woman, making conversation, asked Defford what he was working on, and he, having had a few drinks by then, told her he was looking for an unknown haunted house.

Biting his tongue when he saw that Harry Ansell had over-heard, but the obvious connection that haunting has with death and loss didn't seem to have occurred to anyone. When the subject got picked up and bounced across the table, it came out that the manor house itself was said to have a spectral presence – an old lady in a Victorian nanny's outfit who only appeared when there were children in the house.

'Any use, Leo?' The peer scenting money. Defford telling Grayle how he took a certain pleasure in regretting that a dead nanny didn't quite do it for him.

But Harry Ansell wasn't so easily dismissed.

'I popped out to the terrace for a smoke, and there he was.'

Defford well remembers how Ansell looked that night. He'd lost weight but not substance. Grayle guesses he looked like a grey wolf during a lean winter, intent and purposeful. 'Driven' is Defford's word.

Driven by what? Losing Trinity was losing everything. She never wrote a word for *Cotsworld*, but she sold that magazine just by existing in the background, a conduit to life in an English paradise. Trinity's name had not come up once over dinner, but as they gazed down over Stroud, Defford told Ansell how very sorry he'd been.

There are, of course, different kinds of sorrow, and Defford's must have been coloured with a kind of excitement he'd find hard to conceal when Ansell said,

'I have a haunted house.'

Something was telling Defford not to follow up on it too quickly, but, because they were alone, he felt he could go on talking about Trinity.

'Hell of a loss,' he told Harry Ansell. 'A light gone out.'

There was silence. Defford recalls Ansell crushing his cigarette into the wet, dead foliage of something in an ornamental urn and saying,

'What if it hasn't gone out?'

Grayle pads across, finds the door's unlocked, opening into a short passageway with doors either side, all ajar. She opens them in sequence. What could've been a small kitchen has an array of power points and a sink. There's a bathroom with a pedestal tub in its centre, a toilet, a second bathroom attached to a dressing room with closets, frosted window panes. Only one door, directly ahead, is closed. In fact no, not quite; it's just darker in the room on the other side.

This is likely to be the bedroom. She can make out walls of panelling and one of plaster, evening-pink and veined with bleached oak and—

Oh, dear God…

—a silent group of people standing there.

Grayle backs out, stumbling, chest hurting from a shrivelled scream. Tries to shut the door but only succeeds in slamming it back with a crash against the wall, folding to her knees just as she identifies the skeleton of a four-poster bed, its canopy and backboard missing, an empty cavity at its base.

She stays down there, releasing trapped breath.

Old houses. The filaments in a bulb become faerie kids dancing in a ring, and four rigid bedposts are black-clad mourners gathered around an open grave.

There's nothing else in the dim room but the bed, symbol of a marriage collapsed by death. Grayle's mind inflicts on her an image of Trinity Ansell sitting between the posts at the foot of a vaguely similar bed, richly curtained. Lightly brushing out her long, sheeny hair, swish, swish.

Grayle comes to her feet, pushing numbed fingers through what's left of her own hair. Only a half-dismantled bed, but it's unsettling, and she can't lose the feelings of loss.

Never felt less happy in Knap Hall but makes herself walk deeper into the room. The main reason it's dark in here is that the biggest window has been roughly boarded up, a thick wooden frame hammered in tight to the mullion. The only light comes from one much smaller window at a right angle to it, exposing the uninspiring bushes next to the house and the woodland further back that were visible from the first room.

Which suggests the blocked window overlooks somewhere that might identify the location. Could be Sudeley Castle. A deep-set door right at the end, the darkest part, probably leads to wherever they've taken up the floorboards for the overhead camera sweeping the chamber below.

It's all a big TV studio now, or will be in two or three weeks.

A mothy air in here, like it's whole decades since Trinity Ansell slept in that broken bed. Now her eyes have adjusted, Grayle can see that the carved posts are darkened by an accumulation of grime. Someone has work to do.

The air's actually laden with fine dust. She coughs. The boarded window has hairline cracks of ruby light. She imagines the boards gone, Trinity standing next to her, both of them gazing towards the last home of Katherine Parr, a couple miles away, a trinket in the trees.

What are you thinking, Trinity?

Did she stand here, knowing she was pregnant? Maybe thinking of KP, pregnant by Seymour of Sudeley, though never by Henry, a fat old king with an ulcerated leg, who had one son, not destined to make it out of his teens and could've used another.

Is it possible Trinity's baby was not Harry's?

Talk to me, Trinity.

Haunt me.

No, don't. Jesus God, ignore that, don't.

On her desk in the portacabin, she has two biographies of Henry's last queen, which she's only flipped through but, in all the portraits, Katherine – small-featured, demure, quite kind-looking – is wearing a red dress. In various pictures inside, she's wearing different dresses, all red. Grayle remembers one sumptuous number with gold braid and padded shoulders. And rubies, everywhere.

A distant rustle of voices from downstairs tells her the ten minutes must be up by now. Defford will be looking for her, impatient. Always impatient, now. He's changed. Too many things not going right. Does this place really do stuff to people, or is that just down to the kind of people who wind up here? People and history and suggestion – a word often used by Ashley Palk, editor of *The Disbeliever*, some of whose lectures Grayle's found on YouTube. Some are hallucinations, some are self-deception, but most so-called ghost experiences are down to suggestion, says Ashley, of the tilted head and mirthless smile. Oh, really, does anybody educated actually think that way any more? How marvellous. Everything is marvellous to Ashley, for whom marvels don't exist.

There's movement, woodwork whingeing. Grayle looks sharply back down the bedchamber, wondering if she's trodden on a loose board. But she hasn't moved.

'Who's that?'

Aware of saying it, she doesn't hear it. The room looks longer than when she came in, ending in a purply vagueness around the pale rectangle of the doorway through which she entered. A shadow is dislodged from the corner by the door.

'Leo? Is that—?'

The pale rectangle narrows. It's the oak door itself, slowly closing, sliding quietly into the light-space, the wooden latch falling – *thock*. And then a shift into silence, and the silence is a fabric that wraps itself damply around her, and she can feel, as it touches her, its quick decay.

A tipping sensation inside her head and chest, an outpouring of cold and a connection across years to being in a cab bound for the airport after leaving her father's apartment with its framed blow-up of Ersula in her academic gown. A weight of misery settling around her heart like sludge, a wanting for it to be over.

Life. Please. No more.

She's aware of standing beside the barricaded window, watching, in the slats of sunset, specks of dry dust falling and gathering, motes of misery, all the misery in the room coagulating around her, a smog of sorrow, and it has a vague smell, the distant stench of last year's dead leaves, slimed and skeletal and never coming back. A sick little airless cry is trapped far inside her, as a last vibration of panic inhabits her hands and arms like pins and needles before it becomes an acceptance of the inevitable, and she watches something assembling raggedly between the posts of the bed.

Oh Christ, she's really seeing this…

She's still standing up, but something inside her is on its knees, naked and desperate, too utterly dejected to cry out. She can only see, through eyes she wants to close and can't, not four bedposts but five, and the fifth is a man with his arms by his side, a thin shadow joining him to the blackness above like an umbilical cord from his head into the vaster shadows of the ceiling. The weight of the body slowly bringing the face around for her and the eyes are like capsules of egg white, a liquid desperation, and Grayle feels she might die of fear and this all-enshrouding misery.

24

Two camps

MARCUS HAS LOST weight which, considering his cardiac history, can't be a bad thing. He has only two remaining chins and his cheeks are not so red. But his eyes are still burning with the same angry light under the dense grey hair.

'Strikes me, Lewis, that if it's reasonable to assume a double agent walks away with twice the money, this is going to make you sickeningly fucking rich.'

Quite comforting, it is, to detect the old sulphur in his voice.

'Comparatively speaking, Marcus,' Cindy concedes. 'Comparatively speaking.'

Setting down his mug of Earl Grey, gazing with a genuine affection across the desk of dented beech-wood, which is far too big for this place. Here in the second bedroom, which serves as Marcus's office, extra shelving has reduced the window to little more than a slit.

Better than a caravan, mind.

Marcus scoops up his manuscript, slams it in a drawer of the desk, Cindy raising his arms in protest, bangles jangling.

'I'm not going to steal your ideas, Marcus, I do retain some ethics.'

'Really? Where're you keeping them these days?'

Cindy smiles, eases his chair away from a stack of books. Apart from the English bull terrier, Malcolm, they're alone in the bungalow. The good Sister Anderson is working late at the clinic, which can only help preserve their relationship.

Cindy sighs.

'Opposite poles, we are, Marcus.'

Opposite poles, however, of the same planet. Neither of them will ever join the British Humanist Society or buy a subscription to *The Disbeliever*. And a cause which they support equally is the welfare of little Grayle Underhill.

'Come to meet Mr Driffield, I have. We're having dinner.'

'Who?'

'The television producer?'

'Defford?'

'That's the man.'

'And you're going like that?'

'Brand new skirt, Marcus. Vera Wang.' He couldn't afford a pair of knickers by Vera Wang, but the chances of Marcus having heard of the woman... 'Anyway, dinner's at his house, near Stow. Can't be seen together in public, obviously.'

Marcus sits back, polishing his glasses.

'All right, start by explaining the double-agent business. I was too dazzled by your tawdry jewellery to take it in.'

Cindy considers what Marcus knows, what he needs to know and what it would be better to conceal. He knows, for example, about Cindy's long-term friendship with Trinity Ansell, though not about the diary or its content. Knows how Cindy played young Jo to get himself invited into the house, also that Jo and her boss are keeping Cindy a secret from the rest of the production team, including Grayle, until the eve of transmission. He does not, however, know why.

'They're not idiots at HGTV, Marcus. They employ psychologists to predict how the people they're calling residents will react to one another – who will form friendships, who will be hostile. Anticipate all that, they can, with a fair degree of accuracy.'

'They hope.'

'However, this is a programme considering the existence of paranormal phenomena. I think that if anything entirely inexplicable were to occur the production people really would have no idea how to react. And I think they realize that.'

Marcus smiles, itself an almost preternatural occurrence.

'We can take it, I think,' Cindy says, 'that Mr Defford is not a believer and is fairly confident that nothing inexplicable will take place. However...?'

'Needs to cover all his bases, as Underhill would say.'

'What he can't allow to develop is an us and them situation, with the production team, including his informed researcher, as outsiders. What, for example, if the ghost supporters work together to invent an apparition and support each other's stories?'

'Hard to conspire in that situation, surely. They'll all be wearing these personal microphones day and night. Everything they say overheard.'

'Marcus, Marcus... it can happen without a word exchanged, by the power of suggestion. One person claims to have seen something, the others of a like mind convince themselves they've seen it, too. And then it virtually exists, and they go on feeding it and pretty soon they've all forgotten they've made it up. Which is why Defford needs an insider.'

'Double agent. Snitch.' Marcus blows out his lips, replaces his glasses. 'Traitor. So you're the house rat.'

Cindy strokes the strange, white head of Malcolm the bull terrier who's sitting between his chair and a book tower comprised of the collected speculative works of Colin Wilson.

'It is, as you know,' he says cautiously, 'a part of my tradition to have a foot in two camps. However, I would worry for my karma if I didn't have a reason for being there which goes beyond the goldrush for viewing figures.'

'You mean your personal guilt? Your suspicion that you might have saved the Ansell woman?' Marcus looks pained. 'Lewis, she didn't even bloody die there. And she died trying to abort a baby. You have no idea at all what mental state she was in or if it even connects with the house.'

'I think it does.'

'Why?'

Cindy sighs, makes no reply. His fears about the death of Trinity Ansell run too deep for easy explanation, even to Marcus Bacton, whom he tried to get appointed as researcher. Never imagining that Marcus would conspire to hand over the job to little Grayle Underhill.

'I...' Marcus has sunk back into the shadows behind the lamp, 'told Underhill they'd offered me a place in the house – yes, I know they wouldn't consider someone as obscure as me – and that I'd had to turn them down for health reasons. So they offered me the researcher's job, and... I may have given Underhill the impression I found this either an insult or a distraction from my book.'

The book. Which will, Cindy is sure, have well-developed theories, eloquently expressed, and twenty years ago would probably have found a reputable publisher. Today, even with a punchier title than *In Defence of Mystery*, publishers will wear rubber gloves to carry it to the bin.

Oh, Marcus, Marcus. The researcher's fee would have been far more than he could reasonably expect to make from his book even if a reputable publisher were to accept it.

Little Grayle, however, is the daughter he's never had, while her own father, who's left her in this transatlantic limbo, is the kind of man Marcus despises most.

'*The Vision* was going down the toilet, Lewis. We were actually losing money on it by then. Underhill went back to the States. Anderson arrived from the Midlands, diagnosed I was heading for another heart attack and stayed. We... for reasons of poverty, we sold up and moved out here. Woman held me together. Still does.'

'You'll never deserve her, Marcus.'

'Then Underhill turns up again without any warning. Relationship with her father's broken down beyond hope of reconciliation. Cold bastard.'

'So I gather.'

'She's—' Marcus takes a hard breath. 'Thing is, when you talk to her about it, she'll tell you she didn't realize how close she was to a breakdown. But she wasn't close at all. She was having a fucking breakdown. Turned up here looking like the husk of something. I think she had some idea of relaunching *The Vision* on the Internet, but… its time was over, Lewis. Never go back. And the bastard Internet's no answer to depression.'

'Quite.'

'What were we supposed to do? Toss her into the psychiatric system? As it happens, one of Anderson's clients – irritable bowel – is a man called Neil Oldham. Owns the Three Counties News Service, which makes its money serving shit to the tabloids. One of his reporters had just landed a job on the *Sun*. Oldham's lying helpless on her treatment couch, Anderson twists his arm.'

'A radical solution?'

'Lewis, Underhill's a trained journalist. Decent writer who got waylaid by all the whimsy and windchimes bollocks. This was the other end of the business – hard graft, long hours, commitment required. And she does commit. And the last thing she wanted was space for a private life. It broke the pattern. I think she enjoyed it.'

'So the windchimes are no longer hanging in the porch.'

'Cut her hair short. Looks bloody awful.'

'Drastic.'

'And then all that goes to pieces, and she's about to become unemployed again. Without much of chance, this time, the way things are, of becoming re-employed. So when Oldham arrives for his next treatment…'

'It's all right, Marcus, I know the rest. You made a sacrifice of Christ-like proportions and tried to cover up your part in her rescue. The problem is, this role is not the sinecure you might have thought it would be. Don't get me wrong – I have no doubt little Grayle is doing a fine job, and the money's good. But the house may be more challenging than Defford imagines. And, however you dress it up, reality celebrity television is for losers, some of them deranged.'

'You speak as one of them.'

'Indeed,' Cindy says. 'And the problem with us losers is that we're so much more dangerous than winners, isn't it? And the house… the house is the biggest loser of them all. Always has been, see.'

'Lewis—'

'Do you? See?'

'You're saying this house takes people down with it?'

Time to drive over to Stow to meet Mr Defford. Cindy, who worries about varicose veins, stands up, takes what paces he can around the constricted study, massaging his legs. He can hear the first sullen spatters of night rain on the window.

'Goes beyond that, Marcus. Do you know Belas Knap, at all?'

25
Spent energy

Even in the daytime, most motorways rob you of the country-side, sunk between their banks and obscured by high-sided trucks and trailers. At night they're about speed, lights and not much else.

She looks in the rear-view mirror.

Sees lights through the rain. Just lights.

She's prodding the CD changer on the stereo, trying for something loud and sense-consuming, but all Mumford and Son's songs seem to be about body parts. She switches off. The satnav woman tells her to do nothing much for nineteen miles.

She looks into the rear-view mirror.

It's becoming obsessive.

Her left hand grips the gearstick for support. Gearsticks are just so reassuringly English.

Like ghosts.

Stop it.

She doesn't remember too much about getting out through the enshadowed door at the bottom of the bedroom, only the crawl over the hole between beams, through a tangle of electric wiring, into the empty belly of the hotel. Through twisted, oak-banded passages, sunset-flushed and narrow like bowels, until the house emptied her into a stairway she'd never used before and she fell down the last three wooden stairs, one knee hitting the floor and opening her up to crazily sublime agony. Real-world pain.

She tries the CD player again, at random. It's Foals, an album she's forgotten she had, a song about a guy never feeling better than on his way out of the woods. Never being afraid again.

She turns up the sound, grips the wheel, stays in the slow lane until she's calm enough to consider how someone like Ashley Palk would explain it. Palk with that special smile for making people feel stupid. Talking about suggestion. Out of which comes hallucination.

God, it's so easy, isn't it?

She looks into the rear-view mirror.

Sees the edge of her own face and, behind it, lights, just lights swollen by rain.

'Excuse me, but is there someone up there?'

She said this to the first guy she met on the ground floor, who was Patrick the carpenter, working on a temporary chipboard wall to seal off the main staircase which will have no part to play in *Big Other*.

'Shouldn't be anybody wandering around up there,' Patrick said. 'It's not safe. Floorboards pulled up, exposed wiring everywhere.'

'Only I think I heard someone.'

'You sure?'

'I could've been mistaken. But I'd hate to think… like… if someone's hurt.'

'I'd better go and check.'

'Yes,' she said. 'Might be a good idea.'

With some relief which fragmented when he came down after about five minutes and said nobody was up there. Looking a tad irritated. He'd gone into over twenty rooms. Nobody. Nothing. Grayle mumbling something about sound carrying in strange ways in these old houses and stumbling off towards the sound of real voices.

And you know what? Nobody noticed. Nobody saw anything different about her. Nobody said she was looking pale, nobody offered her a glass of water. Not Kate Lyons, not Peter the sparks, and especially not Leo Defford, taking the A4 cardboard envelope from Kate, handing it to Grayle.

'Don't make a big deal about this. Just make sure she sees the revised figure while you're chatting to her, journalist to journalist.'

She remembers now how there was going to be some straight talking between her and Leo Defford about the need for this journey, like she was going to be set up to take the blame if Parrish pulled out.

Never happened. All she wanted was to put miles and miles of roadway between her and Knap Hall...

... where maybe nothing happened. Nothing outside of stress, overwork and her own failure to harden up the house's meta-physical history. Emotions released by being in a room displaying the ruins of a relationship.

She pulls into a motorway service area, ventures far as she can get from the interior lights, sits behind a coffee and a doughnut and thinks, rationally, about ghosts.

It's like this: haunted houses are fun to read about, haunted house movies useful for providing a reason to hold onto someone in the cinema. And English ghosts are special – if Transylvania has vampires, England has ghosts, the way it has the Royal Family and the bowler hats nobody wears any more. Somehow, from across the Atlantic, these English ghosts... they make you feel kind of thrillingly... warm? Really?

Hell, no. This is what Marcus says after his bit about trusting terror: ghosts are not about someplace else, ghosts are about here. An aspect of here that is almost invariably negative. Ghosts are dampness in the walls, cold shadows on the stairs. Ghosts, when you see them, offer no real hope of redemption, no promise of heaven or a meaningful afterlife. Ghosts are spent energy sucking feebly at yours. Ghosts make the fire go out. And then you carry them away with you like cold ashes from the hearth, and you yourself have become a haunted house.

And still you keep glancing in the rear-view mirror in case there's someone sitting in the back seat. Someone who you've picked up.

Grayle drinks a second coffee. Has to put the cup down when her hands start to shake.

Back in the Cooper, she rolls up the left leg of her jeans and examines the abrasions around the knee, sustained when she fell down the last stone stairs. Still there, still real, still hurting. She remembers trying out her limbs, from which she'd felt in some way disconnected, her body feeling stiff like unfamiliar, starched clothing.

It's quite a small, stone, farmworker-type cottage on a down-sloping lane somewhere between Totnes and the sea which Grayle can smell when she gets out of the car. The English Riviera at night, what a waste.

Not what you'd call lonely here. The nearer you get to the coast in Devon, the more crowded it becomes, and the lights of other houses and bungalows are strung out either side of the former farmworker's cottage that probably stood alone here once, and she can hear music from someplace.

The porch door is already open, globular wall lamps lit either side. It's no longer raining. A woman comes out of the porch, stands at the top of some steps, peering down towards the Mini.

Grayle's seen some recent pictures of Helen Parrish and vaguely remembers her from the BBC news. Seems to be the same woman, despite the clothing. Unless she was in a war zone someplace hot, Helen Parrish, like other TV reporters of her era, would be wearing smart suits and talking in this clipped, tough-as-a-man voice. Or this is how Grayle remembers her. Tonight, Parrish is wearing a loose cashmere cowl-neck sweater and shocking pink jeans. She looks relaxed, raises a cheery hand.

'Grayle Underhill?'

At least she hasn't lost the voice. To be a reporter on the Royals, even ten years ago, it helped if you sounded like one of them.

'Thanks for seeing me.'

'Hardly a problem. I told the woman who rang that tomorrow would be fine, but she insisted.'

'She did?'

Figures. Grayle follows Helen Parrish into the house, into a small parlour, warm with the coloured dust-jacket spines of travel books, bright, plump cushions and a compact, glass-fronted woodstove burning red and orange.

A room for one. Grayle's research says Helen Parrish began as a reporter with the *Western Morning News*, marrying one of her colleagues. Within a couple years, she landed a reporting job on the BBC's West Country local news team, and the marriage didn't survive her move to London four years later. However, latest rumours are that, thirty years on, back home in the west, she's seeing her former husband again, though they're still living separately.

'Coffee?' Parrish says. 'Tea? Or… I mean, have you eaten?'

Grayle thinks of a doughnut bleeding into a plate.

'I'm fine. But tea would be… yeah, please. Um… weak.'

'Grab a seat.' Parrish waves a hand at the comfortably unmatched chairs around the stove. 'Still summer in the daytime, but I'm sure the nights are getting colder.'

'I guess.'

'You look cold.'

Grayle nods. She's felt cold most of the way down here, refusing to turn on the heater in case it had no effect. In case it wasn't that kind of cold. She sits down in an old wing chair with a chintzy cushion. Thinks about how she needs to play this, and it's really quite simple.

The message, the course of action the honest person in her should convey to Parrish, amounts to reaching out and grabbing the ITV holiday-programme-for-the-older-viewer with both hands. It amounts to wearing those summer clothes, staying in the good hotels, sampling the ethnic food for the camera (mmm… good!) admiring the scenery and forgetting you ever heard of Hunter-Gatherer Television.

The envelope is under Grayle's arm. Here's the contract, she should say. Take it out, don't look at the revised figure. Just take it out and tear it up. This might not be a programme you should be doing, in a house that could mess with your dreams for the rest of your life.

But that's not how it works with Helen Parrish. Helen is used to taking control. When she returns and they're sitting either side of the stove's glow with their mismatched mugs of tea and a plate of buttered fruitcake, Parrish stretches her lean body, fluffs up her blue-grey hair, says,

'How are things now, then, Grayle?'

Like they're old friends who haven't met in a while. Grayle looks up.

'Things are… a mite complicated, Helen.'

'Can imagine.' Parrish switches on a reading lamp with an amber shade. 'Not something you can easily walk away from, is it?'

'I'm sorry?'

'I meant your sister.'

Grayle stares at her, the room going into a slow spin.

'You knew my sister?'

'No, no,' Parrish says. 'Not at all. All I know is she was murdered.'

26

Big word

THE MAN CINDY now knows as Leo interrupts their meal to take a call.

The meal, in essence, is a pizza. An upmarket pizza, to be sure, and doubtless expensive, but a pizza nonetheless. Well, Leo's on his own, his woman partner in London, and he was hardly going to employ caterers.

'You're kidding me,' he says into the phone.

He listens. Cindy looks around the lavish farmhouse kitchen, evidently fitted by one of those firms that puts everything behind richly oiled wood so that you need a map to find the refrigerator.

'No, listen, do they want to talk to me? I mean was it actually inside the hedge... fence? If it's just some bloody vagrant or... No, no, don't say anything to anyone, Kate... All right. I'd better come over.'

He hangs up. Some consternation on his face as he strolls back to the banquet-size table where the pizza and trimmings are spread out, a bottle of red wine uncorked.

'Cindy, mate, we have a problem. Not something that happens every day, I'm glad to say. Only, someone appears to have been found dead at Knap Hall. I just need to be sure it's nothing we need worry about.'

Cindy elects to go with him in the white Discovery, leaving his camper in the courtyard at the Victorian stone villa on the edge of Stow. Shouldn't take long, Leo tells him, and they can talk on the way. They take the rest of the pizza and a flask of coffee.

How civilized.

'Sod's Law, eh?' Leo says as they leave the lights behind.

'Or the hand of fate?'

'Don't go sinister on me, Cindy. You ever meet her? Trinity?'

Cindy leaves it a moment.

'Once released my big money balls.'

'What? Oh, the Lottery. I see.'

'A woman on the cusp, even then. I liked her. Why did you decide to use her house?'

Leo goes silent. Must be wondering how much he can disclose to a creature he knows only by reputation. Cindy laughs lightly.

'Only making conversation, Leo. Question of need to know, I realize that. And I'm sure I don't.'

Leo rounds a bend, accelerates.

'Her husband told me,' he says quickly, 'that it was haunted.'

'A big word, that is. Often misrepresented.'

'In what way?'

'Oh, I don't know… we speak of a haunted air to convey that a place has a strong atmosphere that no amount of redecoration can alter. Somewhere you might go in and think, Oh, I feel different here.'

'Yeah.'

'It's only when two or three people, arriving independently, experience the same reaction that it becomes officially haunted, and even then…'

'We're not going into the house,' Leo says. 'I don't want you seen in the vicinity. You can wait in the car, if that's all right.'

'Of course. Must be quite worrying for you. How long have you been working on this now – best part of a year?'

'Could be nothing. Bodies're always being found. I'm just hoping it's no more than someone having a heart attack in the woods. Because obviously if it is one of our people, and the papers finds out, they'll be down on us in force and it won't be easy to mislead them about what we're doing.'

'My solution, in such situations, has always been to give them a juicier story. Rarely fails to divert.'

But it's as if Leo hasn't heard.

'Can't totally trust anybody not to leak it. Some techie who doesn't think he's getting enough money. We'll have in excess of a hundred people on site for this one, all with problems money can solve. Or just problems. You can't monitor everybody all the time.' Leo flicks him a glance. 'Anything I should know about you?'

'Heavens, lovely,' Cindy says. 'I wouldn't know where to start.'

They both laugh. The Discovery glides through the dark and the intermittent rain. Not much traffic on the roads. Glimpses of a milky sickle moon between the trees. They talk, for a while, about people in the business they've both worked with before Leo approaches the reason for this meeting.

'Point is, Cindy, I like to think there's never been a programme quite like this.'

'You could be right.'

'It's a gamble.'

'But if it works,' Cindy says, 'it could make history, could it not?'

'And how likely is that, do you think, on a scale of one to ten?'

'In this house... four? But it can work both ways, see. The problem is that these phenomena have a tendency not to dance to our tunes. And why should they?'

'Perhaps because it's us who conjure them – on some psychological level – into existence.'

'But the only way you'll get that onscreen is through the expressions on the faces of the housemates.'

'Residents.'

'I'm sorry. Residents, yes. Unlikely you'll record anyone walking through a wall, though, see. The best you can hope for is momentarily to shock a sceptic. Have to catch the moment quickly, mind – scepticism soon springs back.'

'So even if the house has a history of psychic phenomena, you don't think it'll play? Even for the believers.'

'All I'm saying is that my experience tells me they don't need us… as much as some of us need them.'

'You mean as evidence that we continue after death?'

'Or even,' Cindy says, 'for us to achieve recognition as the creative force behind a truly epoch-making televisual event.'

Leo's laughter is explosive.

'You bugger! I still can't make out whether you believe in this or not.'

'Oh, I believe in everything, Leo. But, as you must know, it's a gamble.'

'Leo Defford is not a gambler.'

'No, indeed. No successful producer can afford to be much of a gambler nowadays. Leo, pardon me, but I think we go right here.'

'Yeah, you're right.' Leo downshifts as the road inclines. 'You know how to work a ouija board, Cindy?'

'Never done it, to be quite honest,' Cindy lies. 'Though I doubt it's terribly taxing, technically. Upturned glass, bits of paper. Basic knowledge of the alphabet.'

'That'll do.'

Cindy smiles, as the windscreen becomes pimpled by the scattered lights of what might be Winchcombe.

'Am I to understand from your question that if, over the seven nights, we run into what, in television terms, might be described as a dull patch, it might have to be enlivened by someone giving the spirit world a small nudge?'

'It's a remote possibility. A fallback. Or perhaps there are more original ways of appearing to do this. You'd know better than me.'

'The poor old ouija board. All a bit *Most Haunted*, isn't it?' Cindy says. 'I do understand, broadly, where you're coming from and I shall, as the Bard phrases it, think on't.'

'I'd be grateful. We could be a good— Oh fuck, look at this…'

The road ahead has erupted into spasms of blue. There's a skew of vehicles on the grass verges, and two are police cars. A female officer comes over as Leo pulls up and lowers his window.

'Leo Defford. I'm leasing Knap Hall.'

'You have any ID, sir?'

'Loads.' He pulls something leather from an inside pocket of his hard man's canvas jacket. 'Can you give me any idea what's happened?'

'What I can tell you is I don't think it's happened on the property you're leasing. It's just been easier for some of our vehicles to reach the spot from your land.'

'One of my people phoned me and said someone had been found dead. Man or woman? Can you—?'

'Sorry, I can't really tell you anything about that, except we might've thought it was on your land at first.' The officer is shining her torch on Leo's driving licence. 'Thank you, Mr Defford. If you want to drive up through the main entrance, I'll call ahead, see if there's anyone who can talk to you.'

'Thanks.' Leo waves a hand at the other vehicles, a few shadow figures visible now. 'Who are…?'

'That's the media, sir.'

Cindy sees Leo flinch.

'I know,' she says. 'They seem to know about these things faster than we do these days.'

27

Responsibility

IT'S NOT SOMETHING that goes away for long. It's part of who you are. You could win a Pulitzer Prize, get a medal from the Queen, but you're still the person whose sister got murdered.

And this is a small country. Murders get remembered, especially if yours is part of a chain and the killer has a popular handle like The Boston Strangler or The Yorkshire Ripper.

Here's how it probably went: Kate Lyons tells Parrish they're sending Grayle Underhill to talk to her, Parrish thinks maybe she's heard the name before and goes onto the Internet, where there's hardly anything about Grayle, but still quite a bit about Ersula, and whole megabytes about the Green Man, who drew attention to the erosion of British traditions by killing people at ancient sites.

'Where is he now?' Helen Parrish asks.

'Broadmoor. Under constant watch, I guess. He was down here in Dartmoor for a while but he killed a prison chaplain.'

'Oh God, I remember. Kitchen knife. They trusted him.'

'Not a mistake they'll make again.'

Grayle leans back. Being with another journalist makes her realize she is one, has always been one, even during the New Age years on the *Courier*. Journalists, whatever part of the job they grew up in, to whatever level they progressed, share a mind-set, a kind of objectivity. They always see the story. Even when the story is painfully and horribly close.

And, not untypically, Helen Parrish, as the more experienced journalist, has gotten her talking about herself before HGTV has even been mentioned.

'Your sister was an anthropologist?'

'Among other things. She was younger than me. The clever one. The one who progressed. Like when we were kids we both got into mystical stuff but even then she was ahead of me. I read about witchcraft, she became a witch. Till they discovered she was just studying them and threw her out the coven. Or maybe she just quit in disgust.'

Parrish laughs.

'And then,' Grayle says, 'she was the serious academic who went to Africa and Haiti, studying shamanism, in which she didn't believe. And wound up over here as a guest professor at something called the University of the Earth, which was looking to bridge the gulf between serious archaeology and anthropology and… cranks. Cranks like me. And so spent time testing theories about the siting of Stoneage monuments, often in places so lonely that you can… get killed there.'

'I'm sure you've talked enough about it,' Parrish says. 'I just thought we should get it over with.'

Grayle stares into the fire. Nobody at HGTV has ever asked her about Ersula, though they must all know.

'I'm OK with it now. As far as anyone ever could be. I flew over here when Ersula had been out of contact for a while, and I was there when they caught this… creep.'

'And you're still here.'

'Made a handful of good friends. And got no closer to my father who's never actually said he thinks the wrong daughter was murdered, but if Ersula hadn't crossed the threshold from real science back to the place where I hung out, with the crazies, she might be alive today.'

'He blames you?'

'And in spite of it all, I still love all that – the idea of being in a country full of these ancient ritual sites and old stones and all that stuff. I just… tend not to visit them. Not alone, anyhow.'

She's thinking how close Knap Hall is to the famous burial mound, Belas Knap, after which it presumably is named. Just over the hill. Seen it marked on the map. Never been to look. Too much like Black Knoll, where Ersula died. And where she herself saw or hallucinated the image of the girl in the rain. What a messed up person she is.

'So your mission here,' Parrish says, 'is to reassure me – as a fellow fruitcake – that if I agree to go into your house I'll be amongst friends.'

'It's that obvious?'

Parrish pours more tea for them both from a very English brown pot. She's pretty; her face, though, quite lined, doesn't do severity, always relaxes into semi-amusement. She's been around and it doesn't matter who knows.

'So, Grayle,' she says, 'you have an extensive knowledge of different types of apparition and the people who've seen them.'

'As much as anyone ever does.'

'And does that mean you believe in them… in the traditional sense?'

Grayle leans her heads into a high wing of the armchair, closes her eyes for a moment. What a night to throw this one into her lap.

'I have to say… that after all these tens of thousands of recorded experiences throughout history, I think people are crazy not to. But… in the traditional sense? I don't know. I still don't know what they are. Not sure we're meant to, you know?'

'Or whether it's all down to some brain-chemical cocktail?'

'You really lose your job at the BBC because of telling them you'd seen Diana?'

Parrish shudders.

'I didn't tell them. What do you think I am? I was stupid enough to mention it, in a casual, slightly incredulous way to a couple of people I never imagined I couldn't trust. The post of deputy royal-correspondent was discontinued a short time later. Can't honestly say that whatever I may foolishly have said was anything to do with that. Though I accept that the BBC currently has its tongue a long way up the arse of Dr Science.'

Grayle smiles. Marcus also talks like that about the world's number one public service broadcaster.

'Don't know,' Parrish says. 'Perhaps I was just getting too old, perhaps I wasn't very good. Though, in my defence, I'd point to some famous faces who're a bloody sight older and a bloody sight worse. Perhaps they just needed to lose some jobs. I was on a freelance contract, so there was no huge redundancy package.' She nods at the leather file. 'What've you brought me?'

'Another contract?'

'They were talking about topping it up with another hundred grand. God, I mean that is so bloody tempting. We're now in the region of half a million. There's nothing I could do on the box, not now, that would bring in that much. Certainly not for barely more than a week's work. But, then... I have to give them value for money, don't I?'

Grayle shrugs.

'They – we – would want you to talk in some detail about your experience, however much of it you believe was paranormal. They'd probably have you talking about it early in the week.'

'So it'll get in the papers.'

'And maybe double the *Big Other* viewing figures. I guess that's how they're thinking.'

'You guess?'

'Figure of speech.'

Parrish shakes her head wearily.

'On one level, it's a no-brainer, Grayle. Just after they dumped me, I had an offer for a TV commercial. Rescue-cosmetics for the ageing. Because I'm worth it – just about. No, actually not that one, but you get the idea. And a magazine ad for Saga holidays – get photographed standing at the rails of a cruise ship with some smarmy old git in a tuxedo. Felt quite insulted at the time.'

Parrish lights a cigarette.

'And so told them very politely to piss off. Well, actually, not that politely, which I rather regret now. Regret quite a lot. Anyway...' She shudders again, a tad theatrically. 'You know what worried me most when they first contacted me? Forced myself to watch a DVD of *Celebrity Big Brother*, and... celebrity? Is it my age, or do most people only recognize about two of them? I foresaw embarrassment when we were all assembled and none of us knew who the hell the others were.'

'Was that all that worried you?'

Parrish smiles behind the smoke, doesn't reply. Grayle's now-educated guess is that, for this woman, an afternoon travel programme for the cruise-ship generation looks like TV's terminal ward.

Not good.

'Helen, I need to tell you... the producer's idea is that every night you'll all sit around the fireside and one of you will tell a story about how you came to believe in the existence of ghosts. Or how you came not to believe. Some seminal-moment anecdote. And the others get to question you about it, and while a few will be nut-jobs like me some of them're gonna be serious sceptics.'

'And I might even agree with them.'

'Don't agree too easily.'

Parrish blows out smoke.

'It was... just a strange postscript to a strange period in my life. Being a royal reporter, following them around the world, you realize the whole thing is a fantasy in itself and you're part of that. You're inside the magic circle. Very close to some almost mythical figures, the like of which we may not see in this country for too much longer. And then, occasionally, reality intrudes, with some scandal, and you're a hard-news reporter again and you feel you're betraying them. Which is ridiculous.'

'It was a few years ago, right? When you had this experience.'

'Which I've never actually kept at the forefront of my memory. The more times goes by, the less sure I am that I believe it myself.'

'Yeah, I can understand that.'

In a way.

'What's this house like?' Helen Parrish says. 'Are you allowed to tell me anything about it? Have I heard of it?'

Oh God, she so wants to pour it all out about the Ansell bedroom. Could be she's the only person who's afraid of Knap Hall, and that's a responsibility. It's only just occurred to her what a terrible responsibility this is.

'I guess not,' she says. 'But it's… it's not a good place, Helen.'

Her expression must've betrayed something. Parrish is leaning forward, pinching out the cigarette.

'You're saying you think it's actually haunted?'

Grayle pauses. The window is uncurtained, probably to make the most of a sea view. All she can see is a deep blue night sky, but she knows the sea is out there, and it's huge.

'OK… I think… that there is something wrong there. I think something's… disturbed. And I think… I think that, whatever you believe, you can still be damaged by these… situations. In ways you can't imagine. It's my job to try and identify what it is about the building, or what people think it is. And I'm not there yet. Nowhere near.'

'Bloody hell.' Helen's eyes have widened. 'You sound almost as if you're trying to put me off.'

'I guess I'm not supposed to do that.'

'I guess you're not.' Parrish's grey eyes are curious now. 'Let me see the contract.'

Grayle's handing her the envelope when the cellphone rings.

'Get it,' Helen says. 'They might want you to increase the offer.'

They both smile. Grayle pulls the phone from her jeans, slides the answer bar.

'Underhill.'

It's Defford's PA, Kate Lyons.

'Grayle, message from Leo. Are you still on the road?'

'No. I'm… I'm with Helen Parrish.'

'When you've finished, find a radio. Don't do it in there.'

'What's this about?'

'No hurry. Just something you need to know about. It'll be on the news. Leo will talk to you in the morning.'

And the call's over. Helen Parrish is sliding the contract back into its envelope.

'You all right, Grayle?'

'Sure. Nothing urgent.'

What sounds like a grandfather clock is ticking someplace. Behind it she hears what might be the sighing of the night sea.

'I'm not being entirely truthful,' Parrish says. 'I'm only unsure about it until I start to relive it in my head. And you're thinking, isn't it amazing how a substantial six-figure sum clears the mind.'

Grayle says nothing. She wasn't thinking that.

'Do you want to hear this now, Grayle? I mean, do you want to hear exactly what happened between... her... and me? May take a while. Detail tends to blur until all that remain are the feelings. But I swear those were genuine.'

Grayle sits up in the armchair, takes a long, sustaining breath.

'No, no... please. I'm like... all ears.'

Helen stubs out her cigarette and pours more tea.

Couple hours later, Grayle's following the signs towards Exeter and the M5, whichever comes first, the satnav lady silenced to let the radio through. It's a long drive home, but she doesn't want to stay in a hotel tonight. She's want home, a bed she knows, Cheltenham night traffic.

On the passenger seat beside her, the contract, signed. She doesn't know what the figure is, but after hearing the story she can believe Helen Parrish is worth more than most of the others. A well-known, trusted face, a big, big ghost. And someone who can hold her own against the likes of Ozzy Ahmed.

It's a whole different kind of experience, of course. Altogether different from a place of dampness and rotting leaves. But no more life-enhancing. Not really.

She's wondering if maybe she ought, after all, to have shared what happened to her in the former bedroom at Knap Hall, when the Radio Four news headlines come on.

She doesn't have long to wait. It's second lead item.

'A man whose body was found in a wood in Gloucestershire tonight is believed to have been identified as the magazine publisher Harry Ansell.'

She doesn't even remember pulling off the road into a housing estate, just sitting there with two wheels on the sidewalk and the motor running, going oh my God, oh my God, oh my God.

'Police have cordoned off the wood near Winchcombe in the northern Cotswolds, and a formal statement is expected within the next hour.'

Grayle sits looking at rows of house lights through coloured curtains. She didn't know a person could shake like this. Literally shake, so hard you weren't safe to drive.

'It's less than two years since the death of Mr Ansell's wife, the former model and film-actor Trinity Ansell, whose name he took when they married.'

She tries to call Leo Defford at home, but his cellphone's busy.

28

Exorcizing Trinity

SHE KEEPS DRIVING north till she finds the M5 and then what must be the other side of those same motorway services, where she pulls in and makes another call.

'I've been looking for you,' Fred Potter says. 'Thought you might've come out, in the circumstances.'

'Where are you?'

'Where else would I be, Grayle? Sitting on a damp stile on the edge of a wood I'm not allowed into. Police cars, police tape and one of those ambulances for the dead, and it's bloody cold. Where are you?'

'Not close. On the way back from Devon. All I know is what was on the radio.'

'A farmer found him. Doing a last check on his sheep.'

'Where?'

'Don't know if the wood has a name. It's probably less than half a mile from Knap Hall.'

God.

'What happened to him? How did he die?'

'You don't know how he died?'

'Fred, I don't know anything. It sounds like suicide.'

'Yes.'

'So, like… carbon monoxide in his car? What?'

'Cops are not letting anybody through, but I did manage to talk to the farmer. Recognized Ansell straight away from when he was at the hall. Quite a shock.'

'Fred—'

'He was hanging from a tree. Oak tree, I think. Barely light when the farmer found him. Might've been not very long after he did it.'

Fred goes on talking, oblivious to Grayle covering the mouth-slit on becoming aware of how hard she's breathing. And then she jumps in her seat – someone tapping on the steamed up side window.

She starts the car, lowers the glass. An elderly man is asking if she's all right but looking suspicious like it might be a stolen car. It's the shorn hair does it.

'Had to...' Holding up the phone, waving it around to conceal the shake. 'Had to make a call.'

'Oh, righto.' He smiles apologetically; her voice, her accent, seems to have reassured him. 'Thought I ought to check... the speed you came in.'

'I'm sorry. Sorry about that.' And when he's gone, this concerned local person, she says into the phone, 'Harry Ansell...'

'Word is he was in trouble with the bank, and banks don't help you these days even if you're Harry Ansell. We know he'd borrowed money to launch *Cotsworld* in Australia, Canada and... other places. And then Trinity dies... and that just blows the whole conceit, doesn't it? Paradise looking a little sordid. It's a matter of record he sold some of his other magazines to stay afloat. We think he was even looking for a buyer for *Cotsworld* itself. No chance. Not at a price worth having.'

'Harry Ansell hanged himself?'

The word comes back at her: *hanged, hanged, hanged*.

'Grayle, are you all right?'

'Yeah. I'm just...'

She's vibrating. The bedposts are vibrating. All five of them. *Oh God, oh God, oh God*.

'Who gets his empire now?' Fred says. 'Or rather his debts. I don't know. Eddie Burgess – that's his son from his first marriage – is still at university, doing an MA in history. Could take years to sort out... Grayle?'

'Still here.'

'How's it going to affect you? I'm assuming Defford's got Knap Hall on a firm lease.'

'Sure. I don't suppose it is. Going to affect us. Not in that way.'

'He was actually here about an hour ago.'

'Defford?'

'With a woman in his car who I didn't recognize, but... not his wife, and too old, you know, too old to be a girlfriend.'

'Maybe Kate Lyons. His PA.'

'I know Kate. Wasn't her. Anyway, he said he'd talk to me tomorrow. Needs time to think, obviously. He's got to be on thin ice here, if he doesn't want it to get out about what he's doing at Knap Hall. Media's going to be down in force. Bunch of us here already.'

'He'll stick to the cover story about the Trinity Ansell biopic documentary.'

'Anybody asks me,' Fred says, 'I'll obviously tell them that, too. Assuming our arrangement...'

'Sure.'

Unofficially, they have a deal, her and Fred. He passes on information, like about Ansell, stuff which, for legal reasons, he can't sell for publication, and she agrees to give him news-worthy *Big Other* background stuff, exclusive, not to be used till it won't interfere with the programme.

'Defford's got to be nervous though,' Fred says. 'Wondering why Ansell came back here to do it.'

'He might be more excited than nervous. For reasons I'm sure you'll appreciate.'

'Why would you think he'd come out here to do it?'

'I don't know. I don't think Ansell liked Knap Hall, even before Trinity died. How long you gonna be there, Fred?'

'Long as it takes. Hang on, they're just loading Ansell's Range Rover onto a transporter. This could be quite a big story, you know, Grayle. They'll all be sniffing around, and the Trinity death stuff will get brought up again.'

'If I get anything that won't impact on the programme, I'll pass it on.'

'Thank you.' There's a silence. She can hear voices in the background and maybe tyres rolling in mud. 'One thing I'm sitting on. Got a whisper from a mate in the police. I'll probably put it out tomorrow, so not a word right?'

'Sure.'

'He left a note,' Fred says. 'Well, not a note, just an envelope attached to the breast pocket of his jacket with a paperclip. One word written on it.'

She says nothing, thinks *Trinity*.

'The word was Burgess.'

'Oh.'

'Claiming back his original identity before he died? Do you think?'

Renouncing Ansell? Exorcizing Ansell.

Exorcizing Trinity.

'Makes you think, Grayle. Look, I can see Colin Mellor coming down the track. I'd better…'

'Sure.'

Colin Mellor is a police superintendent at Gloucester.

'Call you tomorrow, Grayle.'

'Right.'

She tosses the cellphone onto the passenger seat with the Parrish contract. All that seems so long ago. It feels like her whole life is a series of hallucinations: the dark interior of the small car, the rear-view mirror as she reverses to face the main road. Ersula in her black gown. The bedposts, and a slumping thing.

The rope connecting it to the shadows.

Her hands grip the wheel so hard her knuckles crack. No wonder people don't talk about these things any more. It doesn't help. Maybe one day, when this is all over, she'll tell Marcus. Meanwhile, she'll pack it all away in a box and bury the box. Would so love to do that.

But it isn't going anywhere, is it? And you can't bury yourself.

PART FOUR

Night...

Ghosts are no longer souls.
Ghosts are now an emotion field.

Roger Clarke
A Natural History of Ghosts (2012)

Late October

29

Resentment

When she stands up, the red dress is alive with candlelight.

It's Thursday evening, three days before transmission, two before the first recording with the residents. It's just after dark, and she walks.

She walks out of the same shadows, every time, in that facsimile red dress. No deviation, the way ghosts walk. The swish the dress makes disturbs the candles as she crosses the stone flags, past the shifting logs in the ingle with their sparse yellow flames and out through the doorway.

A unnatural quietness, then...

'A wrap, I think,' Jo Shepherd says softly. 'We're not going to improve on that.'

She's with one of the cameramen, backed up into a corner by the window. There's another one behind the false wall. Someone's recording ambient sound. Outside the chamber, in a different century, the woman in the gloriously expensive red dress – her name is Meg – expels a whole lot of breath, turns to Grayle.

'You haven't got an aspirin or something?'

'We can get you one in the restaurant. Do you wanna...?'

'Nah, it's OK. I know I haven't eaten for a while, but I just felt muzzy-headed. That' – Meg cuddles her arms – 'was absolutely *the* spookiest thing I've ever had to do.'

She's been contracted in the full knowledge that these pictures may never be shown. She's a Londoner. Grayle thinks she's seen her in commercials. Whatever, she's been given a lot of work in reconstructions for HGTV documentaries over the years and can be counted on to keep her mouth shut and be philosophical if she doesn't get to be a ghost onscreen.

They go up the steps, Grayle looking directly away, avoiding the stairs. She's been told the Ansells' apartment has been converted into two bedrooms with the bathroom and toilets in between. She hasn't been upstairs to look. Nor does she intend to.

Outside, in the half-lit walled garden, Meg pulls off her dark wig, looks relieved.

'Usually when you're on to about the fourth take, it's auto-pilot stuff, but in there it just got more and more uncomfortable. As if I was walking in someone else's footsteps and she was... walking beside me. Resentful.'

'Really?'

'I know, I'm too impressionable for this job. I expect it's just...' taps her forehead, 'up there. While I was waiting in the pop-up, I read another feature in the *Sunday Times* or some-where about Harry Ansell and Trinity... I mean you can't take it on board, can you? Both dead now, and none of it's... you know, normal?'

As Jo Shepherd comes out, Grayle says casually to Meg, 'Who do you think it was? Walking beside you.'

Frilly white cuffs slide back as Meg's hands shoot up abruptly into warding-off mode.

'What're you guys trying to *do* to me?'

Meg laughs unconvincingly. She's about to become another footnote in Grayle's haunted house file.

There are three pop-up hotels, one more luxurious than the others, for the residents and senior execs, though from the outside they all look like big crates. Outside, while Meg's getting changed in a ground-floor suite, Grayle accepts a cigarette from Jo Shepherd. Hasn't smoked, bar the odd joint, since her teens, but with two days to go...

'I'm feeling a bit bloody haunted, too.' Jo's kind of tomboyish, short curly hair and an amethyst in her nose. 'Next time we record in there, it's likely to be for real.'

This week, they've had two days of dress rehearsal, with the residents played by various Emilys and Jamies, hamming it up, and Grayle in her booth in the reality gallery interviewing people sitting in the chapel. She had a monitor in there, showing their faces staring into camera, but they couldn't see her. The first time her voice faltered and she started coughing. Afterwards, there was a big forum discussion in Defford's classroom-sized portacabin office, producers and directors encouraged to say what they thought didn't work.

Tonight the first residents are coming off the plane at the Cotswold airport, blindfolded, assisted into windowless vans. Tomorrow night they go into the house, one by one, and recording starts as they meet one another. Then the rushes get edited and all the best stuff goes out from ten p.m. on Saturday, finally going live at midnight.

Grayle says, 'Leo's looking excited, but not in a good way.'

'That's normal. Between now and tomorrow night, he'll be biting heads off. As soon as we're rolling, an icy calm comes over him. That's not in a good way either, but we get used to it.'

Grayle guesses Harry Ansell's death has hit Defford harder than he's showing. Maybe relying on Ansell – in the gallery, *watching* – making some disclosure that might alter the direction of the programme towards the end when the last person is alone in the house and the location is finally revealed. But the connection's severed, no revelation. He's on his own and there are things he doesn't understand. That none of them understands.

Grayle smokes hesitantly, gazing out at the myriad lights of something halfway between a fairground and a small city. Or like a condensed and comparatively soundless rock festival site, and Knap Hall is the stage. Some stage: silent, unlit and cloaked, she feels, in resentment. Resentment has become tonight's dominant emotion.

'Gotta say I never imagined all this… the expense. How lavish it all is.'

Jo wrinkles her nose.

'It's all relative. We're looking at twenty-four hours of quality television. Think what Hollywood spends on less than two.'

'I guess.' The wind's getting up again. Grayle tightens the belt on her woollen coat, shields her cigarette. 'This weather good or bad?'

'Weather's not a particular problem. We'll be OK for heavy rain, snow, thunder and lightning – I mean *that* would be brilliant. The only problem would be, say, hurricane-force winds so that all this gets flattened, with only Knap Hall left standing.'

'That would be, um…'

'Don't even think about it, Grayle.' Jo swallows smoke, starts to cough. 'I'll go only so far with this stuff.'

After Ansell's death, there was nearly a week of heavy meetings, Grayle getting occasionally admitted to the core team, though Defford keeps looking at her like he's not sure she should be there.

So how *will* this big suicide affect the programme, specially in the final stages? On one level, it will eventually make the whole thing more newsworthy, but there are questions of taste to be dealt with. Also the fact that the programme will be going out before the full inquest on Ansell is held. Defford's spent some hours with the coroner's people, forced to explain some of what HGTV were doing at Knap Hall. Taking Grayle along as his chief researcher and therefore an expert on the Ansells. As if.

Defford's being immensely helpful to the cops in return for nothing about the project coming out through the police press office.

He hopes.

Now that Harry Ansell is too dead to sue, the tabloids have been indulging in some lavish speculation about relations between the lone-wolf publisher and his beautiful trophy wife.

Why did she feel she needed to conceal her pregnancy from him? Did *he* know why, and was that what drove him down to the woods with a rope? There was a small panic when a Sunday broadsheet ran a feature with a big dark picture of Harry Ansell walking the grounds of Knap Hall with the house in the background and the headline: *HAUNTED LIFE, LONELY DEATH*. But it was all metaphorical.

The lonely death made a mess of Grayle's schedule, too. Twice she's had to postpone a meeting with Mary Ann Rutter, the writer, though she's spoken to her on the phone – she sounds old but bright – and learned why there are no copies of *Rogues and Roués of the Northern Cotswolds* to be found.

Seems some far-flung member of the Wishatt family – in the US, Mrs Rutter thinks – got sent a copy. And she must know what some of her fellow Americans are like about their English ancestry. Oh boy, *does* she? Probably dining out on being descendants of a titled landowner with connections to Sudeley Castle. As distinct from a serial sex-criminal. So these descendants tracked down every copy of *Rogues and Roués*, which is so much easier to do now, with outfits like AbeBooks. And they bought them all. Every one left on the market.

And probably destroyed them. Mrs Rutter sounds amused, but she must be furious. Grayle decides to go see her tonight or tomorrow – that's assuming Jo Shepherd doesn't demand more rehearsal for her unwanted role as voice-link with the chapel. All the hours she's spent getting abused by junior producers pretending to be Ozzy and Eloise – *Let them talk, don't interrupt*, Jo insists. *Keep yourself in the background.*

If only. Never totally going to trust Jo, after her revelation of just one day ago, about the last resident – Driscoll's replacement.

Oh yeah, the unnamed one now has a name – a name Grayle knows all too well. Could be that Jo Shepherd has been been sitting on this for months.

And yes, it's all too plausible and explains precisely what Defford meant by his Orwellian reference to some residents being more equal than others. Just this one, to be exact. Whenever she thinks about it, Grayle feels like one side of her mind has shut down while the other, with sadistic glee, is putting two and two together to come up with some impossible prime number.

At seven p.m. precisely, she calls Mary Ann Rutter from her cabin to see if she's free tonight, but it's on answerphone. She leaves a message, and then, barely a second later, her phone rings.

Grayle snaps,

'Underhill.'

A pause, then a light, lyrical laugh that goes through her like raw alcohol.

'Now *there's* authoritative. How *are* you, little Grayle?'

As the wind pushes at the pop-up hotel, a tremor ripples down Grayle's phone-hand. Holy shit, he never changes.

'I'm... handling things,' she says.

And he laughs again.

'A meeting,' he says, 'is necessary, I think.'

'A meeting.'

'Call it a date, I would, if I was normal.'

If I was normal. He always says that. It's one of his signature phrases. He relishes it – not being normal. Like the house.

30

Skid beach

A ROADSIDE PUB out near Gloucester. New-looking, cheap meals, pool table. Lamps like upturned chromium barstools glued to the ceiling.

Not the kind of pub where even the lowest-paid TV person would ever dine, and nobody in here looks at all like one. Grayle's finishing a small glass of orange juice at a corner table when the double doors open for this individual – and *individual* is the word – in a tweed jacket and skirt, pearls, gold and silver hair supporting a pink beret.

When they embrace, it doesn't feel right, but when did it ever? He fetches her another orange juice from the bar and a pink gin for himself. She looks at him, refusing to be disarmed.

'Just so I know, Cindy, you got my cell number from Jo Shepherd, right?'

He frowns.

'*Heavens*, no. No one knows we're meeting tonight. Not even young Jo. Make her anxious, it would. No, I did what anyone would do. Rang the London offices of the eccentrically named Hunter-Gatherer Television, put on my best New England accent and said I was your father. Your aunt is dead, by the way.'

'Which aunt?'

'Aunt Mia. All very sudden. They wouldn't tell me yesterday where you were to be found, but eventually gave me the number of the mobile phone they bought for you. Still, fair play, she had a good innings, at ninety-eight.'

A wave of deeply reluctant affection washes over Grayle as his eerie rosy lips form an unsettling smile.

She holds her face still.

No more lies, no more evasion, no more bullshit.

His full name is Sydney Mars-Lewis and he is, of course, a national treasure. At least, he *was*, until he overreached himself on live TV and faded quietly back into the land of his fathers.

She has no idea how old he is, only that, for two decades, he made a precarious living as a ventriloquist. Cindy Mars with Kelvyn Kite – a red kite, rare at the time, even in Wales. A sinister-looking bird with a smart beak and pink-tipped fingers up its ass, whose derisive comments about the greed and foolish extravagance of Lottery winners came back to peck him when tragedy befell a jackpot-winning family.

Who could forget the *Mirror* headline: THE CURSE OF KELVYN KITE? Not easy to come back from that kind of publicity. Which explains everything. On the surface.

Grayle stares into his mild, friendly, inoffensive, *duplicitous* fucking eyes.

'This is all down to you, right?'

'All?'

He tilts his head and still the goddamn beret stays on. Grayle tilts hers to hold his gaze.

'Marcus… me… you. The way it all mysteriously came together.'

Cindy looks stern, like some old-school headmistress in a black and white English movie.

'Are you honestly telling me, little Grayle, that it never once entered your head to wonder why I was not amongst The Seven?'

Jesus, 'The Seven'. Who else could take a shallow commercial enterprise and endow it with apocalyptic resonance?

'Yeah, I know,' Grayle says, 'I should've figured. Nobody ticks the boxes better. Wounded, washed-up, in urgent need of money. One-time big name on Skid Row.'

'Skid Beach, it is, to be more accurate,' Cindy says.

*

Over the next half-hour, under those industrial lights, some big holes in her knowledge get cemented in. How, before *Big Other* was even conceived, before she or Marcus or even Defford knew anything about Knap Hall, Cindy Mars-Lewis was there.

The only one of them who ever met Trinity Ansell. Who walked around the house before it became the core of *Cotsworld*.

His eyeliner's smudged. All the time he's talking she keeps noticing that. Men, however abnormal, are rarely good with make-up.

'Does Marcus know all this?'

'Little Grayle, the thing always to remember about Marcus—'

'He knows. OK. And the reason he kept me out of that particular loop is he… Oh, Jesus, I'm getting Marcus's money?'

She's pulling back from the table, chair legs screeching. The mobile starts ringing in her bag.

'Not *quite* that simple,' Cindy says gently. 'I didn't know, back then, what was involved. And Marcus… well, would he have lasted two weeks with these people?'

She ignores the phone, drags her bag to the floor.

'And the house?'

Suppose it had been Marcus, not her, in the Ansell bedchamber… Marcus with the heart condition… Marcus who says 'trust terror'. Trust it to do what? Take you out?

Cindy's sitting motionless as an antique mannequin in an old-fashioned ladies' outfitters. Watching her, watching it all sink in. Then he leans across the table, pushing aside his unfinished pink gin, bringing down his voice.

'It's an unreliable house, isn't it?'

She nods.

'I'm only a human being,' he says. 'Walked around, did some dowsing. Listened to my senses and the little voice whispering, 'Tell her to get out, sell up, cut their losses, escape to a tax haven.' Would she be alive now, do you think? Do we believe this nonsense?'

'She died trying to get rid of a baby without her husband knowing. Died someplace else.'

'Don't interfere. That's what Marcus says. Only human beings, we are, we don't really have *wisdom*. Bigger influences than us at work. Might as well say, would she be alive if she hadn't said yes to the part of Katherine Parr in a film? We could go on, couldn't we? At the end of the day, a determination to transcend the everyday has its risks, but when you're very beautiful, very rich, very famous and you've pushed your talents as far as they will go, what's left? Good works? Religion? Perhaps what she was doing *might* have turned the house around. Not impossible to alter the atmosphere by force of will. I don't know. I feel inadequate, little Grayle.'

'Are they both there… on some level?'

Her voice seems very small.

'Who?'

'The Ansells. Trinity. And now Harry.'

He doesn't answer.

'When I came back the second time,' he says eventually, 'it was during one of the Weekends. All frivolity and wealthy guests, a film star, a rock star and a band with lutes and virginals. As if she wanted to show me my ill-expressed misgivings were well off the mark. That she'd pulled it off. And there I am, smiling approvingly, with the sense of a funfair erected on a peatbog full of decaying matter.'

On the other side of the long room, two guys have begun a game of pool: *snick, snock*. Cindy tells her about the diary he asked Trinity to keep. How she'd make a couple of entries, put the diary in the post to him and then start another. He brings out his phone, thumbs through some photographed images of handwritten pages, turns the phone to face her.

I can see the hearth with no fire. The room is cold and there's a blue light, a shaft of blue light bathing a low wooden bed. A truckle did they call it? Her eyes are closed, though her mouth is slightly open. And I know she's dead.

She reads it a second time.

'What *is* this?'

'I think she's describing a dream. About Katherine Parr? Probably. She came to believe, on no historical evidence, that Katherine died there.'

'At Knap Hall?' Which wasn't even called Knap Hall back then – was called Dean Farm, or Quarry Farm, something like that. 'Where'd she get that idea from?'

'Seemed to make her happy. The idea of its being Katherine's final refuge.'

'Was she losing her mind? Was the house… doing something to her? Or her marriage?'

'Dreams… may show us what, if experienced in our waking hours, would test our sanity. But, equally, dreams can strip away the buffers our waking selves use to absorb primitive fears.'

'How long before she died did she write this stuff?'

'Not long. Weeks. I wondered if perhaps she'd begun another in those days when she was alone at her parents' holiday cottage. I even got her parents' number from Poppy Stringer – the housekeeper?'

'Wouldn't even talk to me.'

'Cast a peculiar enchantment, I do, over women of a certain age. Except for Trinity's mother. I rang her parents to see if she'd left another diary. Tried to explain, but her mother was angry. Knew who I was and *what* I was – or what people *said* I was. Told me never to ring them again. Finally, I steeled myself to ring Ansell's office, left my number.'

'Not a man for calling back.'

The mobile starts up again in the bag. She grimaces, drags it out to find a terse, reproachful text from Kate Lyons.

'Cindy, I'm gonna have to go. Gotta… sweet-talk one of the

residents. Go down with a driver to pick him up at the Cotswold airport. In a van with no windows.'

'How exciting.'

'Yeah. We're bringing them all in over two nights.'

'Well, then, I shall leave you my mobile number, little Grayle. We need, I think, to stay in touch when I'm in the house and you are not.'

She stands up, nodding, shoulders the bag.

Cindy says, 'Have you seen the Winchcombe Grotesques?'

'The what?'

'The stone monsters on the church tower.'

'Oh. Well, yeah… briefly, I guess, shopping in town. Haven't had much time for sightseeing lately. A lot of English churches have weird stuff like that.'

'Not on this scale. Forty of them, or more, and at least half of them blatantly demonic. That tower's in a class of its own.'

He talks about one of the grotesques acquiring a naked body and stalking Trinity's dreams.

Seems to Grayle that woman had a few too many dreams.

'The relevant diary was delayed,' Cindy says, 'so I knew nothing of this until long after her death.'

'You're saying it links to the house?'

'I have no idea.'

'Like, if she was getting increasingly screwed up… for reasons we don't know – or do we?'

He says nothing.

'Everything she sees is, like, crowding in on her, including the horrific faces on the tower?'

'Starting to think like a TV person, you are. For whom everything must fit into the box.'

'Thanks.'

'I've always tended to take the overview. Look at the landscape and its features. Find the layers. And, no, I don't think Trinity was mad.'

Grayle closes her eyes, rubs them wearily, shakes her head.

'We need to talk about this. I'd like to know everything she said to you. Everything she knew about Knap Hall and what might… what might've been seen there.'

'You probably know more than me, lovely. She told me she'd never seen Katherine, though perhaps smelled her scent. May once – though she seemed far from sure – have caught a glimpse of a handsome young man with fair hair who wanders in and out. Trinity thought it might have been Thomas Seymour.'

'See, this is a new one on me—'

'Layers. Apparitions exist on different layers, in different time frames, independent of one another.'

'I realize that.'

'Of course you do. Now go and meet your guest. We'll keep in touch.'

'We don't disclose we know each other, right?'

'On no account.' He writes his mobile number on a beermat, stands up, brightening. 'They're paying me to behave in that house like the lunatic the public thinks I am. Light relief. Always so important to me.'

'Yeah. I, uh… I feel better you're here. But what— Thanks.' She accepts the beermat. 'I mean what's really gonna happen in there? And, like, should we be trying to stop it?'

'You really think we could? Us paid lackeys?'

'Whatever he says, Defford likes to know what he's dealing with. Sure, he'd love to have a ghost on camera, but he realizes that's unlikely to happen – as do I, for Christ's sake. Like… a ghost is not for everybody, is it? Or do we, like, *want* something to happen to wipe the smug looks off their faces?'

'The way something seems to have wiped the lovely smile from yours?'

He regards her solemnly.

'I have to go,' Grayle says.

31

It lives here

THE COTSWOLD AIRPORT is in the south of the county, not far from Tetbury, the nearest town to the Prince of Wales's estate at Highgrove. Grayle waits as Roger Herridge is led out to the van on the arm of Elsie, from HGTV. Although it's fully dark, he's wearing large sunglasses, like he's blind. And he is; they're glasses with side shields that even a sighted person can't see through.

Herridge is tall and angular, like a tower crane, with swept-back blond-white hair, a jutting jaw. He's wearing a loud check suit, like bookies are supposed to wear at the races. One of those guys who, even though you can't immediately hang a name on him, you look twice at because it's clear he's *somebody*.

He's smiling vacantly, suitcase at his feet, blindly sniffing the night air.

'It's not Luton, is it?'

'Damn, we never thought of that. We shoulda used a carbon-monoxide spray.' Grayle reaches for his hand, shakes it. 'Mr Herridge, my name's Grayle. I apologize for this delay. We're not usually this stupid and I accept full blame.'

He clutches her hand eagerly. Apparently, he's been here a couple hours. Had to leave London earlier than planned, as the normally efficient Kate Lyons failed to realize that this former RAF base isn't licensed for air-traffic at night. All got messy. Seems, at one stage, Elsie had to find a man to take Herridge to the bathroom.

Not a great start.

When the double doors are shut, bars of muted light come on in the tiny lounge that is the back of the van.

'Can I take these bloody glasses off?'

'Please.'

Bench seats either side, a fixed table between them, cupboards and a tiny refrigerator on the walls. Herridge takes off the glasses, shakes out his impressive hair. Grayle sits opposite him.

'You OK, Mr Herridge?'

'Call me Roger. All women do.'

His smile reveals irony and a narrow gold tooth. You don't see many of them any more.

'Would you like something to drink, Roger?' Elsie says. 'We have tea, coffee, wine, et cetera.'

Elsie, who sounded sixteen on the phone, is actually about twenty-five and smart-looking, even a little spiky. Herridge inspects her.

'Awfully strange to see someone for the first time when you've been talking to them for hours. Strange to see *at all*. Yes, please, Elsie. Whisky? Have to be my last for a week. Even if there's booze available in this house I doubt I'll be having any.'

'No, that's cool,' Elsie says. 'It's just there's usually alcohol readily available in this sort of social situation, for the purpose of, you know, promoting general relaxation?'

And tongue-loosening, Grayle thinks.

'Going to need a clear head in there,' Herridge says. 'I'm taking this seriously, anything wrong with that?' He looks across the table at Grayle. 'I *want* to experience something and, if I do, like to be sure it's not my mind playing tricks.'

Elsie's smile is a little worn, like she's been hearing this, at length, on the plane. She opens what proves to be the drinks cupboard, displaying four bottles of good Scotch and Irish, as the van moves away.

'Ice, Roger?'

'Wash your mouth out, my dear.'

Grayle says, 'So you've, um, never seen… anything?'

'Not… to my knowledge. But I do feel they rather owe me one. The ghosts.'

She doesn't need to ask. It's all on file: his deselection by the Liberal Democrats after failing, by a narrow margin, to keep his Home Counties seat at the last general election. The suggestion that certain prominent figures in the party consider his very public churchgoing, his royalist views and his fascination with ghosts account for his failure, as well as being out of alignment with the party's current leadership.

This, rather than the florists? Well, sure, although the papers loved how, when his third marriage failed, he moved in with these two women, cousins, who ran a flower shop. One florist wouldn't even have been noticed, but two… Grayle's researches suggest he's never actually denied the king-size bed rumours, but so what? This is still fairly low-risk stuff compared with what some Lib-Dem MPs got up to in the last decade or so.

Still, florists, somehow that was funny and it had made the jobless Herridge into a minor TV personality for a while – *Have I Got News for You*, all those guest spots. Hadn't lasted, obviously. Sleeping with florists was never going to be a long-term career. With all the alimony, Herridge, too, can use the money and the exposure. As the van heads north, he sips his Scotch, looking strangely happy. Grayle, thinking about Ozzy Ahmed, decides she ought to drop a light warning.

'You realize some of the people in the house are gonna…?'

Collecting a disapproving glance from Elsie, but Herridge beams as Elsie hands him his drink.

'Take the piss out of me? Grayle, I've been a politician for twenty years. Skin like a Kevlar vest.'

'You miss politics?'

'Never left, Grayle. Just don't do Parliament any more. Still pursuing my own form of liberalism, as we like to say. I maintain that science and secularism have joined forces to constrict our lives. For the next week I shall fight, shamelessly, for the ghost.'

She's read his book, *Holiest Ghosts*, about haunted churches and rectories. He's done another about haunted stately homes.

His argument is that the ghost is an essential component of the national heritage and that a respect for the unknown is an equalizing factor, more necessary now than ever in a society inclined to sneer at the ignorance and gullibility of its ancestors.

'I have no idea where we're going.' Herridge finishes his Scotch, wipes away the offer of another. 'But if you want anyone to spend a night in the most haunted room, I'm your man. I'm not afraid of fear. If you see what I mean. I'd genuinely like to see one. I would probably count it as *the* seminal moment in my life so far.'

He flashes a smile.

'We'll, um, bear that in mind,' Grayle says.

Thinking, *Jesus, Roger. Just be careful what you wish for.*

It's kind of thrilling in the grounds of Knap Hall, where Grayle is wandering alone. She feels a little ashamed, but it is. All the lights between the trees are low and calm, the dish aerial on the satellite truck raising a cosmic dimension. You can see the glow of energy, you hear the generator's diesel growl and you can feel a quiver: the power of television. It still exists.

This is just the grounds. Knap Hall is close but in another place, and the glow doesn't reach its walls. Some windows are blearily lit, but most are greyly opaque, like lead. Tonight, it looks small and almost squalid.

You compare these two worlds and it's surreal. All this technology, developed by scientists who would look at Knap Hall with incomprehension and – surely – some distaste. The idea that the people are using the technology, at enormous expense, to peer into the grimy crevices of superstition.

Even the stable block, with its clock tower, has deserted the house, defected to the other side and been honoured for that by being made the centre of operations.

The Live Gallery. Mission Control, home of the producer, the directors, the vision-mixer. All the horse stalls have been taken out, put into storage, old bales of straw transferred to the barn beyond the knot garden. There are now new walls with acoustic panelling. Under soft lights, you see ergonomic seats, desks with sensual curves and enough monitors, it looks like, for a whole city of CCTV. From the doorway, the accumulation of screens is like an open stamp album. Row upon row of monitors, various sizes right up to maybe fifty-inch, some tilting down from the beams.

Bringing Knap Hall out of itself: whole walls alive with close-up images of oak panelling, stone stairs, a reddening log fire, dark sofas, beds, a few shadowy people moving around, robotically arranging things.

Look down to the actual Knap Hall, and it's dead. Grayle realizes, with a breathless anxiety, as she enters the gallery proper, that it lives *here* now, that *this* is the slowly beating heart of Knap Hall, electronically extracted, fed first into the reality gallery, in a long truck outside, and then into here.

'We've had the cameras running for most of two nights,' one of the Jamies tells her. 'On the off chance.'

'Of what?'

'I dunno. Orbs or something? I'm not sure.'

Yeah, right. It also gives them hours of wallpaper shots of empty rooms in different lights. She sees on a few monitors where more of the upstairs windows have been boarded up, but it's no longer rough, it's proper panelling now, matching the walls, as if the windows were open wounds which have healed over. What did all this *cost*?

'Grayle, what've you done with Herridge?'

Jo Shepherd's come in behind her. She's wearing camouflage cargo pants bulging with stuff. Grayle opens up her hands.

'In the restaurant, having coffee?'

The restaurant, which has no windows, is attached by a canvas tunnel to the pop-up hotel where the residents will sleep until they go into the house. The restaurant is a long marquee divided into two eateries, one for the crews, one for the execs and the residents.

Jo looks worried.

'You *left* him?'

'With a minder. Someone Elsie found. I guess she's beginning to feel the strain. Roger can be… a touch wearing. He's like someone from another era. An adventurer. Comic-book hero. Kind of naive.'

'An act. They all come in with an act. MPs are a lot of things, but naive is never one of them. The friendly stuff won't last, never does. As soon as the others come in, he'll find somebody to hate.'

Jo seems, essentially, like a kind person, but she accepts in-house hatred as desirable and necessary.

Grayle nods, the way you have to.

'So who else do we have in so far?'

'Just Helen Parrish. She's OK, she's a pro. She's asleep in her room. Two more who don't live that far away get picked up by van before first light tomorrow. Cindy we meet in Cheltenham at the garage where he's leaving his car. Usual dark glasses job. Can't have him seen driving in here.'

'Who knows about Cindy being… more equal than others?'

'Officially, Leo and me. Unofficially, Leo, me and you. Leo will announce to the team that Cindy's a last-minute replacement for Colm Driscoll. At which point you can legitimately say, "Good God, I know this man." I'm trusting you with my entire future here, Grayle.'

'OK.'

You can't dislike Jo Shepherd. Anybody who's survived working with Cindy on the *National Lottery* and then chooses to work with him again, also live, has to be a strong and capable woman. Or in desperate need of that bonus.

'I forgot to mention,' Jo says. 'Another person you know who'll be working here from tomorrow is Lisa Muir. Reprising her role as… scullery maid? She'll be serving the residents their meals. We're trying to keep it all in the family. For security reasons at first, and then—'

'Shit, Jo, she told me she didn't even like to *drive* past here.'

'Lure of television, Grayle. Put it this way, we didn't need to ask her twice. Leo decided it would be good to reassemble some of the people who were here when the owners were, you know…'

'Alive? Leo told me months ago that all the house staff would be shipping up from London for security reasons.'

'Yeah, well, that was then. The staff won't be seen on camera, so nobody's going to get identified and give the location away. And they're used to keeping shtum. So Darryl, our location manager, discreetly contacted the former staff one by one and only Lisa agreed. Jordan the gardener's already here, so he's getting extra to do the odd-job-man bit. Keep the fires fed. He's been, you know… coppicing? From our woods?'

'And chainsawing, and gathering and chopping logs and barn-drying all summer. I noticed.'

'And the wood gets brought into the house loaded on… that, probably.' Jo points to an ancient-looking low flatbed handcart with wooden wheels, standing to the side of the main doors. 'Suitably rustic. Pretty battered.'

Grayle blinks.

'Like… you do know what that is, don't you? At least, I think it is.'

'Just looks like a wood cart to me. Somebody found it in here when it was a stable, and we were going to put it into storage, and then Leo thought it was kind of in keeping. Knap Hall's cart.'

'Jo, that's a bier.'

'A what?'

'For like wheeling coffins out of houses and into church?'

'Oh God, really?' Jo looks a little unsteady. 'What the hell was it doing still here?'

'I have no idea. Surprisingly, with all the extra work that got dumped on me, there's still a bunch of stuff I don't know about. Which reminds me, there's a woman I'm gonna try to see tomorrow before it all starts up, if you can spare me for a couple hours?'

'Well, try and be back by lunchtime, we might need you to go down to the airport again.' Jo tightens her lips, shakes her curls. 'A bier. Jesus. We haven't even started yet, and this place is already doing my head in.'

'No kidding.'

'No, really, I mean I've always got along fairly well by oper-ating on the basis that if you don't have particular feelings about something – if you just see it as subject-matter, you won't be touched by it. Then, hey… I had *a baby*.'

'Congratulations.'

'Nearly four now, and I like to think, like all parents do, that she's super-intelligent, really advanced. And I'm reading her traditional fairy tales because I like the idea of all that. And it's just weird how things that feel silly to me make her, you know, really very scared. And I want to stop reading, but she won't let me, for God's sake! She wants more. She can't wait till bedtime. And I'm wondering at what age things like that stop touching you.'

'Some people, it doesn't stop,' Grayle says.

Thinking of Louise Starke – Eloise. And maybe her adult self not too long ago.

'And now I'm surrounded by… all this. We're all supposed to be getting focused on… uncanny possibilities. And I think that, to do my job properly, I really ought to be affected the way my daughter's affected by fairy tales, though I'm not because, to me, they're just… fucking fairy tales.'

'They say,' Grayle says carefully, 'that as kids we're receptive to what we later automatically start to block out. If we could return to the child-state we'd become blown away, and all our thinking mechanisms would alter.'

'And we'd probably all be in analysis. Ignore me, Grayle, I'm overtired.'

Grayle nods at the bier.

'You think Leo knows what that is?'

Jo looks annoyed.

'Well now you mention it I wouldn't be at all surprised. Anything to unsettle them. The residents. That's what we're paying them for, after all.'

'Uh… you feel like a coffee?'

For the first time, Grayle's not going back to Cheltenham tonight. She has a tiny bedsit in the second pop-up hotel, won't be leaving Knap Hall until it's all over, ten days or so from now.

'No thanks. Might keep me awake. Been hard enough to get to sleep lately. Keep thinking about… not ghosts or fairies… I keep thinking about the man we have to call the owner's husband. Or the real owner. What he did.' Jo looks around the gallery. 'Now that is *real*. That makes me worry about the weight of human stress.'

'Yes.'

'*You* OK, Grayle?'

'Fine.'

She realizes she must've been scanning the monitors for a picture of the Ansell bedroom. Which she won't recognize, anyway, with a different bed and panelling over the window. Or will she? She feels an urgent need to bring it all out: the smell of slimed leaves, the dangling dead weight, the blurry egg-white eyes, but it…

…what good would it do, for either of them? Just another fairy tale.

Jo's not looking at her, which might be just as well. She's watching the screens.

She says, 'Did Leo tell you…?'

'That… the owner… wanted to come in here? To watch.'

'You want spooky, that *is* spooky.' Jo's face flickers in the myriad monitor lights. 'I don't believe in this stuff, Grayle, I really don't. But I'll tell you one thing. When we're rolling, I'm always going to make sure I'm *never* sitting next to a bloody empty chair.'

Friday

32

Fouler seed

THE WEATHER'S ALTERED. It's like the fall happened overnight, the air dry but dense with breeze-blown autumnal dust. Some years, the leaves stay on the trees until well into November; this morning, you can see them floating like moths outside the windows of Mary Ann Rutter's terraced cottage.

'Now, if you've read my book,' Mrs Rutter says, 'you'll know what a devilish man Sir Joshua Wishatt must have been.'

Grayle nods. This Wishatt is a key player in *Rogues and Roués*. He was a squire of sorts. Or liked to think he was. Married to a woman from a good family, whose ancestor had been a lady-in-waiting to Katherine Parr at Sudeley Castle, Wishatt lived here in the eighteenth century. His son and heir left Winchcombe after a fire destroyed the family home on the outskirts of town. After that the Wishatts simply disappeared from the area.

'Or rather the *name* did,' Mrs Rutter says. 'Do you see?'

'I think maybe I'm starting to.'

It was seven-thirty this morning when Mrs Rutter returned her call, waking her up, startled, in her shoebox bedsit inside the economy pop-up. Maybe just as well, there's a whole lot to clear today and another hour would've put Mary Ann on the back-burner.

She could be eighty-plus, a former schoolteacher living in what a sign says is an old cloth-weaver's cottage across the main street from Winchcombe church. She has a husband, Billy, maybe older, who's sitting by the fire in its cast-iron range, and smiling to himself. His wife doesn't seem to sit down at all.

She's fluttering and flapping like a small bird, over a polished gate-leg table on which are scattered open books with pages turned down and curling papers which look like stuff gathered to line a nest.

'I've always made it my policy, Miss Underhill, never to retell a story for which there is *no proof*. Which is why the very worst of Sir Joshua Wishatt is *not* in my book.'

Her eyes are excited. Apparently, it's been some years since anybody asked about that book, which, she says proudly but also kind of warily, is the seventh and raciest of her works. She's heard, of course, about the TV people up at Knap Hall, making their programme about the life of Trinity Ansell, which she's sure everyone in this town will be eagerly awaiting.

Wedged between the table and a wall of musty-looking books, Grayle gets the feeling Mrs Rutter is quite pleased that some Wishatt descendants in the US have been shocked enough to buy up every copy of *Rogues and Roués* they can lay their cursors on.

Mrs Rutter peers down her glasses at the assembled data.

'Wishatt was, you see, fond of women. Wrongly fond.'

'"Wrongly"?'

'Essentially, a follower of that old custom known as droit de seigneur. Which, by the eighteenth century, was not widely practised, even here.'

'That's um…?'

She knows, just doesn't want to seem too clever. Nothing worse than a smart-ass foreigner. Mrs Rutter tells her about the lord's perceived right to have his way with the wives and daughters of tenants. Her husband nods his head over an unlit pipe. He wears a flat cap. The atmosphere is like the inside of a chicken shack. Grayle wonders how long there'll be living rooms like this outside of folk museums.

'He loved – to paraphrase Shakespeare – widely and too well,' the old lady says. 'Surprising how many folks in this area can claim him as an ancestor. Here…'

Her brown hands quiver and swoop on something on the table. Lifting it carefully. It's the size of a prayer book, thick, uneven pages held together, because of its split spine, by rubber bands. Mrs Rutter lowers it in front of Grayle, adjusts her glasses, jabs a forefinger.

'There...'

Handwritten, very faded. Grayle bends to the book but doesn't touch.

When mother came home and found me washing myself I broke into weeping and told her Silas Waller the dirtiest boy in the school did put his arms around me and call me his cousin.

Grayle looks up.

'It's a diary?'

'From the year 1838. Many people who could write kept a diary in those days, especially the girls. Given to me some twenty years ago by the owner of an antique shop in Tewkesbury. Worth nothing to him, but he guessed it would answer some questions for me, and he was right. The writer *appears* to be called Constance, surname unknown, but I have my ideas.'

Mrs Rutter turns a page of the diary.

'Read here...'

When mother had dried my eyes she told me to pay no heed to the Waller boy for she said my grandfather John might be one of Sir Joshua's misdeeds but the Wallers were sure to be from the fouler seed of Abel Fishe.

'Now,' Mrs Rutter says. 'Do you see?'

Hell, yes, she does. Her own research, in libraries and on the Net, has thrown up the name Fishe several times, but nothing much about him. Just one of those quaint names that turns up in old records and lists.

Abel Fishe.

Abel's Rent.

'I think… he was either the owner or the tenant of Knap Farm in the early eighteenth century, do I have that right?'

'That's correct. And was also Sir Joshua's steward. Awarded the lifetime tenancy of the farm by Wishatt for, I would guess, given the circumstances, a peppercorn rent. For services rendered.'

'He's not mentioned in your book, though, is he? Nor is Knap Farm.'

Mrs Rutter frowns.

'It wasn't called Knap Farm before Abel Fishe's time.'

'*He* called it Knap Farm?'

'We have to assume that. It wasn't much of a house back then, mind. More than a hovel, but not very big at all. Fishe lived alone there. Although it seems he was not alone all the time.'

Guessing this doesn't mean ghosts, Grayle finds herself stiffening with that reprehensible kind of tremulous excitement that reporters come to recognize when a story, no matter how distasteful, begins to form on its own. She picks up what might be a similar feeling coming off Mrs Rutter.

33

Domestic chores

THE PHONE, ITS ring muted, is trembling in Grayle's hip pocket. She claps a hand over its bulge.

Stop it, leave me alone. This could be important.

Mary Ann Rutter says, '*None* of this is in my book, you see. Partly because it's *not documented*. And partly because some people in this area still don't like to talk about it.'

'Some things,' Grayle says, 'need to be talked about.'

'Miss Underhill…' Mrs Rutter bends across the table, brings her voice down to a whisper, 'while, as a historian, I've never been afraid of the controversial, neither I nor Billy was born here.'

Grayle suppresses a smile. This sure doesn't seem like the home of incomers.

'So how long you been here?'

Mrs Rutter works it out on her fingers.

'Fifty-seven years.'

'Right.'

'Billy was the new policeman. I was a very young school-teacher. Do you mind if I ask you again what this is for, my dear, in relation to Mrs Ansell? My memory of long-ago things is rather stronger nowadays than…'

'We're looking at… not only what Trinity Ansell did at Knap Hall but the effects it had on her. If you see what I mean…'

'Ah.' Mrs Rutter leans across the table. Hints of a shared conspiracy. 'We used to see her, you know. She would come into the town and spend extraordinary amounts of money at the local shops on items we could *not* imagine she had need of.'

'Like she was just doing it to help the local economy?'

'Perhaps. She was rather distant, but I think perhaps that was shyness. We don't think famous people can be shy, do we?'

A tapping by the hearth. Billy Rutter is knocking out his pipe.

'Tell the girl,' he says.

His wife tosses him a reproachful glance.

'Miss Underhill, this is *not documented*. This is… what do they say?'

'Word of mouth?'

'Oral history. Which is not always to be trusted.'

'I understand that fully.'

'No doubt you'll have heard this before.' Mary Ann Rutter clasps the diary to her cardiganed chest. 'But it's no less true for all that. Mrs Ansell was trying to make a beautiful world in a place that was not beautiful.'

'I… have heard it put… almost that way.'

'When I had the chance – angry with myself now, look – I said nothing. I stood next to her in the ironmongers once and we exchanged pleasantries about the weather and which bird feeder was best. But I did not tell her what I might have told her.'

And she probably would at least have listened to a local historian.

'She would have thought me mad, of course. A mad old woman.'

'What would you have told her?'

'I would have told her to bring a priest to Knap Hall, to have it… you know?'

Grayle nods but says nothing. Waits. She's become good at that.

'And about Abel Fishe,' Mrs Rutter says at last. 'And the women, I would have told her about them. If she thought me mad, what would that matter? She'd remember what I'd said. She might have acted on it.'

248

Billy Rutter clears his throat. Picks up a leather tobacco pouch, shiny with age and use. Starts to fill his pipe.

'Wishatt needed somewhere to take his women,' he says into the pipe's bowl. 'So as word wouldn't get back to his posh wife.'

'Who was so necessary to his status,' Mrs Rutter says.

Grayle's mouth has gone dry.

'I think she knew, of course,' Mrs Rutter says. 'But as long as it was not *seen* to be happening. As long as it took place somewhere hidden.'

'Knap Hall?'

'No longer purely oral history… because of this diary. Which I did not have access to, or even know of, when I wrote my book. Well, I shall never write any of this now, but I'm glad that it corroborates what I *did* write in my book about Wishatt. I feel easier in my mind. It *should* be known, you see. These matters should not be hidden for ever. Or if the stories are passed on as gossip they'll lose whatever truth they possessed and become legends. But if it all comes out in your programme…'

Ah. Right.

'Well… you know… if I forgot to mention this,' Grayle says, 'we will, of course, include your name in the programme credits, and there'll be a payment of—'

'No, no *no!*'

The old lady's almost taking off from the ground in horror, pages flying out of the diary like feathers, Grayle rushing to scoop them out of the air.

'Hey, look, I'm sorry if I—'

'That must not happen! None of this must be seen to have come from me. And no payment is necessary, is that understood?'

'I'm sorry.' Grayle goes down on her knees to pick up a page. 'I truly didn't mean to—'

'People don't dispute what they see on television.'

'Well, I think they do, but—'

'Here. Keep it.'

Mrs Rutter pushes the depleted diary at Grayle, who accepts it, but...

'I can't take this.'

'Yes, you can, it's worthless, except as evidence of something that must not become legend. You're doing me a favour. You're taking away the responsibility. Do you see?'

'OK... I.... I'll handle this whichever way meets your approval.'

Down by the fire, Billy Rutter smiles and nods. Policemen, most of them, have a need to see justice done, even after centuries, and not always in the most direct way. Grayle has a friend who was a cop – a distant friend now, sadly.

But this still feels wrong. Mary Ann Rutter thinks this is going to be a serious documentary about a woman who tried to rehabilitate a bad house, a shunned house, and turn it into something beautiful. Does Mrs Rutter seriously blame herself, in some way, for the tragedy of Trinity Ansell?

'Well, OK...' Grayle holds the diary in both hands. 'I'll bring it back soon as I've read it.'

'No need to bring it back at all. I won't need it again.'

'Mrs Rutter, when this talks of... Abel Fishe's *fouler* seed...'

Defford will so love that phrase. If she tells him. Which will depend on how Mary Ann Rutter qualifies it.

'Miss Underhill, you realize that apart from the diary, there is no doc—'

'Word of mouth will be just fine. Fouler than Wishatt's, that's what it's saying?'

'There is...' Mrs Rutter pulls a spindle-back chair from under the table and finally sits down, composing herself. 'There's a kind of wickedness that often passes unnoticed because it's... so abhorrent that it's upsetting to consider and we convince ourselves it cannot be happening. There was a local saying once – or so I'm told. "Abel's Rent". People would say – in a disparaging way – "Oh, he had it for Abel's Rent." Meaning for no rent at all. For *a service rendered*. Often, in later years, this might simply involve the avoidance of tax, which I suppose was a way of sanitizing it.'

'OK.'

'In the eighteenth century, as steward, Abel Fishe would visit Wishatt's tenants to collect the rents. And if a tenant had difficulty finding the money after a bad harvest or something, payment might be arranged… in kind. Through the services of a wife or a daughter. Might be said she was performing domestic chores. Do you see?'

'Yes.'

'And after Wishatt had made use of them – with or without the knowledge of the husband – Abel Fishe would… have his commission.'

'Just to get this clear – I'm sorry, Mrs Rutter – we're talking… carnal commission?'

'Of the most brutal and distasteful kind. Or so it's said. Please do not ask me what that means. I don't know. It isn't spoken of. The more I've uncovered of history, the more I've learned that the past can be a most unpleasant place. But I've also realised that keeping secrets about it helps no one, except those responsible for the wickedness. And having the *responsibility* of a secret… that is not a good position to be in. *There*…' She opens her arms. 'Perhaps we're helping one another.'

'And this abuse took place not at the homes of tenants, but…'

'At Knap Farm. As it was now called. Oh, yes.'

'Why? I mean, why did he give it that name?'

'Knap means the top of a hill. And, all I can assume is… the farm is not far from Belas Knap.'

'The longbarrow. The burial chamber.'

'I don't know why he gave it that name. Except perhaps to make people think it was connected to Belas Knap. Which, back then, local people avoided, as some do today, for superstitious reasons. A haunted place. All kinds of stories, widely told in books now.'

Check this out.

251

'What I don't understand, Mrs Rutter, is how it was all covered up at the time. Abel Fishe.'

'Oh, they were pragmatic times. No thoughts of equality for women in those days. And people were afraid. Sir Joshua Wishatt was a powerful landowner, Abel Fishe was his retainer. If anyone complained or even talked too much… well, there are even stories of a couple of people – women – disappearing. You'll find hints of it in the diary. And, of course, all the talk at that time was of something else.'

'Disappearances… linked to Abel Fishe?'

'I can't be certain. It isn't documented. Even Wishatt wasn't talked about till I was daft enough to put him in my book. He even fell off the church wall, he—'

'He fell off the church wall?'

'Well, a likeness of him, in stone. Some of them are supposed to be caricatures of local people who perhaps weren't popular.'

'You mean the so-called grotesques?' She's not getting this. If Wishatt was only around in the eighteenth century… 'Aren't they all late-medieval? Well before Wishatt's time.'

'You're quite correct, yes. But what they used to say, look, is that someone carved one of Wishatt, because they thought that was where he *ought to be.* You see? Where he belonged. This was after he was dead and the son gone, too. But it wasn't very well made, they say, and it fell off and never got put back. It's probably in the river.'

The cellphone's shivering against Grayle's thigh. She should maybe get it this time.

'So Wishatt's still remembered,' she says. 'Um… what about Abel Fishe?'

'Oh well…' The hint of irony in Mrs Rutter's smile is dispelled by an uneasy twitch. 'What they say about Mr Abel Fishe is… that *he* was up on the church already.'

'I don't…' Sensing this is likely to take some time. 'Mrs Rutter, I'd really like to pursue this, but someone's calling my cell— my mobile phone?'

Mrs Rutter looks mildly cross.

'Ah, these dratted little phones. Demand more attention than a baby.'

'I'm so sorry.' Grayle drags it out. 'Underhill.'

'Grayle, where the *fuck*—?' Defford in person, no happier than he's been all week. 'Kate's called you twice. You do realize you should be recording the fucking chapel prelims?'

'I'm in Winchcombe, Leo, middle of some research. I thought—'

'You're fucking everyone up for something that should've been done weeks ago?'

'I thought it wasn't until this afternoon.'

'We rescheduled an hour ago. Get your arse back here.'

Gone.

'Mrs Rutter…'

'I know, I know… Off you go.'

'Can I call you later?'

'If I'm not shopping, I'll be here. Billy doesn't answer the telephone.'

'Meanwhile, could you just tell me, very briefly, what did you mean by Abel Fishe being on the church already?'

'Old wives' tale.' Mrs Rutter's on her feet, guiding Grayle to the door. 'Just an old wives' tale, and I'm just another old wife who shouldn't pass this nonsense on.'

'Is it? Nonsense?'

'Of course it is.' Mrs Rutter opens the front door into the street, and there's the church on the other side of it. 'People used to say he was there.'

'So if I call in there now, is it likely I can see him?'

'It's more usual, I'm told,' Mrs Rutter says, 'to pray that you don't.'

34

A form of containment

'MY NAME IS Cindy Mars-Lewis, and I claim ancestral rights to slip through the curtains between worlds.' Cindy shakes his head in apparent horror. 'Heavens, what *does* that sound like?'

Grayle doesn't respond. She's been told not to ask any questions for about the first ninety seconds. Let them establish themselves.

She's in the reality gallery, inside the big truck. The reality gallery controls the house, its heating and lighting and also houses the booth from which Grayle does her interviews with the residents in the chapel. In front of her, the mic with its bendy stem and its mesh screen to stop the pops on consonants. Cindy's on the monitor screen in front of her, wearing his pearls and his beret and his tweedy spinster suit. All you see either side of him is the new/old panelling over the Holy Trinity stained glass.

'Now, in case I'm not allowed to expand on this later,' Cindy says, 'I should tell you that Celtic shamanism – or any kind, really – is a state of mind, a way of perceiving. It's about walking the corridors of ancestral memory. Living at the joining point of different spheres of existence. A state of mind, a state of consciousness. A state of *being*.'

He stops.

A small, domed green light blinks in front of Grayle.

She takes a breath. Will these be her first words on TV?

'Cindy, the more observant of us might've noticed that you're a man who habitually dresses in women's clothing. And, um, wears make-up and pearls and bangles?'

'Well, there we are.' Cindy beams, spreads his hands, which are in soft tan gloves. 'A foot in both camps, isn't it? About living on the cusp of worlds and on the fringe of society. In the old days, the shaman was, if not exactly an outcast, then certainly someone on the periphery of the tribe, respected but regarded with suspicion and often feared. And would dress accordingly.'

'On the, uh, cusp of the sexes?'

'Exactly. Well, now… I'd *love* to be respected and feared, but, sadly, that aspect of it just never seems to come right. Regarded with suspicion, however… well… story of my life.'

His eyes register sorrow in the second before another face slams up in front of his, filling the screen. This face has huge malevolent eyes, a yellow beak and what you can only describe as punk plumage which jitters as the beak springs open with an insane cackle.

'Never was a problem for me, lovely!'

Grayle sighs.

'Hello, Kelvyn.'

There's a break while the editors mess with the rushes and someone moves in to collect Cindy from the chapel. He'll be guided through the house in the opaque glasses and sent back up the windowless plastic tunnel that connects the house with the restaurant and the pop-up hotels. Maybe they should also put glasses on Kelvyn Kite, ventriloquist's evil dummy and mystical totem-bird.

Suddenly, Grayle feels better. Explaining Cindy and Kelvyn for however many million viewers can't be a bad start. And the more you think about it, the more suited to this show Cindy appears. He lives his whole life with weirdness; the other residents just have to get used to it. And they will.

At one week, this show will run for less than a third the length of a *BB* series, but Jo Shepherd's told Grayle it takes no more than a couple of days for individuals to become institutionalized.

Over the past months Grayle's watched five series of *Big Brother*, mostly celebrity. They all have people who look rational to begin with, but at some point, you start to wonder why some have never been taken into psychiatric care. And *they're* just living in a big kindergarten.

Problem is it's contagious. Month or so ago, she downloaded details of a study by the Max Planck Institute for Human Cognitive and Brain Sciences and some university in Dresden, which had found that just being around a stressed person could stimulate your body to release the stress hormone cortisol. This is never more apparent than in a *Big Brother* house.

Grayle steps down from the truck, pulling on her woolly hat, but doesn't wander too far in case the stress-vessel Defford's somewhere close. She shelters from the wind under a big, creaking ash tree which she'd never noticed until leaf-loss turned its upswept boughs into an impressively complex candelabrum.

Takes out her phone and calls Mary Ann Rutter. But Mrs Rutter's out food shopping.

'Always says I don't answer the phone,' Billy Rutter says. 'That's because she don't trust me to remember who called. You got her in a state earlier, Miss Underhill.'

'I'm sorry.'

'No, no, she likes that. Getting into a state. That Abel Fishe. They didn't know what a psychopath was, did they, them days?'

'Um… Mrs Rutter seemed to be suggesting that… it might go a way beyond that.'

'I'll tell her you called,' Billy Rutter says. 'I'll write it down.'

After leaving the Rutters this morning, she had to pass Winchcombe church to reach her car. The church is right next to the road. A mellow old church with a very traditional-looking weathercock on top of the tower. A lucky bird: it's spared the horror of looking down at all the stone faces, scrunched and twisted, pop-eyed and slack-mouthed.

A weird humour at work here. Like Cindy said, there are definitely two different kinds of grotesque, some obviously representing human beings, male faces leering or, in some cases, looking terrified.

And now she has a connection between these horrors and Trinity Ansell, and the connection is a man called Abel Fishe. She needs to talk to Cindy about him. Only problem is when.

At the door, before she left, she asked the admirable Mary Ann Rutter if it wasn't just some local joke about the face of Abel on the church wall. Mrs Rutter said if it was a joke it was a very old one and not, given what the man did, all that amusing.

The ash tree rattles in the wind. Grayle recalls the stone faces in the air, the second kind, the demonic ones, with their stunted wings and stubby horns and the black holes in their eyes. Devilish, rather than pagan. What are images this distasteful doing on church walls? Are they to frighten people away from sin or repel whatever evil they represent? Or is it about imprisoning evil in stone rising from sacred ground? A form of containment.

But they're just stone images. People don't get scared any more by sculpted stone. Probably not even little kids like Jo Shepherd's daughter.

Unless they mutate in dreams. Acquire a body, with all the functioning parts. Like Cindy says, dreams are another state of consciousness. Anything can happen to you in a dream but, when you think about it, rarely does because some mechanism wakes you up. Dreams die on the cliff edge.

But where does Abel Fishe stand?

Does he have a body, too?

The new face in the monitor is serene. Fine, white-blond hair swept back, angular earrings. A quite low-cut cream dress, a white cardigan around the shoulders.

'I'm Dr Ashley Palk. I'm a psychologist, author of several books on the nature of belief and I'm the founder and editor of *The Disbeliever*, an Internet magazine for people who realize our fate – not my favourite word – and that of the planet are entirely in our own hands.'

It's a clipped accent, with only a hint of Scottish. Edinburgh, maybe. Grayle has in front of her the first briefing document which says,

Dr Palk, 35, has appeared on several documentaries to debunk the claims of so-called psychics. Specifically, she showed that the famous Cambridge Poltergeist was a product of communal hysteria among students at a private music college. Palk has degrees in psychology and anthropology.

'I imagine I've been invited into the house to cause a certain discord and annoyance amongst believers in the supernatural, but actually I'm a very easygoing person.'

Ashley smiles a wide, white, grimacey kind of smile. A kind of explanatory smile for people of inferior intellect, and she tilts her head to one side whenever she produces it.

Grayle says, 'Ashley, can we take it you don't believe in ghosts or anything that might... occupy another dimension?'

'Do you want the short answer or a cosmological dissertation?'

Not your job to get into arguments, Jo says.

'Can I put it another way. How would you feel if you were the only resident? If you had to stay here for a week entirely alone at nights.'

Palk gives this some thought.

'I would be a wee bit afraid,' she says. 'I'd be afraid of the possibility of somebody getting in, for the purpose of robbery or worse, and me not being aware of that because the house is probably very big. And I'd be afraid of rats – hate rats. But I wouldn't be afraid of anything you might describe as metaphysical.'

Grayle says nothing. Ashley Palk considers some more.

'However, after a few days, I might well be telling you I'd be less bothered about being entirely alone here than having to listen any more to some of my more credulous companions. Not that I know who they are. But the thought of who they might be – *that* is a wee bit scary.'

'So, briefly, how does a house like this get a reputation of being haunted?'

'Well, as I just said, if I was alone here I'd be afraid of robbery or rats. In earlier times I'd have a whole range of phenomena to fear – with the full permission of the Church. The Church *wanted* people to be afraid of the unknown, and the Church was a dominant influence on everyone's life. Now, as we all know, there's been a dramatic decline in churchgoing in recent years. Ghosts are now seen as... almost comical. Cinematic effects are far more scary.'

'So what would you say to someone who thinks he – or... or she – has experienced something, in this house, which can't be attributed to any human source and has left her feeling deeply disturbed?'

'Well that would depend on—'

'And we're talking about someone who would consider herself – or himself – to be an intelligent person who's... been around.'

'Well, I think most of us would consider ourselves to be intelligent, so that has to be relative. But I'm afraid I would have to begin by looking at that person's emotional condition.'

'So you'd think they were crazy?'

'Oh, my dear, I would never use that word,' Ashley Palk says.

And does the explanatory smile that says,

Well, of course, I would consider them to be either extremely stupid or in need of psychiatric counselling.

'Thank you, Ashley,' Grayle says.

35

Women and ghosts

SHE COMES OUT of her booth in the reality gallery, jumps down from the truck into the damp afternoon. Needing to talk to Defford, but you don't just walk in on him any more. Defford has a personal portacabin. The biggest. Until recently he just seemed like a guy, now he's God in his celestial city. You don't approach him any more, you're just grateful if he sends for you.

But she can't wait for the next time he does that. She grabs a Jamie coming out of the reality-gallery truck, asks if he can find Kate Lyons and get her a half-hour with Leo.

This is complicated. She doesn't even know what she's going to say to him without sounding like a person in need of psychiatric counselling. She wants to tell him not to trust the house, and she doesn't know how. She can't explain it. *Don't challenge them, never try to befriend them*, Marcus says. Marcus who never claims to have answers, who thinks the processes of human logic cannot be applied in these situations.

Try telling that to a TV producer.

On the inside, Defford's personal portacabin could be a penthouse suite. Red leather seating, pictures on the walls of HGTV's previous successes including Defford's last one for the BBC which had hospital cooks competing against each other to provide cheap, healthy dishes. First patient to throw up, the chef was out of the game, something like that.

'Don't have much time, Grayle. A million things to tweak.'

Defford waves her to a small plush chair without arms, in the well below his big desk. Kate Lyons is sitting in a red leather swivel chair, an iPad on her knees. The are two more ipads on Defford's desk, and two TV monitors. Grayle wonders if there's a camera somewhere focused on her now, and Defford's watching her expressions in close-up.

Paranoia.

She has no laptop with her, no notes, only the peeling diary Mary Ann Rutter gave her, held demurely on her lap like a prayer book.

'First off, Leo, I don't wanna rock the boat.'

'Grayle…' Defford's leaning back, tilted smile, the eyes wary and harder than the white hair and the gold earring. 'You *can't* rock the boat. The boat leaves in just over three hours' time. Either you're on it or you aren't.'

'If you, um… if you wanna continue with that metaphor, this is not as much about the boat as the sea.'

'The sea.'

'Or, like… what's down there. In the dark water.'

'In the house.'

'When all this started, what we had… what I brought to you and you seemed to like… was Trinity Ansell and her perceived connections, living and dead, with Katherine Parr.'

'Two charismatic women bridging half a millennium.'

She scans his face for irony. None is apparent.

'Women, and ghosts,' she says, 'are not the same.'

'Look. What you came up with, the tie-up with Katherine Parr, that was what persuaded me it'd been right to go for Knap Hall. I needed a little-known haunted house and I was intrigued by Ansell's suggestion that his late wife might be one of its ghosts, even though he was clearly holding back on his reasons for thinking this. The fact that we now had Katherine Parr as well…'

'But I think I made it clear at the time that KP could be wishful thinking on Trinity's part. That maybe Trinity *wanted* her to be here because she played her in a movie.'

'Although, Lisa… what's her name…?'

'Lisa Muir.'

'Yeah, Lisa Muir thinks it's rather more than that, obviously.'

'Not as I recall.'

'Oh.' Defford looks vague. 'You haven't seen that interview?'

'Interview?'

'No, you wouldn't have. Sorry. We shot it way back.'

A big cold space is opening up in Grayle's chest.

'You're saying... you're saying that Lisa Muir, who told me she could never talk about this stuff on TV without she'd burst into tears—'

'No reflection on you, Grayle. We're quite experienced at changing people's minds.'

'With money?'

Defford shrugs.

'But you didn't tell me. You *purposely* didn't tell me.'

'It's a whole different area of production.' He looks pained. 'You're research. We made the approach through a friend who knew the girl's parents. We do what's most expedient. In the case of Parrish, we thought she'd connect with another journalist, so we sent you. We go for what's most likely to work. And then, once we had Lisa Muir, it was quite easy to get Pruford.'

'*Pruf—?*'

Grayle's lips have gone dry. She closes them.

Defford's sigh is close to a yawn.

'Yeah, we have Pruford, too. Soon as he was back in the country, we were on him. Everyone has a price. The story about the woman who photographed the two images in the doorway, he tells it well. Be very convincing overlaid with pictures of the relevant doorway. And Meg. And a little wizardry.'

Which he wasn't going to do. He told her specifically there'd be no special effects.

'So you put that together,' he says, 'with Lisa Muir's story about her and Trinity talking to Katherine Parr through a ouija board... Grayle, don't *look* at me like that. It was early days

262

when you talked to her. She didn't really know who you were. She didn't think her parents would like it. Lots of problems like that. Once they were all sorted, she opened up. It's what we do, we sort things.'

Grayle wants to die. She thinks, *Need to know. Need to fucking know.*

They didn't tell her because they didn't want her messing with what they'd gotten neatly parcelled up. That's what this is about. She struggles for composure.

'Am I allowed to ask what they learned from the ouija board?'

Because, unless Cindy's playing by the same HGTV rules, Trinity never told him about this.

Defford shakes his head.

'I dunno, usual garbled rubbish. What was significant, according to Lisa, was that whenever they had a ouija session, Trinity would have dreams. Very vivid, usually involving Katherine Parr. Then Trinity would say she was seeing Katherine in the house. Like they'd opened up a way for her to come in.'

It fits. Sure it fits. Grayle clutches the diary and thinks of another one, more chaotic, less coherent, kept by Trinity Ansell at the behest of Cindy. You can't second-guess ghosts, but people are easier, and it's clear Trinity Ansell wanted Cindy to help her bring something of KP into Knap Hall. And Cindy wasn't playing. Then, the next time he went back, when the UK's most prestigious guest house was up and running, she was saying, Look, I did it. I did it by myself. To the happy sounds of Renaissance music.

Sure. It all fits. But then, as the diary reveals, something changed: *I can see the hearth with no fire. The room is cold and there's a blue light.*

Something ended. Something died. Something that was represented in Trinity's dreams, according to Cindy, by an image of the dead body of Katherine Parr.

'So what did you want to tell me?' Defford asks. 'Bearing in mind how close we are to recording.'

Jeez, you can almost see the digital clock pulsing in his brain

'I went to see a woman this morning. An historian.'

She sits on her pride and tells him as briefly as she can about Sir Joshua Wishatt and Abel Fishe. About Abel's Rent. Tells him this man is, pre-Trinity, possibly the most significant piece of history she's been able to uncover relating specifically to Knap Hall. Only the way she's feeling now, it doesn't come out with as much enthusiasm as it might've done earlier.

'And when was this?'

'Don't have precise dates, yet, but we're looking at the eighteenth century.'

'The eighteenth century,' Defford says. 'So that would be around two centuries after Katherine Parr. And three before Trinity. She know about this guy?'

'Fishe is believed to have brought women here. Here. To Knap Hall, as he was now calling it. And he was abusing them. Here. And whereas today abuse can be like a guy pinching someone's ass…'

'I realize all that. Did Trinity know about him?'

'If you're saying did she know his name, his personal history, I guess not. But if you're asking was she affected by… whatever remains of him and what he did, that's a whole different—'

'I'm not asking that,' Defford says.

She keeps trying.

'See, you're looking down to another level of… murk. You could be looking at what's represented by all this talk among the staff of things in the house getting dirty very quickly. Heaps of soil appearing on the floor, the windows becoming hard to see through. Maybe you recorded somebody talking about that, too. I wouldn't know, I'm just the researcher.'

He doesn't react.

'OK,' Grayle says, 'I don't know whether any of that actually happened or whether it was just in the perceptions of the staff who thought they were having to do too much cleaning, but it's what worries me a little, so I thought you oughta know.'

'OK. Thank you.' Defford glances at Kate Lyons, who remains expressionless, then he leans back again. 'Grayle, I have two problems with this. 'A, wrong century. B, wrong sex. In television, we don't look to complicate things. The more straightforward the background, the fewer people involved, the less history to absorb... need I go on? We have two famous women in a house which is Tudor in origin. That is, *not* eighteenth century.'

'No, but—'

'And we start recording programme one tonight. You do realize what "tonight" means?'

He snatches up a copy of one of the cheapo TV guides, almost the whole of its front page given over to the black silhouette of some historic house which clearly is not Knap Hall and a big headline:

WHO DARES GO INTO THE
BIG OTHER HOUSE?

It's the first of these she's seen. There's been a few speculative pieces in the papers over the past weeks but it's the first time she's seen the name. Defford puts it down on his desk.

'And there are big spreads coming up in the weekend TV supplements. I've done an interview for the *Sunday Times*. Done and dusted. I need to draw a line under this, or it'll run away with itself. Your job now is to try and match what's happening in the house over the next week with what we know about Trinity Ansell and Katherine Parr. And tailor your chapel questions accordingly.'

'OK.' She stands up. 'That's what you're paying me for. But so I know where we're headed, let me just re-check the formula. As well as debating the existence of ghosts in general, from the outset, you want the residents to start forming a picture of what might've happened here, right?'

'Correct.'

'And then, at the end of the week, you'll reveal the truth about where we are – how close they got, if any of them do – and we see the footage of Meg the actor in the red dress, and we hear Lisa and Pruford. And then we come to the Ansells, and Harry's death by probable sui—'

'We're being careful about that. I don't propose to speculate about Ansell's death. Leave that to the media. It'll add a certain resonance, but I'm sticking with his wife.'

'Right.'

Why should she care now? After more than half a year, her role in this project is nearly over. Why not just back away from it all? Like lying back in some hospital bed with your eyes closed and submitting to the…

… the disease.

Dis-ease. You walk into someplace to produce a piece of light entertainment disguised as something deeper, and you find you're close to something old and sick that nobody wants disturbed. Least of all Defford. No excitement in his eyes. It's not about seeing what happens, it's about control. Always was. He should've realized by now that *Big Brother* rules just won't work here. Virtually none of them.

He hasn't.

Grayle looks into his deceptively amiable features under the innocent lambswool hair. She remembers the first time they met and him saying he wanted to know everything there was to know about this house, all the history, all the legends, all the reasons to be afraid.

'So you're… happy.'

'I'm as satisfied as I can be at this stage. I don't think we'll get anything better. All this eighteenth-century abuse stuff, sure, bear it in mind, but don't go looking for it. I really don't want to have bring in an emergency team of actors in different costumes to shoot rape scenes against a background of whatever this dump looked like in the eighteenth century.'

'Well, I just wanted you to be aware of it. Being as how you like to be one step ahead.'

'OK, I'm aware of it.' He consults his iPad. 'Kate, get me Paul at C4, will you?'

Grayle's aware that, for Defford, she no longer exists in the room. Kate Lyons already has the door open for her and outside it's raining now.

36

Walk but they can't sue

SHE RUNS OUT, through the rain, to her ash tree, the only place she feels safe to think. And to feel confused and useless. Ash trees... something about them: when they die it's from the inside and they become hollow, something like that. Eloise would know. M.R. James wrote a famous story about an ash tree with a dead witch inside.

This one seems to have resisted whatever ash-blight is going around. Its branches heave up around her into the rain, most of its leaves have been shed. Is that liberating for a tree facing winter? Is it liberating to know when you're not wanted any more, when nobody wants you to think outside of the box?

What now?

Maybe call Marcus Bacton. It isn't the ash tree that says that.

When she tells him about her day so far, his laughter's a bark, like Malcolm the terrier came through on an extension.

'You talked to Lewis about this?'

'Oh, yeah, I've *talked* to him. I've interviewed him in the chapel. Have I *really* talked to him? No.'

What's more, she doesn't see how she's going to. Not today, not tonight, not any day or night until this is all over.

It's the phones. When they go into the house, *the Seven*, they have to leave their phones behind. Well, sure, it makes sense. They can't have any contact with the outside world. The phones are kept in a safe in Kate Lyons's office inside the Leo Defford cabin. Twice a day, with the residents' agreement, Kate will take them out and check for messages.

The residents have been asked to inform their loved ones, agents, lawyers, etc. that they'll be unreachable for a week except in dire emergency. In which case all calls should go through an HGTV number. Anything possibly urgent found on the mobiles will be monitored by Kate and crucial messages passed on.

'So you see the problem. Assuming Cindy would have his phone back after our chapel session until he went in again, I was about to leave a message to have him call me… and then it hit me that the next time Kate Lyons went through his calls she'd spot my damn number. Then Defford would know we were talking behind his back. Which now would be even worse.'

Marcus grunts, like conclusively.

'You're stuffed, Underhill. No point at all in arguing with a megalomaniac. Do what he says. Then grab the money with one hand while lacing up the bastard running shoes with the other.'

'That's it? That's the summit of your advice? Grab the loot, don't look back?'

''What d'you want me to say? Knew from the start what you were getting into. Spent two years working with cynical hacks, had your hair symbolically butchered. No, look, essentially, Underhill, your work there is done. Why prejudice your bonus?'

Yeah, right, why? What can she do here? Who can she help? Only the dead.

She stares out over the Hunter-Gatherer village to an empty field, the wind dragging dense grey rain across it like a tarpaulin, along with the voice of Mary Ann Rutter.

If she thought me mad, what would that matter? She'd remember what I'd said. She might have acted on it.

Too late now, Mary Ann, Trinity's dead. Also Harry. The small wood on the other side of the grey field is where they found him hanging, the tautened rope disappearing into a mesh of dark branches and the dusk.

It should *be known, you see. These matters should not be hidden for ever. Or if the stories are passed on as gossip they'll lose whatever truth they possessed and become legends. But if it all comes out in your programme...*

Which it won't, not now. The programme will be a travesty, a fabrication. And, sure, you can see why it probably has to be. And yet...

... keeping secrets about it helps no one, except those responsible for the wickedness. And having the responsibility *of a secret... that is not a good position to be in.*

No. It sure as hell isn't. Grayle watches wet trees and sees Mrs Rutter flapping amongst the remnants of her research, absurdly delighted that an old responsibility has been lifted from her old shoulders by a younger woman who isn't subject to local pressure and might run with it.

'Only you wouldn't do that, Marcus, would you?'

'Do what?'

'Take the money and run. That's not what you're about.'

'All I was thinking...'

He dries up. She's guessing that what he was thinking was, do I want to be responsible for Underhill winding up on Prozac again?

Which, let's not forget, she took just once. *Once*, OK?

She says, 'What if all Trinity Ansell and Katherine Parr had in common was that they were both victims of this house and something in it?'

'In which case, whatever it is can't be this Abel Fishe, can it? When Parr died, he was still two centuries in the future.'

She sighs.

'That mean Fishe was a victim of it, too?'

'Let's not go that far. Man doesn't sound like a victim to me.'

Grayle pulls down her woolly hat over the phone at her ear.

'A ouija board. A freaking *ouija board*. Trinity and her little friend Lisa, and maybe the third finger on the glass is Jeff Pruford's. Both of them saying more on camera, prepared to tell millions of viewers more than they felt able to confide to me. Maybe because I'm like *foreign*?'

Marcus is silent for a while. Rain pools around crispy leaves at Grayle's feet.

'However,' Marcus says at last, 'there's nothing to stop someone else – someone not in the house, not on the Defford payroll making a few tentative inquiries. Is there?'

'Oh.'

Thing about Marcus, the word *tentative* doesn't exist in his dictionary.

'On the basis,' he says, 'that this outsider can make use of anything he might find… in defence of mystery.'

'In his book?'

'Planning a chapter showing how people, non-believers usually, have always manipulated the paranormal for their own purposes, confident there isn't going to be a comeback. Spirits can walk but they can't sue. HGTV can do what they want with dead Ansell and dead Parr. Move them easier than puppets. These TV programmes, there has to be a conclusion, otherwise it's a pointless exercise. Especially if it's lasted a whole week.'

'An ambience of mystery… maybe that doesn't translate to TV.'

'Can't.'

'I'm trying to tell myself it wasn't gonna be like that. Could be Harry Ansell's death changed everything. Ansell had a reason for inviting Defford to use his house, and it surely wasn't only because he couldn't find anybody to buy it. And now Defford's never gonna know what that was, and that makes him feel insecure.'

'Anyway,' Marcus says, 'there are things I can look into. You'll take your money, they'll take theirs. And I can blast the bastards out of the water from a safe distance.'

'Worthwhile publisher might like that.'

'Never once occurred to me, Underhill.'

'Of course it didn't.'

A rising wind heaves at the ash tree's branches.

'I do get the feeling, Underhill,' Marcus says, 'that there's something you haven't told me.'

The damp field looks like dead, grey skin.

'I guess,' Grayle says. 'OK, here we go…'

37

The eighth person

SIX HOURS TO recording, early dark outside. No more than a dozen people under low lights in Leo Defford's executive office. Key people. The producers, directors, senior Jamies, senior Emilys sitting around a plan of the house surrounded by photographs, all pinned to display boards, replacing the pictures of competing NHS chefs.

Defford's final briefing. Pep-talk time. Grayle's been permitted to sit at the back with the more lowly members of the team. Defford's on a high stool, a clipboard of handwritten notes on his knees, rectangular reading glasses on his nose.

'OK. Now I've said most of this before at various times, as you know, but I'm saying it again so nobody forgets what this is about. The viewers think they've seen everything. They think we've seen every conceivable permutation of the haunted house scenario. If they still think that after the first hour they'll switch off in their hundreds of thousands.'

Actually, he's told Grayle he reckons they have a full two hours to hook the Saturday night viewers. What will grab them initially is the first interaction of the residents. Virtually everybody will recognize Austin Ahmed, Helen Parrish and Cindy Mars-Lewis. The others they'll've heard of. And their individual introductions in the chapel will signal the discord to come.

Defford leans back on his stool, tosses away his notes, the way smart-ass political leaders do at party conferences to show how personally confident they are of the way ahead.

'Intelligent viewers think they no longer fear the supernatural. They're continually assured by smooth scientists and serious newspapers that it's all primitive myth. It's a secular society now, and there's no going back from that. No God, no ghosts – not if you want to work for the BBC.'

Nobody laughs.

'Which I don't, any more,' Defford says. 'Been there, done that. But I accept that some of you might, so please be sceptical. See, I don't care how many of you claim to believe in ghosts or how many think it's all balls. I don't *want* to know. I don't want to hear opinions expressed or arguments for or against until we're out of here at the end of next week. That's not your business. Your business is to produce hour after hour of unmissable television.'

A few of them start to applaud, but Defford stops them with a raised hand.

'Now what do I mean by that? There's so-called reality television that everybody knows *isn't*. We all know these people are playing their parts in a pre-structured scenario. Some of our seven residents will also be under this impression. Some of them will think they're only doing this to rescue their careers, show the world what great entertainers they are. I don't intend to tell them otherwise, but I do want to see the situation gradually beating it out of them. Do you know what I'm saying? At no point do I want any of these fuckers to think they can upstage *the house.*'

Jo Shepherd raises a hand as she's maybe been programmed to do.

'Are you saying here that the house is… the eighth character?'

'The house is the *primary* character. When people at home switch off at the end and go to bed, it's the house I want to invade their dreams. The candlelight, the old glass between the mullions, the embers in the hearth.'

Defford stands up, goes over to the plan of the house. Most of it's shaded to highlight the important bits, the oldest part of Knap Hall which consists of the main ground floor chamber with the dining hall on the other side of the inglenook and the Gothic doorway where two women, only one of them alive, were allegedly imaged by the visitor from the American Midwest.

'The main door out of the chamber leads to the half-spiral stone stairway… here. Continues past a locked door accessing the more modern parts of the building where we don't need anyone to go. On the other side are toilets which we've divided into male and female. The passage continues to a rear door, accessing the walled garden and the chapel. This will be electrically controlled by us, as will the door of the chapel.'

One of the Jamies asks if this means the residents won't be able to go out for air or a cigarette. Only in the daytime, Defford tells him. He doesn't want anybody attempting to scale the wall at night to try and find out where the house is. If they want to stick their heads out of their bedroom windows for a smoke that's entirely up to them. If they're lucky enough to get a window.

'All right, upstairs. Seven single bedrooms, two created out of the former owners' own apartment, five more off the passage across the landing, the door at the end of which is double locked, sealing off the rest of the house. All windows with views extending beyond the grounds have been boarded.'

'So what we have is – essentially – a time capsule,' Jo says. 'The oldest part of the house, Tudor or even late medieval. The place of ghosts. Which some of the residents might well feel they're aware of. They'll be asked to share any impressions.'

'Don't get me wrong,' Defford says, 'I don't want people *seeing* things all the time. Don't want any of this cable-TV shit where everybody jumps at an airlock in the pipes and then, "Oh look, it's a fucking *orb*."'

Laughter.

'What I'm saying… when – if – somebody sees or hears or feels something, I want it to be an *occasion*. I want everybody either frozen to their chairs, or astonished or furious at the stupidity of the others. The expression I don't want to see on anyone's face is beatific calm.'

Grayle's been told that the live sections aren't aired in real time. There's a short delay in case anyone says or does something unsuitable even for Channel 4 after midnight. And there are specific *Big Other* no-nos. Defford tells them how close they can go to the old *BB* format and what they should avoid.

'I *don't* want burps and farts on the track and shots of guys scratching their balls. Though a glimpse of flesh is OK if it appears to be in response to something. We don't expect to see any ghosts, but we don't rule out anything. What we *know* we're going to get are the responses of people who think they *have* experienced something, and the reactions of people who think this is insanity.'

This audience – even Grayle, now – is techno-savvy, so he doesn't need to explain about pictures being fed simultaneously into as many as twenty channels as the Seven start to socialize and small alliances form. Everyone wears a personal mic. All conversations get recorded. Different directors will be assigned to follow emerging storylines or developing relationships, with editors constantly at work on the rushes, selecting the best moments for the following night's programme. Jo and then Defford will make final decisions on what's used. Everything, however, will be saved in case something that appears innocuous at the time proves to be significant in light of what happens later.

One of the Emilys raises a hand.

'Leo, what are we actually telling them about the house?'

'To begin with, as little as possible. They'll learn it's an old house – at least as old as it looks – with a history of unhappy events and psychic phenomena. On the history, the viewers will be one step ahead – they'll see some of our pre-recorded images, suggestive of period, but never identity. At the end of each night – in the live part of the programme – the residents will be asked to review their impressions. Anyone who seems to be close to the truth will be called into the chapel for in-depth questioning by Grayle.'

'What if nobody gets close?' Emily asks.

'Someone will always get close to something, even if it's only guesswork. The fact that they've been called in will indicate they're on the right track. However, yes, it's possible we might lose momentum. I'm not going to worry too much about that at this stage. These people are doing it because they want to be noticed. Things *will* happen. But we'll meet here every day to hear your views on how it's going and discuss any ideas on how we might expand the picture and tighten the screws. We want them to be challenged in all kinds of ways.'

It's becoming clear to Grayle that Defford has contingency plans she hasn't been told about. He obviously isn't going to mention the possible use of Cindy as an engine of change. The unethical side.

'What about the evictions?' a bearded Jamie asks. 'How often?'

'One every night. Possibly two,' Defford tells him.

The technical part of this, the counting of phoned-in votes, is being handled from London. When a resident gets dumped, he or she is straight back up the tunnel and into the pop-up. They won't be prisoners, they can walk around the grounds, but they can't go the other side of the gates. Perhaps short interviews will be recorded with each of them as they emerge, and then longer ones the following day with a view to finding out if and how their opinions have changed.

The final Saturday night will see just one person left in the house. The winner, if you like, although spending a night alone in Knap Hall doesn't sound to Grayle like any kind of prize. In theory, this is the resident whose opinions best represent the attitude of the viewers. Next Sunday, when it's all over, they all go back into the house for the final revelations about Knap Hall, and the last night will be a review of the week, intercut with clips from this session.

'Evictions,' Defford says, 'are usually the most exciting moments in *Big Brother*, but even more significant for us, in that they'll show which way the nation's leaning – towards belief or scepticism. Yes, there'll be votes for people the viewers just want to keep in the house for entertainment value. But not too many, we hope. At the end of the day, it's the eighth person – the house – that wins or loses.'

Defford sits down.

There's applause. Grayle slides out into a night fresh from the rain, full of star-spatter now and no illusion of control.

38

Fragrant

'SO,' ANDERSON SAYS. 'Did she or didn't she?'

One small lamp burns weakly in the sitting room of the bastard bungalow. Marcus is in his dressing gown, feet up on an old church hassock, Malcolm alongside.

Not what he was expecting from Underhill. Bloody well wasn't.

'Never thought of her as particularly psychic. Very few of these New Age types ever are. They *think* they are, but there are times when all that incense and tinkling windchimes bollocks actually works the other way. A barrier.'

'But she's no' that way any more, Marcus. *You* achieved that.'

Anderson hands him cocoa, which he doesn't like but arteries or something apparently do.

'But the poor bitch has been pushed back into the liminal world, and I did that, too. Me. Why? I'll tell you. Because when you hear the word "television", you think it can't be real. Land of make-believe. Essentially harmless.'

'All right.' Anderson sits down. 'Let's take this slowly, examine the possibilities one by one.'

Marcus sips the cocoa with distaste. The nursing profession, of course, has always had its liminal moments. It's nurses rather than doctors who share the weird beauty of death, inhabit the halfway-house.

'Go on,' he says.

'All right, starting wi' the rational, is it some kind of déjà vu?'

'What, you mean Underhill learns that Harry Ansell's topped himself on the end of a rope in a dark wood and imagines having had a precognitive experience in his former bedroom?'

Anderson shrugs.

'If so, what's that imply about her current mental state?' Marcus says. 'Recurrence of manic depression?'

Which he likes to think never quite set in. Likes to think they caught it in time. Is quite proud of the way two years of coalface-journalism gave Underhill a seemingly protective shell.

'Or,' he says, 'is it something in the atmosphere at Knap Hall, some condition of the place, that plays with you? And to what extent is that conditioned by what's happened there in the past? I mean as distinct from locational influences, geophysical stress.'

'You hate terms like "geophysical stress".' Anderson activates her e-cig. 'We both know what you *want* it to be. Why not just accept it, Marcus?'

He peers at her down his glasses. It worries him that she actually seems to enjoy life here. She's had her hair dyed crimson which, though he's never going to admit it, he rather likes.

'All right,' he says, 'let's say it *is*. Let's say that Knap Hall is… polluted. In which context, I really can't see we're looking at what remains of the fragrant Parr. That has to be wishful thinking on the part of the Ansell woman. Even Lewis thinks that. So that leaves us with—'

'How do you know she wis fragrant?'

'Fuck's that mean?'

'I'm no' entirely sure. But you're the one's always going on about no' taking history at face value.'

Marcus thinks about it. Point taken. Perhaps he should look into Parr's last days at Sudeley Castle, even though he can't believe there's anything historians have failed to find in this most poked-over period of English history. But then, bastard historians are selective.

'Also,' he says, 'we have this man Fishe, to whose activities the word "fragrant" can hardly be applied.'

He's told her the stories Underhill had from the woman in Winchcombe, but Anderson still looks sceptical.

'Did he even exist?'

'What's the matter with you tonight?'

'You just wannae be involved, don't you? Indirectly. Which is the only way ever works for you. You need tae be operating some kind of… subversive rearguard action.'

'Oh, for—'

'*You…*' Anderson's up in her chair, waving the e-cig, 'were never gonnae work for the TV, not in a million bloody years. You were just waiting for them to leave you an opening. Like dissing wee Grayle, so you can claim it's your responsibility for gettin' her into it in the first place. In fact, I wouldnae—'

'Balls. And yes, he did exist.'

'Who?'

'Fishe. Tenant farmer at what is now Knap Hall, 1756 to 1789. Nothing else about him on the Internet. Not that I can find, anyway. Not going to give up, obviously.'

'Got yourself a purpose now, I can see it in your evil wee eyes. I'm just trying tae make sure you don't dive in too far, too fast, you know?'

'If you don't dive in too far, bugger all use diving in at all.'

'Wis she scared?'

'Who?'

Marcus looking into the wobbly lamplight. The bulb's on the way out, starting to whine. It's an old bulb, not energy-saving but at least isn't full of bastard mercury. Malcolm growls.

'Grayle.' Anderson leans forward. 'When she saw whatever she saw, wis she scared? That's always your key factor, is it not?'

'Could hardly bring herself to talk about it.'

'That's no' normal. For Grayle.'

'Bloody isn't.'

The lamp bulb… this has happened to him before, he thinks stupidly, when he's approaching something odd. Or maybe it's some warning device in the ear canal.

'Been in the attic,' he says.

'Aye, I noticed.'

'Going through the files, all the old *Vision* correspondents. *Thought* I remembered the name Rutter from somewhere. Used to send us snippets of Cotswold folklore about wells and saints. Before Underhill's time. Think if I phoned her, it's possible she might remember me?'

Anderson eyes him in the dimming light.

'Wid anyone ever forget you, Marcus?'

39

Death canal

A YOUNG PRODUCTION assistant with a half-grown beard and cans around his neck, takes Cindy into the ante-room to the plastic tunnel.

'My,' Cindy says, 'how exciting is *this*?'

He's been here before, of course, while waiting for his interview with Grayle, and the young man looks at him as if he might be taking the piss. Cindy remains solemn.

The windowless room has a few chairs and equipment including a monitor on a desk, its screen dithering over half-formed images. He glimpses firelight on polished panelling.

'You're in second, Mr Lewis, which means you get to watch the start of the recording.'

'What a privilege.'

'I might as well tell you the first person to go in is Eloise, the singer and TV presenter. She's in the tunnel now.'

The boy looks at him in search of recognition. Fortunately, Cindy once guested on *The House Wizard*, an edition involving the cleansing of a former maisonette where a woman had stabbed her husband to death in the bath. He recalls Eloise telling him miserably that viewing figures had been disappointing and there probably wouldn't be another series after this. Well, these things happen. What looks like a good idea in concept often falls flat in execution. Leo Defford has good reason to be on edge.

'And do I get to watch the fair Eloise crossing the threshold?'

'Yeah, sure, no problem.'

'Thank you.'

Cindy takes a seat in front of the monitor. He's been told it won't be especially warm in there, so he's wearing his tweed jacket and skirt with thick leggings and a scarf. And his beret, of course.

In the monitor, he can hear static and the criss-cross of studio voices, and then, in isolation, the words 'sixty seconds'. The boy adjusts his headphones, looks excited. In the gallery, they'll all be watching the big digital clock. It's only a recording for the opening programme of *Big Other* tomorrow night, but it's live *now*, with all the tension this implies. Nobody wants a second take because of some avoidable cock-up.

The screen goes black, as the countdown starts from ten.

Then it's not simply a black screen but the view down a dim passage. The emptiness of which emphasizes the difference between this and *Big Brother*, where you have masses of young people bouncing up and down with excitement at the proximity of real, live celebrities… the level of whose insecurities, at this moment, would astound them.

'Seven… six… five… four… three…'

Silence as the screen comes to attention. A distant light, and old-house noises, probably amplified. Faint creaks, footfalls, maybe amplified a little. Candles on the walls are protected by glass funnels, of a kind that wouldn't have been around in Tudor times, but that doesn't lessen the effect, as the camera peers at them, circles of lights expanding and dissolving.

It goes on for quite a while, far longer than necessary. Tomorrow, the commentary will be added – a sonorous scene-setter, voiced up, Cindy's been told, by Matthew Barnes, a one-time radio newsreader more often heard nowadays on lower-key TV commercials. Barnes will be a muted, neutral voice, not a personality. Never upstage the talent.

Leave all that to *Big Other*.

Movement at last. A woman comes out of shadow, walking slowly down the passage, her back to the camera. She has on a long black skirt which makes it look as though she's gliding. A black crocheted shawl is around her shoulders. Something bulky hangs from her right hand.

At the bottom of the passage is a door of age-greyed oak, with iron studs, long metal hinges half absorbed into the wood. The door is ajar, and the gap is the source of the light. It's all traditional, but nicely done. The woman doesn't touch the door. She turns slowly towards the camera. Her head's bowed so you can't see her face for near-black hair.

'Cold,' she mutters crossly. 'Why do these places always have to be so bloody cold?'

She puts down what she was carrying, and it stands beside her in the shadows, like a child all in black. It's a guitar case.

The beardie extends an arm.

'Time to go in, Mr Lewis. Good luck.'

'Thank you, boy.'

The tunnel squeaks in the night breeze. Cindy walks into what he supposes is a kind of birth canal for *Big Other*. The phrase 'death canal' passes through his head and makes him smile. Well, he likes to think it's a smile, as the tunnel darkens.

It's been done so well that he hardly notices when plastic turns to stone and he's inside the house.

He doesn't notice the camera at all, which is *very* clever, as he must now be in the stone-walled passage in which he'd seen Eloise just a few minutes ago.

The difference is that there's a larger light at the bottom, the door thrown wide. He thinks he remembers now: a couple of steps into a hallway or ante-room and then the door into the chamber which was Trinity's large parlour or reception room, with its inglenook.

In which there is now evidently a fire. He sees it for real now, lighting the panels, flickering on the stones.

Cindy stops for a moment, listens, as if some predictive part of him knew the scream would come.

PART FIVE

… after…

I realize that all this will mean less than nothing to the sceptical reader. Well, that's all right. It is the sceptics' right to disbelieve, just as it is mine to print what I believe. I am not proselytizing on behalf of ghosts. You can lead a full, happy and useful life without believing in them. But I should like to point out that scepticism is largely a negative matter. People do not believe in ghosts because they have never come across them.

Diana Norman
The Stately Ghosts of England (1963)

40

Iscariot

YOU WOULDN'T CALL it cosy, but…

… you almost would. Certainly in comparison with the room he first entered with Trinity on that hard, bright January day nearly three years ago, the mildewed panels all sepia-drab and the hearth dead.

The second time he was here, it was rich and rosy, all tapestry wall hangings and brocaded cushions. But that was in the summer, and there was no fire in the ingle then, either.

So this is the first time he's seen it with logs ablaze, red ash aglow. There's a sofa with two chairs either side arranged roughly around the inglenook. Modern furniture, distressed. Tudor seating as it would have been if they'd known about springs. Physical discomfort is not what this is about.

The room looks less cavernous, more woody, more intimate, yet more active. Could be all those unseen glass eyes in the panelling holes, in the crevices between the chocolate-bar beams, and behind the false wall where the duplicitous mirrors are reflecting flames.

He remains in the doorway, listening. The only sound in here is breathing. Steady, controlled breathing, the kind which, in Cindy's world, is often a gateway to meditation.

Or for the quelling of emotion.

He goes in and finds Eloise hunched like a woodland animal trying to blend with the foliage. Tight into the corner where the panelling meets the oaken screen. Both arms wrapped around the solid guitar case, holding it in front of her like a riot shield.

Her head lifting slowly as he walks in. Then the dark eyes are widening and the breathing stops.

'Good God.'

Cindy stands with hands on hips.

'How *are* you, lovely?'

'Well. I never thought of *you* for this.'

'There's flattering.'

She rises, smiling wanly through the straggled black hair. He takes the guitar case, helps her up.

'Now then, Elly. Trying to work out, I am, what it is that you're seeing and I am not.'

She scowls.

'Do *not* tell me that's down to ignorance.'

She's looking at the fire which, as fires go, is not the hardest to miss.

'Didn't mean to yell like that. Rage as much as anything. The *bastards*. They must've known. They have experts. Or should do.'

She points to the cut logs assembled against the stones of the ingle. Cindy walks over. There's no hiss from the fire; these logs are well-seasoned, two summers or more. He lifts one.

'Oh.'

Now he sees.

Its bark has grooves as deep as tyre tread.

'Oh dear.'

'Thank Christ,' Eloise comes to her feet. 'I thought it was just me.'

In the live gallery, the directors are looking at one another. There are four cameras covering this, and they're getting the lot: four images, four different angles, wide shots, close-ups, face shots, fire shots, log-shots. Grayle's getting puzzled, backward glances from both Defford and Jo Shepherd.

In a seat behind their desk, she basks in it, in no hurry to explain. First time today she's felt halfway needed.

Jo leans over the back of her chair.

'Fire? This is about fire? Is this to do with Eloise having a thing about fire? Because of the witch-burning?'

290

'I'm more inclined to think,' Grayle says, 'this is about *what* they're burning.'

'It's wood.'

'Gimme a minute.'

Grayle opens her laptop. On the sound-feed, over the clunk of Cindy laying the log back on the pile, Eloise is talking, like an incantation.

'You don't bring it in. In the house. You *don't*.'

'I've heard that.'

'You don't burn it in the house. Same story. Wherever you go. Unlucky.'

'But it also has healing qualities,' Cindy says.

'That's the fruit and the flowers, isn't it?'

'And the leaves repel insects. And the green wood may cure warts.'

'But *you don't burn it*.'

Now you're hearing genuine distress.

'No,' Cindy says soberly. 'It is generally agreed, in most areas, certainly this one, that you don't burn it.'

Defford signals Jo Shepherd to keep tabs, beckons Grayle and points at the door. Grayle gets up from her chair as Eloise's voice is raised to the beams, and it's not a steady voice.

'Somebody… needs to get this out. All of it. It's not a joke, *do you understand?*'

Grayle sits down on the steps of the reality-gallery truck, wet against her ass but she needs to operate the laptop.

'Judas Iscariot,' she says. 'Remember him?'

Not expecting a reply from Defford and she doesn't get one. He's standing in front of her, legs either side of these heavy-duty pipes carrying power lines and fibre-optics or whatever.

'Judas Iscariot was said to have hanged himself from an elder tree, and some sources say that's where it started. Elder trees are bad news. Which is unfortunate really, because the bastards are everywhere.'

'That's what the wood on the fire is?'

Defford's come to lean over her shoulder to see the Folklore of Trees website she's found. Grayle points.

'See there? See those deep grooves in the trunk? No other tree in this country has bark quite like that. The elder's known as a fairy tree in the Isle of Man, a witches' tree in most of Britain and Ireland. An elder tree growing too close to a house might cause consumption to claim the dwellers therein – it says here. And yet they courted bad luck by chopping it down. You can't win with an elder.'

'The woman's a bloody witch, anyway.'

'She's a hedge witch. It's a state of mind. I couldn't find that she was ever part of a coven. Witch in the folklore context usually means plain evil. Elder is often called the devil's wood.'

'Is it really?'

'Just tell me you didn't know that.'

'Fucking hell!' Defford smashes his right fist into his left palm. 'Talk about a happy accident.'

He looks up at the stars, a big, open-cut of a smile on his face.

Grayle says, '*Happy*?'

'Grayle, it—'

'"Accident", even?'

'If it was possible for this programme to get off to a better start, I'd like to know how. Did you *hear* that scream, the way it resounded off the stone?'

'If that's what you want.' Grayle closes the laptop. 'I mean, I realize you're the producer and all, but you don't think maybe it's a little too soon?'

'Aw, Grayle you really don't think—'

'Strikes me as a hell of a coincidence that the first two people in the house are those most likely to identify elder as the devil's wood.'

'You think it was deliberate?'

'*They* do, Leo. How you gonna handle that?'

'Fuck's sake, Grayle, the only person this side of the cameras who knows anything about this witchy stuff is you!'

'Far's you know.'

'And I take it *you* didn't arrange with – what's his name – the gardening guy?'

'Jordan.'

'To have Jordan bring in a pile of elder.'

'Somebody did. Now whether they knew what effect it would have—'

'Whoever they are there's a small bonus coming their way. Did you see her *face*?'

'And it was not a professional reaction, Leo – she wasn't playing to the camera, even I could see that. She truly believes, like a lotta people, and maybe me too, to an extent, that old traditions didn't just get made up. She sees nothing but elder wood on the fire and more of it stacked up on the hearth, and something tells her this whole project will not go right.'

'Like a curse?'

'Or even,' Grayle says, 'like a set-up. And isn't that what the viewers are gonna think, too?'

Defford's fingering his earring. She's been following his reactions from the start of this, all the way from surprise to mystification to something close to joy.

'Yeah,' he says, 'that's a possibility. We'll need to consider how to get that point over. Because obviously I have no reason to think that wood was deliberately chosen. '

'You're gonna have the wood removed, Leo? Jordan's still here, is he, to handle that?'

'He has a caravan. He's on call.'

'You mind if I go ask him if anyone here told him to bring elder wood into the house? Because I'm guessing he knows what it means. Country boy and all.'

Defford takes a step back.

'And if nobody told him?'

'Well, that would mean either he thought none of the residents would be au fait with rural superstitions that even I know about… or that he did. And if *that* is the case…'

'All right. Yeah. Sure. Talk to him.'

'Thanks.'

'However,' Defford says, 'you might just be pushing it a little, Grayle. Be aware of that.'

'He's always been OK with me.'

'Didn't mean Jordan.'

Defford's eyes are unblinking and he isn't smiling.

Cindy's thinking, inevitably, he supposes, about Harry Ansell.

But that wasn't an elder, was it? That was an oak.

He's aware, for the first time since he entered the house, of the personal mic he's wearing, the size of a bluebottle, glad that it doesn't pick up his thoughts, hoping to God he doesn't talk in his sleep.

This is not a good start, is it? Is it really possible it was deliberate?

'When the others come in, it might be as well not to mention this,' he murmurs, knowing full well that by this time tomorrow his murmur will have been broadcast to the nation. 'I think they've got the message. I think the wood will be taken away in the night.'

'Too late,' Eloise says. 'Damage is done now.'

41

Electric pig

MARCUS IS BACK from the loft with a big old book. One of those books he knew he had somewhere. Bought second-hand a few years ago, maybe fifth-hand judging by the state of the binding.

Andy notices he's panting a little. Aw hell, what's that matter? All those years of being Sister Anderson, the stink, the drips, the bedpans and the old guys who drooled, and you're worried about a wee bit of panting? Could be he'll never have a heart attack again. Then again, he just might.

She follows him into his office where he slaps the book on his desk. Just where his own book was, the last time she was in here.

The manuscript of *In Defence of Mystery* is gone. The whole thing. Marcus always likes to see an actual paper manuscript piling up. Every time he finishes a chapter he prints it out, adds it to the pile. Satisfying as the stack thickens, but also a threat, as Marcus admits sometimes, late at night. *Finish me*, it says, *finish me or I'll finish you.*

Not how she'd imagined it was going to be. Writing a book seemed like something she thought he could relax into. But, because it doesn't get finished, because he goes to bed knowing he'll have to wake up to it next morning, it's become this source of unending anxiety. He wakes up in the night, thinks of something he's got wrong, and he's babbling into the wee recorder he keeps by the bed, and then he can't get back to sleep and goes and writes. Not good.

'Where's it gone? The book.'

'Drawer. Tired of it nagging me. Look at this.'

The title of the tome Marcus has brought down from the loft is *Annals of Winchcombe and Sudeley* by Emma Dent.

'Famous Victorian matriarch of the family which still owns Sudeley Castle. Persistent old dear. Probably not unlike Rutter, if considerably richer.'

Overhearing his phone call to the woman called Rutter, Andy was amused to register that she'd thought he was dead – Marcus, furious at this, snarling *minor… cardiac… blip* into the phone.

'I asked Rutter,' he says now, 'how, if this man Fishe was so close to demonic, did he get away with what he was doing with the local women? How come a bunch of vigilantes didn't go up there and lynch the bastard? She reminds me his employer, Wishatt, was a magistrate, wielding considerable power. Also that people were superstitious about Belas Knap and Knap Hall and believed Fishe under the protection not only of Wishatt but the devil himself.'

'How's the devil come into it?'

'Belas Knap – where's the name come from? Some people say "bel" – beautiful. More likely Baal, the storm god. In the eighteenth century, when nobody was seeing paganism as cosy, that would've been as good as saying Satan. Demonic, anyway.'

Marcus switches on the black Anglepoise lamp that used to stand on Andy's desk at the hospital for so many years. So much a part of her that when she left they gave it to her. At first the hospital administrators had refused even to sell NHS property, so a couple of consultants pinched it. Marcus loves it.

'Lot of legends and ghost stories attached to Belas Knap. As recently as 1998, a woman clearly saw a group of monk-like figures approaching the mound but disappearing before they reached it. Quite significant. Suggests God-fearing folk can't get close. For hundreds of years, probably the only people who went up there alone would be bastards like Fishe – the ones who'd given up worrying about their immortal souls and believed it would give them what they craved. And who's to say it didn't?'

'Craved?'

Marcus is looking a wee bit devilish himself. Gets like this when he's on the trail of something, snuffling around from one place to another like an electric pig. For a while he was unsure about this Abel Fishe, thinking maybe the guy had come to embody the misdeeds of several people, possibly all of them connected with Knap Hall.

Now he's decided Fishe was halfway demonic and this is linked somehow to his naming of the house after Belas Knap.

'Bodies buried there. Outpourings of devotion to Baal or whatever they worshipped to improve their hunting.'

She knows it, of course. Marcus dragged her up there once, in the days when he was still taking it slowly. She recalls thinking there was something smug about it. Didn't like it that much.

'Whatever energy's accumulated there,' he says, 'might be neutral in itself, but it'll swell whatever reservoir of toxic energy's inside a man like Fishe. He'll come away from there feeling he isn't on his own. He's united with something. And that whatever he's been doing, he's *meant* to be doing it. And he'll keep going back for more.'

'You don't even know he ever went there. Maybe he was scared like the rest of the folk.'

'Then why would he name his house after it?'

'Wasnae even his house.'

'True. Wondered about that. How would a tenant be in a position to change the name of someone else's farm? Put it to Rutter, who suggested that Fishe knew enough about Wishatt to be able to make certain demands. That Wishatt was sufficiently afraid of Fishe – or of what Fishe had become – to accede to his every whim.'

'You're still flyin' a kite.'

'Of course I'm flying a bastard kite. With nothing to go on but Rutter's word-of-mouth history, what option do I have?'

Andy turns away to conceal her smile. This is not exactly living with the mystery.

'All right.' Marcus is rapping a pen on the Sudeley book. 'Let's say Fishe is controlled by urges, and one of them keeps drawing him back to the mound, like a junkie to a drug dealer…'

Andy nods for the sake of domestic peace.

'But you're right, Anderson. We don't know enough about him. So thought I might as well drop an email to old Teddy Everly. Knows everything, remembers most of it. When he's sober.'

Teddy Everly is this old drunk from Stroud, most famous for his book, *In Search of Rosie*, in which Teddy challenges the author Laurie Lee's assertion that the obliging young heroine of his classic Cotswold memoir *Cider with Rosie* was a composite character.

Marcus slaps down a printed-out email.

'This is his reply.'

Marcus, you old sod.

Certainly heard the phrase 'Abel's Rent'. Always meant to look into it. Never got round to it.

But if this Fishe was a farmer near Sudeley in the 1750s-plus, could he have been a mate of another farmer name of Lucas?

Check out Dent's *Annals of Sudeley*, etc. Back pages.

Doesn't take much imagination.

'Which,' Marcus says, 'brings me back to something Rutter said when I asked her why there wasn't a lynching party for Fishe. Apart from him being Wishatt's man and the superstition about the burial chamber, she said that there was something causing considerable excitement and no small amount of awe happening over at Sudeley.'

He opens up the *Annals* a few pages from the end, flattens them out. Andy sees a primitive-looking drawing of what looks like an old longcase clock lying flat. There are two flaps in the case which have been opened to reveal, at the top, not a clock face but a human face and, lower down, a hand.

'What is *that*?'

Andy pulls out her reading glasses to magnify the faint, tiny lettering under the drawing.

'Why'm I no' getting a good feeling about this, Marcus?'

Marcus sniffs.

'I'd say a strong stomach was required. If you hadn't been a nurse in Glasgow.'

42

Losers

'OPEN IT, SHALL I?' Cindy asks.

Through a speaker cunningly set into a wall hanging, the unchallenging voice of the former radio announcer Matthew Barnes has invited them into the dining room where, on the narrow oak table, under a low-hung hoop of candles, there are bottles of red and white wine, glasses, two jugs of beer and a vellum-coloured envelope.

'You know you want to, Cindy,' Ozzy Ahmed says.

Cindy has never met Ozzy before. He seems an affable person. Some comedians can become tiresome in minutes but the boy's humour is dry and stays out of your face.

Ashley Palk places the envelope, addressed to no one, in Cindy's hands.

Cindy says. 'Should we be seated for this?'

There are seven matching chairs, wooden, rudimentary, a grey cushion on each. As they sit down around the table, the Seven, Cindy's already slitting the envelope with a thumb, unfolding creamy notepaper.

'Well, children, quite simple, it is. First, we are asked to state briefly how we would define ghosts.'

'Bollocks?' Ozzy says diffidently. 'That brief enough, or would you like me to reduce it to a single syllable?'

'I think that sets the pattern admirably, Austin. Eloise?'

She's calmer now, but wary, inevitably, after the incident of the elder. She's shed her shawl to reveal a crocheted black top, through which her black bra is visible. Her nails are black. Once a goth...

300

'Spirits of the dead,' she says unequivocally.

She's chosen the seat at the bottom of the table, well away from Ozzy and Rhys Sebold, whose radio session with her was sent to Cindy a week ago. She hasn't spoken to either of them directly. Biding her time, no doubt.

Cindy nods gravely, looks next at Roger Herridge – suit and tie, big hair.

'Place memory,' Herridge says. 'Recording in stone. Imprint.'

'So without personality?'

'Only in the most obvious sense. If this was, say, the ghost of an angry person, you might get a sense of excitation... wrath, disturbance. Which might be hard to live with, even though essentially harmless in a physical sense.'

'Invariably?'

Roger's smile is rueful.

'One should never say that.'

'Thank you, boy. A good answer. Helen?'

'God... I dunno.'

Helen Parrish looks more relaxed than any of them. And rather fetching in a sloppy jumper and black jeans, Cindy thinks. In fact, if he was normal...

'Try.'

'Well, you know... I do think there's something. Levels of personal experience as yet uncharted by science, how about that? All those centuries of ghost stories, you can't just dismiss it all out of hand.'

'I think I just did, didn't I?' Ozzy Ahmed says.

'Only because a put-down is usually funnier. You strike me as a man who must always go for what is funnier. In the interests of sustaining an income, surely.'

Ozzy blinks. Helen shrugs.

'And, as they say, I know what I saw. And it doesn't bother me greatly if you all think I'm deluded because I can't prove otherwise. If this was something we could easily get a handle on, we'd all know by now.'

'You *can* get a handle,' Eloise insists. 'If you want to. Perhaps you don't, which is fine.'

'We should perhaps…' Cindy raises a finger, '…build *up* to the arguments. Mr Sebold?'

Rhys is wearing one of those crisp, striped shirts with a white collar. His body is gym-slim, his hair thick but short, razored at the sides. Good-looking boy and well aware of it. His mouth is wide, as befits his big voice, tossing Cindy a loose smile.

'So where do *you* stand, Mr Lewis?

Of course. Rhys is an interviewer. *He* asks the questions. Cindy feigns embarrassment.

'Me? Oh, heavens, all of the above. And more. Ghosts are various and complicated. But also, I suppose, relatively simple. They inhabit areas of our senses which have become moribund through disuse. They live in our derelict houses.'

'You're saying we make them up.'

'Far from it. What I—'

'Because we *do* make them up. For whatever purpose suits us at the time. That's my answer. We invent them.'

Rhys stand up and walks away from the table, as if his work here is done. Cindy calls after him.

'Or do they invent us?'

'What's that mean?'

'Haven't the faintest idea. Now…' Cindy peers around the table. 'Who's left?'

'Just me, I'm afraid.'

'*Ashley*. My apologies.'

She's looking fresh and relaxed in a magnolia dress, swingy blond hair, no jewellery. A schoolteacher on holiday. She sips white wine.

'As a psychologist, I could bore you all at length, but I shall restrict m'self to words like "projection" and "auto-suggestion".'

'As distinct from "hallucination" and "self-delusion"?'

'That would be offensive.'

302

How nice we are being to one another, Cindy thinks. And how nice the room feels, quietly Elizabethan, not oppressive. He wonders: was the elder a device? And whose? If so, it could hardly have worked better: a sudden darkness followed by some companionable light relief – which no viewer will trust. He consults the creamy notepaper under the circular candle-holder which haloes them like the biblical light in a Rembrandt.

'Next question. Again, quite simple. Apart from the money, why are we all here?'

Sitting beside Jo Shepherd in the live gallery, Grayle watches on another monitor as Jordan arrives in the chamber with his bier and its cargo of fresh logs. The thick door between the two adjacent rooms is shut. Jordan's alone.

Well, not entirely. Let's not forget the cameramen behind the false wall with its inset two-way mirrors. *They* are the ghosts in here.

To make this kind of traffic possible, boards have been cut to use as ramps to get the bier up and down the few steps. What this suggests to Grayle is that Defford knows full well that this is no ordinary wood cart and is hoping one of the residents knows enough about historical death-procedures to get spooked and spread it around.

Jordan unloads some wood that Grayle doesn't recognize. Pale, flaking bark, silver birch? The camera's behind him, so that his face is not seen. He looks timeless in a leather apron and a kind of old-fashioned watch cap – not the type of headgear Grayle's seen him in before – so you don't even get to check out his haircut.

A camera between the ceiling beams observes his hands piling the elder on the bier for removal, which itself must be an infringement of some folkloric no-no. The fire's burning low, the main elder log already collapsed into pink and orange ash. Jordan uses one of the new blocks of wood to push it back. Then he nests the block in the hot ash, arranging a funnel of smaller ones either side.

'In case you were wondering, Leo actually hadn't planned that,' Jo whispers to Grayle. 'The elder incident. He loves how it happened, but he's disturbed that it did.'

'How much *does* he have planned?'

Jo comes on all wide-eyed.

'Did I say he had anything arranged, Grayle? I don't think I did. That would be against the whole ethos of the programme.'

'Sure,' Grayle says between her teeth.

Damn right it would.

'Let's not dress this up,' Helen Parrish says under the kindly candlelight. 'We're all losers. We're trying to recover something of our professional lives before we're unfit to be seen on the box after four p.m.'

'Except for him.' Eloise nodding at Ozzy Ahmed. 'He's doing rather well, it pains me to say.'

'Yes, indeed.' Cindy running with it. 'Austin's behaving terribly badly, he is, simply by turning up here and robbing a decent loser of an opportunity to get back on his feet. Thoughtless, see. Selfish.'

Ozzy looks wry, says nothing. Fundamental rule: if you can't think of anything funny to say, look wry and say nothing. But he'll be looking for a way to establish that Cindy is not the house's number one comedian. Eloise, who's drunk a little wine, waves her empty glass.

'I know why he's doing it.'

The reflections of at least five candles glimmer from that glass. There's a scraping noise from the inglenook.

'His marriage is over,' Eloise says, impish glee behind seaweed hair. 'No mother-in-law to torment any more. He needs a whole new act. He needs *us* – all of us, except possibly his mate, Rhys. We're new material. Soon as he gets to his room he'll be making notes, scribble, scribble, scribble.'

'Unfair,' Ozzy says at last, more of his native Manchester coming through. 'I actually *like* mixing with people like you.

Used to enjoy visiting me mum-in-law, meeting the coven.'

'He's a hypocrite,' Eloise says, succinctly.

Ozzy grins, waves a hand casually, as if he's swatting her.

'Never said they were sane, but I enjoyed their company.' Shaking his head, smiling nostalgically. 'Muppets.'

Cindy notes that he hasn't given them a better reason for his presence. Neither has he denied his friendship with Rhys Sebold or his intention to use this gathering of eccentrics in future comedy routines.

Aware of movement in the fireplace, he turns his head, but is disinclined to mention it. Ashley Palk also glances at the fire. Could be production people, whose presence they're expected to ignore, just as nobody commented on the rumbling from next door a couple of minutes ago. This is television.

Helen Parrish says, 'They going to tell us what happened here? A murder? How old's the house, anyway?'

Eloise and Herridge answer simultaneously. She says late medieval, he says Elizabethan. He bows to her.

'Let's compromise on Tudor. But you could be right, could be older. Stone-colour suggests... hard to say, could be Oxfordshire, Gloucestershire, Wiltshire, Somerset. And if you want to know why *I'm* here, it's very simple and nothing to do with money or being political driftwood. I want to see a ghost.'

Eloise turns to him, interested.

'You never have?'

'Absolutely fascinated by them since childhood. Written three books about them. Made a practice, whilst travelling the country, of sleeping in the most haunted room of every haunted inn I could find.'

'And a haunted flower shop,' Ozzy murmurs, 'where you wake up and smell roses from the pillow on the left and gardenias from the pillow on the right. Spooky.'

Roger Herridge laughs, and it's not forced either, Cindy notes.

'I suppose this begs the question, Roger – why do you still believe?'

'I haven't seen God, either, Cindy, but I still go to church.'

'That,' Rhys Sebold says from over by the door, 'is ridiculous.'

'You may think so.'

'Not that, Roger – well, that *is* ridiculous, but I meant what's happening through there. Come and have a look.'

He's opened the door. From the chamber on the other side comes an uneven, weighty rolling: wobbly wheels on stone flags.

Ozzy Ahmed gets up, followed by Roger Herridge. The women don't move, being above all this. Cindy turns his chair to observe.

'There's a kind of yokel here,' Rhys says, looking into the main chamber. 'Quiet, now, we don't want to scare him away. What you doing, mate?'

No reply. Rhys doesn't give up; he's an interviewer.

'Chop this wood yourself?'

Ozzy opens the door wider, amusement squeaking in his throat.

'What *has* he got on? It's like a fucking troll uniform.'

'Let's not torment the poor chap,' Roger Herridge says. 'He's obviously been told not to speak to us. He's just bringing in more logs.'

'No he's not, he's taking them out. What's that about? Nice cart, though, cock.'

Roger bends into the room.

'That's interesting.'

'What is?' Rhys says.

'It's a bier. Funeral bier.'

'What, you mean for carrying…?'

Rhys takes a step back. Cindy hears the cart rolling away down the passage.

'Corpses,' Roger says.

'You're kidding.' Ozzy peering in. 'This a joke or what? Is there also a secret panel in the wall and when some bugger opens it a fucking skeleton falls out? No, geddoff his back, Rhys, they probably don't want him to speak to us, avoid paying him Equity rates.'

The women are quiet, Eloise's eyes dark and smoky, watchful behind the candles' aura.

Cindy ponders. Evidently, a man has been sent to replace the elder logs with something less offensive. But on a bier? He hears the rolling, grinding sound in his head, those wooden wheels. Were they, the Seven, meant to be aware of this going on, and in a fairly sinister way? If Defford hasn't mentioned any of it to him, well, why should he? Defford is a seasoned professional. He'll have constructed his sets with care. It's in his interests to create a general air of uncertainty and apprehension. And, amongst the residents, a fermenting mistrust of one another – essential, that.

'It's OK,' Roger Herridge says. 'He's gone.'

They come back into the dining room, Rhys Sebold closing the oak door, letting the wooden latch fall like a little guillotine. He looks annoyed. Cindy hears Eloise's indrawn breath, gives her a warning look: say nothing.

Ozzy rubs his hands.

'I really like the idea of the funeral buggy.'

Roger Herridge turns to him with understandable suspicion.

'No, I do,' Ozzy says. 'You reckon when we get evicted, we all go out on that? Laid out? One by one?'

Strangely, nobody laughs. Ozzy doesn't give up.

'Roger with a little bunch of flowers on his chest?'

'Let it go, mate,' Rhys says.

43

The rusty fender

JUST BEFORE MIDNIGHT, Eloise is summoned to the chapel to talk to Grayle.

How they do this, a bell bongs and the voice of Matthew Barnes – he sounds like a monk – comes through the speaker in the tapestry. '*Eloise to the chapel, please.*' It's a recording. Barnes has done a summons for each of the residents, so he doesn't have to be there the entire time. In fact, Grayle's never seen him – or maybe she has and just doesn't recognize him; he's a radio face.

The green light comes on. Grayle pulls in a breath.

'Good evening, Eloise.'

'Is it?'

'Not been a great one for you, huh?'

Eloise has pulled back her hair, applied a rubber band. Been into the bathroom, washed her face clean of make-up, though her eyes are still dark. She looks like a corrupted schoolgirl, still vulnerable in spite of everything she's said yes to.

'Look,' she says, 'I'm not mad, you know.'

'We do know that.'

'Old beliefs, they weren't just invented. They came out of a time when people were sensitive to the moods and the vagaries of nature. When you had to fit in with the natural world, when people didn't think they could trample over everything, and fracking and all this abuse.'

As suggested by Jo, Grayle gets Eloise to explain the folklore surrounding the elder tree, Judas Iscariot, all that stuff. It can be edited and fitted subtly around what happened at the inglenook.

'We don't yet know how that happened,' Grayle tells her. 'But we apologize for any offence. Eloise, what do you think of the other residents?'

'They're OK. I mean, they're OK so far.'

'Are there any of them you seem to connect with?'

'Well, I knew Cindy before. He doesn't change. He knows his stuff. Roger Herridge seems fairly well-meaning. Not as much of a conman as I'd expected. I've never met a politician who was honest. Maybe he's realized what's important. Helen Parrish… I don't know. She seems OK, but I don't really know where she's coming from. I'm going to wait and hear what she has to say.'

'Ashley?'

Eloise wrinkles her nose.

'She's just the token sceptic. Just comes out with psychological crap. I've heard it all before. Doesn't impress me. Just hides a completely flat mind.'

'Which leaves…'

'Yeah, I know who it leaves. I'd forgotten about them. They're just nonentities, those guys. You can tell why they're mates, both just out for everything they can get. Atheism's cool right now, OK, let's have some of that.'

'They've offended you in the past?'

'I did Sebold's radio show and Ahmed was on it, and they took the piss out of me, non-stop. I didn't expect intelligent. Sad bastards on late-night trash radio. They'll go through the next week determined to see nothing and sneer at any of us who do. Well, fuck *them*.'

'Do you have any feelings about the house itself, Eloise?'

'It's not a warm place in any sense. I don't feel it welcomes us, or what you're doing here. But then I'm not sure any house would. Which sounds a bit hypocritical after agreeing to take part. I can probably give you a better opinion after spending the night here.'

*

309

The night.

This isn't like *Big Brother*, where they sleep in dormitories, all together. This isn't about turning them back into kids. Each has a separate room, with an en suite bathroom and a bell to awaken them for breakfast. Cameras will watch over them as they sleep, but there are none in the bathrooms. This is not about voyeurism.

At least not in *that* sense.

Most of them go up before one a.m. to rooms with boarded windows, a wardrobe each, a mirror and a bedside table with a lamp. The single beds are plain, with headboards of antique pine; nobody gets a four-poster.

The residents emerge from their bathrooms mostly in robes or dressing gowns. On one monitor Eloise is switching out the lamp before sliding into bed. On another Ozzy Ahmed is not scribbling in a notebook.

When the lights go out, there's no infrared to make people look like they're in another dimension. At least Defford stuck to that.

He's quit the live gallery now, leaving a couple of all-night producers and Jo and Grayle amongst the screens. Grayle watches the house tightening into the dark. Ashley Palk comes out of the bathroom into quite a large bedroom, the single bed looking isolated in one corner. She's wearing a long, dark nightdress, low cut. As she crosses the room, Grayle realizes which room this is, looks away. Perhaps Ashley's the best person to have it.

Only two people remain in the chamber, chairs pulled close to the ingle, the fire bronzing their faces. Late-night chat, like after the kids have gone to bed. Helen Parrish has a cigarette going.

'I suppose I came out of normal journalism too soon, all those years ago. Once you've been a TV-face, you're over for everything else.'

Cindy nodding, his beret on his lap.

'Couple of years ago,' Parrish says, 'I applied for a sub-editor's job on an evening paper. Turned me down. The editor said he couldn't believe I'd be satisfied with the subs desk.'

She stretches out her legs, easing off her shoes.

'Thought you'd want *his* job?' Cindy says.

'Worse than that – I think he thought his managing director would want me in his job.'

'He was probably right. Household name, you are. An asset.'

'What nobody gets,' Parrish says, 'is you can still be a household name when the income's completely dried up. People're still pointing at you when you're sitting on the scrapheap, and you find yourself smiling back at them, with a rusty car bumper up your bum.'

Cindy laughs.

'You could do after-dinner speeches.'

'Please, God, no. Not that, not ever.'

Grayle finds them kind of touching. Two middle-aged ladies, except one isn't. Nothing is as it seems. Helen contemplates her tweedy companion through her smoke.

'You actually gay then, Cindy?'

'What?'

'I've often wondered. I mean, there you are in your senior-secretary's outfit. I remember you on the Lottery show in all your glitter. *Are* you? Or is it a double-bluff?'

One monitor shows Cindy up close, gazing thoughtfully into the bed of spangled ashes. Catches the twitch of his glossed lips.

'Never really warmed to that word, to be honest,' he says.

'Gay?'

'I appreciate the irony in it, of course, and "homosexuality"… well, that still sounds like a criminal offence. But "gay", I think, has had its time. Always sounded too much like a squeal of petulant defiance. Look at us, we're all so happy! You straights will never be as happy as we are! Reaching the stage, I think, where all that needs to be left behind. Too shrill for the times.'

Grayle's nailed to the screen. Of all the questions she's never liked to ask… Marcus, too, though she's sure Marcus really doesn't want to know one way or the other. Now, here's Helen Parrish and Cindy, both well aware of the personal mics and the

311

potential size of the eavesdropping audience, opening their hearts into the embers, like only the ghosts can hear.

'Do you know that song, Helen, by John Grant? "Glacier"? Marvellously eloquent, profoundly melodic gay whinge. Its chorus extolling the pain of his situation. A glorious agony.'

'You still didn't answer the question.' Helen says.

'Well, you know, lovely, thinking about it, I've always preferred "queer". Oh yes, queer, I am and no mistake. On every level.'

Helen Parrish laughs.

And Grayle laughs, too, delighted as Cindy and Helen sit in companionable silence, watching a log collapse, splinters like fireflies.

'You gonna use that, Jo?'

'Depends what it's competing with. That's the stock answer. I'd love us to use it, wonderful cameo, but it might just wind up getting saved for the out-takes programme when it's all over.' Jo spins her chair to face the full bank of screens. 'Tomorrow's opener goes like this: first half atmos and introduction of residents, and the core of the second half has to be the elder-wood sequence. Some of the shots of Eloise's face before Cindy comes in – that really was magic. The kind of fear nobody can fake.'

'I figured maybe you'd want me to get Eloise telling the story of the witch's house. I was gonna—'

'No need. We've shot a sequence of her at the cottage – didn't you know that?'

'No I didn't. Like the rest of the background, I just wrote it up and handed it in. I know I'm only the researcher, but I'm starting to feel kind of resentful about all the stuff I haven't been told about. Like half of this was going on behind my back.'

'Only half? Hell, Grayle, we all feel that. It's a totally paranoid industry. Don't let it get to you, OK?'

'Sure.'

'Anyway, we bought some local news clips of firemen poking around in the smoky ruins of the witch's cottage after the blaze.

And Eloise with her commemorative sign, raging about the hunting set, looking like she's completely lost it. Performing her Alison Cross song in a field. So quite a nice package on the backstory.'

She tells Grayle a senior director called Mike is already at work on the Eloise thread. They're loving how it all comes back to fire. Mike will be following this angle all week.

'Ozzy give you a nice out, with the line about getting carried out on the bier?' Grayle says.

'Yeah, I really like that. Ozzy knows what he's doing. Could've been scripted.'

Jo comes out of her chair, offering Grayle a cigarette to take outside. Grayle declines. Jo tells her Leo wants to have Helen Parrish telling her Diana story tonight for the Sunday programme.

'Maybe we could use the fireside sequence with Cindy there. At the end, just before we go live. Unless we have an embarrassment of riches. The angle with Parrish is whether she dares to believe. Whether she trusts her own senses. Is she going to come down on one side or sit on the...?'

'Rusty fender?'

'Ha! Get some sleep, Grayle.'

'What time you want me in the morning?'

'Twelve will do. We don't plan to do much by daylight.'

Under a sparse but spiky rain, Grayle goes back to her room in one of the less-luxurious pop-ups, all lined up like outsize bathing huts. Strips and washes and puts on her ten-year-old, long T-shirt with the cabalistic Tree of Life down the front – relic of a previous life.

Walks to the window. Gazing out over the TV city that never sleeps, she sees, in the middle distance, what can only be Jordan Aspenwall pulling his bier up from the house. He would've had to wait until everyone was in bed before building up the fire, installing the fireguards, making sure all was well. As well as it could be.

Long hours for Jordan. She has questions to ask him and wouldn't mind getting dressed again, but this doesn't seem like a good time.

She wonders how it affects him, being called a yokel and a troll, knowing this will be on TV tomorrow night. Waits for him to come past but he doesn't. Flattening her face to the window, she finally locates him sitting on the tail of the bier, parked on the edge of an area lit by security lamps which, she guesses, must be overlooking his beloved knot garden.

44

KP

MARCUS GRIPS THE metal shade of Anderson's old black Anglepoise for warmth. The heating went off hours ago. In the heat of discovery, he didn't notice, but now pertinent facts are emerging more infrequently and, at two a.m., he's cold.

Not often he's still around at this time. The old night nurse, Anderson, often prowls the early hours, claiming she can get more done when he's out of the way. Now she's in the kitchen making more bastard cocoa, or possibly tea to tempt him out of here.

But he doesn't want to go, leaving the friends of Farmer Lucas still in hiding.

Bastards.

His desk is cleared of all but the book, *Annals of Winchcombe and Sudeley*, and his computer. Not much you can't discover now in cyberland, if you have the patience, but these are not important people.

Like hell they're not.

Malcolm's sitting by his chair, bony head on his left thigh. Malcolm's unsettled by all this.

'Ten minutes,' Marcus tells him. 'Then we'll go, and you can piss at your leisure all over the streets of Broadway.'

Lucas, Lucas, Lucas…

Too common a name. What were this man's motives in the first instance? He think there might be money in a dead queen?

All Marcus has found out so far is that, in the latter half of the eighteenth century, this Lucas appeared to have farmed land at Sudeley Castle, probably living at the castle lodge, all of it owned at the time by Lord Rivers, whoever he was. The castle, on which Parr had spent much of her bequest from Henry VIII, had been wrecked during the English Civil War, left derelict, continuing to decay during Rivers's time. Likewise the chapel in the grounds where Parr now lies in her showpiece tomb, fashioned as recently as Victorian days.

Whether the original tomb was trashed by Roundheads or was just not built to last doesn't seem to have been reliably recorded.

However…

In the summer of the year 1782, the earth in which Qu. K. P. lay inter'd. was removed and at the depth of about two feet (or very little more) her leaden coffin or chest was found quite whole, and on the lid of it, when well cleaned, there appeared a very bad though legible inscription of which the under written is a close copy

VIth and last wife of King Henry the VIIIth 1548.

This is from a 1783 account attributed to a man called Brooks, apparently an eyewitness to what happened at Sudeley the previous year, someone official. Marcus looks at the drawing of what Anderson thought looked like a longcase clock with small door that opened to a face that was a human face.

Mr Jno. Lucas (who occupied the land of Lord Rivers whereon the ruins of the chapel stand) had the curiosity to rip up the top of the coffin, expecting to discover within it only the bones of the dec'ed, but to his great surprise found the whole body wrapp'd in 6 or 7 seer cloths of linen, entire and *uncorrupted*, although it had lain there upwards of 230 years. His unwarrantable curiosity led him also to make an incision through the seer cloths which covered one of the arms of the corps, the flesh of which at that time was white and moist. I was very much displeased at the forwardness of Lucas who of his own head opened the coffin.

Marcus has read it four times. Seems bizarre that Parr was originally given such a cursory burial and then ignored by later owners of the castle.

As for the condition of the body after over two hundred and thirty years encased in lead, with just the earth below it, this is the level of preservation normally only associated with the remains of saints.

In the *Annals*, first published in 1877, he finds a poem attributed to a Mrs Clara Payne.

> In Sudeley's ruin'd chapel, lo! 'twas there!
> Royal Katherine's neglected tomb they found,
> More than two centuries had pass'd while here,
> Reposed her corpse within the hallow'd ground.
>
> Yet time had not her lineaments effaced,
> She seem'd as slumb'ring in Death's tranquil sleep—
> For perfect might her features then be traced,
> So well in death, their form of life they keep.

Even more remarkable considering a report made to the Society of Antiquaries in 1787 recording that the spot where Parr lay in her shallow grave had been used for the keeping of rabbits which 'made holes and scratched very indecently about the Royal Tomb'.

There's also a tradition of an ivy berry falling into the opened coffin and a subsequent inspection revealing an ivy wreath around the head of the Queen.

However, Brooks seems to have returned to Sudeley for another look at the corpse, by which time the poor woman seems to have been, not unexpectedly, in a state of considerable putrefaction. The smell makes Brookes's son, who was with him this time, 'quite sick'.

Hardly surprising when you read about the lead coffin being opened several times by then.

'Bloody tourist attraction,' Marcus tells Anderson.

She's given up waiting for him to come out, lowers a tray with a teapot, mugs, biscuits to his desk, nudging the *Annals* to one side.

'Still be here in the morning, Marcus.'

'It *is* the morning, and I don't care.' He stares down at the book as if its pages might start to putrefy before his eyes. 'Don't want to accuse anybody of something they didn't do.'

'Oh no. You widnae do that. Against your very nature.'

'But, bloody hell, Anderson…'

Reversing the book, pushing it at her.

Again in 1792, the tomb was violated; the tenant then occupying the Castle, in the most incredible manner allowing a party of inebriated men to dig a fresh grave for the coffin. The details of their work are too dreadful to give or dwell upon; but the tradition lingers in Winchcombe that each one of the Bacchanalian band met with an untimely and horrible end.

'Probably bullshit, the last bit,' Marcus says. 'All the same…'

'If you're thinking what I'm thinking you're thinking…'

'As there'd be very little left on the bones by then, no, I'm not. I've found another version on the Net suggesting all they did was turn her upside down. Having a laugh. I'm thinking back to the early days after that very first opening of the lead coffin. When she was, ah, fresh and moist.'

'No.' Anderson wiping the air. 'I don't wannae hear this.'

'Abel Fishe is Lucas's neighbour. Within walking distance. Both tenant farmers. Land might even've been adjacent. Lucas was obviously fascinated by his discovery. Who does he tell first? Probably not his wife.'

'He tells his friend the notorious sex addict?'

'They didn't even have to be friends. A lot of people owed Fishe – Abel's Rent? Equally, a lot of people were shit-scared of him.'

'Marcus you are never gonnae prove—'

'I'm not a historian.' Marcus slams the flat of a hand on the desk, making the tray rattle. 'I don't *have* to prove it.'

45

Dirty linen

GRAYLE AWAKENS TO the sound of techies tramping through the mud, a dawn chorus of techie jargon. In the window, Saturday morning is seeping in through a sky like an old brown plastered wall.

She's had maybe five hours' sleep. The image in her head, detritus of a dream, is of a blackened log in a cold hearth. She feels isolation, a sense of betrayal. As she rolls out of bed, heads for the bathroom, something is coming together, the way these things do in the cold light.

Relating to the elder. A word she's growing to hate. The viewers will watch that stuff tonight, thinking it's a trivial issue. And it would've been trivial to virtually anybody walking into the house last night, had they even noticed what was on the fire. Trivial to everybody, except for Eloise.

OK. Grayle stands barefoot on the vinyl floor. If you assume it's no accident that Eloise was the first person sent in, it suggests strongly that the wood incident was a set-up.

And if you assume it's no accident that the second person in was Cindy, well that's where it starts to smell. The whole thing is too subtle. Nobody ever asked *her*, as researcher, to find out the relevance of different types of wood when applied to fires.

In fact, you can't imagine anybody on the HGTV team coming up with that idea. Too esoteric, too far out of the box.

Only Cindy would know about it.

Cindy who went in second.

Cindy the double agent.

Grayle spins the faucet in frustration, throws cold water on her face.

In the restaurant, she sees a couple of directors and an editor who've been working all night, cutting the rushes to show to Defford before they can go catch up on some sleep. She also sees Lisa Muir coming out of the plastic tunnel after delivering breakfast to the residents.

'Oh,' Lisa says, like she's trying to remember where she's seen Grayle before. 'Er, hi.'

'Lisa…' Grayle's making no effort to hide her no-shit mood. 'I think we need to talk.'

'Oh. Do we?' Lisa's baby teeth form a vacuous smile. 'Sorry, I thought all that was over. Thought I was just being paid to serve meals and things, now. Am I wrong?'

Grayle spots someone beckoning her from the doorway. Jo Shepherd, wearing what looks like army kit. She sighs.

'I'll catch you later, Lisa. Don't leave town.'

Lisa smiles at her like she's some faded old person whose significance is waning fast, then walks away with a toss of the hair – something Grayle can't do any more. Why is Lisa behaving younger than she is?

'You'd better come and look at this,' Jo says.

They're alone in the live gallery amongst paper cups and illicit cigarette butts. Jo brings up a hard-disk menu.

'Just in. This morning's rushes. We were interested to see the individual residents' reaction, waking up in the house. Mostly, nothing significant. *Except*… OK, look at this, tell me what you think.'

Ozzy Ahmed's room. Room two, turn right at the top of the back stairs. Plain walls, but lumpy stone underneath, deep-set window with the view-concealing boards.

A bell dinging, the bedside light coming on, an arm emerging from the duvet with an extended, mocking finger. Jo flicks forward to Ozzy standing by the side of the bed, wearing red shorts, a small paunch hanging over the waist. No personal mic. He walks over to the door, stares at it then tries the handle, but the door remains closed. There's a key in the lock. Ozzy bends over, seems to be turning the key. Opens the door. Closes it, pulls on the handle. Scratches his head, his face serious. Stands still for quite some time, before turning back into the room. Seems to remember the camera, looks up into the wrong corner and smiles.

Then he goes into the bathroom.

Grayle shrugs.

'What was that about?'

'Don't know. It was as if he thought someone was trying to get into his room in the night. Out of interest, I got one of the guys to flip through the dark hours in Ozzy's room. No sound from him, no sound of anybody messing with the door.'

'He's not laughing, is he?' Grayle says. 'But then, deadpan's his thing.'

'It's not deadpan either.' Jo plays it back. 'Watch his face. Not fear, but it's certainly consternation. Like he's thinking, Is somebody winding me up.' She stops the recording. 'OK, we'll leave that. Here's Ashley, not too long ago.'

They watch Ashley Palk as she bends over her bed, in her silky nightdress, picking up the edge of one of the pillows between finger and thumb. Disdain on her face as she pulls the pillow over the edge of the bed, lets it fall to the bedside rug, shudders, scowls.

Grayle turns to Jo.

'What's that on it?'

'Stain. You can't see it clearly. When Palk was up and about, we sent Lisa up to bring it down. Carefully. I've seen it. It's faded now – not as dark as it looks here, but it was definitely there.'

'A stain on the pillow.'

'In an indentation.'

'She reported this?'

'When she went downstairs, Helen was there. Palk's like, had *your* bedding been washed? Claiming she didn't notice it last night – early this morning – because she was too tired. But oh, how disgusting. How *cheap* of them. And yes, she's right, it would have been a pretty bloody cheap trick. If it hadn't been a new pillowcase, fresh from the wrapping.'

'You're sure about that?'

'We got the housekeepers on the phone.'

The housekeepers are a company, based in Cheltenham, on 24-hour call. They're booked to come in every day. Grayle figures they don't recycle old bedding. Jo grimaces.

'They were quite annoyed. Like their hygiene standards were being questioned. All the pillowcases are new. Leo's wondering what we do next. Send it for analysis?'

'I'm guessing you wouldn't find anything unusual. Nothing foreign to the room. Nothing you couldn't scrape out of a dusty corner.'

'You encountered this kind of thing before?'

'Well, similar. It's never, like, moondust or anything. What's Palk saying?'

'Nothing specific. She's just disgusted at having slept on it.'

'On what? How's she describe it?'

'As a dirty pillow.'

'Where it looks like a man's unclean head has lain. That mentioned?'

'You said it. She didn't.'

'But is that what it looked like?'

Grayle feeling the questions being ripped out of her.

'I've only seen it on here,' Jo says, 'but yes, apparently it did. Like a man with dirty hair had lain there and rolled his head from side to side. But I don't want even to *think* about that.'

'Anyone know apart from Helen?'

'She won't say anything. But think if it had been Eloise?'

'Nothing disturbed Eloise?'

'Full night's sleep, it looked like. Like everyone else, far as we can tell.'

On several monitors, Grayle watches the residents gathering in the dining hall, summoned by bells: Ashley Palk with a cardigan around her shoulders, helping herself to toast, Eloise searching for muesli, Herridge and Sebold doing the full English. Ozzy Ahmed sitting alone with a coffee.

The place is a hotel again. Grayle feels a pressure – to say something, do something. Let in some hard daylight.

'OK. Jo, you need to tell me. Is someone doing this? Has Defford hired somebody, like he's hired Cindy, as insurance? Is stuff getting messed up deliberately. Is there a game plan?'

Jo stands up, walks out, hauling her tote bag after her. Doesn't speak until they're outside, like you don't diss God in the temple. The sun is palely visible in the brownish sky, like an old coin in the sand at the bottom of a wishing well. Jo lights up a cigarette, gazing out over the site.

'I've never worked with him before. But he doesn't have a reputation for sharp practice, or Channel 4 wouldn't touch him. On the other hand, I agree you don't go into something like this without fallbacks.'

'But he hasn't told you about anything.'

'All I know is about Cindy, because it was my job to set him up.'

'So Defford could, far as you know, have other deals going with other residents?'

'Anything's possible, but I can't see it. Everybody informing on each other, it would just make a farce of the whole project. Let's not ignore the other possibility which is that Palk did it herself.'

'Messed up her pillow?'

'When you think about it, they all want *Big Other* to be a massive success, attract record viewing figures, re-fire their careers. And if that means helping it along the way…'

'Palk's an arch-sceptic. A *professional* sceptic.'

'So she lets us build this up into a spooky head-on-a-pillow situation and, towards the end of the week, she's saying, You suckers, how easily you fell for my little scam.'

'You really think Palk would do that?'

'I'm not ruling it out, Grayle.'

'OK, yeah, it's possible.'

Now she thinks about it, you look back over Palk's lectures and her pieces on YouTube, it was all acerbic stuff at one time. No leeway given; anyone so much as sent their kids to Sunday school was a hopeless crank. But not here, where even the condescending smile's been less in evidence. Grayle thinks of the Antichrist, Richard Dawkins. One day it's all withering scorn, then he's describing himself as a secular Christian, who loves the liturgy, just a shame about there having to be a God. That other guy, de Botton, playing the same game. And, to a sceptic, it *is* a game.

What a goddamn can of worms this is.

'Leo's calling a meeting about it, anyway,' Jo says. 'How we air the dirty linen, as it were, without appearing to declare an opinion. At some stage today you'll be talking to Palk in the chapel. You'll be told what to ask. I'm just forearming you'

'Thanks.'

Walking all around it.

Hands in coat pockets, Grayle walks all around the TV city, past the truck with the satellite dish, around the pop-up hotels, out towards the woods where Harry Ansell hanged himself. There's a partially-collapsed drystone wall, the boundary re-inforced by a wire fence, and the trees the other side: larch, oak and elder – ubiquitous, she's seeing it everywhere this morning, with the grooves, the leaning branches, like they were all bowed by the weight of Judas Iscariot.

Above it all, the sun is a lustrous bubble. Like the eyes of the...

Did she *see* that? Those egg-white eyes, as the head swung?

Did the head swing? Did it? Or does your mind just make these moments meld? You hear about a hanging, and you gather it into the sickening mix, out of which false memories spawn.

But under the surface scum, there are small moments of actuality. This is how it happens. It isn't Amityville. Nobody dies, no animals are hurt in the making of this haunting. It's about small things: the wrong wood, a soiled pillow, stone demons in your dreams.

In a hip pocket of her jeans, the cellphone rings; she fumbles it out, stares into its screen, doesn't recognize the number.

She wraps an arm around a fence post.

'Underhill.'

An echoey ambience.

Miss Underhill, the voice will say. *Harry Ansell. I think you left a message for me.*

But then nothing. Somebody misdialled. She loses the call.

Clouds are closing the sun's cold eye when the cell goes again.

Jo says, 'Grayle, can you get back here?'

Trying for clipped and businesslike, not making it.

46

Guilty

'ON HIS WAY there now.'

Jo standing by the reality-gallery truck, holding the door open with one hand, the other pushing the air like she's sweeping Grayle in.

'This is Defford's idea?'

'Soon as he saw the rushes, he's demanding we pull Ahmed into the chapel before he talks to anyone else. In case he's winding us up. Leo's getting very sensitive about being pissed about.'

'It look to you like he was winding us up?'

'Doesn't matter. Go. Start off quietly, but push him a bit, you know what he's like.'

'What about Palk?'

'Palk can wait. Palk's less volatile.'

'So, like, where's he now – Leo?'

Jo points to the stable.

'And he'll be listening.'

In the booth, Grayle sits down, throws on the cans. In the monitor, Ozzy Ahmed is arranging himself in the churchy-looking chair. He's wearing his Jesus Saves hoody. He leans back, his brown eyes unmistakeably wary.

The green light comes on. Grayle clears her throat.

'How are you this morning, Ozzy?'

'OK.'

'Good night's sleep?'

'Not bad.'

She waits, counts the seconds, one, two, three. OK.

'We, uh… we all saw you doing a few odd things early this morning.'

'Thought you didn't shoot in the bathroom.'

'Ozzy, we saw you trying the bedroom door. Locking it and unlocking it.'

'So?'

'Did you not feel secure in your room?'

No reply. Ozzy's fingers are drumming on the arms of his chair, both hands.

'*Was* it a good night's sleep?'

'Nobody has a good night's sleep in a strange place. With the emphasis on *strange*.' Pause. 'Especially when some bugger's trying to make it even stranger. Know what I mean?'

'No. In what way?'

Ozzy seems to realize what his fingers are doing, how this might suggest nerves. He clasps his hands across his middle, shaking his head slowly.

'You really are buggers, aren't you?'

Grayle's about to reply and then bites it off, staring into the dome where the green light comes on. Nobody watching her from outside the booth which suggests they wouldn't know how to advise her.

On her own with this, the first real challenge. Ozzy looks into camera.

'Cat got your tongue?'

'Ozzy, what do you think we're doing to you?'

'I thought that wine last night tasted a bit bloody funny.'

Don't argue.

'You think I'm really, really stupid? This is worse than that fucking troll with the funeral cart.'

She says nothing.

'Out-of-work actors,' Ozzy says.

'Actors.'

'Only this one's got a speaking part.'

'Ozzy, who are we talking about?'

'The woman. As you know. Tell me I'm being stupid. Go on, tell me.'

'In your room?' Grayle feels a skein of sweat on her forehead. 'You saying you saw a woman in your room?'

'You know what?' He sinks down into the chair, arms folded now. 'I think I'm saying nothing without my solicitor.'

'Was that this morning or in the night?'

'I don't have to play this game.'

'I think you need to explain.'

'No comment,' Ozzy says.

And keeps saying that to whatever questions she asks until someone activates the red light and she winds it up.

Defford's waiting in the live gallery, and Max, the psychiatrist, is with him.

'Tell me what you think is happening, Grayle?' Defford says.

Bags under his eyes. Day one, the programme not even aired yet, and he has bags. For a moment Grayle feels kind of empowered.

'How'm I supposed to give you an opinion on that when *I* don't know what you're doing either.'

Jo's eyes flashing warnings. Grayle thinks, the hell with that.

'Ahmed figures you're doing something to him. I mean like, *are* you?'

'No.' Defford stands up. 'No, we aren't. It's not the purpose of this programme to mislead the residents. And you know everything you need to know to give an opinion. Why is he angry with us?'

'He obviously thinks we're playing with his head.'

'Max?'

'I'd agree.' Max is wearing a white sweatshirt that says HOUSE SHRINK. 'He either thinks that or he wants us to think he does. And it didn't look like that to me. He was very serious.'

'I was clearly getting nowhere fast,' Grayle says. 'Whatever he thinks he's seen, he doesn't wanna discuss it. He feels used. He's like you, Leo, needs to feel in control. I— Sorry I'm doing Max's job here.'

Max says, 'It doesn't take a psychiatrist to know that Ozzy also needs to occupy his stage persona. He needs to be funny. He wants us to think he's always funny – and most of the time he succeeds.'

'Not much of that in evidence this morning,' Defford says.

'You noticed that.'

'That's why we're all here. We have to react to the unexpected. So you really think he feels he saw something in his room?'

'And that makes him angry,' Max says. 'Because Ozzy's a non-believer in the paranormal, God, whatever. He looks at Eloise and he sees elements of his famous mother-in-law, and the very thought of winding up in that state... So yes, anything even faintly anomalous and he's scared. And angry, as you saw.'

'So, what's happening?' Defford sits down again, thumbs pushing into the chair's seat like he's trying to choke something. 'We need to know.'

Grayle flops into a swivel chair.

'OK, he's a pro. He knows there's a camera or two in his room. Why wasn't he playing to them?'

'As we've established,' Max says, 'he's a comedian who doesn't need a script to be funny. If he can't say anything clever, he says nothing. And he really hates being in that situation.'

Defford says, 'You think maybe he awoke, forgot what this was about? Forgot he was on camera?'

'That's a possibility. Might've been a dream. With hindsight, Grayle, you might've asked if he remembered any dreams.'

'If you wanna take over in there, Max, fine with me.'

'Thank you, but no. My sort of questions are not what Leo's looking for.'

'Too rational, huh?'

Max grins, then thinks of something else.

'It's also a possibility that the attitude of consternation that Ozzy's showing in the bedroom is actually masking some other reaction that he really doesn't *want* to show.'

'Like what?'

'Not sure I want to say, Leo. Don't have any evidence.'

'Equally, Max, we don't have time to piss about.'

'All right. Some emotions are harder to convert convincingly to anger than others. Anger, however, *is* an excellent way to smother fear.'

Grayle notices that this doesn't seem to displease Defford.

She says, 'He was checking the locks on the door. Presumably to see whether he'd locked it before he went to bed. Which he does appear to have done. Suggesting strongly that nobody came in. In the night.'

Max nods.

'That's how it looked to me.'

'You think he'd've even mentioned it, if Leo hadn't decided we should haul him into the chapel?'

'Hold on, guys.' It's Jo, watching the screens. 'I'm guessing he's about to unload something.'

The residents are gathered in the chamber. First time Grayle's seen them here in daylight. Not that there's much of that with the false wall, just a faint greening of the air beyond the candle-light. Fat candles now, in a huddle on the drinks table. Grayle realizes there's no clock in here. This could soon get seriously disorienting.

The first words she picks up are from Ashley Palk.

'And they won't admit anything?'

'Buggers.' Ozzy Ahmed sprawled in his chair. 'But at least we know where they're coming from. Won't get fooled again. As they say.'

'Not where *I* understood they were coming from.' Roger Herridge looks concerned. 'Or I wouldn't have done it. This is supposed to be a situation where we open ourselves up to the possibility of psychic phenomena. *Not* a bloody ghost train.'

In the gallery, Defford winces. A camera finds Cindy, inoffensive in a mauve twinset, adding an innocent log to the fire.

'Austin,' he says, 'do you recall dreaming at all last night?'

Ozzy stares at him.

'Meaning what?'

'In unusual circumstances, a strange and disconcerting place, dreams can be remarkably vivid.'

Ozzy looks suddenly weary.

'Yeah. Whatever.' Sinks into his grey velvet armchair, eyes closed. 'Let's call it a dream. Let's give them a get-out. Benefit of the doubt, man.' Opens one eye to peer at Cindy. 'Or whatever you are.'

'Austin, could I perhaps ask you… how well could you see this woman?'

'Dunno.'

'What was she like? All I'm thinking is… well, dead of night, with the lights out, no windows… how would you know she was there?'

'Didn't get where I am today without knowing when there's a woman in my bedroom.'

'As you're obviously not taking it seriously…'

The camera pulls back to find Roger Herridge, his face reddening. Ozzy looks up from the depths of his chair.

'Don't be a twat, Roger, I'm just not letting it get to me, all right?' He sits up. 'All right, it was a shadow. And a scent. Perfume. Really, really wouldn't like to think it was you, Cindy. Guilty.'

Silence.

'It's a perfume. By Gucci. Guilty. How would I know a thing like that? Because my wife wore it occasionally, when we first started going out. Never forget that one, do you?'

He's silent for a while, his dark brown eyes uncertain, like a dog wondering if it should go for someone's throat, Grayle thinks.

'Not one I wear,' Cindy says softly.

'Anyway.' Ozzy sits up. 'Obviously not the first time I've dreamt about it,' he says. 'Guilty.'

'God,' Grayle says.

She looks at Jo, then Defford and, finally, at Max.

'First he's accusing us of trying to mess with his head, putting someone into his room. Then, when Cindy plants the idea it could've been a dream he hardly argues at all. Takes the easiest way out. What's that say, Max?'

Max is running his tongue over his upper front teeth. Quiet in the gallery, quiet in the house.

'Not an easy one, Grayle.'

'Only, I'm no shrink but what it says to me is Ozzy's been going through all the motions in an effort to convince himself that he didn't experience anything remotely paranormal last night.'

'And failing,' Max says.

47

Shrine

THEY WERE MAKING a documentary about the cult of Diana. And it *was* a cult, in the original sense. She was a goddess – much more of one than any Hollywood film star, because she was the real thing: the fairy-tale princess. And then the fallen angel. That wonderfully sordid death in a tunnel with the boyfriend and the international paparazzi buzzing around on their motorbikes like a cloud of stinging insects.

'Horribly cinematic,' Helen Parrish says.

She tells it so well, sitting on a cushion at the edge of the hearth. Probably pieces of her old TV news scripts coming through.

'I didn't cover the funeral, of course – wasn't grand enough. Wasn't enough of a name.'

Rhys Sebold palms his stubble. He hasn't shaved since he came into the house.

'You a bit pissed off about that, Helen?'

'No. Of course not. You get used to it. I knew they'd offer me one of the menial jobs, doorstepping the fans who'd travelled hundreds of miles with their tributes and their sandwiches. "What did Diana mean to you?" Couldn't face that. Threw a sickie – two days of migraine. First time I'd ever done that. The documentary was years later and that was my idea. Didn't think anyone would go for it, but…'

She pauses for a sip of wine, her glass blood-red in the fire-light. Ghost-story time, the first one and so nicely done, Grayle's thinking. The nest of shivering candles on the drinks table, all those in the overhead hoop extinguished. Jordan did this while the residents were eating next door, arranging chairs around the fire. Helen was called into the chapel to be told she was first.

It's only seven o'clock but feels like the other side of midnight.

Cindy says, 'Did you have much to do with her? Diana?'

'Oh yeah.' Helen's smile is tilted. 'We all did. I mean the regulars. I don't know whether she really did like the media or whether she just chose to like them because she thought Charles and The Family preferred to view them through bullet-proof smoked glass. Whether she only courted us to piss them off I still don't know. But, yes, there were days when she was your mate.'

Grayle thinks of Trinity, what Lisa the scullery maid said. She notices Eloise turning away, looking bored by Helen's cascading memories.

'You'd show up and she'd give you that cute look over the shoulder, as if she's about to roll her eyes, *here we go again*. She liked the photographers best – the long-serving royal snappers. Tabloid guys especially. She knew what they wanted and she always made sure they got it. And when she wanted to be photographed in a particular way, with a particular person, to piss off Charles, she'd give them the nod and they'd be there for her.'

'All true then,' Ozzy says.

'Mostly. We had a few short discussions, she and I. She was opening a new school for kids with learning difficulties down in South Wales and she said to me, "Don't you get fed up with this, Helen, day in day out?"'

'And you said?'

'Well, I wasn't going to say, Don't *you* get fed up? I told her I enjoyed basking in the reflected glamour, and she said "liar", and gave me a little punch on the arm. You rather glowed when she did something like that. I mean, nobody royal ever *touched* you in those days, for heaven's sake, not even some duchess on the fringe of the action. I'm a hard-bitten hack, and I've still got that jacket in my wardrobe. Stupid, isn't it?'

'Little circles, Helen, where Diana's knuckles connected?'

Ozzy's mood has lightened.

'Don't knock it, my boy,' Roger Herridge says, 'If she'd touched *your* arm you'd still be having sexual fantasies about it.'

Ozzy opens his mouth like he's about to say something involving flowers then shuts it again and shakes his head with a little puff of breath.

'So you were shooting at Althorp,' Cindy prompts. 'The seat of the Spencers.'

In the live gallery, Grayle hears Leo Defford mumbling something about wishing Cindy wouldn't add pertinent details for the viewers.

They've allowed two hours for this. Should be ample.

It will go out in the second programme, Sunday. By then the story will have been released to the press for Monday's papers. Doesn't matter what Parrish says, Defford told the team at tonight's briefing, she's talking about it for the first time.

'Could be looking at a couple of front page leads – *Star*, *Sun*... *Mail* even?'

'*Mail* will blurb it on the front,' Grayle forecast, 'but the story will be inside. It's no splash, except maybe for the Star, but it has legs. I guess even the *Guardian* will use it someplace, having started the whole thing off with that diary piece which may or may not have gotten Helen fired.'

Surprising herself at how well she's picked up on the psychology of the British popular press.

Now, sitting behind Defford and Jo in the live gallery, she listens and knows this is on the level. Whichever of them sneers, Helen will ride it. The way only the truth can. Or the *perceived* truth.

Helen says. 'Althorp, yes. Where she'd been buried about five years earlier. There's a lake and an island with this little white classical-looking temple on it. A real shrine.'

Grayle thinking of Katherine Parr at Sudeley.

'This day I was doorstepping people. It's probably Britain's most recently established place of pilgrimage. I saw a woman in a wheelchair. Knew what I was after. Wanted her to say she believed Diana could heal her, you know?'

Eloise turning round, showing interest at last.

In the gallery, Defford leaning across to Grayle.

'Good-good?'

Grayle nods. Helen being a professional, earning her money, displaying her human side. Giving value. Also, it will make people like her. On TV she seems to have come over as kind of stiff and proper. That's the consensus, anyway. Maybe it's what's expected of royal correspondents.

Ashley Palk says, 'So this was what? Scene-setting? I'm guessing you were more than just presenter?'

'I was directing, too. Indy production for the BBC. Yes, you're right. Near the top of the programme we needed some short vox pops to demonstrate the kind of following that Diana still had, even so long after her death. We talked to the woman in the wheelchair for about five minutes. She obviously knew what we were looking for, but all she said was, "You do get a sense that she's here, don't you? I think she'd want to be here for us. She wouldn't like to think we'd all come for nothing." And I remember wishing I *had* been here for the funeral, instead of pretending to be sick because I didn't want to be a minion.'

Helen looks around the room, briskly shakes her hair.

'I don't *get* headaches, you see. Don't drink much these days, but even when I did I didn't get hangovers. Yet I had one that day – maybe too much sun, but it felt like I was being paid back for inventing a migraine. We weren't getting any great vox pops, so I walked away through the crowds to try and think of something. A question to set them off. The atmosphere was quite heavy by then, sultry. The surface of the lake like brass.'

'And like a halo over the island?' Ozzy Ahmed says wistfully.

Bringing Eloise half out of her chair, hissing.

'*Shut the fuck up, you moron.*'

'Yes,' Herridge says. 'Let's hear this.'

Helen shrugs.

'I'm quite happy to stop. Been quite a tiring day. Surprising how exhausting it is watching people trying to revive their crumbling careers.'

Delivered with such genuine weariness that nobody says a word.

'Helen,' Cindy says softly. 'Please go on.'

Helen leans back against the stonework, tilting her head so she's looking above all theirs, addressing the dim beams.

'I'm not going to do the build-up. There was a woman. Standing with her back to me, facing the lake. She was wearing an ankle-length fitted dress. Cream-coloured with a narrow brown diagonal stripe. She didn't turn around, but I heard her voice, very clearly. She just said, "Hello, Helen, how're you these days?"'

Helen leaves a silence, knows the cameras need to record reactions. They won't want to spoil this, Grayle thinks, so they'll probably go for placid Cindy rather than sardonic Ozzy.

'Oh, it was her voice. No question. That light, faintly collo-quial tone she used sometimes, talking to the press when she was in a good mood. "*Hello*, Helen…" not "Oh, *hi*, Helen," no drawly stuff. Nobody else there. It was tremendously still. Like a cocoon of silence. So every word was distinct.'

Ashley Palk says gently, 'Was the voice in your head? Were there other people nearby who might've…?'

'There *were* other people. Just a few, not a crowd. If you're asking did they react as if they'd seen something, I don't remember anything like that. But I know it wasn't like the way a producer's voice sounds in your earpiece. I don't remember it as being in my head. I just… it's like I was in another world, another place. Or rather *we* were. Her and me. It was her place, her world – she wasn't in mine.'

'Like… a spirit place?'

'No. A kind of… middle place. That was also Althorp. Another Althorp.'

'Did it feel good?'

This is Eloise abandoning her chair, dragging the cushion down to the stone flags.

'Don't know,' Helen says. 'Didn't think about it that way. It wasn't a religious experience, if that's what you're asking, except in the way the lake and the sky seemed to have become one place. She turned around. I thought there was mist... Her eyes were looking towards me, but... through me, somehow. And I realized it was a veil. You know the veil she wore with her wedding dress, covering her face so she looked... shy. Demure. Something like that. And she was still talking, very quickly, as though she needed to get something over to me. Something she needed to say, but her voice was getting fainter, and I saw that she was fading back until she was just a... a paleness. I don't recall what she said. I can hear her saying it, in that confiding, between-you-and-me voice, but I don't know what it was, except for these four words, over and over: "nobody can see it, nobody can see it." And then gone.'

Helen shrugs. Nobody speaks.

'I mean me,' Helen says. 'I was gone.'

Next thing she knows she's lying on a brocaded sofa. They tell her she fainted and the St John Ambulance guys carried her back to the house. Hot day. Too many people. Hallucination. Mirage. Her cameraman has some shots of her passing out. Never been shown on TV, those pictures. But a couple of visitors caught it on their videocams, and they've been on YouTube. Grayle's not seen them, never thought to look. Unbelievably remiss of her.

'Slipping to my knees,' Helen's saying. 'Not gracefully, not how you imagine someone fainting. And then sideways on the grass at the edge of the lake, frock up around my waist. Undignified.'

Grayle jumps, something touching her left knee. It's Jo's hand reaching behind her seat with a scrap of paper, one of those Post-it notes. Grayle takes it, reads: *Check mobile when poss. She crumples it.*

Ashley's saying, 'You've been very honest, Helen, very fluent, obviously. You've explained what you think happened. You've disclosed that you had a headache, that it wasn't going well, that you weren't getting the interviews you wanted.'

'Oh, we were getting them, we just weren't getting any surprises. Nothing that would make people sit up and take notice. No wow factor. No miracle and wonder.'

'That must've been alarming.'

'Just disappointing.'

'Would you say you were… close to a minor panic attack?'

Helen looks wry.

'I don't get panic attacks, Ashley. I'm a professional. I get faintly irritated attacks.'

Ashley laughs, approaching from another angle.

'Diana was very much in your head that day.'

'She was in everybody's head. It was her shrine.'

And so it goes on. Helen never departs from what she sees as the plain facts. She makes no attempt to attach any greater significance to them. Asked if she thinks she's psychic, she says she has no idea what that means.

Seeing Ashley Palk about to say something, she gives her a direct look, pre-empting it.

'Well *of course* it could have been in my mind. It obviously was in my mind because nobody else saw her. But does that negate it as an extra-normal experience? What do you want me to say?'

Grayle watches Cindy sitting next to Helen on the hearth, no cushion. Can't be comfortable.

'It could indeed be in your mind,' he says. 'But what put it there? What made it so vivid? So *separate*. Should we perhaps consider the effects of the atmosphere of the place itself, a place subjected to such floods of emotion… all with one focus.'

Palk sighs at this.

'And the idea that something of her remains there,' Cindy says. 'As well as her final resting place, it's her ancestral home. An old family. Ancestors are important.'

340

'Only,' Palk says patiently, 'to a professed shaman.'

Doing her smile. Cindy takes no notice.

'And what happens when all these powerful elements connect, like wiring? Have you ever fainted before, Helen? Anywhere? The stench of bodies in some war zone?'

Helen looks annoyed.

'If I'd ever fainted in a war zone, Cindy, it would have been the last war-zone I was ever sent to. Men were allowed to pass out in those days without damage to their careers, women never. No, that was the first and only time I've ever fainted.'

'You were losing confidence in the programme,' Ashley says. 'If it gets off to a bad start—'

Helen raises both hands, as if in benediction.

'All right, you've explained everything for me, Ashley. I'm not going mad. It was a hot day and I was getting stressed-out. It happens. And I probably only saw Diana *after* I passed out, although I remember it as being before. How's that? Is that OK with you?'

Ashley Palk makes no reply. Looks, for once, lost for words. Grayle's hearing Ozzy Ahmed earlier today. *Let's call it a dream. Let's give them a get-out.* Does Helen know she's reacting to a challenge in almost the same quiescent way? Does Ozzy recognize…?

She looks for him but he isn't there. Looks around the semi-circle of chairs, the firelit faces and his isn't one of them, and there's an empty chair. Roger Herridge is agreeing with Cindy; he knows Althorp well, talks about the almost magical serenity of that setting, as Grayle leans forward to tap Jo on the shoulder.

Defford catches the movement and turns at the same time, Grayle waving a hand at the screens.

'Any chance we can get a wide shot? Sorry, but I can't see Ozzy.'

'Can't…' Jo glancing rapidly from screen to screen. 'Can't be far away…'

'We're supposed to be watching him, for Chrissakes.'

A few seats away, one of the directors gets the point of this, looks at Defford, who nods, and then the guy's pushing switches, wrapping cans around his head, talking low-voiced into a mic. Within seconds there are wide shots, two of them, one from above, but the light's not good in this one, especially with several candles gone out, pushed off the table as if by someone hurrying past, lying on the flags like old bones, one rolling under a chair as they watch.

The other picture's from the false wall, and it's brighter but all blurs at first, vague shapes trying to coalesce. On other screens, movement, lights, the screech of chair legs, shouts. You can see all that on other monitors, but Grayle doesn't take her eyes off the rubbery blurs as the camera tries to make sense of them.

'...uck's the matter with him?'

Rhys, big voice distorting.

'Leave him.' Roger Herridge. 'You don't know what...'

Then the voices are dusted away by a close whisper.

'*Bleeding.*'

Not a wide shot any more. No more than the width of a face.

Ozzy's face so close to the false wall it's like he's trying to deliver an open-mouth kiss to the camera lens.

He backs off, eyes wide and glassy.

'She was bleeding.'

'Tears,' Grayle breaths. 'Jesus, God, look, there are tears in his eyes.'

Defford's on his feet, his face looks paler than his hair, and he's impossibly excited.

'Put out a call for Max.'

'*She was bleeding!*'

Ozzy swaying, then down on his knees, sobbing.

48

Dirty lantern

THE ATMOSPHERE IN the live gallery ought to be electric and, in a way – not a good way – it is. It's like they got all the wiring wrong and nobody noticed until now.

Mutiny? Is that the word? Whatever, he's ignored it. Ignored the bell. Ignored the Matthew Barnes recording, repeated twice: *'Mr Ahmed to the chapel, please.'* If it wasn't just a recording and he wasn't just a hired voice, Barnes would be screaming obscenities through the wall by now.

Glancing from face to face in the gallery, Grayle notices how close trepidation is to anticipation, excitement to dread.

Leo Defford and Jo Shepherd are watching a monitor screen featuring Ozzy Ahmed curled like some kind of crustacean on his bed, face hidden by a pillow and the arm wrapped around it.

'What are we supposed to do about this?' Jo says, a little shrill. 'What can we do? Dock his pay? Would he care?'

'End of the day,' Grayle says, 'we need him more than he needs us.'

'Never a good starting position,' Defford admits. 'Someone told me, play safe, stick to losers. The slippery slope, looking down. I laughed.'

He digs the fingertips of both hands into hair that might, after all, be prematurely white. Less than two hours from the first transmission. That, at least, is safe: a full recorded programme put together, with the emergency extra hour added. No way can they go live after midnight, not now. Events already have overtaken them.

Leo Defford – oh God, how dangerous is this? – is *one step behind*.

'Looking on the bright side,' Jo says, 'one way or the other, it will be magnificent telly. Eventually.'

'Not,' Defford says heavily, 'if the guy turns out to be a basket case, emotionally flaky or drunk... This programme is not about the pity of somebody coming apart.'

He makes an executive decision.

'Get Parrish in.'

At first, Helen Parrish looks oddly appropriate in the chapel, priestly in her grey cowl-neck sweater. They've altered the lighting so that you can see the pews behind her Gothic chair, receding into shadow. But, if Defford's looking for stability from Helen, her hollow-eyed half-smile is not encouraging.

'I don't know that I can help you much with Ahmed. Didn't really see how it happened.'

'We'll get to that,' Grayle says. 'Helen, after you finished your story you seemed drained.'

'Mmm.'

'But relieved?'

'That I'd finally unloaded it, yes. When you've been carrying something around for so many years...'

'When Ashley suggested the whole Diana incident was likely to be more about your own emotional state than, say, the location, you didn't seem inclined to argue.'

'No, I wasn't.'

'Why was that?'

Helen thinks about it over a long, tired breath.

'Didn't seem worth it. I suppose I didn't care what she thought. Or anybody. Just glad to have told the story, in a very public way. I could argue all night and it wouldn't alter Ashley's world view. What's the point? She is what she is.'

'When you say—'

'Doesn't matter how anybody else explains it, who believes it and who doesn't. It's all just opinions. Scepticism, atheism – they're just opinions, they're not based on any kind of empirical knowledge. Anyway… it's out there now for the crows to pick at. Joined all the other ghost stories out there.'

Helen looks sad but somehow not unhappy. She's on a different level. Grayle's fascinated. This is the programme doing what it needs to do.

'Helen, earlier, when you were getting started, Ozzy made a smart remark, and—'

'Smart remarks. There you go again.'

'You still feel that?'

'About Ahmed? Hmm. Not sure. Bit of an eye-opener, wasn't it?'

'What did you see?'

'Saw there was someone missing from the circle, and then I saw him at the bottom of the room, and he seemed agitated. I thought his shoulders were shaking. Looked like he'd just got up without a word and started walking towards something. Not looking where he was going, knocking some of the candles off the table. And of course they went out, reducing visibility even more. And then I saw that he was genuinely crying. Thought it was laughter at first, but he doesn't laugh much, does he? Not his style.'

'You think he saw something. In the room.'

'Perhaps he did. I don't know. Or maybe something he saw or even something one of us said brought back some aspect of his own history that he'd buried.'

'Like what?'

'I don't know anything about his past. *Something* must've broken up his marriage, and I'd be surprised if it was just his mother-in-law jokes. Makes you…'

Helen goes quiet.

'Go on.'

'It does rather make you wonder if there isn't something in this house – or what we're doing here – that opens up doors into your subconscious mind. When I was describing what happened at Althorp, I really felt I was there. All the colours were alive – green and blue and white and so vibrant I wondered if all of you could somehow…'

Helen's shaking her head, hands raised.

'I think I should shut up.'

'No, keep going, Helen, please.'

Through the windows of the booth Grayle sees rapt faces in the reality gallery watching her from both sides. If this programme has half the impact on the viewers…

'Were you at any stage wondering if maybe you'd brought Diana herself into—?'

Stop. Don't put words into…

'When Ahmed was mumbling to himself,' Helen says, 'he was talking about a woman.'

'Bleeding.'

'Yes. Bleeding. I was thinking about Diana in the crash in the tunnel in Paris, but then I would, wouldn't I? Had he entered my… field of vision? I don't know how these things…'

'None of us do.'

'Oh God,' Helen says, appalled, recovering her old self, 'please edit this, or I'll never work again.'

'… but we have to channel our thinking according to the logic of the situation,' Defford's saying, back in gear now as Grayle slips into the live gallery. 'If anybody saw anything, the chances are it wasn't anything to do with Diana. If we're looking for something that answers to the logic of this house, that's not it. Jo, let's open up a storyline here. Get somebody moving on it.'

Grayle slumps into her chair staring at him. It's like she can see his aura, and it's brightening again, a lurid yellow.

'You're thinking Trinity, aren't you, Leo?'

'I'm thinking that's definitely got to be something worth following.'

'Blood,' Grayle says. 'Abortion? That didn't even happen here? And wasn't it pre-empted, anyway, by a heart attack?'

He doesn't reply. Grayle thinks of contagion. Something happens and Helen Parrish thinks of Diana and Defford thinks of Trinity Ansell and Ashley Palk thinks of the power of suggestion.

'I think I need the bathroom,' Grayle says.

In the nearest portaloo, she switches on her phone. First chance she's had to check out Jo's message.

> Get rid of this when you've read it. My job's on the line
> here. Ten minutes into transmission go round the back of
> the house. Gate into walled garden will be open. So will the
> chapel. Go in.

Ten minutes in. When Defford's watching the first programme go out. When nobody will see someone walking round to the walled garden and the chapel. When nobody will miss her. What's *this* about?

Outside, the wind's on the rise, sending clouds scurrying across a fugitive moon. Grayle walks away from the porta-village to where she can see the house, only one corner of it lit and that dimly, like a dirty lantern.

It's not about ghosts right now, it's about people and how they react to their confinement and one another. Maybe that's all it will ever be about: seven people trapped inside the glass of a dirty lantern.

When she gets back into the stable and the live gallery, Defford and Jo and a couple of the directors are on their feet, watching the pictures. Jo glances over her shoulder.

'He's on the move, Grayle.'

'Ahmed?'

'He could be coming down.'

49

Hurt

OZZY'S IN THE doorway, standing like some introverted only child at his first party. JESUS SAVES on his chest in white, with a fish symbol.

For long moments, nobody speaks to him.

Most of them have been talking about him behind his back, for the benefit of several million viewers, but now they're embarrassed. Because what he did *was* embarrassing.

It's like the tension has frozen the screens. *It's artificial*, Grayle thinks. *It's just reality TV, for Chrissakes.*

Even Rhys Sebold says nothing – Rhys who's been defending Ozzy against the ridiculous claims that he might actually have been affected by this house. Rhys is in a black shirt open to a chained symbol that's unlikely to be religious. He looks down at his feet in patent leather then over at Ashley Palk for back-up.

In the end it's Cindy who walks over to Ozzy.

'How are you, boy? Feeling better?'

The room's brighter now, all the fat candles back on the table, lit, and a match applied to the eight stubby candles projecting from the overhead hoop. Roger Herridge did this, without asking anyone.

It's just over one hour to transmission when Ozzy clears his throat.

'I wouldn't mind telling my ghost story. If that's all right.'

It isn't all right in the gallery.

'*Shit.*'

Defford's chair is pushed back. According to the schedule, Ozzy isn't due to say his piece until tomorrow after the Helen Parrish story has broken, thus swelling the viewing figures. And now a call's come in for Defford from Channel 4. He's going to be out of the loop until after the first programme's gone out, the other side of midnight. He's going to miss the end of this, which means that he's *two* steps behind. He bends to Jo.

'Just... don't get this wrong.'

Like she can alter anything. Like any of them can. Grayle's glad when he's gone. It eases the pressure on them to try to adapt everything to what Defford calls the logic of the situation.

It's back to dirty lantern logic, now, which is no logic at all.

Ozzy says his school, up in Yorkshire, used to be a grammar school, then the poshest kind of state comprehensive. It was in an old building, late eighteenth century originally, some Victorian additions with flat-roofed 1960s projections.

It had a haunted room.

'Science lab,' Ozzy says. 'Biology.'

He's agreed to sit down, but not too near the fire. He's broken up the arrangement of chairs set up for the storytelling session and sits in the centre of the chamber, on a hard chair. His back's to the screen with its camera holes, so it's all down to the false wall mirrors and the eyes between the ceiling beams.

'I think it was only said to be haunted because it had this... skull. His name was Reg. Reg the skull. He was in this glass-fronted cupboard high up on one wall, and it was said that sometimes Reg would disappear from his cupboard and he'd be found somewhere else. Which I think actually did happen once, but that was some lads on their last day at school, having a laugh.'

Ozzy expels a little amused puff of air. In the gallery, Grayle takes Defford's vacated seat next to Jo. This is weird, it's like nothing happened earlier, like Ozzy's mind just blanked it out. What if he does have some *condition*?

'Used to be a lot of made-up stories about Reg – how he was the first school caretaker who fell off the roof, brains all over the quad, which explained the patched-up bits in his skull. So attached to the school he'd bequeathed his body to the biology department. Bollocks, obviously, but that's what the first-formers got told. And how Reg's ghost would be seen in the corridors with his rattly toolkit. There was also a complete set of human leg bones in a long drawer at the other end of the room, and another story was that other bits of Reg were hidden all over the school, and when his skull disappeared it was because he was trying to reassemble himself.'

One of the cameramen finds a close-up of Ozzy's face, sweat-free and relaxed.

'So the school was raising money for a minibus for educational trips, and me mate came up with this idea about how four of us would be sponsored to spend the night in sleeping bags in the lab… with Reg. Well, the teachers couldn't refuse, but equally they couldn't leave us alone on education authority premises all night. So one particular teacher agrees to come and check on us. He's dead now or I wouldn't be telling you this. I'm going to call him Cyril.'

Ozzy describes how they made a space in the centre of the room for the sleeping bags, and brought sandwiches and cans of Coke. One of the lads had this torch with coloured filters, and he kept shining it up on Reg so there'd be this evil-looking red skull grinning down at them.

'Or green – that was the worst. You'd go to the lav and come back and there'd be this slimy light down the side of the door. Oh – should've said – it was a full moon – we had to do it on the night of the full moon, so it wasn't much better when the torch was off. Old Reg grinning up on his shelf in a moonbeam, the black holes of his eyes. I didn't like it. Well, I was a timid kid, I'm not scared to admit that. Makes me annoyed now to think of it. Wimpy little Arab.'

Grayle wonders how recently Ozzy's kin were practising

Muslims. To her knowledge, he hasn't made any jokes about his family.

'So during the night I put off going to the lav as long as I could, but we'd drunk a lot of Coke, and in the early hours I was in agony. All the others were asleep and I couldn't hold out any longer. Got up, tried not to look at Reg. Go shuffling off down the corridor. On my way back, I encounter Cyril doing his rounds. Asks me if I'm all right. Says I'm looking a bit scared and I'm going, no I'm all right, sir, thank you, though I really didn't want to go back in the biology lab. So when Cyril asked me if I'd like a mug of hot chocolate in the staff room...'

'Oh dear.'

This is Herridge, ex-Eton or someplace like that. Ozzy gives him a look.

'Yeah right. And we go down to the staffroom, and we sit down on the big plush sofa with our mugs of chocolate, and then the fucker's all over me.' Ozzy looking up, full into camera, brown eyes full of pain. 'All over me.'

Squeezes his eyes closed.

'Dynamite, or what?' Jo whispers.

The monitor on Jo's left has Ozzy's audience, the camera finding Ashley Palk as she lifts a hand for attention.

'Ozzy, I'm not being prurient, but when you say— I mean, what did this man actually do to you? You *can* say. In fact you should.'

Ozzy hesitates then shrugs.

'Made me toss him off, Ashley.'

'And you went along with that?'

'Listen, I was scared *shitless*. I mean, already. Ghostly old Reg, you know? I was twelve! Twelve-year-olds were different back then, we didn't even take drugs. Cyril... he wasn't the gym teacher, but he played rugby with the sixth form, bought them pints down the pub. Big bloke, everybody's mate, you know the sort. And in the staffroom we were far enough away from the science labs for nobody to hear me scream.'

'You didn't report him, afterwards?'

'Easy to say that now, but you didn't back then, did you? Popular teacher, Cyril. Everybody liked him. It was like bloody Jimmy Savile groping his way round the country, and lots of people knew and not a word cos he was such a lovely bloke, so-called.'

Ozzy stands up into silence.

'And that's why I don't like ghost stories.'

In the gallery, Jo breathes in slowly.

'Media are going to be down on this like a strike force.'

The quality of light in the chamber has altered, or so it seems to Grayle. It's brighter, yet bleaker.

Rhys Sebold breaks the silence, going over to shake Ozzy's hand.

'Well done. I think your experience illustrates an important point about the way predatory paedophiles use a child's fear of the supernatural.'

'It was the other hand, actually, Rhys,' Ozzy says.

Getting some nervous laughter, but Rhys has a point to make.

'They use ghost stories, the way cults use religion.'

'Let's not go overboard,' Roger Herridge says. 'Your rather weak attempt to equate the supernatural with sexual predation says, I think, rather more about you. This man evidently was just an opportunist.'

'Given me a few nightmares, though, Roger, over the years,' Ozzy says. 'Reg and Cyril have become like an item. In my subconscious, if you like. And now Cyril's dead, just as dead as Reg… OK, I *don't* believe in the supernatural. But it still scares me. That make sense?' He sits up. 'No not scares, it *disgusts* me. Makes me go cold. Like a phobia.'

'It's a trigger,' Rhys says. 'One's become a trigger for the other. Perverted sex, perverted beliefs.'

'In which case…' Behind him, Eloise is looking entirely

unsympathetic. 'I mean, what the hell are you doing *here*? Because it's trigger after trigger, here, isn't it?'

'Maybe that's *why* he's here,' Rhys says. 'To exorcize it. I'm using that word in its most rational sense.'

Looks at Ozzy who finds a wry smile.

'If you think this guy knows me better than I know myself, you're probably right.'

'OK.' Helen Parrish raises herself up. 'So you feel better now, Ozzy? Now that it's out in the open?'

'Not sure about anything, Helen. All I think I'm saying is that you don't have to believe in something to be scared of it. Buggered if I'm going into therapy, mind.'

'Yes, sure, I get all that. But it doesn't tell us anything about the woman, does it?'

'Woman?'

'Here? In here? Over there? The woman you thought you saw? Who you thought was bleeding? Help me out here, Ozzy, I've lost the plot.'

'I don't know what you're on about.'

Grayle and Jo look at one another. A flurry of movement in the monitor, Eloise on her feet.

'Oh, you so bloody do, Ahmed! You're in total denial. I'd be *very* surprised if all you'd had over the years were dreams.'

'Oh, Elly, you're such a—'

'No!' She's standing directly in front of him. 'You can't just blank it out. You can't go on fooling yourself for ever. We're all psychic to an extent, and if you just go on hanging out with negative people like Sebold, you'll wind up an alcoholic or getting sectioned, trust me.'

'Yeah, go on,' Rhys says to Eloise, 'go for him while his defences are down. There's no such thing as psychic. There's only fraud.'

'Oh, you are such a fucking idiot, Sebold.' She spins at him. 'Big mouth, opinionated, politicized... but going nowhere. Occasionally useful for winding people up on tabloid radio, but blind to what's right in front of you. And he… *he* can go on denying it until they take him away.'

This is personal, Grayle a little scared at how fast the situation's escalating. They haven't been together two full days yet. Even on the celebrity *Big Brothers* she's seen, it usually takes over a week to reach this level of antipathy.

She watches Rhys Sebold trying to control his rage, small tightenings in his narrow face. Eloise's little fists bunched, a line of perspiration above her upper lip, like she's been made-up for some hothouse drama. Is that a moment of love–hate electric sexuality, a pulse of blue light between her and Rhys? As if everyone else in the room has felt the charge, they're all separating, a wide shot showing the diaspora. An experienced director called Lee is supervising, giving rapid instructions. A muted excitement in the gallery.

'Hang on.' Jo's pointing. 'Listen to this.'

One camera's never left Ozzy. Now Helen Parrish has pulled her chair close to his, is talking quietly to him. Ozzy's staring at the false wall, its mirrors reflecting candlelight as a blaze.

'Two way mirrors,' he's saying. 'That's what they always do on *Big Brother*, isn't it? There's a narrow walkway behind, where cameramen creep like perverts. I hate that side of it.'

'No worse than CCTV in a shopping centre,' Helen says. 'We're all under surveillance now, soon as we leave home.'

Ozzy's screwing up his eyes.

'Maybe, if you're at the right angle, you can see through a two-way mirror. See who's on the other side. Would that explain it?'

'Wouldn't know. I've never worked with secret filming.'

'Or maybe,' Ozzy says, 'I just fell asleep looking into the mirror. Didn't get much sleep last night. Maybe I drifted off. I don't know. And then drifted back. In and out of it. Sleep and wakefulness intersecting. You know what I mean? Gets confusing.'

Grayle and Jo exchanging glances. What's he saying? Helen's interested, too.

'How false memories are made. Ozzy, what *did* you see in those seconds? Out of interest, what did you actually see? I'm not trying to trap you or anything. Not trying to prove you saw a ghost or that you're actually psychic, which would be point-less, but…'

Ozzy smiles at her.

'Don't like it when you lose the plot, do you, Helen?'

'Hate it. Takes me back to when I was a young reporter on a big story and all the national papers would be there, and they all knew each other, and you felt they all knew what the story was and you didn't. Don't expect you to understand that. It's just nerves playing tricks.'

Ozzy turns his chair to her.

'I thought I saw a woman. In the mirror.'

'The same woman you saw last night, in your room?'

'Dunno. Maybe. But that wasn't much more than a scent.'

'Yes, I know, but…'

'This was a woman in white. Looked at first like a robe, but I think it was a coat. A long, white mac… trench coat kind of thing.'

'What kind of woman? How old?'

'Couldn't make out her face. But young, I think. I thought she was real at first, maybe one of the technicians. Definitely looked more real than that bloody troll with the logs last night.'

'So, as you don't believe in the paranormal…'

'I don't believe in Jesus.' Ozzy looks down the front of his hoodie. 'I don't believe anyone gets saved. Yeah, I went for a closer look.'

'You ran at her.'

'Before she could get away. I'm like, What's up? What do you want? She didn't say anything but she slowly opened her coat, and she… she was naked underneath? Yeah, I know, I *know*… Thing is… it didn't matter, her being naked. What mattered was that she was covered with what looked like bruises, and she was bleeding, and it was like *that* was what she wanted me to see, what she wanted me to know. That she'd been hurt.'

'I see.'

'You don't.'

'Erm… I hate myself for asking this, but…'

'Not Diana, Helen. I know we'd all been listening to you, and you told it very vividly, but no, not Diana.'

'You cried.'

'Did I? Shit. Maybe because I'd realized she wasn't there. That she was just in my mind. Felt the hurt coming off a woman who didn't exist and it just broke me up. That's what tiredness does. And brain chemicals. I'm a mess, Helen.'

The wide shot shows several people in that chamber pretending disinterest whilst clearly straining to hear what's coming crisply through to the gallery from those personal mics.

Jo says, 'This is almost too much for one night, don't you think?'

Grayle leans back.

'Helen did my job for me. No wonder he didn't want to go into the chapel. I guess you want me to find out if Trinity Ansell ever wore a white trench coat.'

'Leo will.'

'I'll do what I can.'

'You check your phone?'

Jo glances at Grayle's bag where the mobile sleeps.

'Right. I got the message.'

Neither of them has mentioned the text. Everything's accelerating before their eyes, and it may not be making the kind of sense that Defford wants. Or any at all.

The clock says there's less than eight minutes to the first transmission.

50

Surfeit of detail

THE ESTABLISHING SHOT. Is that what it's called? Looks like a still until you notice the off-white light in a window is not static. A shivery light. The gables are flat silhouettes against a cold night sky. Even an architectural historian would not recognize the house from this.

'This is a *haunted* house.' Matthew Barnes's soft voice spelling it out for the millions. 'And whatever that means, we want to know. Really *know*.'

The front door swinging open to yellowy, smeary light. No music, nothing naff. Grayle feels a small seismic shudder: God, it's happening, programme one going out to the millions, and although it's not live, it *is* live, the house entering the ether.

A woman in the passage: Eloise, her back to the camera. Another camera picking her up from the stone hallway on the other side, top of the steps. She has the right face for this, expressing an acceptance that anything could happen tonight.

And it will. When the viewer watches her discovery in the fire in the ingle, it won't disappoint. You see the anomaly through her eyes. It will set that tone of very real instability.

Reality TV is deceptive. Only editing allows that passage to access this hallway. But, hell, it looks good.

Cut to clouds scudding across the moon. Normally the sky might be speeded up, but the elements were playing ball when this was shot, just last night, the clouds really shifting.

In the house, more lights come on, room after room but only in that one corner of the building. The dirty lantern.

Grayle slips away.

In the chapel, one bulb burns in a small safety lamp set into a recess like an aumbry – where the communion chalice normally lives.

Grayle's never been here at night before. It feels, more than ever, like a sanctuary. More of one than anywhere in the actual house.

He's waiting in the corner of a pew, hands primly on his skirted knees.

'Gone to the toilet, I have, little Grayle. Never easy to get away. Someone always notices if you're gone. The toilet's all we have. Pull down the wooden lid, we do, and sit there and relish the silence. Come to this, it has.'

Above him, facing the screened window with the camera behind, is the inquisition chair, empty as a dead king's throne. Grayle sags gratefully into the pew opposite Cindy.

'Is it as bad in there as it looks?'

'It looks bad?'

'Getting weird, Cindy. These are not airheads.'

'Two days to become institutionalized. That's what they say, isn't it?'

'Yeah. Something like that. Listen… What did Ozzy see?'

'Now that,' Cindy says, 'is interesting. He does indeed give every indication of fighting against himself.'

'So you think Eloise could be right. He's in denial?'

'Not cool to be psychic, is it? Not what a cynical stand-up comedian needs in his life.'

'So does that' – Grayle leaning forward – 'does that explain his anti-religion gags, his witchy mother-in-law routines? I *talked* to his mother-in-law. Seemed, in spite of all he said about her, to have a respect for him. Said he was clever. But what happened in there… that didn't look at all clever to me. Looked like something was taking him apart.'

'Indeed. What's Mr Defford's view of it?'

'When I was in there, he hadn't seen it. He's watching his first show go out. But it's obvious who he'll think the woman was. Or who he'll think the woman needs to be for our purposes.'

'Trinity.'

'You know if she ever wore a white coat? Raincoat, trench coat?'

'I don't know. I remember a dark cloak, that's all. Keeping a low profile, I am, for now, little Grayle. A haunted house – what is it? An imbalance, perhaps. Might be no more than atmospherics caused by something physical like a crossing of natural watercourses underneath. Might be something… less natural.'

Cindy frowns. 'Trinity's a victim.'

'She's still around?'

Sometimes Grayle can't believe she can still talk like this. She looks across at Cindy in his mauve and pink woollens, Cindy who can make you believe anything. Even in the dimness, his features are soft and kindly – not effeminate, but not what you'd call uniformly masculine either. Monkish, perhaps, although when he smiles it's the smile of a tarnished monk who knows that an abbey is the very last place he should be.

For once, he doesn't answer.

'You don't have strong feelings?'

He crosses his legs, in pink tights under the skirt.

'I'm rushing into nothing. Ever since Trinity died, I've felt inadequate, as you know. I didn't see. Now I find myself withdrawing into a corner. Useless, as Marcus often says, for any of us to pretend we know what we're doing.'

'Least of all HGTV.'

He laughs.

'Tension, friction, the combustion of negative emotions. What fun.'

Silence. Here in the chapel, in the sanctuary, she believes. And she's afraid for them, these overpaid losers.

'But the reason for this,' Cindy says, 'the reason I've had to employ all this subterfuge… I do need your help. Need you to visit someone for me.'

'Well…' She's wary. 'If it's not too far, it might be possible. They'd apply manacles if they could. That is, we can get out, but they like to know where we're going.'

'Leave early, my advice. Before they're up. They've taken our phones, see.'

'I know.'

'Mrs Lyons goes through all our messages to see if there's anything urgent. Missing nothing that smells of betrayal.'

'I realize that.'

'So when she found a particular text, marked urgent, from a certain Mrs Emma Moore, I was called in here to see if it was life-or-death important. Naturally, I said not. Said Emma Moore was just a long-time fan who pestered me. Of no consequence.'

'But in fact…?'

'She's the daughter of Trinity's housekeeper, Poppy Stringer. Whose name would be recognized at once, throwing suspicion on both of us.'

'So Stringer knows you're here?'

'I told her. I went to see her a few days ago. Poppy's a strange woman, see. Loyalty's important to her. More important than anything. Her husband was disloyal in some minor way and almost immediately became history. And it seemed to me there were some things she hadn't told me because of Harry Ansell. Because he'd been her employer. It occurred to me that now Harry Ansell was *dead*…'

Didn't push her, just left his phone number, and she gave him the name of her daughter who he's never met. Mrs Stringer, he reminds Grayle, is a very old-fashioned person, discretion her watchword and therefore closer to the Ansells than any of their other former employees. Defford would have liked her to lead his catering team, but she wouldn't come back. If he was paying her, she'd feel under pressure to answer questions about her former employers, the Ansells.

'Wouldn't talk to me, Cindy, that's for sure.'

'Well, exactly. I'm… grateful to young Jo for arranging this meeting. And I think I'm taking too long in the toilet. Even for an upset stomach.' He stands up. 'Evidently, Poppy has something to tell me. You'll have her phone number?'

'But she wouldn't talk to me.'

'She will now, I think,' Cindy says.

The gate to the walled garden has been left unlocked and she gets out onto the footpath at the foot of the pine-topped hill. Moving quickly; it's started to rain and she has no coat.

No flashlight either, other than the tiny one on her cellphone, useful for lighting up a key in a lock and not much else. The half-moon which guided her here has been swallowed by cloud. Knap Hall rears behind the wall, to her right.

Right? That's wrong. In her hurry, she turned the wrong way. *Shit.*

Just one light visible, far back in the house, glad when, at the end of the building, the path broadens and a sliver of escaping moon lights a gathering of eerie little growths like dwarf monoliths.

The knot garden, with the open-fronted barn on the other side of it. Just need to get around the garden and she can start to run through the hardening rain.

Then the cellphone's shrilling in her jeans. Damn. She pulls it, shielding it with an arm. The screen says: *Marcus.* She picks up the call.

'Just gimme a minute, Marcus.'

Walks around the knot garden and takes him out of the rain, into the barn. It's now packed to the entrance with straw, old bales stacked up forming interior walls. She switches on the little flashlight in the phone, looking for a place to squeeze in; it's LED and better than she figured, showing the barn to be older and higher than she thought from outside. Oak trusses which, presumably, once supported a hayloft, long gone.

She enters a narrow alley between the stacks of small bales, some probably brought in from the stable block when it was cleared.

'Marcus?'

'You able to talk, Underhill? Thought you'd be watching your programme.'

'Long story.'

'Commercial break. The woman playing hell about elder wood on the fire. That a set-up?'

'I don't know.'

'Anyway, made me think I ought to leave a message for you, get you to call me tomorrow. Didn't expect an answer. Where are you?'

'I'm, uh, in a barn? Sheltering from the rain.'

Smell of must, air full of dust. Very dry but, hell, it's cold. She slips into a space between straw-towers. The floor feels harder underfoot.

Marcus tells her he's spent most of the day reading old farm documents. Found an expert who emailed him scans of documents going back to the late 1700s, showing evidence of transactions between A. Fishe and John Lucas, both tenant farmers.

'Transactions?'

'Stock. Sheep, mainly. Just needed proof they knew one another. Unlikely they didn't, their farms being so close.'

'This is significant?'

'Lucas was the farmer renting the land around Sudeley Castle from the then owner, Lord Rivers. Lucas was the man who discovered, in a shallow grave, the remains of Katherine Parr, in a coffin like a lead body-bag. And exposed the body. In a remarkable state of preservation.'

'Like a saint. Allegedly.'

'The word "moist" is used.'

'Maybe too much information, Marcus.'

'A surfeit of detail indicates it's not mythology. I've emailed you some of the letters from Lucas to Lord Rivers, and also the reports of various antiquarians. Doesn't make edifying reading, Underhill, but I think you need to.'

He tells her how proud Lucas seems to have been of his discovery. How many people he showed it to over the period of KP's final decay. He tells her about – *Jesus* – the reports of molestation. He's thinking of what might have happened when the body was newly discovered, her face and body good as—

'Marcus, I'm not a *queasy* person, but…'

Oh hell, something's fallen to the ground with the familiar, always slightly upsetting, sound of breaking glass.

Marcus didn't hear, goes on talking.

'The word "antiquarian" was a general cover-up for various busybodies and opportunists. One, as you'll see, claims he was one of the first to learn of the discovery of Parr's body. Rushed to the castle, to find it was gone. Nobody about to ask. When he returned a week later, it was back and he was told it had never been moved. Where did it go?'

'What are you saying? They thought she was in such good condition after two hundred years that she could, like walk? Marcus, look… could you just hold on a minute, I think I broke something.'

She lowers the phone, switches on the LED flashlight.

On the flagged floor – a floor swept clean – a framed photo lies, its glass smashed. She bends to it, with the lamp, sees a face in a faded colour photograph. She shakes away fragments of glass, uncovering a youngish woman, dark hair pulled back into a white ribbon.

Where did this come from? As she stands up, holding the picture, postcard-size, by its frame, the light finds an alcove in the straw walls, four bales arranged into a square base, a blue cloth over it.

Blue with gold edges. Like an altar cloth.

Grayle throws the little light around, illuminates a small silver dish. A leather-bound pocket Bible. A prayer book.

Another tier of bales rises behind the cloth, and there's a foot-high wooden cross pushed into the straw.

What…?

Grayle switches off the light, brings the phone to her ear.

'Marcus?'

'Something wrong?'

'Marcus, I just walked into this barn, and it's full of piled-up straw bales and in the centre… I just found an altar? A Christian altar?'

'In a barn?'

'Not even used as a barn any more, just a store. No reason for anybody to come in here, apart from shelter, and even then…'

'Old?'

'Barn's old. The altar, not at all. No dust. And there's a picture of a woman in a frame? I don't know who she is. It's like a goddamn shrine. Somebody swept the floor.'

'No one knows about it?'

'No one told *me* about it.'

'You know what, Underhill, I'd get out of there. Check it out tomorrow. In daylight. With someone else. Then call me.'

'Right. OK. I think I will.'

She feels tight inside. Shrivelled up against the cold. She starts thinking of what might be under all the straw. She thinks of a two-centuries-old moist woman.

Too much information.

51

Not to be understood

A WOMAN IN a black parka is standing at the bottom of the lane, close to the hedge, hooded against the wind-driven rain. Grayle slows the Mini, brings down her window, identifies herself.

The woman nods, and Grayle leans over and lets her into the car.

'*This* wasn't forecast,' the woman says.

She doesn't lower her glistening hood until they're out on the bottom road. Grayle glances sideways and finds she doesn't look like someone called Poppy Stringer. Her hair is long and fine and near-white. Her face is long, too, and serious. She wears no make-up, nor really needs it. She's like some mature noblewoman from a Renaissance painting.

Grayle called her an hour ago, after first checking with Jo Shepherd to make sure nothing crazy occurred in the night. Poppy Stringer told her she'd be attending communion at St Peter's, ten thirty. Too late; Defford would be screaming by then. Eventually, she said she'd meet Grayle in the lane and they would walk.

But it's too wet and windy for walking, if you need to talk at the same time.

'I'd have come to your house, Mrs Stringer.'

'Doesn't matter.'

It's a local accent, but refined, voice low and sure. Grayle doesn't even know where her house is, only that it's one of a group of former farm cottages.

At the bottom of the road, Grayle looks both ways.

'Where should I go?'

'Not through Winchcombe. Too many people know me there.'

'OK...'

She turns left, up towards Cleeve Hill, not quite understanding why Poppy Stringer should not want to be seen in a car with a someone whom almost no one in Winchcombe is likely to recognize.

It's hard going. Or maybe just hard to concentrate this morning. Too many overlapping images, mostly dreadful. She had a tortured night in the pop-up, thanks to the stuff Marcus sent to her laptop. Like he says, none of it can ever be proved, but it sure sours your sleep.

She'll need to call Marcus when she gets back. Also talk to someone, discreetly, about the altar in the barn. Maybe Jordan. Or maybe, considering the barn's proximity to his knot garden, Jordan already knows. So maybe not Jordan. Not yet.

'I watched your programme last night,' Mrs Stringer says. 'The poor elder.'

'Pretty widespread piece of folklore.'

'I still burn it, sometimes.'

Grayle glances at her, slowing the car.

'You burn the devil's wood?'

'One can resist the devil without having to run away from him at every turn. The harder you run, the faster he follows you.'

'Oh.'

Grayle drives on for a couple miles until she's looking down on what, in better weather, would be a wide view over the melanoma housing and the fields where Lisa Muir's family farms. Sensing a big question approaching, she pulls into a lay-by alongside a copse, shuts off the wipers, kills the motor. Waits till it comes rolling towards her like a bowling ball.

'What are they trying to do at Knap Hall, Miss Underhill? Are you allowed to tell me?'

No, of course she isn't.

'Call me Grayle.' She watches the windshield misting over, sealing them in a grey capsule. 'I think they would like it to appear that the house may be haunted by Katherine Parr. And also Trinity Ansell.'

'And what does Mr Lewis say about that?'

'Cindy? Uh... he isn't sure.'

'He was kind to the girl who was afraid of the wood.'

'I, uh, think he'd like to've been kinder to Trinity Ansell.'

'She would have invited him to the house more often, I think.'

'If Harry Ansell—'

'Mr Ansell didn't know him, Grayle. He was suspicious.'

'But not you?'

'He tends to wins you over, Mr Lewis.'

'One of his... skills. Would've come himself this morning, but they don't get to leave the house till it's all over.'

Poppy Stringer's hands are in her lap. She's unzipped her jacket, but not by much.

'He's been in touch with me, Mr Lewis, a few times. In relation to Mrs Ansell's diary. Her third short volume. Which she sent to me from her parents' cottage, not long before she died. To keep safe for her. She didn't know if she'd ever show it to anyone. Even Mr Lewis.'

'But she trusted you.'

'We'd become closer than I'd expected we would. We were never friends. She had many friends. But not many people she could rely on.'

'You did eventually read the diary?'

'Some time after her death. I had a decision to make.'

'I mean, you didn't think of handing it over to the police? If there was something there to explain the circumstances of her death?'

'That would've helped nobody.'

'Not even Harry Ansell?'

Poppy Stringer bites her upper lip and then talks to the misted glass.

'No, it would not. He was my sole employer by then, and he'd always been considerate to me. But she clearly hadn't wanted him, of all people, to see the diary. It would... not have made him happy. Yes, it did outline the circumstances of her decision to abort her baby. How that was to be done. Secretly. Why she felt driven to it.'

'Where is it now? The diary.'

'I destroyed it. That was the decision I had to make.'

Grayle's hands tighten on the steering wheel. Cindy, she guesses, doesn't know this.

'Perhaps it was wrong of me, but I didn't think that at the time. Mr Ansell was a broken man. I didn't want to harm him any more.'

But now he's beyond harm. And the diary's gone for ever. No wonder Cindy wasn't getting anywhere with her.

'Harry Ansell talked to you about it? After she died.'

'He came to see me twice. He'd never said much before – not his way. But he began to talk about his wife. About the house, mainly. What he thought about the house. How he'd tried to like it but hoped she'd soon grow tired of it. How it eventually came between them. How he once rented a house in the West Indies for them both to live for several months, to get her away. She refused to go.'

'Wouldn't leave Knap Hall? She still loved that place?'

Poppy Stringer turns to face her, sorrowful.

'He told me how much it was costing, simply in repairs. It was rewired twice. Replumbed. It resisted refurbishment. Mrs Ansell didn't see it. She simply wasn't used to failure. I doubt she'd ever had the experience of it. So many sure steps. Higher and higher. Thinking she could transform the house the way she'd transformed herself. It wasn't arrogance, as such. She just...'

'Thought it was part of her?'

'That was a delusion encouraged by… some people.'

Grayle remembers Lisa: *We wanted them to go on loving the place. We wanted them to stay. Like I say, it was a brilliant job. We thought Mrs Ansell was turning the place round. Just by being there.*

'But you… as a local person…'

'Oh yes. I knew what Knap Hall was.'

'So why did you want to work there?'

'I didn't. Mr Ansell found me. Through his magazine, he knew a lot of people, including a former employer of mine in Cheltenham who sold his hotel to a chain. Which I didn't want to work for, so I left. When the new Mrs Ansell became obsessed with developing something wonderful out of Knap Hall, my old boss warned Mr Ansell it did not have a good history. In a business sense – that was the only way to get through to him. He was told he should be careful who he employed. Don't bring in people he didn't know about.'

'But local people would know the history.'

'Some local people know what to avoid. The unwary are the ones most likely to be hurt. Or those drawn to… these things.'

'So this retired hotelier directed Ansell to you, as a safe pair of hands in, like, an unsafe place.'

'Well, I lived locally, and didn't have to sleep there. He paid me extremely well. I said I'd stay for six months, though I didn't, to be honest, think they'd last six months at Knap Hall.'

'And the longer they lasted, the longer they stayed…'

'It isn't like the films, Grayle. It isn't names written on the walls in blood.' Popper Stringer shaking her head in sadness. 'It's slower than that. More sly. More furtive. Slow and… cumulative. Not to be understood.'

'Trust terror. Little else is safe.'

'I'm sorry?'

'Something a friend says. Uh… Harry Ansell was spending time away. Increasingly. I was told that. Business meetings in New York.'

'The impression I had was that he thought Mrs Ansell was safer in Knap Hall... when he wasn't there.'

'Jesus.'

'He didn't believe it, in his mind. But perhaps it's not about the mind as much as the body. A man's body which he thinks is his to control.'

'Oh God. What did he do?'

'I only know what the diary said. At first I tried to tell myself it wasn't true. An exaggeration perhaps. He was, essentially, a kind man.'

'You're saying he wasn't kind... when they were alone in their apartment at Knap Hall?'

'We can't know what mental state Mrs Ansell was in at the time. By then.'

'And in that room...'

Poppy looks at her. Grayle wants to tell her about the room. Can't.

'And she didn't seem to think she could have children, you see,' Poppy says.

'She told you that?'

'*He* did. After her death. She'd never been interested in children before. But suddenly decided there should be an heir... to Knap Hall. Madness. Nothing happened. He thought it was his fault they couldn't. Low sperm count. I think he was glad.'

'But she did get pregnant. Gossip at the time said it wasn't his baby.'

'That wasn't true. At least, not the way these stupid people thought.'

'The diary said it was Ansell's?'

Poppy nods.

'It described a particular night. A terrible night. Perverse. *Dirty*. That was her word.'

Grayle thinks of the night of the banquet. Trinity all aglow in her Katherine Parr dress, drawing the eyes of every man in the room, according to Lisa Muir. And Ansell *very much in the background.*

Poppy says, 'Do you want the details of what he did to her?'

'I... no. If you had the diary... but you don't.'

'She said – wrote – that she couldn't have a child that was conceived in those circumstances. She said she thought she'd be seeking a divorce. And still didn't seem to realize...'

'That it was the house?'

The weather brings a fuzzy shadow-branch bowing low across the misted windshield, scratching at the glass. How could Trinity Ansell be in so much denial? She *believed*, for Chrissakes. She believed in tarot readings. She believed in Cindy Mars-Lewis.

'When she died,' Poppy says, 'Mr Ansell's grief was smothered by a rage at what Knap Hall had done to them. Never expressed, he wasn't that kind of man. He was always calm. But it was as if there was a tornado inside him.'

'I used to see him. In Cheltenham. I'd've been scared to approach him.'

'He hated the house then. Would have demolished it, I think, if it hadn't been a listed building, protected. I didn't understand at first why he'd agreed to lease it to the TV people to make a documentary about Trinity. Make a film about what must surely be his worst memories.'

'I wondered about that a lot.'

'I didn't realize until I read the programme schedules that we'd been misled about what kind of programme it would be. *Big Other*?'

'The location isn't disclosed.'

'Where else could it be? It's the same company. Same people. I checked on the Internet. It's trash television.'

'Yeah, we hope it won't be, but I agree that's how it looks. That's how it'll get the massive viewing figures. And Ansell... told my boss he thought it was haunted by Trinity.'

'Yes. Yes, he would.'

'You're saying this was to be his revenge on the house? Wanted to see what happened in Knap Hall with HGTV inside? Wanted the house he hated thrown open to millions of people? He wanted to watch. Wanted to see it go out. From the gallery – the room where all the pictures come in.'

'To see what it might do,' Poppy says. 'What it might do to other people.' She pauses as the tip of the low branch flaps against the windshield. 'People who didn't matter.'

Now it's all too clear why she left a message on Cindy's phone.

'But he never got to watch, Poppy. He hanged himself. Close to Knap Hall as he could get. Like he was delivering a last message. A warning even. He must've been in some screwed-up state. If he felt there was no coming back from it.'

The rain's drumming furiously on the car roof. It's too late now for Poppy to attend Holy Communion at Winchcombe.

PART SIX

... night

Ghosts have confounded centuries of criticism. Modern science's attempts to exorcize them has foundered, just like Reformation theology, Enlightenment philosophy and Victorian mass education... As long as people believe in ghosts they will continue to exist.

Owen Davies
The Haunted (2007)

52
Betrayed?

It's started and, like a defective rollercoaster, is dangerously unstoppable. You look ahead in panic and want to start climbing down the girders.

'At least a dozen people phoned in last night to say they could see anomalous lights in the chamber,' Jo Shepherd tells Grayle outside the reality truck, late that Sunday afternoon. 'Faint lights. Hazy shapes.'

'Like orbs?'

'Probably. I'm told even one of the camera crew thought something odd was happening at one stage.'

'Where?'

'A woman, Jess, working behind the false wall. Leo's considering whether we should get her into the chapel or if that's underlining the fact that the Seven are not alone. Personally, I don't like it.'

'You don't like the idea of televising someone who's working on the programme?'

'Grayle...' Dark bags of overwork have formed under Jo's eyes. She's wearing an extra sweater. 'I don't like the idea of anything happening *on our side of it*. Makes me uncomfortable. Makes me think about it as something more than television.'

'What, like all lunacy should be contained behind a screen? Like there's some spiritual demarcation line between reality TV and reality? Jo, essentially the camera crew's in the same room.'

Jo turns away, her shoulders shaking. Muttering what sounds like 'shit, shit, shit'. She hasn't asked what Grayle learned from

Poppy Stringer, but she's promised to try and find a space to get Cindy quietly back into the chapel.

Not going to be easy today, though. Grayle's barely left her booth in the reality truck since lunchtime. Defford wanted different views on Helen's Diana revelations, which are airing tonight. Embargoed highlights should now be on their way to the media with a one-minute DVD clip from the show, Helen saying, *Her eyes were looking towards me, but... through me, somehow. And I realized it was a veil. You know the veil she wore with her wedding dress, covering her face...*

Tonight's programme will wind up just before the Ozzy incident, including the first part of Grayle's interview with Parrish in the chapel, a taster for tomorrow night, which, basically, will be the Ozzy Ahmed show.

Defford's still trying to get Ozzy into the chapel, but he's ignoring all entreaties, as he knows he can. Hell, even without the Diana factor, Ozzy's story will be bigger than Helen's. How will they ever top Ozzy?

Maybe they won't need to. His story doesn't end. He had another restless night, according to Jo. They have shots of him getting up in the early hours, putting on his light then just sitting on his bed, clenching and unclenching his fists, closing his eyes and rocking backwards and forwards. Going to sleep, eventually, with the light on. Jo says she's never seen a man more afraid of showing fear.

Grayle's been watching some of the rushes from today. Ozzy talking to Roger Herridge who at first seems miffed at the idea of Ozzy seeing what he can't. But the truth is this is something he's had to live with for many years; in the end he's patting Ozzy on the back, telling him there's only five days to go. Telling him that at least he'll leave with something to think about.

Quite a sad person, Roger, but more philosophical than Rhys Sebold – white-faced with fury, according to Jo.

So they pull him into the chapel.

'You feel in some way betrayed, Rhys?'

'In what way?'

'By Ozzy?'

Rhys does a loose grin, the old cool restored.

'I'll be honest with you. Thought it was a wind-up at first. But then, when it didn't stop…'

'A wind-up? You thought Ozzy was lying?'

He just carries on talking, through the question.

'… I felt surprised and disappointed. I've known Ozzy for years. Now, however, I'll admit to being worried. He's had some anxiety with his divorce and losing custody of the child. And he's been working harder than ever, as if he can just ride over personal problems. Provincial shows, six, seven nights a week. Too much. Behind that deadpan delivery, he can be manic.'

'So you think it's stress related?'

'Well, of *course*, it's stress related. Listen, nobody likes to see a good mate cracking up. So it's my hope that the viewers will take pity on him and evict him ASAP.'

They're coming up to the first eviction. Viewers will be asked to vote for the removal from the house of whoever they find the least convincing. Begins to look like Defford's idea of votes for or against belief in the paranormal might actually work.

'But they don't show pity, do they?' Rhys Sebold says. 'Too much fun watching a celeb coming apart under pressure.'

'How do you see the pressure?'

'All right, look. People like Eloise and Roger Herridge are desperate to prove something. Even Cindy Mars-Lewis doing his wise old owl thing on the side of supernature. It was obvious that in the early stages there'd be an element of excitement and anticipation, before it all falls flat, as it will. As these things invariably do.'

'Rhys, if I could just point out—'

'No, let me finish. Ozzy's an instinctive entertainer. He can't help himself. He doesn't believe any of it, but there's some part of him that's always committed to giving an audience its money's worth.'

'You think he's fooling himself? That what you're saying?'

'I've known him a long time. If he thinks he isn't being funny, he panics. He instinctively creates opportunities. If the real world isn't funny enough he'll construct a fantasy world in which he totally believes. Ashley Palk can probably explain this better than me. Personally, I just don't want to have to see him snap… on television. I'm sure you do, but I don't.'

She remembers him that day on the phone, when he laid into her for making inquiries about his past. *So you want to be sure I'm not psychiatrically challenged. Well, let me ask you… would it – should it – matter if I am? Is yours the kind of programme that still considers mental health something that should be hidden away?*

She's thinking of a way to remind him about this, without reference to a private phone call, when his voice is overlaid in her cans by Jo telling her not to argue, to break this thread, switch to more personal stuff.

'Rhys,' she says, 'why does all this make you so angry? I don't mean just the idea of Ozzy having a psychic experience. Why does the whole idea of any kind of supernatural presence here make you so aggressive?'

He smiles crookedly.

'You took a long time to get around to that. All right. If you want to bring God into this, fair to say Rhys Sebold does not do God. Or angels. Or ghosts. There *is* no Big Other on any level.'

'And no life after death?'

'Of course not. Listen, I've had Professor Richard Dawkins on my show. I've talked to Professor Brian Cox. These are men with planet-sized brains and immense erudition, and if they were desperate enough to appear on *this* show, it wouldn't last two nights before this place was seen as just a… a not very pleasant house.'

Grayle figures they might disagree about what kind of brain qualifies as planet-sized, but she lets it go. Never argue.

'Your anger... there's also a personal side to that?'

'Of course there is. And I have to say I blame myself totally for what happened to Chloe, my partner. I will never forgive myself. I make no excuses.'

She's sure he said those very words during that edgy phone conversation. No need to get him to go into it all again; the story's well known and, just like with Eloise and Alison Cross's cottage, they've shown a collage of news clips explaining his arrest for possession of a class A drug the night of Chloe's death.

'And I should emphasize I don't use drugs any more. Nor will I ever again.'

'And are you speaking now to Chloe's sister, Rhiannon, who encouraged you to—'

'No, I'm not.'

'—to go with her to a spiritualist medium in the hope of achieving some kind of closure?'

'That made me very, very angry. The way these appalling people exploit grief. All so-called mediums are either self-deluded or fraudulent. It sickens me that what began as a fad, in the aftermath of the First World War, is still active in our so-called enlightened society. The last thing I'd *ever* do is besmirch Chloe's memory by listening to some trickster pretending to channel messages from her. She's *dead*.'

'Better wind up here, Grayle,' Jo says.

Grayle goes down to the fast food part of the restaurant, orders up a toasted cheese sandwich and takes it to a corner table. Thinking she might call Marcus. But then Defford comes in, evidently looking for her. Brings a coffee to her table.

'Grayle, we have to make a decision about Ahmed.'

'You just watched Sebold?'

'Interesting, but...'

She looks at him, curious. Isn't this what he wanted?

'I got Max in immediately. He says that unless Ahmed seems likely to harm himself or anyone else, we should simply stay out of it. Don't force him to do anything, don't pressure him to come into the chapel. Max says it's actually probably best that you don't get to ask him difficult questions. Let all that come, if it comes at all, from the other residents. Let things work themselves out.'

'That seems sensible. For now.'

'However, in the light of what Sebold says, I want you to find out if Ahmed's ever been in an abusive relationship.'

'Oh.'

'He's volatile, he's single-minded, he uses people.'

'You're thinking this woman he keeps seeing, the bruises…?'

'I don't *really* like the idea of it being an echo from his past – some old girlfriend, maybe even his wife, who he got a bit rough with. And while it could still be great television…'

'Too complicated.'

'Yes. So we need to know. Was there a period in his life, before he was famous, that – perhaps because of drink or drugs – he's wiped from his memory? Has he ever hurt a woman?'

Grayle cuts a slice of her sandwich.

'You ask Max about this?'

'Max thinks it could simply be a woman he hurt emotionally and he's projecting that as physical – bruises and blood.'

'But if we find there *is* something?'

'Then we wind down the Ozzy story. Let it either come out in its own way or die a natural death. I don't want us relying too much on Ahmed for metaphysical interest, and then that side collapses.'

'You think maybe Sebold knows and that's why he's trying to kill the story? Not everything about Sebold has to be self-centred.'

'See what you can uncover. Should take us onto the next stage, anyway. As long as he doesn't get evicted tomorrow.'

She'd forgotten about that. Viewers can vote on the phone or online, where they can briefly explain their reasons. Max will do a reaction analysis at the end of tomorrow's programme. Then the evictee walks straight into the chapel to vent into the camera, before spending the rest of the week being cosseted in a pop-up suite until the great reunion at the weekend.

'Leo…' She pushes her plate away. The programme's started on a roll, he doesn't seem too unhappy. She may never get a better chance to approach this with him. 'On the issue of complications…'

'You're not going to spoil my night, are you, Grayle?'

'How's Ozzy been today? I didn't get a chance to see much of the rushes.'

'Quiet. People being very careful around him. Nothing dramatic. What's your problem?'

Without mentioning Cindy, she tells him about Poppy Stringer and the diary.

Watching the excitement building in Defford's eyes as she talks. Can almost hear the rattle of the *Big Other* rollercoaster, as he finishes his coffee, leans back in his cane chair, signals to the waitress for some more.

'This woman thinks Ansell's suicide was not entirely about facing financial ruin?'

'Possibly not even at all.'

To cover for Cindy, she's told Defford she left her cellphone number with Poppy in case the housekeeper ever changed her mind about talking to the programme. She hadn't expected this. Which is true.

'She thinks Harry Ansell abused his wife?'

'*Trinity* suggests that.'

'Why's Mrs Stringer come forward now?'

'Kept quiet out of loyalty to Ansell, but now Ansell's dead. Also, she's figured out what we're doing here. Thought it was just gonna be a documentary about Trinity Ansell, now she's put two and two together. Realized this has to be the *Big Other* everyone's talking about.'

Defford's excitement is fading to wariness.

'Is this about money? Any suggestion that if we don't grease her palm she might share her knowledge elsewhere?'

'Not that kind of woman, Leo. Never came close to mentioning money. She just… wants to do what's best. I guess.'

'For whom? Both Ansells are dead. And if the diary's destroyed, we're talking about Ansell's *alleged* abuse of his wife. Could all be imaginary.'

'Leo, I'm just passing it on.'

'Will she record an interview for us?'

'Didn't even think it was worth asking. If you want me to, I will, but—'

'Leave it for the moment. I just… I don't like coincidence. Abuse, domestic violence, Ahmed's bruised woman. Too much in one day.'

'Yeah, I see that.'

'And yet, if we ignore it… Thank you—'

He stops talking while the waitress puts down coffee. The waitress is Lisa Muir. She doesn't look at Grayle.

'Ahmed,' Defford says when Lisa's gone. 'He's never described the woman he thinks he's seeing.'

'No. Um… Leo… can we consider this in relation to something never explained to my satisfaction? Which is why Ansell offered you his house for *Big Other*.'

'Yes.' He nods. 'We need to do that.'

Reliving his encounter with Harry Ansell on a terrace above the lights of Stroud makes Defford look youthful and once again blown away with the dark potential of all this. Remembering Ansell's response to him saying, about Trinity, *Hell of a loss. A light gone out.*

And then Ansell's reply: *What if it hasn't gone out?*

'Went through me like a knife, those words.'

All too resonant. Grayle sips coffee, unsure where to take this.

'I'm still on the fence about Trinity, how much to believe. But I do believe what Poppy Stringer told me. I think Ansell came to hate this house, with a passion.'

Defford's nodding slowly.

'There was no way that he wanted to keep Knap Hall as a memorial to Trinity. It was only ever important to him because it was important to her. He'd stripped the place within weeks, taken away nearly all the furniture, sold it or given it away to charities. He wanted to get rid.'

'Only nobody wanted to buy. People came to take a look and I'd imagine what they saw didn't help. Someone let the old darkness back in. What did he actually say?'

'He asked me how long I'd need the house for. I told him six, seven months. He threw a figure at me, and it wasn't giveaway. I said I'd have to talk to the network. Trying to buy some time, because this was a very unexpected development, you know? But he wasn't going away. He asked me precisely what I wanted it for, and I... look, I'm not really a businessman, I'm an ideas man. I took a chance and told him what I had in mind. When he started to smile, I thought, well, that's it, fucked. Worth a try.'

'So he knew what *Big Other* was gonna be.'

'Of course he did. He just nodded.'

'You saw him as a friend?'

'Grayle, I don't think he had friends.'

What should she say to him now? *You think he wanted the house to do its worst? Wanted bad things to happen to you and your programme? While he watched?*

'You worry too much, Grayle,' Defford says.

53

No wall

MONDAY MORNING, Helen Parrish is big news.

All the papers have her story – Grayle pleased to see the *Mail* blurbing it on the front, like she'd predicted, and a full-page piece inside. The *Guardian* have a quote from the BBC who maintain this is the first time they've heard the Diana story in full and would not wish to comment on its credibility as Helen Parrish no longer works for them.

Helen knows nothing about this. No papers are allowed into the house. It's strange when you hear everyone talking about it outside and on the radio and breakfast TV, but in the house it's been overtaken, is already history. The house and the outside world are in different time zones.

Defford is said to be well pleased. By tonight *Big Other* will be the TV programme to watch. By tomorrow night, after Ozzy, it will be the programme which must, on no account, be missed. He's kept out of Grayle's way. It's clear he doesn't want to talk about the Ansells' marriage.

So Grayle concentrates on Ozzy Ahmed, calling up his former mother-in-law, the witch. Answering service. Again. Rang several times last night with the same result. She's away? On holiday? At the end of October? Who goes on holiday at the end of October? Only…

Only a goddamn witch. End of this week it's Hallowe'en. Samhain. The Celtic feast of the dead. Ozzy's mother-in-law's probably on her way to some mass pagan gathering at an obscure stone circle in the middle of Wales or someplace.

Mid-morning, Grayle gives up. Maybe Sebold knows something but if he didn't mention it yesterday he's hardly likely to talk about it today. No obvious gossip on the Internet, either, even though she's put some pointed and probably libellous suggestions into Google.

Ozzy's spent most of the morning reading in his room, a book he's borrowed from the small library in the chamber: *The Scole Experiment: Scientific Evidence for Life After Death.* He makes tea in his room, misses breakfast but comes down for lunch. He's a little quieter than usual; when people involve him in conversation he responds but doesn't seem to be engaged.

Later that morning Eloise goes to the darkest corner of the room and sits on the floor, eyes closed. She's wearing a black velvet dress, and her fingernails are also painted black. You can almost hear the intake of Sebold's breath as she shifts her position on the rug to something approaching lotus. Later she asks Cindy if he, like her, is aware of a brooding presence, something waiting.

Grayle doesn't hang around for Cindy's answer. He'll be evasive. She puts on her coat and carries her phone through a slow, cold drizzle, to the ash tree, planning to call Marcus. Too tired to ring him last night, after Defford.

When she reaches the ash tree, she sees Jordan Aspenwall walking alone towards his knot garden. She follows him.

'Jordan, I swear to God…'

He says nothing. The rain hisses on the barn roof.

'I did not dream this,' Grayle says.

She burrows in the straw, encountering only more straw. She feels ridiculous. Jordan watches her, impassive.

'How many people do you have working here, Miss Underhill?'

'Dunno. A hundred?'

'I suppose some of them are bound to be devout.'

'What, like they're holding little religious services in the barn to protect their souls against what's happening in the house?'

He says nothing. Stupid of her not to take a few flash pictures of the makeshift altar.

'There was also a picture. An old photograph, framed. Of a woman. Which I accidently broke. Heard it fall.'

By the light of Jordan's flashlight, she looks for broken glass on the barn floor. A floor which, the other night, was swept clean and is now padded with straw.

Nothing.

'Yeah, well, I'm sorry to have bothered you,' Grayle says.

Too disheartened now even to ask him about the elder wood.

Late afternoon, Roger Herridge is called into the chapel. No reason, it's just his turn, and the director following his progress in the house says he could use some more about Roger's mindset.

'I'm a churchgoer, yes,' Herridge says.

Grayle doesn't know why she asked this as a preliminary. Maybe the vanishing altar put it into her head.

'Roger, how does faith in God equate with a belief in ghosts?'

'Hmm. Not easily, as it happens. Not many ghost stories in the Bible. But, flimsy and transient as they are, ghosts do appear to be evidence of some form of afterlife. Perhaps the best we're going to get during this one.'

'But you've never experienced an apparition.'

'No. As I've explained, it's why I'm here.'

'And why you exchanged rooms with Ashley Palk?'

He looks resigned.

'Yes, we did that. I offered to swap with Ozzy Ahmed, but he refused. Quite angrily. Ashley was more accommodating as long as there was fresh bedding.'

'Ashley doesn't believe that the soiled imprint on her pillow was any more than—'

'Dirty laundry? I disagree.'

'What do you think it was?'

'For what it's worth, I think she probably wasn't alone in the bed. Didn't say that to her, of course. But time and place can overlap. Particularly in a room where something significant took place – or *takes place*. Continually.'

'You've been in the room for two nights now. Has anything... occurred in that time?'

Looking forlorn, Roger shakes his head.

'Sound like an idiot, don't I?'

'You don't sound too much like a politician,' Grayle says before she can stop herself.

Roger recoils.

'All right, let me deal with that. I was a Lib-Dem MP. Always understood liberalism as a matter of providing enough money, through increased taxation if necessary, to give people the freedom to be what they want to be. Even if what they want to be doesn't conform to what the majority of Liberals consider politically or morally acceptable. My fascination with ghosts has never endeared me to some of my colleagues who respect your right to a belief system but despise you for having one.' Roger trembles slightly. 'Don't get me started. I think that, far from being nonsense, ghosts connect us with our past.'

'In what way?'

'If we only experience history through old buildings, antique furniture, old books, we're missing the reality of it. Emotions live on. Tragedy doesn't go away. Nor does evil. Sometimes we're side by side with our ancestors and our moods are affected by what they did. Think about it.'

'Thank you, Roger.'

'Thank *you*.'

Stepping down from the reality truck into a dimming afternoon she's met in the mud by an apprehensive-looking Jo Shepherd.

'Come with me, Grayle.'

'Where?'

'You need to see this. Although you didn't see it, OK? I'm not supposed to share it. I'm not even supposed to have copied it.'

They've given Jo a small cabin. One desk, one chair, one laptop, switched on. When they're inside, Jo slams the door, locks it, waving Grayle to the chair as she fingers up a document. Steps back quickly as a solemn-faced dark-skinned woman appears on the screen.

'Jess Taylor.'

'Who?'

'The camerawoman you were to have spoken to. If Defford hadn't decided to do it himself.'

'Oh, the one who… saw something.'

'In the main chamber. From behind the false wall. Put the cans on, I don't want anybody overhearing. Plus, *I* don't want to hear it again.'

'Why did Defford have to interview her?'

'Because she was under contract, one of the team.'

'I see.'

She doesn't.

'You will,' Jo says.

The woman's evidently uncomfortable at being on the wrong end of a camera. Or maybe just uncomfortable. Her accent is London, middle-class. Her skin is very dark, African rather than West Indian.

'Thought it was the log guy at first. Or the log guy's assistant.'

Defford's voice: 'He doesn't have an assistant.'

'Thank you for that.'

She's in the chapel, but with no mood lighting. This is bright and hard, for clarity. She's very thin and fit-looking, sinews in her neck like piano wire.

Defford: 'What was he wearing?'

'Could've been leather. Brown and worn. Some kind of boots. He had fairish hair.'

'Where were the residents?'

'Supper. In the room next door. I'd been told to get some GVs of the room while it was empty. Only it wasn't. So I waited for him to leave. Which he did after a few seconds.'

'So why would you think—?'

'Because, Leo, it walked' – her voice rising like a siren in the cans – 'through the fucking wall?'

No reply from Defford. Grayle turns to look at Jo, detaches one can.

'Quite,' Jo says.

Jess Taylor's glancing from side to side in the chapel. Not really liking it or what she's here for.

Defford: 'And that was it?'

'No.'

'You're saying you saw it again.'

'Yes. In a different part of the room. Half formed.'

Defford waits.

'I… One hand, no legs.'

'Take your time.'

'Don't patronize me, Leo.'

'Older than she looks,' Jo says. 'Eight years with Al Jazeera.'

'So not…'

'Not exactly inexperienced.'

'I'm trying to get this right for you,' Jess Taylor says. 'Picture me on my own in my little bunker behind the false wall, where I knew nothing could see me. Hard to believe that at first – first time for me with two-way mirrors. But by then I'd spent a couple of days shooting people who couldn't see me, so I was adjusted. But this…'

'This was different?'

'Oh yes. First of all, remember I'm seeing it through the camera. You always think you're OK behind a camera. Invulnerable. You're obtaining the shots, that's the important thing. It's how cameramen get killed in wars, obtaining the shots. What you see is not what gets you. I was actually saying that to myself. *What you see is not what gets you.*'

'What you're seeing is usually harmless.'

'Usually. Certainly this… sort of thing.'

Defford: 'You've seen one before?'

'My gran. I was about thirteen. It's not uncommon for kids. 'This was…' Jess lifts a hand into shot. 'Look at that. Still shaking. Don't remember the last time that happened. These things… it creeps up on you, then it takes over everything. All your senses. Takes you out of yourself and into *its* place. Not like anything else you'll ever experience.'

Grayle stiffens. *Yes.* Yes, that's how it was. Thank you, Jess. *Christ.*

'You're not going to use this, are you?' Jess manages a wispy smile. 'Or you wouldn't be doing the interview. It'd be the American woman.'

'Maybe we should do it again, then. With Grayle.'

Jess takes the kind of breath that conveys astonishment moving towards outrage.

'I said I'd talk about this once, Leo, and then never again. Nor am I going back in that room.'

'Jess—'

'So if you've nothing else for me, outside the house, I'll be on my way. Just glad I'm not using my own kit. That camera, by the way' – she's half out of the chair – 'you should get rid of it. And *don't* trade it in. I mean get rid.'

Silence. Then,

'Why do you say that?'

'When I saw it again, it was suddenly *fully* formed. And unclothed. Walking through the candlelight, as if the candle was part of it. And it was this… this side of the mirror. My side. With me. In other words, there was no mirror. No wall. And the camera… the camera was utterly freezing. So cold it felt hot, you know what I mean? Like in the dead of winter when you're trying to prise something out of the ice, and it freezes your fingers. And they go numb. *That* cold. The camera was that cold.'

'You were frightened.'

'Now what do *you* think, Leo?'

The sound distorting as she gets up and it's over.

'Sometimes, Leo just doesn't think,' Jo says.

'Where is she now?'

'Gone. I mean really gone. Gone back to London.'

'He *let her go*?'

'She's a freelance. She gave him a full account of what happened—'

'Very professionally. Fulfilling her contract.'

'And then she quit. Grayle, I could not possibly be more convinced.'

'No wall,' Grayle says. 'You notice that? There was no false wall there even last week. Let alone centuries ago.'

'So… whatever it was lives in that room as it used to be. God, I never in my life thought I'd be having a conversation like this.'

'And she's right. He needs to get rid of that camera. And not switch it on again.'

'We checked the rushes. Nothing. I asked Leo what we were going to do with Jess. He said we're going to sit on it.'

'He's that stupid?'

'I think he means we save it, for possible use at the end of the week. If it seems appropriate. We don't have pictures of anything – he kept saying that – at the end of the day, we just have somebody talking about seeing something. Somebody nobody's heard of.'

Grayle stands up, slams down the lid of the laptop.

'This because it doesn't fit into the story so far? Because it's a man?'

'Because we don't know who he is or how he fits in. An innocuous fair-haired man in leathers.'

'You think he was innocuous? You wanna watch her again?'

'God, no.'

'What if *I* know who he is? Was. *Is.* Time we stopped backing away from this. End of the day, the worst that can happen to the credulous is embarrassment.'

'We go and talk to Leo?'

'Uh-huh.' Grayle shakes her head. 'Let him come looking for us. What I think is you need to fix up another meeting with Cindy. Any way you can let him see this?'

She's nodding at the laptop.

'Might be possible, but it'd be a risk. The chapel's going to be in demand tonight. We go live for the first eviction, and the timing of that's still floating.'

'Can we get him out the back? Outside the walled garden?'

'If Defford finds out we're going behind his back, it'll be the worst of all worlds. I mean, OK, my world view's turning upside down, but apart from that what's going to happen? What can Knap Hall and a man with… yellow hair… really do? Apart from not giving us the kind of television we had in mind.'

'Well, Jo,' Grayle says. 'Why don't you ask Harry Ansell? Why don't you ask Trinity?'

That night, from the very top of the programme, they screen Ozzy story's, beginning with those 'previously on *Big Other*' moments when he's behaving oddly in his bedroom, finding him knocking over candles at the end of Helen's Diana story. Joining the audience next day for his memories of Reg, the caretaker's skull, and Cyril the paedophile. Ending with that intimate public confessional with Parrish. *I'm a mess, Helen.*

Defford thinks it's the finest programme he's ever produced.

He has several bottles of champagne brought up from the restaurant to his office, to which everyone will be invited.

Just as soon as the first eviction's out of the way.

54

Fruitcake thing

FIRST THING TUESDAY morning, Grayle is called into Defford's office, where Kate Lyons sits, hair bunned and skewered, behind Defford's big desk, a printout in front of her.

'We have a problem, Grayle. I've handed it over to the lawyers, but Leo thinks you should be in the picture.'

'Eloise?'

'No, Eloise is still taking it rather well. She didn't make any friends and she says she's getting better vegetarian food out here. No, it's this. Have a seat.'

At first, she thinks it must one of the viewers' emails, backing up a choice of evictee, but, no, it's someone using the same *Big Other* email address to alert them to what he says is a gross libel.

'Obviously, it isn't a libel,' Kate says, 'as the alleged victim is no longer alive. Even so, if it's true it's unsavoury and poses certain questions that we'll need to answer sooner or later.'

The name on the email is pafswinton4@btinternet.com.

He doesn't waste words.

I was sickened watching your programme to hear the name of a good man blackened in the worst possible way. I am a former schoolfriend of Austin Ahmed and was one of the four boys who spent a night in the 'haunted' biology lab. As the youngest and most impressionable of the group, I doubt if I slept at all that night. It's still very vivid in my memory, and I actually remember Ahmed going to the toilet in the early hours. He was scared, too, and was away no longer than about three minutes. I even remember looking at the clock.

So hardly enough time to enjoy a hot chocolate in the staff-room and then administer a hand job to 'Cyril', whose real name was Dave Turner. Dave, who died three years ago, was still teaching at the school when I started work there myself as a maths teacher and we became good friends.

I can tell you for a fact – and would say the same to his face – that Ahmed is LYING. If neither he nor you is prepared to put this right, I shall be obliged to refer this matter to the national press.

Paul Swinton

'What's Leo say?'

'He tends to leave these things to lawyers. He isn't too worried. It's Ahmed's word against this chap, and Mr Turner's dead. His friends would be expected to stand up for him. Even if he does go to the press it may not come to much.'

'I dunno, Kate. When you look at this morning's spreads…'

Every national paper except the *Independent* and *Morning Star* carries the story from the very careful press release OK'd yesterday by Defford. Again there's been no time to follow up the story. The tabs love it, the *Express* asking,

WHO IS MYSTERY WOMAN 'HAUNTING OZZY'?

And in the *Mirror*,

PSYCHIC? DON'T MAKE ME LAUGH!

All of them pointing out that the comedian still refuses to explain the figure of an abused woman messing up his nights in the *Big Other* house. All the papers carry a quote from the programme – the singer Eloise accusing Ahmed of being in denial, Rhys Sebold suggesting he's simply stressed out. A formal statement by producer Leo Defford emphasizing that a psychiatrist is standing by. Compared with all the world's problems, it's trivial stuff, but it'll still have commuters snatching copies from rail-station racks. Days like this, Grayle wishes she was back out there, trying to write shit like this.

'This guy Swinton,' she says. 'Don't wanna get in the way of the lawyers, but would anybody mind if I tried to talk to him? Don't imagine he's exactly a friend of Ozzy's any more, but maybe that's what I need.'

'You didn't tell me,' Kate says.

Within an hour, Defford calls a key-people conference to tell them they're going live for most of tonight's programme. Raising both fists joined at the wrists.

'We have a huge audience in handcuffs now. I think it's time to live dangerously, don't you?'

Getting the applause he expects. Grayle starts to join in but her hands won't connect. If Defford detected any hint of danger, no way would he consider going live.

In her cabin, she Googles Ozzy's old comprehensive school near Leeds, asks for Paul Swinton, but he's teaching. He sends a message through the school secretary that he doesn't want to talk from work but passes on his home number.

In the restaurant, Grayle has a vegetarian breakfast with the newly evicted Eloise, looking surprisingly fresh-faced and relieved, seaweed hair tied back.

'I guess you know where we are and everything?'

'Funny.' Eloise spreads hummus on a rice cake. 'I met her once. Trinity Ansell. I hoped she'd ask me to come and play at one of her weekends. No chance. Too left-field, me.'

'Probably just as well, when you think about it. If you *had* played here and HGTV found out – and they would – you'd've been dumped long before contract stage.'

'Actually I've been close enough. In my druid days, a bunch of us once went up to Belas Knap. The burial chamber? Genuinely weird place. You go on the wrong day, it won't like you. I mean *really* won't like you. Go inside you'll get wrung out. A guardian goes for you, my mate said. Maybe more than one. It's an important site.'

Grayle smiles. Knows all too well about guardians. Some horrific spectre, perhaps installed by human sacrifice when the chamber was first raised, however many thousand years ago, to protect the site. Dig up the wrong stone you'd see it in your dreams for ever.

'They're not a joke,' Eloise says. 'Trust me.'

Problem is nobody does. After Eloise got voted out last night, they screened Max's analysis. He was in a room Grayle had never seen before. A small room, which looked old, but in a Victorian way and could well be in a more modern part of Knap Hall. There were bookshelves all around Max, stacked with medical-looking tomes without dust covers and a few jacketed titles on psychic subjects.

Max said some people, predictably enough in these cynical times, found Eloise a little flaky in a New Age, neo-hippy way. Others saw pro-pagan politics at work. Several contrasted her aggressive attitude with that of Ashley Palk, who was always polite and appeared to listen to other people's points of view even if she thought they were insane.

If Eloise was secretly delighted to get the hell out, she hid it well, biting her lower lip and leaving the chamber, raising a flaccid hand only to Cindy before picking up her guitar case.

'There appears to be a consensus,' Max said brutally, 'that the *Big Other* project will probably proceed in a more balanced and considered way... without Eloise.'

'Tossers,' she said in the chapel. 'I don't hold out much hope for Britain any more.'

But now she's slept on it and confirmed that her crazy fee won't be affected by an early rejection.

'I was never in it to try and revive my career. Nobody wants esoteric TV programmes any more, and next to nobody buys CDs. I'll have enough money to restore Alison's cottage and buy some land. Plant fruit trees. Find a new relationship. You can really start again, can't you, with a few hundred grand in the bank? I mean for two days' work?'

'Ozzy Ahmed,' Grayle says. 'What's your verdict?'

'He got me out, I think. I accused him of not facing up to what he knows.'

'What do you think he knows?'

'He knows what he wants. When you see a glint in his eyes, it's hard and metallic. He's here for a reason and it's not money. In a way I like him. I even fancy him a bit. But I'd never trust him. Any more than I'd trust that house. Somebody said a cameraman quit?'

Grayle says nothing. Eloise starts to unscrew a jar of honey. It resists her.

'I mean this is not *Big Brother*, is it? Nobody's going to want to be the last in there. Any more than you'd want to be alone in Belas Knap.' She puts down the jar, looks up. 'When I came out last night, they let me look at the house from the outside, and I just... I just started quaking. I don't mean shivering, much stronger than that. And I'm thinking, hang on, I didn't feel that way when I was actually inside. Not even when I found the elder. What's that mean? Two days, and I come out and it's like walking into the sunshine, even though it's night and pissing down. What's that mean?'

'You tell me.' Grayle picks up the honey jar, gives the lid a twist. 'A lot of people lived and worked here when Trinity Ansell was here. You might say it got her in the end. You might even say it got Harry Ansell.'

'They were probably good people in their way. They were certainly throwing good energy at it. Brought jobs, too. Maybe they were supported by their employees.'

Grayle thinks of Lisa Muir.

We wanted them to go on loving the place. We wanted them to stay. Like I say, it was a brilliant job. We thought Mrs Ansell was turning the place round. Just by being there.

All that positive energy, and the dirt still gathering. Dead rats and birds and soil. She gets a sudden image, nothing mystical, nothing psychic, just dreadful, of a fair-haired man pulling a cart with big wooden wheels up the hill from the ruins of Sudeley Castle.

'Forget it,' Eloise says. 'I don't know what I'm saying.'

'No.' Grayle twists hard at the jar's metal lid, feels sweat below her shorn hair. 'Keep talking. You don't love this place, do you? None of you. Most of you are just here for the money.'

'Takes more than that,' Eloise says. 'Greed's not good, but it's not necessarily evil. And for some of us it's just despair. I'm a fruitcake, sure, but when we were doing *House Wizard* I picked up evil in a few places. And again at Alison's cottage. She was murdered, I know that. I'd walk through that village and I'd know the people who torched her house – the killers – were there. Just like when I looked back at the house last night, I knew, for the first time I knew what it meant when they say your flesh creeps.'

'But you didn't feel that when you first went in? When the worst thing in there was elder wood.'

'No. You're right. I didn't.'

'Which suggests there's something in there – something negative, let's just call it *negative* – that wasn't there when you first went in. Alone.'

'That's a cranky thing to say, Grayle.'

'Yeah, I know.'

'You still connected with Marcus Bacton?'

'You remember him?'

'I course I remember him. And how you couldn't use my story because his magazine was closing down. I never forget a crank.' She looks suddenly forlorn. 'And, yeah, I know when I go back to that cottage, with my ill-gotten gains from Hunter-

Gatherer, it'll probably mean bugger all. All that planting fruit trees, finding a nice guy to help pick the apples, that won't happen. I might go back and they'll break down my resolve, those bastards in the hunt. Or kill me. Like Alison.'

She laughs, a little shrilly.

'So don't go back,' Grayle says. 'Learn a lesson from Knap Hall.' She waves the honey jar. 'Let's see if they have one of these we can actually get into.'

She finds Jo Shepherd in the live gallery, watching Ashley Palk talking to Cindy.

Ashley going, 'Let me say that I didn't start out as a sceptic. As a wee girl, I was fascinated by the supernatural. And UFOs. Didn't draw much distinction between them. I used to think it was an adult conspiracy. That adults knew the truth about the things that frightened us and when we grew up all would be clear.'

Something of Ersula in Ashley, Grayle thinks.

'Unfortunately,' Cindy says, 'the older we get, the more uncertain everything becomes. There is always a period, during childhood, when everything seems quite clear.'

'Children don't believe in the same way, Cindy. A ghost is a special effect. They know that a special effects department can do anything now. So a ghost – in the way that ghosts are allegedly experienced – is a rather inferior special effect.'

'But surely, part of the ghost experience is the sensation evoked by the encounter. Something special effects cannot yet replicate. Big Other, if you like.'

Jo says, 'I worked with him every week on the *National Lottery*, and I still don't know to what extent he's for real. I still don't know if he's just a transvestite or a proper transsexual. I don't know what bits he has under his skirt. And I don't really know what a shaman is.'

'Someone who mediates between the tribe and its ancestors on a spiritual level.'

'Like a medium?'

'Only less cosy. You're usually not thinking of ancestors in the sense of like your great-uncle, your grandma. Maybe local-ized energies to which we can turn in times of crisis. It's not so crazy. Some people choose to see it more in terms of psychology than religion.'

'Always a get-out, Grayle.'

'But the point is that a shaman's essentially a loner. Someone on the periphery. Often an outcast. Shunned because he's neither one thing nor the other. Both feared and despised. Unless he works in light entertainment.'

'Anyway, we'll see a lot of him tonight. He gets to tell his ghost story.'

'Live?'

'Leo thinks he's what we need right now.'

'What's that mean?'

Grayle looks down at the seated Jo. The worst of what she just said is that Cindy *live* is not someone accessible. She won't be able to consult Cindy at all tonight. Won't be able to tell him about Poppy Stringer or Jess Taylor.

Jo doesn't look up.

'I think it means that before the night's out,' she says heavily, 'Cindy gets to talk to the dead.'

55

Old and twisty lane

'AN IMPORTANT PART of their working lives, you see,' he says softly, 'was the management of death.'

He pauses, looking from face to face, and a camera follows him around the semicircle. They've all been asked, in a Matthew Barnes recorded message, to wear dark clothes tonight. And have generally complied. This means you can see only their faces in the firelight, which makes you really look at these faces. Normally, when you first meet people, you observe their taste in clothes, hairstyles, adornments. In this light, it's the real people, all faces naked, now that the woman with the sapphire in her nose has been removed.

None of them as compelling as the face of the man talking. A man in… late middle-age? Grayle realizes she doesn't know. He could be fifty, he could be approaching seventy. He's outside of normal time. Or something.

'I use the word "undertaker",' he says, 'as distinct from the term "funeral director". Always do more for you, they would, the old undertakers, than today's funeral directors with their coffin-catalogues and their plush reception rooms with the pot plants and the pastel walls. And "undertaker" is so full of an unintended profundity.'

His accent is Welsh at its cosiest, the Welsh of the old mining valleys in the south. But the Wales he's talking about is the wilder Wales, further north and further west where, it seems, he ended up spending a significant part of his childhood.

'So think of the Fychan brothers as farmers and undertakers. In the old way. They made coffins from local timber, and they carved headstones from local stone. They had their workshops in the outbuildings at the family farm. A hill farm, this was, on a ridge beyond Machynlleth. Most impressive against a blood-red dawn, when it would look like an extension of the rocks themselves.'

Grayle sees a sardonic grin on Rhys Sebold's thin, firelit face. A craggy face tonight; he still hasn't shaved. Now his head is sunk into the blackness of his chest and it's being slowly and scepti-cally shaken as the monk-faced man talks of the Fychan brothers and a relationship with death that went back generations.

When Cindy smiles... that smile seems almost calculated to induce unease. He can be very funny, but his smile is rarely part of that.

'My parents, see... they did not find it comfortable to spend too much time in the company of the Fychans. We kept our holiday caravan in the farthest corner of their field and my mother would not go alone past their buildings. Not even in full daylight. Which would have troubled the Fychans, had they known, for they were kindly people.'

Ozzy Ahmed leans forward to put another log on the fire. It's an oak log, heavier than he expected, Grayle figures, and he drops it. Raises an apologetic hand and leaves the log rocking on the hearth.

The fallen monk smiles, in his accommodating way.

'I suppose that what did it for my mother was hearing a story in the local pub. Or it might have been the post office. These were the days, you understand, when every village had a post office and a pub, and there was always time to chat. And my mother was told the story of how the Fychans were given notice of an impending client.'

Usually Emrys, it was. Grayle's heard this before. Emrys Fychan, who had been the sickly one in the family. Attacks of asthma – well, not good for a farmer, with the hay, or a carpenter, with the dust, so Emrys would do the books, the accounts, and the cooking. He never married, nor formed an attachment, so nobody was ever there when he awoke in the night. Usually to the sound of sawing.

Cindy leans forward, and you can see the shadow of his arm, making the sawing motion, up and down.

'A slow and rhythmic sawing in the little stone workshop across the yard. And a *light* in there. Well, the first time he hears it – little more than a boy, he is – up he gets and down the stairs he goes and makes a tentative journey through the summer night towards the window of the workshop, where a small light gleams – the softest white light. *Well...*'

Ashley Palk is sitting in an armchair, one leg crossed over the other, hands clasped around a knee. She's enjoying this.

Cindy opens up his hands.

'... no one there, of course. And when he reaches the window there's no light. And the sound of the sawing has ceased. Gone. And the workshop door, of course, is locked. And so he returns – rather troubled as you might imagine – to his bed. And the next time he's awakened it's by an urgent banging on the farmhouse door. Samuel Jones, it is, the farrier, with the news of the sudden death of his father in the night.'

He leans back.

'In the course of one summer I would be told many such stories. Mostly by the Fychans themselves. A long-ago summer. It was only the second day of our holiday in the caravan when my father decided we should walk out over the hills to Staylittle. Not a particularly difficult walk on a fine summer morning, but here's Idris Fychan at the gate – a big man, grey beard and a very old cap like a broken slate. And Idris is moving the air with his hands. "Not the day for it, Mr Lewis." And my mother, who has made up a special picnic, laughs him away, and Idris sniffs and shrugs and looks a little sad. And, of course, my mother it is who slips down a crag, smooth as glass, and breaks an ankle, and me who is sent running back to the farm to summon an ambulance from Machynlleth.'

He tells them how the holiday came to a premature end – for his parents, at least. How his mother who, he later learned, was pregnant at the time with his sister Carys, was taken home to Merthyr by his father. Travelling without Sydney, as he was then. His father, worried he would not be able to cope, had accepted the offer by the wife of Idris Fychan to look after the boy for a few days until things were organized.

'Well, the few days turned into a few weeks. Until the end of the school holidays, in fact. I was twelve years old and learned more in those weeks than in all the rest of my schooling. And years later went back to the Fychans for more advanced tuition.'

'In what?' Rhys Sebold asks. 'The telling of tall stories?'

'Learning to be what I am. For my sins. And they are many.'

The camera lingers in the honey light, exploring the wooden panels, the lofty inglenook and a solid chess table for the drinks. A nice shot of five silhouettes grouped around the monkish man as he rises and straightens his tweed skirt.

'What I am,' he says sadly, again.

Grayle's alone in her micro-cabin with a TV.

No multi-views tonight. She's been thrown out of the stable. A live broadcast needs too many people, working like a machine.

They'll come for her if and when they need her. It's strange watching alone on a single screen in a prefabricated cupboard in a low-lit village above the house, the dirty lantern. Which is in here now. Odd how a single screen, after so many, concentrates the mind.

The phone rings on the desk.

'He was a little sod,' Paul Swinton says. 'Got beaten up a few times for it, but he couldn't stop himself. Smart remarks, you know? He could always hurt big kids with his tongue more than they could hurt him with their fists.'

'That's talent,' Grayle says.

She tried to get Swinton earlier, before the programme started, but his phone was engaged and she ended up leaving her number on his machine. Is he calling back now, nearly ten thirty, just to show he's not watching Ozzy?

'We used to be big mates. I went to his wedding. I was almost his best man, but then he got Neil Gill, instead, who he used to write comedy scripts with, and we drifted apart. He was a big star, and I was just a maths teacher at his old school. He always hated maths.'

'Mr Swinton,' Grayle says, 'we were very disturbed to read your email.'

'I didn't want to write it, but Dave Turner was a good man. One of the best, and there's no way he liked little boys, not in that way. Not in any way, now I come to think of it, he was an old-fashioned teacher.'

'You know why Ozzy Ahmed might've made that up about him?'

'Like I say, I've had nothing to do with Austin for years.'

'Anybody you can think of who might shed some light on it? See, we rely on the residents to tell the truth.'

'He *did* lie. Quite a lot, no doubt about that. If he thought a lie was funnier than the truth, he'd lie.'

'That kind of figures. But doesn't make me happy.'

'I'm glad you're taking it seriously.'

'More seriously than you know. If he's lying about this, he could be lying about other things.'

She has his confidence.

'Have you spoken to Neil Gill? They don't work together much any more, but I think they're still mates.'

'You know that for sure?'

'I'm still in touch with Neil. He was at school with us. He should've been with us and the skull that night, but he had a cold. At least he said he had a cold. I think he just didn't want to do it. He never liked that skull.'

Grayle notes that Ashley Palk is now regarding Cindy with what looks almost like affection.

'Tell me, Mr Lewis. Are you on a retainer with the Welsh Tourist Board, or is it more informal?'

The reply takes a while to come.

'Ms Palk. All too clear, it is, that your knowledge of the new Wales is distressingly scant. In my experience, the Wales Tourist Board is wary of such primitive throwbacks as the Fychan brothers. Does not invite people to Wales to be intimidated. Wrongly, in my view, mind – a certain kind of English visitor relishes the sinister. But there we are.'

He looks around.

'The Fychans' parlour was not unlike this room, in age, at least, though much smaller and more rudimentary. Walls of rubble stone, an ancient, faded rug over cracked flags. The house was reached by an old and twisty lane. Some say that spirit-paths are straight, but the Fychans found that it often helps to disorient them.'

'Who?' Roger Herridge asks. 'The spirits?'

'The ashen husks of the departed are rarely to be welcomed.'

'This is *such* bullshit,' Rhys Sebold says.

'But, Rhys, it's why we're *here*.' Helen Parrish is on her cushion on the edge of the ingle with a small glass of white wine, distantly amused. 'As nobody's given us a clue about what's supposed to haunt this house—'

'NOTHING haunts this house except us.'

'—should we not be not be trying to find out? Earning our money?'

'Come on then.' Rhys is up on his long legs. 'Come on, then, spirits. Bring green bile from my lips. Spin my head. *Possess* me.'

'Let's not descend to the juvenile.' Ashley uncrosses her legs, sits up, thoughtful. 'Cindy, tell me, if your friends the Fychans were here now, what might they do to contact the spirits?'

'But they wouldn't, see. The shaman is not a medium. Consider it presumptuous, he would. Let the individual dead lie.'

'Bullshit,' Rhys says irritably. 'So much incredible bullshit.'

'Let's not condemn it all out of hand,' Ashley says.

'Oh, sorry.' Helen looks up, perhaps just slightly tipsy. 'I thought you'd been condemning it all out of hand for over a decade.'

'I'm always open to correction.'

'*Ashley*,' Ozzy Ahmed says silkily, 'I didn't know you were into *correction*. I myself—'

Ashley raises hands for hush, looks around, face to face, ending at Cindy's.

'*Should* we make an effort?'

'Never claimed to be a medium.' Cindy straightens his skirt. 'A little too cosy for me. Too *drawing room*.'

'Table turning?' Ashley turns her chair to face his. 'Ectoplasm? Didn't you once produce ectoplasm through the beak of… what's his name?'

'Kelvyn Kite. Left him in his box, up in my room. Has a tendency to be confrontational. That was comedy, Ashley. Not always useful in our situation.'

'Well, let's see what we can find.'

Ashley comes elegantly to her feet and into the ingle, prodding a smouldering log to one side, a camera closing in on her hands reaching for the handle of a small iron door in the stone. Grayle doesn't even remember a door in there.

'I noticed when we came in from the dining room tonight…' Ashley's voice crisp from the personal mic as she messes with a metal latch, '… that the wee cupboard in here, the door was open. I think one of us was meant to notice, don't you? Here we are.'

As Ashley emerges, arms full, Grayle's getting a sense of sequence, almost scripted drama. Which is not possible.

Helen says, 'God, what the hell is *that*?'

Ashley brings it out, lowers it to the chess table.

'Oh, that *is* a rather lovely one,' Cindy murmurs.

It fills Grayle's screen: a wheel of what looks like grey stone, covered in glass or perspex. A pentagram in its centre. Curly letters around its perimeter. Isolated words.

One says, NO.

Another says, GOODBYE.

'I want to smash it already,' Rhys Sebold says.

56

The haunted

THE GLIDING TRIANGLE on which you place your forefinger – the planchette – has a hole through which a captive letter or symbol can be viewed.

Cindy watches little Ashley, so pert in her black knitted dress, touching it with an ovalled nail.

'I'd say five people, maximum, can fit a fingertip on here.'

'Making me the sixth,' Rhys Sebold says. 'How thoughtful of it.'

'I'd be happy to stand down for you, Rhys,' Ashley says.

'You will not, Ms Palk. This was your idea. If you simply want to prove that it doesn't work, well, fine. I'll watch.'

If, Cindy thinks, Mr Sebold can detach his gaze from her breasts.

'There *is* actually a simple way to prove it doesn't work,' Ashley says. 'Unfortunately, it only applies where you have the wee bits of paper in a circle, with a letter inscribed on each one. If the letters are visible to the participants, it will indeed begin to spell out credible messages. Turn the pieces of paper over, letters facing down, and its literacy is out the window.'

'All *that* proves, lovely,' Cindy tells her, 'is that spirits don't have X-ray eyes. Why should we assume that they acquire higher senses? Or even a higher intelligence. I tend to think of the earthbound dead as rather dim, and basic in their desires.'

'Or if we're all blindfolded,' Ashley says. 'That would also work.'

'Tedious, though, lovely, and the viewers would be deprived of the expression in the eyes of whichever of us is told that he or she has only two weeks to live.'

'That happen often?' Helen Parrish asks.

'Only to those foolish enough to ask when they're scheduled to depart this world. Spirits can never resist ruining someone's night, the scamps.'

Cindy watches them peering and prodding, as if the device might light up.

He's noticed this before with live television; it generates its own nervous energy, a feverish need to *do something*. There can be no editing. Each moment of inactivity is a moment lost for ever. The air is electric with possibility.

Only a matter of time before this thing appeared. He wonders how long it's been there, in that discreet cupboard. High quality, it is, for all its vulgarity. A superior toy, doubtless the best Leo Defford's people could find on the Internet outside of the antiques trade. For all his professed disdain for psychic programmes, Defford can't afford to let two hours of live television pass without incident. Cindy remembers what he said when they were motoring towards what would prove to be the cooling corpse of Harry Ansell.

You know how to work a ouija board, Cindy?

He actually knew less then than he does now after some hurried research which has left him rather more respectful of the so-called 'talking board' than he expected.

Five chairs are arranged now in a circle around the chess table away from the fire. Cindy hesitates before sitting down.

'Physical contact is recommended. Usually suggested, it is, that our knees should be touching under the table.'

Ozzy Ahmed looks stern.

'Steady on, Cindy.'

'Also, some groups begin with a communal prayer.'

Rhys, it is, who advises dispensing with this futile formality, leaving Cindy to suggest that those who wish to might pray silently. Roger Herridge nods, then loosens his tie, tosses back his hair and sits down, flashing his cuffs as if preparing to deal cards.

'How do we start?'

'I always imagine two verses of "Abide With Me",' Helen says. 'Was that in an old film?'

If it was, nobody else seems to have seen it. Ashley Palk positions the chess table directly under the candle hoop.

'I think we should formally decide what we're hoping to achieve by this. I'm assuming… contact with whatever haunts this house?'

'That,' Cindy says, 'presents another dilemma of which we should be aware. Normally, an outlet is offered to whoever or whatever might seek one… *if* its intentions are positive. If it wants to help us.'

'In other words,' Herridge says, 'discourage the demonic?'

'A time-honoured preliminary, Roger, in ritual magic. Which – make no mistake – this undoubtedly is. The first ouija boards known by that inexplicably silly name were apparently manufactured in America during the spiritualist boom of the early 1900s. But the principle goes back into the mists. Pythagoras, I believe, used something similar.'

And dangerous are they? Well, yes, even if the worst it can do is unlock doors to the subconscious. Who knows what inner-plane connections the subconscious might make? Poke a forefinger through the veil and you may have difficulty withdrawing it.

'I don't think,' Herridge says, rubbing a cheek, 'that we have any reason to suppose that whatever is thought to haunt this place is terribly friendly, do you?'

'Is that what we all feel?' Cindy asks.

Helen shrugs.

'Never felt too pleasant to me.'

Cindy is uncertain about this. It's not really the house itself. They don't use buildings, they're not really squatters, these entities. The famous technical-sounding term 'stone-tape theory' used by Roger is misleading. Invented for a TV drama. Stone has its qualities, but a haunting requires the haunted: people, life force.

He feels suddenly quite weary of this, wishing he was normal. Wishing he'd never been exposed during his formative years to the utter strangeness – though not so much in West Wales – of the Fychans. Envying the clean-cut certainty of Ashley and Rhys, sterile though it might be.

Never mind. Too late now. He is what he is.

He taps the planchette.

'A triangle, see? In ritual magic, a spirit is summoned into the triangle – whether on a table or the temple floor – and held there. The planchette is this same magical triangle in miniature. Seldom spoken of, this, especially in toy shops.'

'So if we each have a finger on the thing,' Helen says warily, 'then we're inviting whatever it is to…'

'Cross our threshold. And we don't even know who it is we are inviting until they're here. Madness, isn't it?'

Rhys picks up the planchette.

'A bit of bakelite or something. With a hole in it. I can't tell you how scared I am.'

He drops it back on the board. Cindy moves it to its original position away from the symbols.

'Now then. Customary, it is, to familiarize ourselves with the movement of the planchette. So if we all…'

Ashley and Roger and then, after some hesitation, Helen, apply a forefinger. Cindy looks at Ozzy Ahmed.

Ozzy pushes up a sleeve of his hoodie, holds up a finger in that well-known mildly obscene gesture, looks at it then lowers it to the planchette.

'There we are,' Cindy says. 'That's— Oh, my goodness…'

With their five extended fingers aboard, the triangle has gone skating wildly away. Ozzy jerks back his finger.

'Little bugger!'

He looks genuinely alarmed, which is interesting. For Cindy, the nature of Ozzy Ahmed's scepticism has never quite been established. Cynical, yes, but evasive rather than unequivocal in his dismissal of the others' beliefs. Resistance rather than outright rejection. A comedian's traditional role is as bewildered victim: Ozzy cowering from the madness of his mother-in-law, scepticism as a shelter.

'Not used one before then, boy?'

'Never even seen one before.' Ozzy nods at the board. 'Where it says "goodbye", why's that in big letters?'

'So you don't forget, when you're finishing, to close the door behind you.'

'And if you leave it swinging?'

'Then you risk allowing something to remain in the room… unsupervised.'

'With respect, Cindy,' Rhys Sebold says, a thin wire extending under his voice, 'there's a very sound argument for saying guys like you are borderline fucking insane.'

Cindy doesn't look up.

'Rhys, would you be prepared, as an outsider, to keep notes on any answers received?'

Rhys mutters, flattening his back against a wall of the inglenook. Cindy scowls.

'"Borderline". Damned once again with faint praise. Now, then, who is to ask the questions? One person, it should be. A chorus causes confusion.'

'Not Ozzy,' Herridge says. 'Unless I've been reading the wrong books, they're not famous for their sense of humour on the Other Side.'

'No indeed. Sullen, they are, the earthbound, sometimes hostile. Can be like trying to quip your way out of a stabbing.'

'Has to be you, Cindy,' Ashley says. 'What's your definition of earthbound, by the way?'

Cindy talks, in a non-committal way, about the astral plane, the nearest etheric layer to this world, a clearing house for the newly dead, also accommodating those who would rather not leave, or remain joined to the earth-plane by obsession, compulsion, perversion, et cetera.

'Wait.'

This is Helen Parrish, shaking her head in faint dismay, as if coming down from some narcotic plateau.

'Hostility... demonism... obsession... perversion? Is it just me who thinks we're rushing into this stuff because we think it's our role in the battle for viewing figures?'

Good point. Cindy takes the chair opposite the inglenook, where the fire's burning quite low and smoky. While he doesn't believe the ouija to be hell's cellar-hatch, necessarily, this air of irreverence is perhaps misplaced.

Roger Herridge sits back, his hair a stallion's mane in the candlelight.

'The antagonism of someone like Rhys doesn't surprise me – I understand his reasons and I sympathize, of course. Ashley's enthusiasm – possibly *feigned* enthusiasm – doesn't worry me a great deal either. How can we possibly be harmed by childish nonsense? But I really don't think I'd want to ride roughshod over Helen's reservations.'

'All right, point taken,' Ashley says. 'We don't *have* to do this. However...'

'Yes.' Cindy folds his arms. 'Roger raises an interesting point. Why *are* you so keen to employ the talking board, Ashley? As someone for whom words like "psychic" and "spiritual" mean not much. I do think a little... candour might be in order at this stage.'

'You're a hard man, Cindy.'

'How flattering.'

'Look... all right... yes, I think the idea of spirits invading our space is complete rubbish. But I'm willing to consider the possibility that this... thing... can act as a sounding board, if you like, for our personal anxieties. That we can project our feelings through it and get beyond our normal inhibitions.'

'A channel for the subconscious?'

'Not all of us find it very easy to explain our feelings un-assisted. Look at Ozzy.'

Cindy turns to Ozzy.

'Difficult week for you, boy?'

'Not especially.'

'Spent the most profitable years of your career, you have, dissing all those cranks... and now here you are faced with the prospect of becoming one. Stressful, indeed. A bit like poor Paul on the road to Damascus. "Please don't let this happen to me, I'm an accountant."'

'You're a bugger, Cindy.'

'How much flattery can a man take? Listen, I think I'm deducing that Ashley would like us to try and contact whatever has been invading your space. Purely as a psychological exercise. Correct, Ashley?'

Cindy feels the sharp gust of Rhys Sebold projecting himself from the wall.

'For Christ's *sake*—'

'Rhys, you don't believe in Christ. Do you?'

'You just... you leave him alone, all right? Just keep your noses out. He's tired, that's all. Came here exhausted by overwork. He feels he has to perform constantly. If you want to watch a man crack up, melt down, just carry on with this...'

Silence. Ozzy is sitting between Ashley and Cindy, who feels the boy go tense. But when Ozzy looks up, his face is a scrubbed slate.

'Thanks, mate.'

Raising a bloodless hand to Rhys. Rhys nodding, perhaps not noticing that his best friend in the house is peering at him as if unsure who this is.

A pregnant moment of live television, it is, the viewers thinking, *Yes, he's right, this funny, amiable man might indeed be on the edge of a breakdown.*

But please, please, don't deprive us of this spectacle.

Cindy puts his head on one side, venturing no opinion either way. There's a vote later tonight for another exclusion, is there not? He doesn't mind being seen as what Marcus Bacton might describe as a national bastard, but equally he doesn't want to leave these people alone with a ouija board and an obligation to perform.

Ozzy stands up, stretches.

'Aye, all right, let's do it. What's to lose?' He looks over at the false wall with its duplicitous mirrors, addresses the glass eyes and their controllers. 'Just give us a few minutes, fellers, to psych ourselves up. Run some commercials, eh?'

57

Close to the land

GRAYLE HITS THE key, and the phone speed-dials and, hell, if someone doesn't answer this time...

'Whoever you are,' he says, 'can I call you back?'

'Mr Gill?'

'Tomorrow would be good, but not too early.'

'Mr Gill, my name's Grayle Underhill from HGTV. The *Big Other* programme? I'm calling about Ozzy Ahmed?'

'Oh. Yeah, I'm watching him, or I will be when the ads are off. What did you say you did at HGTV?'

'I didn't. I research. I take it you've been watching the whole show, night after night?'

'Most of it.'

'And you're still close to him, is that right?'

'In a strictly platonic way.'

'Mr Gill, Paul Swinton gave me your number. He's very unhappy about Ozzy's claim on our programme that he'd been abused by a teacher he called Cyril.'

'Yeah, he would be upset about that, Paul.'

'Because it's not true?'

'Not for me to say. And if I were you—'

'See, we're also a little unsure about Ozzy. We need to know if he's OK.'

'Everybody's unsure about Ozzy. He loves that. Now, if you—'

'And because we don't want him to cause any damage to himself or—'

'Or your company.'

'—we'd like to know if any other people he's been close to could be adversely affected by what Ozzy's been saying.'

Mr Gill laughs.

'Well,' he says, 'try not to take this personally, luv, but I can imagine that you, as a production company, could be very seriously affected by somebody's failure to figure out where Ozzy's coming from before they threw him into the bearpit that is *Big Other*. And like you say, he's my mate. And you – pleasant as you might sound – are not. Goodnight.'

'Mr Gill—'

God*damn*. She calls up the live gallery, asks for Jo Shepherd, is told that Jo isn't taking calls right now. Well, no. Jo will be sitting next to Leo Defford, watching male and female fingers descending on the planchette, like they're meeting for some kind of finger-sex, Defford going, 'good-good, good-good'.

In a sudden, frenzied need for blood-sugar, Grayle rips into one of the Big Sur cereal bars sent by her old boss, Lyndon, now with the *LA Times*.

Something deeper, more intelligent, more issue-led.

Oh, sure. The old ghost-show fallback: if nothing's happening, bring out the ouija board. It's fun, cheaper than a medium and doesn't need a hundred-page instruction manual. But then neither does a gun.

What really annoys her is that the ouija was quite obviously introduced with the collusion of Ashley. It was supposed to be only Cindy who was more equal than the others but it's now clear that, in the interests of staying ahead, Defford's been hedging his bets all along, playing more than one of the residents against the others. Keeping cards up different sleeves. *Bastard*.

Grayle abandons the Big Sur bar. An hour or so ago, before the programme started, she emailed Marcus, telling him about Poppy Stringer and Jess Taylor, the camerawoman. Now she calls him on the cellphone.

*

'Are you male?' Cindy asks.

The triangle hesitates before arrowing in on NO. It makes a very faint scratchy sound, like a mouse under floorboards.

Ashley whispers, 'Do we need to ask if it's a woman?'

'Are you female?'

YES.

'Are you known to any of us here?'

YES.

Ashley looks at Cindy, who shakes his head. No, he isn't going to try to narrow it down. Not yet, anyway. They lie, you see. They'll finger an individual out of pure mischief. Instead, he says,

'Did you die of natural causes?'

NO

'Violence?'

Again, there's a moment's hesitation before it replies in the positive. It always moves directly to yes or no, their fingers clearly resting so lightly that it seems impossible to tell if anyone's pushing. Doesn't look like it. Under the table one of his knees is touching Helen's, the other Ozzy's. He's asked for them all to concentrate on Ozzy, his interests, his welfare.

'Did the violence occur here?'

NO

This is the third apparent spirit to come through. The others made no sense, as if the planchette was only warming up, and were soon terminated: *Goodbye.*

'Was someone here witness to the violence?'

Hesitation, then

NO

Ashley: 'Go on, Cindy, you're walking all round this. Don't be a wimp. Ask if it was murder.'

'Is someone here…?'

…the cause of it, he was about to say, but the planchette is already moving, as if impatient with them. Cindy allows his finger to be dragged along to the letters of the alphabet.

G

U

Roger Herridge says, 'Gun?'

I

L

'God,' Helen says, 'this is genuinely unnerving. It is actually as if it has a mind of its own.'

T

Y

'Someone's guilty?' Herridge says. 'Of what?'

The planchette is static.

'Don't you see?' Ashley is inflicting upon them her famously condescending smile. 'It's the perfume. The perfume Ozzy was smelling in his room. Guilty by Gucci. As worn, memorably, by his ex-wife on their first date… what, fifteen years ago, Ozzy?'

Ozzy stares ahead, into the fire.

'Something like that.'

Herridge says 'But guilty of *what*?'

The planchette moves to the letter A, then the letter B. In this chamber, against this wan light, it's already acquired a distinct, mischievously knowing personality. They are the Seven again, the planchette is the new seventh. The others have given birth to it.

U

Cindy watches his finger amongst the others as if it's no longer his. He examines the faces of the others, nobody taking it lightly, even Ashley's hazel eyes conveying a suspension of disbelief. The planchette is an emotional magnet, drawing them in. Helen's knee and calf are against his.

S

'Abuse?'

YES

Cindy says quickly, 'Do you possess a white coat?'

The planchette quivers.

'Raincoat?'

Fitfully, the planchette spells out a message that makes none of them laugh.

ON

LY

A

SH

RO

UD

With impeccable timing, a candle sputters in the hoop, its flame reduced to a slender spiral of smoke.

'Went darker then,' Marcus says, 'did you see?'

'I'm not sure.'

Both of them watching the same picture on TV sets miles apart. This is a little crazy, Grayle's thinking. Could be that nothing at all will happen bar a few more creepy messages. Equally, it could be that something will happen that won't be obvious onscreen and maybe not until days afterwards.

'You remember the brother and sister I talked to, 'bout four years ago? Messing with the ouija board, then both are troubled by persistent poltergeist phenomena in their separate homes.'

'Yes I do. Proved nothing.'

The camera pulls back, the picture opening to an overview of the company around the table.

'There, you see,' Marcus says. 'At least one candle's gone out.'

'What's that mean? Some absorption of energy? Or someone left a door open.'

Grayle wondering what they might all be seeing if Jess Taylor was shooting through the wall now. Nothing, probably. That wasn't how it worked.

'This room,' Marcus says. 'Was this where the Ansell woman saw Parr in her coffin?'

'I don't know. Cindy thought that was a dream, anyway.'

Though she's never forgotten the entry in the diary that Cindy showed her. She can close her eyes, recall most of the words.

... cold and there's a blue light, a shaft of blue light bathing a
low wooden bed. A truckle did they call it? Her eyes are closed,
though her mouth is slightly open. And I know she's dead.

'And, anyway, in the dream it was a bed… a truckle.'

'As she saw it. Perhaps she'd never seen the engraving in the
Annals of Parr in her lead coffin. Not what we'd think of today
as a coffin.'

Grayle watches Roger Herridge standing on a chair applying
a match to the dead candle in the hoop.

'You still think that when KP's body was missing for a while,
it was because Fishe had… borrowed her?'

'Yes, I do, actually. It fits with what he is.'

Is? *Is?* Abel Fishe is more than two centuries dead.

The phone is damp in Grayle's hand.

'You can start to see things that aren't there, Marcus. We all
do that.' Trying to hold her voice steady. 'We don't know
anything about him. Nobody does. He's a bogeyman. Anything
you care to say about him goes.'

'Is there still a cross-country path between Sudeley and Knap
Hall?'

'I don't know. Never been much of a hiker. Why?'

'He'd just load the coffin on to his cart, throw some straw
over it, wheel it up there.'

His cart. His bier. *No.*

'How was all this hidden, Marcus? Why isn't Fishe in the
history books?'

'Underhill, he's not *important* enough. He's just a sex addict
with a particular taste for women beyond his social class. "Abel's
Rent" – even has official dispensation for doing what he does.
It's just like… like the BBC employed Savile, and the NHS
allowed him into its hospitals and he acquired an executive role
at Broadmoor. Arguably the most prolific sex criminal in the
country, doing what he does almost in full view of the nation.
How was *that* hidden for the duration of the bastard's lifetime?'

'Yeah, I know, and dead women, too, allegedly, in the hospital morgues. Necrophilia. I see where you're going.'

'Not necessarily.'

'Marcus, I can't take this tonight, OK?'

'"Entire and uncorrupted" are the words in the *Annals*. After 230 years. Naturally, I've been reading up on tales of uncanny preservation. People didn't have access to scientific theories about delayed putrefaction. They simply thought there was supernatural or religious significance. Think of the body of St Cuthbert carried around the countryside intact and undecayed for years by the monks. Immense sacred power. Now Katherine Parr… a queen of England… survivor of the extraordinary Henry VIII. Lying there, "entire and uncorrupted" and…'

Please God, don't let him use the word moist.

'I'll go no further down that road for the moment.'

'Thank you,' Grayle says.

'But necrophilia may not be the right word.'

'Oh that we should sully this man's name…'

'He has a fascination with death. Perhaps as a rite of passage. And he's steeped in this countryside. He's grown up with Belas Knap, a place where bodies were taken, but not a grave as we think of one. Also perhaps a place of rebirth. The so-called false entrance, shaped like a vagina. A very obvious entrance, but not one that a *man* can use.'

On the TV, Grayle watches Roger Herridge brushing himself down, taking his seat at the table, his back to the smouldering hearth. The camera lingers on the circlet of small flames, like a halo above the group. Seven candles alight.

'So, OK, we have a sacred sexual orifice.' Even after Ersula, Grayle's happier with the prehistoric stuff. 'Sealed against men, but open to the gods. Yeah, that makes sense, Marcus.'

'Good.'

'And I'm sure an illiterate redneck like Fishe would know all about it from his extensive private collection of antiquarian manuscripts.'

'Underhill… no one's saying he was an historian or even a magician. He was *close to the land*. He followed his instincts. Death, Underhill. And sex. That's what this is about. All he'd understand. Sex and death. Something eternal about that combination, don't you think?'

'And Knap Hall?'

'His place. His temple. Sanctum. Lair. No links with Sudeley. Katherine Parr was never there hosting dinners in a red silk dress. Never here in a bed. Never even there alive. *Now* do you see what Knap Hall is?'

58

Say goodbye

HELEN LETS BOTH hands fall below the table.

'Someone's doing this.'

'But it's a spirit, surely.' Rhys Sebold from out of shot. A camera finds him still over by the fireplace. 'Perhaps even *Diana*? Anything's possible in a haunted house, Helen, *you* know that.'

Helen's long dispensed with the wine glass, no longer looks at all tipsy and, when she turns to Rhys, her voice is cold.

'Perhaps we should swap places.'

'I'm enjoying myself too much here.'

'No, come on…' Helen pushes back her chair, stands up. 'You know you want to.'

'Then you know me better than I know myself, Ms Parrish.'

A blur and a small mic-crunch as Helen steps out, then her face is caught side on, angry, a pearl earring spinning.

'You're not giving value for money, Rhys. You'll be remembered as rather peevish, and the BBC will never give you your radio programme back, and you'll wind up on the graveyard shift at the jewellery channel. I'm sorry, but you're going to do this.'

Ashley laughs.

'Better do it, Rhys. Or, even worse, you're going to look like a closet born-again Christian.'

Rhys Sebold puts on a grin – remembering he's live on TV, Cindy thinks, as Rhys drops into the chair next to him.

'Christians are, of course, entitled to their eccentric faith,' he says.

'Tactful of you to remember that, boy. Now let's hope' – Cindy's finger has remained steadfast on the planchette, across from Roger Herridge's – 'that our friend has not deserted us.'

He looks across at the fire, and it isn't there. The inglenook is dead. The walls are pale brown and roughened stone. There's a lumpen chair and a table and hangings like scraps of rotting clothing on an old skeleton.

He blinks, stays calm as Ashley's voice comes out of thick air.

'You ready, Cindy?'

'I'm sorry… yes.'

Flaking red logs are back on the hearth. All is as it was. He steadies his breathing, waits as Ozzy and Ashley replace their fingers on the triangle, followed, flamboyantly, by Rhys. He thinks, *female*. He thinks of a woman in white, holds her at his centre.

'Are you angry,' he's asking, 'at the manner of your death?'

YES

So immediate that Ashley's finger is left behind. And then, quickly, before he can lose her, he asks,

'What's your name? Can you tell us that?'

Grayle wonders why he's taken so long to get around to this. In the live gallery, Leo Defford will be on the edge of his seat, waiting for the planchette to land on the letter T, from Trinity, or at least K, for—

A

Oh.

Helen's writing it down on a cigarette packet.

A

The planchette returns, and there's a pause.

N

The planchette returns more slowly. When it starts to move again, it seems to trundle like a miniature version of the wood-man's bier.

G

'A N G?' Herridge says, 'Angela?'

And then it all goes crazy, the table tilting upwards, even Ashley Palk squealing, and then the table rocks back and the camera in the ceiling sees the planchette take off like a small bird as the ouija board goes sliding over the edge, hitting the stone flags with more force than you would imagine, and shocked faces go whipping past on Grayle's screen.

The planchette clicks on the flags, chairs are pushed back.

Ashley Palk separates herself from the others, goes to stand by the Gothic door to the dining room, breathes hard for a few moments, tucks disarranged fair hair behind an ear.

Ashley says, 'Thank you, Austin, but let's leave it at that, shall we? You've done enough. Show's over.'

You can almost see the anger like a dust storm in the room, but none of it's coming from Ashley Palk. Ashley's standing in a capsule of calm at its core.

Grayle points at the screen.

'Look at her. She couldn't be more happy.'

Grayle's been summoned to the live gallery. The programme has just over a half-hour to run. Or more if they want it. Might turn out to be the last thing they do want but if Leo Defford knows for sure then Grayle figures he's a major loss to TV drama.

He's on his feet, the monitors around him like a map of the landscape of insanity.

'Why?' he says.

'Because… I guess she came here with a purpose. Amply fulfilled, it looks like.'

'Asked me if we could make a ouija board available,' Defford says. 'Said someone was playing games. Claimed she didn't know who.'

'Oh, she knew.'

'Then why didn't *we*?' His fist smashes down on a curving desk. By *we* he means Grayle. 'You're giving me all this shit about the wrong ghost, while Palk's stealing the fucking programme from under us?'

427

It's true. He's so wrong about everything, but this is still true. Grayle watches Roger Herridge coming into shot, addressing Palk.

'Go back to the beginning, I think.'

This is a very different Herridge, hard-voiced, focused. Quizzing Ashley Palk like she's been hauled up before some Parliamentary select committee he's serving on.

'I'm quite happy to do that,' Ashley says. 'Let's start with the perfume. Ozzy's had a bad night. Keeps thinking there's a woman in his room. He identifies her perfume because it's the one worn by his ex-wife when they first started going out together. Well, obviously it can't be her. She's very much alive and wouldn't be seen – if you'll excuse the term – dead in Ozzy's room. And he's given no indication of pining for her – certainly not in the divorce court.'

Defford turns to a director.

'Ozzy… tight shot.'

Here he is, on his own by the chess table, the ouija board at his feet. No clear reaction on his face, but Grayle has the feeling that the habitual crooked little half-smile is no more than a twitch away.

'Not fazed,' Jo Shepherd says. 'Not fazed at all.'

'But more to the point,' Ashley says, 'when that first date was happening, Gucci's Guilty wouldn't be launched for another ten years at least.'

Jo says, 'Bloody hell.'

'I know that for a fact…' Ashley's sweating, very slightly. A glow. 'Because a friend of mine had an early sample pack and I bought some for my wee sister's birthday, the year before she got married. So Ozzy was either hallucinating or lying. I started to watch him very closely. I'm a trained, practical psychologist. This is what I do. Behavioural science.'

'Whose idea was it to get Ashley into the house?' Grayle asks.

Defford's expressionless.

'Mine. She took a while to agree.'

It's like a lecture in there now.

'… began to notice the discreet ways Ozzy would let his own experiences filter into other people's stories – his hijacking of Helen's Diana stuff is a prime example. All very clever. Giving the impression of a man secretly grappling with the worst personal crisis he's ever faced. He's convincing us this is the very last thing he wants to talk about. He's shocked and embarrassed and deeply unhappy – an unbeliever, the very *idea* of something paranormal happening to him, of all people. And gradually he gets us all – *and* the viewers *and* the media – on his hook, believers and sceptics alike. He persuades us to *prise* the details out of him, clearly against his will. His friend Rhys thinking we're bullying him.'

'What's the *matter* with him?' Jo shaking her fists. 'Ahmed. Why doesn't he *say* something?'

'If you'd asked me a few minutes ago,' Defford says, 'I'd have said they were in it together. Ashley, Ozzy and possibly Sebold, too. Wonderful publicity for *The Disbeliever*. A new direction for Ahmed's genius. But the way he's behaving now makes you wonder.'

He's right, Grayle thinks. If Ozzy's just done the greatest performance of his career, why's he letting Ashley take all the credit?

Herridge says, 'If you knew he was making it all up, why did you keep quiet for so long?'

'Roger, I'm a psychologist, not a detective. I observe, I assess, and I test what I'm getting against my and others' experiences. Sure, I've convinced m'self he's lying, but I'm not going public with it until I can convince the world. I'm even thinking, OK, he's created this ghost, he's given her a white mac and a history of physical abuse… is it possible *he's* the abuser?'

Defford's nodding.

Helen Parrish says, 'Is that likely?'

'It was possible,' Ashley says, 'but I wanted to give him the chance to take it further. To bring this woman, as it were, to life.'

They keep jumping to Ozzy, but it's like a still; he doesn't seem to have moved.

'Ouija,' Defford says.

Still on the floor at Ozzy's feet, the planchette on its back.

'I may have lied about the ouija board,' Ashley says. 'If I gave the impression it was something I'd no experience of, that was my only untruth. I've worked with my fellow psychologist and ex-illusionist Richard Wiseman and others in exploring the paraphernalia of the seance room. Spent many an hour over a hot planchette until I could easily identify who – whether intentionally or subliminally – was manipulating it.'

'And, ah' – Cindy's voice – 'you're in no doubt?'

'No doubt at all.'

'Who pushed the table over just as Ozzy's guest was spelling out her name?'

'You were there, Cindy, was it you?'

'Angela?' The shot widens to take in Roger Herridge, hair down over his face, his head inclining now to Ozzy's and tilting to one side. 'You *prick*.'

Then Rhys Sebold's shouldering between them, but Herridge is already walking away, tossing back his mane.

Nobody needs an explanation. A liquid glint in Herridge's eyes he passes under the candle spears which are themselves beginning to drown in molten wax.

'One of Roger's flower ladies,' Grayle says dully. 'I think her name's Angela.' She turns away. 'Ahmed really screwed us all, didn't he? Came in with the sole intention of screwing us.'

'We've had at least ten calls or emails,' Jo says, 'from people putting names to the woman he keeps seeing.'

'Let's see how Sebold's taking it,' Defford says.

But Rhys's thin, edgy face is hard to read. Street-cred at stake here. Grayle's guessing Ahmed didn't disclose his intentions to his self-styled friend, which is going to hurt. But is it better from Rhys's point of view to conceal that? Let viewers think he's part of the scam.

Ozzy doesn't look at Rhys, or anybody. Only the ouija board by his feet. Bends slowly and picks it up, stands looking down at it between his hands, before dropping it on the flags and hacking the heel of his right shoe into its face until spidery cracks appear.

He kicks it away, faces the false wall.

'Get me out, please.'

Jo looks at Defford.

'Can he?'

'Of course he can. We can hardly be seen to be keeping prisoners. Besides, they're voting on the second eviction as we speak. Chances are it'll be him.'

'Doesn't look like he's prepared to wait, Leo. Clearly doesn't want to get into explanations.' Jo glances at the nearest screen, winces. 'What's that fool doing?'

Roger Herridge is looking down at the wounded ouija board, prodding it with a suede toe.

'You didn't say goodbye to it, Ozzy. Got to say goodbye or the spirit doesn't go away. Eloise would be furious if she were here.'

'El-o-ise,' Ozzy says, his voice almost musical, 'got kicked out for being a mental bitch. I, on the other hand, choose to go without assistance. Is anybody even listening to me? No?' He looks around, retrieves a half-empty wine bottle. 'This anybody's?'

'Helen's, I expect,' Sebold says. 'Keeps Diana in there.' He turns at a movement. 'Haven't you done enough for one night?'

Ashley stops, couple of paces from Ahmed. Between him and Rhys, she looks slight and unexpectedly vulnerable, like she's realized she might have no friends left in here.

'Come on,' she says. 'You almost pulled it off, didn't you?'

Ozzy doesn't turn to her, but he can surely see her in the mirror.

'I mean, what was I supposed to do, Ozzy, once I knew?'

He stands tossing the bottle from hand to hand, shaking out a smile. Directly in front of the false wall, he's huge in three screens.

'I think what we'd all like to know is why you did it? M'self, I really don't think it was just to prove you could get away with it, and I… we don't want you to go, Ozzy.'

Three cameras record Ozzy Ahmed bowling the wine bottle overarm at the two-way mirror. In two of them, his arm hides his face, its expression. Looks like slow motion, Grayle thinks, like he's feigning it, until the bottle full of green candlelight leaves his hand.

Three boom mics and two personals snatch the sounds of exploding glass, but the pictures are just splintering abstracts, the only coherent one showing Ashley clawing at her face and the blood and glitter between her fingers.

59

Last fruitcake

FROM HER WINDOW at the pop-up, she sees a line of grey in the north-eastern sky. It might be pre-dawn; it might be a false dawn, just like all the others.

It's too hot in here for near-winter. She takes a short shower, sits on the edge of the bed in T-shirt and briefs, calls Marcus. She's promised to call him, however late, but won't push it. She'll let it ring twice and then hang up.

'So how many left in there, Underhill?'

'Jeez, didn't even hear you pick up. Where are you?'

'Downstairs. It's all downstairs in the bastard bungalow. Anderson has the defibrillator plugged in. Time is it?'

'Four a.m.... sometime around there. Maybe five. Who cares? What did you say?'

'How many left in the house?'

'Three. Helen, Herridge and, uh, Cindy. Defford said they had to go through with the vote. Jo thought with Ahmed out, that would suffice, but Defford said they had to stick by the rule. End of story.'

End of Sebold. Hardly went out with good grace, but what did he really expect? Oddly, Max figured it wasn't the viewers' general feeling that he was party to Ahmed's scam that did it, it was implying that Helen was a lush. Everybody likes Helen. Sebold should have known that. Helen's your older sister, ageing gracefully, wiser but never throwing it at you.

'Where's the duplicitous Ahmed now, then?'

'Luxury block next door. Soon's he comes out the tunnel, Defford's waiting for him. I don't know all of what was said, but

Defford got what he wanted, which was a promise from Ahmed that he'd go before the cameras tomorrow – today – and explain. Different person when he was out of there, according to Jo.'

'You weren't there?'

'I was at the gate with the cops. Maybe it was on the news?'

'Not that I saw.'

'Too late, maybe. What happened, hundreds of people phoned the cops, accusing Ahmed of assault... malicious wounding... worse? Never stand up in court, but he'd still've faced a night in the slammer if Ashley hadn't gone out to the walled garden insisting she wouldn't be pressing charges. Standing there wrapped in some guy's sheepskin coat. "No, truly, officer, I'm fine". Blood seeping through the dressings. Marcus, a mirror, for God's sake? She coulda lost an eye.'

'Ahmed have any idea what he—?'

'Says it was an accident, he didn't plan to let go of the bottle. Deeply upset and traumatized. Yeah, right, but also denying the woman in white was a scam. Tells Defford he didn't know where she came from. Doesn't believe in ghosts, God or Allah, but he doesn't know where she came from. Defford thinks he's lying. Even I think he's lying. Why, why *why*?'

'Where's Palk?'

Ashley's overnighting in the pop-up medical suite, but insisting she has to go back in the house else scepticism will be seriously under-represented. Grayle rocks back on the bed.

'Jeez, Marcus, I am more than a little sick at heart. Over six months of my life. *Six months.*'

'Could've told you it was a hiding to nothing. We're not—'

'Not meant to know, yeah, yeah. Never gonna work. But, hey, the show's still a major success story. Viewing figures doubling. No wonderment, no sense of the world being bigger than we thought, but what's that shit matter?'

Marcus doesn't laugh either.

'You know why that is, Underhill? Why nothing's come of it? Two sides. Eloquent and reasonably well-educated people with opposing viewpoints. Neither wants a reason for doubt. But neither wants to show weakness in front of the other, so nobody takes it seriously. Just a game. Except for the poor Starke woman, and look what happened to her.'

'Worse than that, Marcus, it turned into the competition it was never gonna be. Now, at the halfway stage, we have what looks very like a winner. Let's hear it for fragrant atheist, Ashley Palk. Whom, against all my instincts, I've actually kind of grown to like. Listen, I better try and get some sleep. People to interview. Maybe even Ahmed.'

'Wish they'd let me interview the little shit.'

'Yeah, that would be, uh…'

'I'm sorry, Underhill.'

'Hardly your fault. And you don't even get paid.'

She still hopes to give him half her money, help get him and Andy out of the bastard bungalow. She doesn't think she can tell him anything from the Knap Hall experience to make his book worthwhile. A haunting isn't cold spots and vases falling off shelves, it's what happens inside people, and that doesn't translate to the screen. If the cameras had been working when she was alone in the Ansells' bedroom and she saw what she would later come to think of as Harry Ansell's hanging body, heavy with regret, sagging with sorrow, liquid grief in dead eyes…

… all you'd see in the live gallery would be different views of broken bedposts and a woman with a white face.

When Marcus has gone, the sky in the window slit is the colour of tar. The white line has disappeared from the northeast.

Grayle lies back, shuts her eyes on it all. Will the last fruit-cake in the tin please pull down the lid?

60

Script over it

SOMEHOW, SHE SLEEPS, for maybe three hours, and when she awakes, to a banging on the door, the day's started without her.

Jo Shepherd, in her TV-fatigues, is outside, displaying the kind of anxiety that doesn't usually come before nightfall.

Grayle peers out. This is worse than nightfall. There's dense mist, dark autumn mist, no sun behind it. Jo's almost screaming through it.

'Ahmed?'

'What?'

'You seen him?'

'Jo, I saw enough of the bastard last night to last me the rest of my life.'

'I'm serious. We left him in his room with tea and drinks and whatever he wanted, and he seemed tired but calm, said he'd talk to us – that's you – on camera this morning. We've fixed up a small sitting room for it, in the unused part of the house, near Max's office.'

'Great,' Grayle says dully.

'But he's not in his room in the pop-up, and we've checked the restaurant and all the obvious places. I thought maybe you and he...'

'What?'

'Were talking, before the interview. I don't know.'

'Can he get off the site?'

'Anybody can get off the site, Grayle, it's not a bloody concentration camp. But he hasn't got a car here, and we still have his phone.'

'But not his credit cards, I'd guess.' Grayle yawns. Fucking Ahmed. 'Lemme get dressed. Where you gonna be?'

'Out looking for a new job, if we don't find him.'

Ten a.m. finds them in Defford's executive office: Defford, Jo, Kate Lyons, Max,… and Grayle. Funny how, when the shit's all over the fan, you've become part of the core team, one of the need-to-know circle. The windows are opaque with grey mist, all the lights are on.

'I wouldn't want to scare you,' Grayle says, 'but it isn't far to walk into Winchcombe. He could easily get a cab there. Or even a bus.'

'Thanks for that.' Defford's pacing. 'Why would he want out? What am I not getting? He knows full well that pissing off before it's over puts him in clear breach of his contract.'

'You think he cares about that?' Grayle's gaze floating up to the ceiling. 'He just doesn't want to tell us why he did what he did.'

'Shit, Grayle, he was always going to have to, at some stage. He knows that, too.'

'Naw, think back, Leo. What Ashley did, what she sprang on him, on all of us, he was *so* not expecting that. Far as he knew, she was there just to piss off the crazies, not her fellow sceptics. Soon's he sees they're not on the same side any more, all his wit and his gags desert him. You could see him, like *whaddo I do, whaddo I do?* No obvious answer presents itself, so he's like get me out, get me out. Remembering he's on live TV.'

'That's what Sebold says. Sebold says he was having a very public breakdown.' Defford fists his desk. 'And why the fuck did we let *him* out?'

Sebold is already threatening to lay this on the media, saying there were clear signs that his friend Ahmed was going through an emotional crisis.

Only there weren't any signs, Max, the shrink, keeps saying.

'I could give you a list of obvious symptoms he wasn't displaying. Well, you probably don't have time to hear them…'

Defford's expression agrees.

'Put them in writing, in incontestable shrink-speak.'

'Though I do think Grayle's right about last night,' Max says. 'Previously, when Ahmed was clamming up, you could see that was deliberate – he was being enigmatic. Last night was the first sign that he was not in control. And that's not where Ozzy likes to be. He's like you, Leo, he plans ahead. No heckler ever walks out of a gig uninjured.'

'And who did he think *was* in control, Max – *Big Other*?'

'Maybe he did,' Grayle says.

And gets stared at.

'Well, maybe Eloise was right. Maybe he was, to an extent, in denial. The idea that something he doesn't believe in is screwing him up…'

'Do me a favour, Grayle,' Defford says. 'Don't go there. Don't go anywhere *near* there. Not today.'

'Leo, it's what the damn programme's *about*!'

'You really haven't learned much since you've been here, have you, Grayle?'

Grayle shuts up. Least it wasn't anything *she* did that drove Ahmed out of the house, off the entire site. No one saw him leave but that's no surprise. The firm handling security is more concerned with anyone getting in.

Defford has people discreetly checking out cab firms, train stations. He's awaiting a call from Ozzy's agent. Only Defford could know what to say to Ozzy's agent in a situation like this. Sebold's also been asked if he can think of any friends Ozzy might go to. London-based staff are keeping an eye on Ozzy's north London home.

'If it's not a breakdown,' Jo Shepherd says, 'it has to be concealing something heavy to make him throw it all away.'

'He *didn't* throw it away,' Defford says. 'Ashley blew it all apart. And then here she is, being all nice and sympathetic and "don't go, Ozzy". Smug bitch. Even I'd smash the bleeding mirror.'

Grayle jerks. *Bleeding mirror.* Something about that climactic moment still disturbs her in a way she can't work out. Maybe she'll get Jo to play it back. Sometime.

'I'm not panicking at this stage,' Defford says. 'We have three days to get him back. Somehow we'll do it. Meantime, we just script over it, and we rebuild tension in the house by letting some of the background in.'

Grayle looks up at him.

'Trinity?'

'Been out of the picture for too long.'

Grayle lets her eyes close on him.

Never really was in it, Leo. It's the wrong picture.

'So much unplanned drama here now, it won't be long before the media find us. I don't want them blowing our cover. I want *us* to be seen to do that, at our own pace. So we start feeding it in, slowly. Katherine Parr, then Trinity. All right? Jo, let's start working on that.'

Grayle opens one eye.

'Would help, surely, if somebody had picked up on any of it.'

'I doubt any us thought that was going to happen. It was a device. A conceit. We're never going to prove there are ghosts here. Or that there ever were.'

'I see.'

'Nonetheless, it demonstrates how you can give a concept a whole new lease of life by introducing a blanket theme.'

'So, uh, what is Big Other?'

'Well, that's it. Big Other is the *theme.*'

'Oh, right.' Grayle turns to Kate Lyons. 'Kate, do you – or anyone – have a list of the viewers who rang or emailed to say they could identify the woman Ahmed may or may not have been seeing?'

Kate looks down at her iPad.

'We should have. If we do, I can email them to you within the hour.'

'Good. Yes,' Defford says. 'Let's get Max to talk about that.

Nice example of how viewers can be conditioned. All right, most of these people are basket cases, still…'

'We should understand each other then,' Grayle says.

Wonders how much of her pay they'll dock if she quits tonight.

Outside, she sees it's not just ground mist, this is fog. This is what happens sometimes in the fall when there's no wind and no rain. She checks her phone, hoping for Marcus, but finding a number from the past, calling it back from under the ash tree.

'Who told you, Fred?'

He laughs. HGTV are supposed to have a hush-agreement with the cops, who don't want the lanes clogged with sightseers either. But Fred Potter's police contacts seldom get their names on press releases.

'Nobody got arrested,' she tells him, 'and Ashley's injuries aren't life threatening. So no story.'

'Glad to hear that.'

'No, you're not.'

'Anyway, this is just a reminder that we still exist and have all the background beautifully written up. First sign of anything leaking, we have to press *send*.'

'Always made sense to me, Fred. Press it now, if you want.'

'Oh dear.'

'I'll explain one day.'

She's being signalled. Kate Lyons's head around Defford's door.

'What's Mr Ahmed's mood this morning?' Fred says. 'Just to keep me up to speed.'

'Uh…' Grayle stares into the greyness. 'I guess he seems a little out of it today. You know?'

'Sebold,' Kate shouts. 'Five minutes.'

This is the small sitting room Jo talked about, in the part of the house that still looks like it used to be a hotel, the furniture in here too comfortable to be Tudor, the wall panels too regular to be handsawn from a tree.

'Can't wait for it all to be over, actually,' Sebold says. 'It's not at all what I thought it was going to be.'

She knows he wants her to ask him what he thought it was going to be, so she doesn't.

They're both wearing personal mics and there's a cameraman – just the one – behind her, focused on Rhys on the sofa. Which means, dear God, that for editing purposes they're going to ask her to do questions and noddies. *Hell,* no. Forget it. No way is she appearing on TV looking like she's here to clean the toilets.

'What did you feel when Ashley revealed Ozzy's scam?'

He's in a Western-looking cord shirt and khaki pants. He looks relaxed but alert, tipping his head to one side.

'How do you *know* it was a scam?'

Rhys in his familiar I-ask-the-questions mode. Trained journalist – what he does, what he is. Except he isn't, Grayle thinks, feeling qualified at last to have an opinion. A trained journalist must never appear to hold a point of view. Hard to avoid Sebold's.

'You think it *wasn't* a scam?'

'I *never* thought it was a scam. It wasn't funny enough. When Ozzy says something that isn't funny, you start to wonder if he isn't feeling well.'

'So when he said he wanted out…'

'He'd reached breaking point. I keep telling people this.'

'Why do think he agreed to come on this programme?'

'You want the truth, look at his background. His father was an immigrant. Immigrants come here to work and they work harder than anyone. They don't stop.'

'But Ozzy's dad's a doctor… an eye-surgeon.'

'And they don't work hard? Are you kidding? He told me his old man was appalled when he said he thought he could make a living as a comedian instead of having a normal career, a respectable career. Which explains why Ozzy, from the start, would take every offer on the table. Even when he was earning more than his father, he couldn't stop. He's…' Rhys sitting up, tapping a palm with two fingers '…the most successful of anyone here. Progressed from comedy clubs to major theatres in the major cities of the world. Regular on all those TV shows in which a panel of celebs swap allegedly unscripted jibes. He works all the time. He *couldn't stop*. I'm going, Ozzy, *take a fucking holiday*. He couldn't. It was like an illness.'

'That bad? Really?'

'After two days he'd be performing for the guests in his hotel to convince himself he hadn't lost the ability to entertain. I think he saw this as a break. The only kind of holiday he could handle – one where he was getting paid serious money to sit around making smart remarks. But that would never be enough.'

'Rhys, that doesn't explain why he was creating ghosts.'

'You're not… you're not *listening*. "Performing for the guests in the hotel". I think it was just instinct. He wakes up, he thinks *am I working*? *Am I earning*? Before he knows it, he's invented something he thinks is expected of him, and then he has to keep it going. It's an illness.'

'What's he gonna think when he hears you saying this about him?'

They've agreed not to mention that Ozzy quit the project. That way this can, if necessary, go out tonight and no one's the wiser.

'You know what?' Rhys says. 'I don't care. I'm willing to put up with being hated for a while if it saves him from himself. I'm only sorry Ashley wasn't aware of his condition – which you'd think she would be, as a psychologist. Perhaps she just chose to humiliate him. For personal reasons.'

'So I can take it you don't' – she has to ask – 'think it was anything to do with the house?'

He doesn't even answer. He's expressed no curiosity about the house or who might've lived there. Some journalist.

When Grayle leaves – quickly, to avoid any noddies – she goes out by the front door. The door seen in that vintage edition of *Cotsworld*, all softly golden as the guests arrive, Trinity Ansell inclined generously towards them, like she's about to offer a hand to be kissed.

In the fog, Knap Hall's stone looks raw and jaundiced. Jordan the gardener, pulling a bier-load of logs towards to the house, looks like he wishes he were someplace else. Grayle waits for him.

'Thankless task, huh?'

Jordan lets go of the bier's wooden handles, wipes his hands on his tartan overshirt.

'Bloody thing.'

'Even I can tell it was never meant for logs. But, see, that's your role, Jordan. Sinister bastard.'

It's likely he didn't intend to smile. Encouraged, Grayle pulls a block of orange-coloured wood from the pile.

'This safe to burn?'

Jordan leans back against the bier, looks up into air the colour of cream of mushroom soup.

'I don't wind up that easy, Miss Underhill. You must know that by now.'

'Else you wouldn't still be here, right? See, I figured you might walk out that first night after Ahmed and Sebold called you a yokel.'

'En't such a bad thing to be.'

'Least a yokel knows about elder?'

He doesn't reply.

'What I figured,' Grayle says, 'two options: either somebody slipped a couple elder logs onto the bier, or you were told to do it.'

Jordan nods.

'One of them options, aye.'

'Thanks.'

'It's no big deal. You can find that stuff in most books on folklore, or from the Internet. Wouldn't take much psychology to choose Eloise as a suitable target.'

'And, of course, you – as a man of science – wouldn't have a problem with that.'

No response. When you see Jordan in the mist, this stocky, brick-shithouse kind of guy, you don't see a man of science so much as a *genius loci*. The spirit of a place, the protector. Which is equally inappropriate; what would Jordan want to protect here?

'You talked to Poppy Stringer recently?' Grayle asks.

He shrugs. 'See her now and then.'

'She, uh, felt some kind of obligation to the Ansells, as regards Knap Hall. Which clearly doesn't extend to HGTV.'

'You thought it might?'

She shakes her head. What she was really asking was why is *he* still here? Really doesn't strike her as the kind of guy who could justify becoming a joke on TV purely for the money. The knot garden? Doing it to watch over the knot garden he made for Trinity? Which she could see from above – as knot gardens are meant to be seen – from her apartment. Not quite enough, is it?

She's wondering what questions she might ask him if he was in the chapel, camera on, sound on, and right now can only think of one.

'Jordan, do you really like being here?'

The fog swallows it.

61

Pure, bright water

PULLING ON HER woolly hat, belting her old blue coat, she walks back up the drive towards the TV village, looking more like a military base on a day like this. Suddenly, it's the dead-end of autumn. The bones of the landscape are poking through the fog, the trees are skeletons in grave-clothes. She doesn't remember ever feeling depressed before in quite the same way. The sense of loss is all-enshrouding, the sense of something that could have been thrown away for the sake of personal vanity. And it *is* vanity. Showbiz people, public people, it's always vanity.

'Doesn't look any more hospitable, Grayle.'

'Oh.'

It's Jeff Pruford, Trinity's old manager… steward… coming across the tarmac drive with no visible limp, glancing down at the dull stones of Knap Hall.

'The places we'll come back to for money, eh?' Pruford's wearing a bomber jacket and tight jeans, carrying an overnight-type bag over a shoulder. 'Going in tonight, to talk to your residents. Tell my story about the ghost in the phone. But with no names, no hints of location.'

'He'll get around to that.'

'Mr Defford?'

'He's, uh, changing the direction of the programme. It's what he's good at.'

'You don't look too happy about it, Grayle.' He falls into step with her. 'Why don't we go into Winchcombe for some lunch? When I've checked in.'

'I would like that, Jeff, but I think they have things for me to do.'

'Some other time, maybe.'

She glances up at him. He has a thing about tired, scrawny women with slashed hair? He still has that soldier-cool. Does Defford think he won't be recognized by people who knew this place when Trinity was queen?

Entering the TV village, he looks around at all the trucks and cabins, the dish aerial.

'Bloody hell. How many people you got here?'

'Over a hundred. I'll show you who to tell you're here. But first, could I…?'

'Anything for you, Grayle.'

'The picture. In the phone. What did they really look like, those women?'

'It was more like a painting, really,' he says. 'Trinity Ansell looked gorgeous. The other woman… didn't look like a real woman. Least, that's what I feel now. No vitality about her. Not like you.'

His eyesight was damaged, in the bomb-blast?

'Was she recognizable in that picture, Jeff? I mean, we're talking about Katherine Parr, right? That's the inference.'

'Who I mustn't mention by name tonight. Look, I'd be exaggerating if I said I recognized her, any more than you can recognize anybody from, say, an effigy on a tomb.'

'She was like that? An effigy?'

'If you mean pale and cold-looking, yeah.'

'And resentful. You said that when we talked.'

'That was the only strong impression I got.'

'And Trinity's mood?'

'Funny one, that. I'm not great with words. Tremulous? All quivery?'

'As if she knew the other woman was there?'

'Wouldn't like to say.'

'Did you notice Harry Ansell that night?'

446

'Harry, eh?' Pruford stops next to the reality van, its door shut against the fog. 'That was a bugger, wasn't it? Him topping himself. Don't know if it surprises me or not. If he was ever depressed, he wouldn't even admit it to himself.'

'What was he like that night?'

'He was like some of the other blokes there. Or maybe more so. The red dress, you know?'

'Go on.'

Jeff Pruford looks both wry and reticent.

'He was keeping in the background, the way he did. But – I might be wrong, and if I am, I'm sorry – looking to me like he wanted to tear it off her there and then.'

No, he wouldn't be wrong. Not this guy. He'd know.

'Uh… they say Trinity was never really happy again. After that night. That banquet.'

'I never said *he* looked *happy* about it,' Pruford says. 'It was just rare to see him betraying any sort of emotion.'

'Like he wasn't… quite himself?'

'What was "himself?"' Pruford says.

When she gets back to her cabin, a document's come through to the laptop from Kate Lyons. One hundred and twenty-seven people who recognized Ozzy's lady. Who think she's a dead daughter or a dead mother. Grayle opens a few – all the Angelas coming in now.

They won't all be basket-cases, some just people looking for something to shore up their crumbling beliefs, in these dismal days. They'll follow *Big Other* to the end of the week and turn off their TVs feeling worse than if it had never been screened.

Defford's assuming – and he's probably right – that the majority of his viewers will not be like this and think they very much got their money's worth in terms of human conflict.

But it's just possible there'll be someone else like Paul Swinton, from Ozzy's Ahmed's past. Glancing down the names on the list, Grayle spots one that's a little familiar, not sure where she'd heard it before. She thinks it's Welsh and under-lines it as the phone rings.

'Ashley Palk,' Kate Lyons says crisply.

Ashley's cuts are superficial, which means they didn't require stitching, but there are other wounds; Grayle can tell that soon as the door closes on them.

The camera's still in the sitting room where she talked to Sebold, but this time there's nobody to operate it. Ashley has asked to talk first, unrecorded. She has minor dressings on her cheek, jaw and under an eye. Wearing a grey bathrobe, no make-up, she's hunched into a corner of the deep sofa patterned with heraldic beasts.

'I don't know how far he would've taken it,' she says. 'I knew he was clever. I know he learned all that Wiccan terminology to send up his mother-in-law. I'm guessing he read up on those famous cases where a group creates a' – she double-fingers quote marks in the air – '"ghost" and then people outside the group start claiming they've seen it. Maybe he was hoping viewers would ring in saying they'd seen the woman in the white mac.'

'They may have. I'm checking. Uh... the perfume, that's pretty conclusive. And the way he consistently followed the pattern of letting people drag information out of him. The ouija board... how'd you do that?'

'That's one of the things I didn't want you to ask me about on camera. Sometimes you just have to wing it.'

'So you didn't know he was pushing the planchette.'

'I do now.'

'But you couldn't really be sure with five fingers on there.'

'No.'

'OK – and this is what I don't understand, Ashley – you let him start to spell out the woman's name – ANG, like it's gonna be Angela or Angie. And then you decide it's time to wind up the charade and you upset the table.'

'No.' She sits up quite sharply. 'No, that wasn't me.'

'Ahmed?'

'Him or his mate, Sebold, who was already annoyed at Helen forcing him to sit down with the idiots. I'm not sure of anything except it definitely wasn't me. I wanted to know who Angela was.'

Grayle nods.

'Me too. I thought for a moment it might've been Roger Herridge. Angela's the name of one of his flower-shop girlfriends. But then why would Ahmed give the spirit the name of someone who was far from dead? Unless he knew he was about to be exposed – which neither of us thinks he did.'

'That was coincidence, I think. It was Roger who first suggested the name Angela, perhaps because it was so familiar to him.'

'Can we go forward to the incident in front of the mirror, when Ozzy Ahmed finally blew? Can you take me through that?'

'I'll try.'

Ashley arranges herself on the sofa. She's holding a brocaded cushion in front of her, like a teddy bear.

'What did you think,' Grayle asks, 'when Ozzy was demanding to be let out of there?'

'A wee moment of triumph, I suppose. Nearest I'd get to a confession. And then I thought, well, that's just a personal triumph. Look how clever I am, you know? Wait till Wiseman and Chris French see this, and all the other shafters of charlatans. But where's it really taken us? How happy is Defford going to be with me for taking out his star performer? And do we know what's behind it? I wasn't sure we did.'

'So you decided to try and talk him down from the ledge, as it were?'

'They made me watch it this morning. Pathetic, wasn't it?'

Grayle's playing the scene in her head, recalling for the first time how it kept replaying itself spontaneously through half dreams. The mental tape jamming on one specific instant that she still isn't sure actually happened as she thinks she remembers it.

'How did you feel when he brought back his arm with the wine bottle in it? What did you think would happen?'

'I thought he wouldn't do it. Too laid-back. Not a violent man at all. Everything about him's rather gentle, apart from his tongue.'

'What did you feel like when the bottle left his hand?'

Ashley's cushion creases as her arms tighten.

'Very cold, actually. *Very* cold and surprisingly... shocked?'

'That a strong enough word, do you think, "shocked"?'

'OK, frightened. I was very frightened.'

'Frightened of Ozzy?'

'Frightened of what he'd become, yes.'

'In that instant.'

'Yes.'

In Grayle's head there's an image from the monitors of the expression on Ozzy's face as his arm passes over his head. How it rapidly changes – only one monitor showing this – as if the lowering arm has wiped away the familiar half-smile and underneath it is...

'Ashley, you were standing just slightly behind Ozzy as he threw the bottle. Were you also looking in the mirror?'

'I don't remember.'

'You didn't see his face in the mirror?'

'I...'

'You only saw the back of his head?'

'I suppose. It all happened incredibly quickly.'

And yet in slow motion, too.

'See, if I was in that situation, Ashley, I'd want to know what I was dealing with. Like what was in his eyes. And his eyes were surely in plain view in that mirror.'

'The room was dark. Just candles.'

'But you'd the spent the whole night in candlelight, your vision would've adjusted. And the light collects in the mirrors, too, and reflects back into the room, which doubles the amount of light. Or is my science not up to this? My sister Ersula could've given it to you in whatever the light equivalent of decibels is. C'mon, Ashley, what was his expression as the bottle left his hand?'

'You're good at this, Grayle. Closing in on things.'

'My old man never thought so. Go on…'

'All right, there was a sort of greeny hue on the face. From the candlelight picked up in the green glass of the wine bottle, as it… That probably was what intensified it.'

'Intensified it how? I mean, what did it intensify?'

'The determination, I suppose.'

'Determination.'

'And the… the single-minded, the focused… malevolence?'

A door opens. In the light, posh Scottish accent, the word sounded quite beautiful, Grayle thinks, like a slow cascade of pure, bright water over smooth stones.

'Not a word you'd normally associate with Ozzy,' she says gently.

'No.' Ashley's gazing into nowhere, with no realization of what she's actually saying. 'That's why m' first thought was that it wasn't his face at all. You know?'

62

The runes don't work

CINDY HAS HELEN alone again, in front of the fire with a pot of tea. Old friends, they are now.

Ashley has not yet returned. Roger, bored and disillusioned, has gone to his room for a nap before the night's recording begins, perhaps hoping something seductively spooky will invade his dreams. Poor Roger. Cindy would like to help him, perhaps show him some exercises to open up certain alcoves of his being, but he's not sure that this, in the end, would be helpful. Roger has his own concept of the beyond, which this house might spoil for ever.

'I've been day dreaming a lot,' Helen confesses, sugaring her tea. 'Not something I tend to do, much. Thinking about Diana and Althorp, how people connect to places. Hard to imagine anybody connecting to this place.' She takes the tea to her cushion on the ingle's rim, stretching out her legs, balancing the saucer on her knees. 'There's no love here. I mean you could feel almost sorry for it.'

'Must have been attempts over the years,' Cindy says, 'to love it. To bring it alive.'

Wishing they weren't wearing personal microphones and he could tell her about his friend, Trinity.

'What I feel, Cindy, is that you could pour in love by the bucketful, and it would all be absorbed very quickly and all you'd have left would be some… damp gunge.'

'Ah, Helen…' Cindy purrs at her perception. 'Marry you, I would, if I was normal.'

'Blimey.'

'No, you're right. Is that the house itself, do you think? Or something in it? Or someone?'

'I don't think it likes women,' Helen says.

'Or perhaps likes them too much. But does not love them.'

Cindy feels a shifting in his spine; the house's concurrence. Glances meaningfully at the false wall, where a mirror has been replaced, lifts a friendly hand.

'Listen well, televisual folk. Wisdom, see.'

They hate that, the TV boys. After four days in here, you're supposed to have forgotten they ever existed. But he doesn't forget and neither does Knap Hall, the name of which must never be breathed aloud this week. The house is irritated, injured even, by the television people, with their ubiquitous hidden wiring and their universal eyes. An intrusion, disrespect, a slight against its sovereignty. When Mr Ahmed put the bottle through the mirror, he was hurling it for the house.

Or for what lives here. A spiritual life-form, low enough now to relish what Helen calls the 'gunge'. He will not distinguish it with a human name, although he suspects it's had several. Of all the levels in the house, this is the lowest, but its vapours rise, and we breathe them in and see what we would not want to see.

Helen leans her head back against the stone.

'When Ozzy Ahmed was talking about an abused woman, I felt… that women have been abused here. I keep thinking about that, Cindy.'

'Abused women… or Ozzy.'

'Ozzy. The performance of his life? I don't think so. When he was talking to me, that wasn't a performance. Yes, he was being *careful* – when you've done as many news interviews as me, you know when people are watching their words – but it wasn't entirely made-up. Something was… burning inside him. I didn't expect that.'

'Mr Sebold thought he was approaching a breakdown.'

'Such concern.' Helen smiles. 'Usually commensurate with the level of fame. TV and radio presenters, while pretending to be above all that, love to collect celebs. They're just part of the celebrity support mechanism, but they like to think they're far more important than that. I wonder what they're saying to one another now. Are you allowed to socialize when you're evicted?'

'I think we all have to come back at the end of the week to share our feelings, so perhaps not. Can't see how they could stop it, mind. Any more than they could stop us gossiping about executives of Hunter-Gatherer Television. Just rely on us, they do, to be decent human beings.'

Helen turns to face him. So clear-eyed, she is.

'*Is* this a haunted house?'

'All houses are haunted. I'm sorry…' He wiggles his hands. 'I know what you're asking. I think, despite some rather baffling developments over the past day or two, most viewers would think not. Human fireworks, but little else.'

'It feels haunted now,' Helen says. 'If you weren't here I'm not sure I could stand it.'

'Well, that's been the problem, see. Too many of us, filling the place with our baggage and our back-stories. Our electric emotions. When Eloise came in alone, she reacted alarmingly quickly to something she, personally, perceived as horrifically wrong – the elder wood on the fire.'

'And the viewers at home, most of whom wouldn't recognize an elder branch from a cactus, thought she was bonkers and threw her out. But was she?'

'No. The elder was a personal conduit to something deeper.'

'So the intention,' Helen says, 'is that, at the end of the week, one person – the viewers' chosen one – will be left alone here for one night. Should it be Roger, do you think?'

'Roger would want it to be Roger. Personally, I would not.'

'All right.' Helen takes his left hand. 'What do you think?'

'What?'

'What is it? What do you think it is?'

Cindy looks down at his silly skirt. What an old phoney he must seem. And yet isn't that the point of all this… that the hard line sceptics like Richard Dawkins and Ashley Palk should regard him with ridicule rather than hatred, thus allowing him to walk amongst them?

He looks down at the jagged red seam of fire under patient old oak logs which rarely flare. Remembers that momentary glimpse he had yesterday, as the planchette trembled between worlds, of the dead hearth, the pale-brown walls, the rude and empty chair and the rotting hangings. Visions from the vapour.

Doesn't do individuals any more, only essences, which is why he was no use to Trinity, who wanted her house to be haunted by Katherine Parr. No Katherine Parr here, that bright January day when he first visited. Only the vapours from the sludge.

'I think,' he says, 'that there is something here – something blocked here – that is incompatible with civilized behaviour. Something very old, as old as… as Stonehenge.' Dear God, he almost said Belas Knap. 'There are some places from which energy can be drawn, for either good or ill. At one time, you suspect, there was little to separate good and evil, the primary desire was for survival, continuity, in the face of heartless nature. Ask the drug addict who beats and robs some old widow to pay for his heroin… ask him if he is evil. No, he'll tell you, I am a victim of circumstance. But the evil is there, see, and all we can hope is to grow away from it.'

'Evil is here?'

'Evil…' Her hand feels warm, animated on his. How to express this… 'Evil grows here. A seedbed for it. So thick, so concentrated like a rich, dark compost. I don't know how it can be removed. Or if.'

Beyond the house, Grayle breathes in the fog, harsh and peppery. Things tend to disappear in the fog and are broken down and absorbed and lost for ever.

Like the interview with Ashley, the rehearsal. Which only existed for Grayle, momentarily, in such a translucent form.

When they finally recorded, with two cameras, nothing was the same. The mood had gone. However she phrased her questions, the words came out different, like myriad autumn leaves turning back into drab green.

The luminous word 'malevolence' had congealed into 'angry'.

She can still see Roger Herridge, some time before that moment, looking down at the trashed ouija board, words coming out of him whose significance is already passing him by.

You didn't say goodbye to it, Ozzy. Got to say goodbye or the spirit doesn't go away.

Grayle walks away into the fog, woollen hat down over ears that haven't known cold like this since she was a kid.

This is all so unreal now. Down by the main gate, a security van is parked out of sight under coniferous trees and someone's walking up. She thinks at first it's going to be Ozzy Ahmed, returning, shuffling out his phoney-bashful little smile. But it's a woman in a dark poncho with her arms inside it and thigh boots which allow her to move through the undergrowth like she's floating.

'You looking for Ahmed?' Eloise says.

Grayle shrugs.

'He's gone, hasn't he? He's pissed off.'

'Uh, so it seems.'

'I hope he's walked into the river. But his sort never do. Unless somebody's pushed them.'

'You saw what happened. I mean, they let you watch TV?'

'Yeah, like in prison. I did hear what he called me. Mental?'

'I don't think he knew what day it was.'

'Not a good enough excuse. I won't forget.' Eloise looks back over her shoulder. 'Funny... you go about twenty paces through the gate, and it's clear. It's not a nice day, but there's no fog.'

'Just hill fog, huh?'

'You know what I think?' Eloise parts the knotty fronds of her black hair to expose a mouth-twist that starts out mischievous and then isn't. 'I think it comes from the house.'

She keeps on walking towards the village and Grayle towards the main gate. Eloise wasn't exaggerating. From the other side of it, you can see middle-distant hills. The outside world will get another hour's daylight while Knap Hall is embracing night.

Up in the TV village, where the air is all the colours of frog-spawn, Kate Lyons spots her, calls her over to Defford's cabin.

'One more here for you, Grayle.'

'I'm sorry?'

'Interesting message from a viewer. Not quite sure what to do about it.'

Kate's hair is unusually mussed. Odd, too, that she seems to be seeking advice from Grayle.

'Rhys Sebold's phone.'

'You still have his phone in the safe?'

'Nobody gets their phone back until the week's over.'

'You checked Ozzy's?'

'Of course. No clues, unfortunately. But Mr Sebold has received a message from a woman called Rhiannon Littlewood, who's the sister of his late—'

'I know.'

'She's also emailed our viewers' line, as you saw, so I specifically checked that. It merely says, as so many others do, that yesterday's seance was not the fraud Ashley claimed it was, and that the woman who began to spell her name is a real – if dead – person. On Sebold's phone she's demanding, rather hysterically, I thought, that he call her back about the seance. Which, of course, as it relates directly to the programme, rather than a personal matter, is something we wouldn't want a resident, even an evicted resident, discussing with someone on the outside. They know the rules, they've had months to inform friends and relatives.'

'He doesn't get to call her?'

'I don't think he should, do you?'

'Kate, how about *I* call her?'

'I did wonder whether you might want to do that.'

'Do I get to read the message?'

'I think you should. I'll leave Sebold's phone on my desk.'

'I'll take good care of it.'

'Grayle...' Kate Lyons is peering at her. 'Are you all right? You look... unsteady.'

'It's the fog. Makes everybody look...'

'Have you eaten?'

'Is it lunchtime?'

'It's nearly four o'clock.'

'Short days, huh?'

'And long nights. You might like to grab some rest. Leo has some plans for tonight.'

'Kind of plans?'

'Well, as he said, to move on from the Ahmed upset, change the tenor of the programme. Leo always likes to be...'

'I know.'

Rhys Sebold's iPhone lives in a monogrammed leather case. Figures. Grayle takes it into the restaurant, orders a pot of filter coffee, collects a salad sandwich and finds a table in a corner.

There's a text and an email from Rhiannon. The text, short and splattered with exclamation marks, is appealing to Sebold to call her back, while the email is quite formal.

Rhys,

I know and respect your reservations about these matters and I know I am the very last person you would want to hear from but I feel I have to tell you how dismayed I was when you chose to ignore those very obvious initials when the 'spirit' was asked to spell out her first name.

I actually don't consider myself gullible but equally I would not sleep easily if I'd ignored something as obvious as this.

I think that one day you might come to regret it. Please at least call me.

Rhiannon Littlewood.

OK, some unanswered questions here.

The restaurant's almost empty. TV people don't seem to do afternoon tea. Grayle gets out her own phone.

No answer. Her coffee pot comes, served by Lisa Muir in her neat, not quite Tudor apron. Well, OK. Good a time as any.

'You wanna get another cup, Lisa? Have a seat?'

'Sorry.' Lisa bares her baby teeth. 'I have other people to…'

The only other people in the restaurant are three techies who, even as Grayle watches, are pushing back their chairs, gathering together morning papers and stuff.

Grayle stands up.

'Tell you what, Lisa. Have my cup. I've had so much coffee today my bloodstream's like the M5.'

'And what can be done about it?' Helen asks.

Cindy drinks his tea slowly.

'Now, *there's* a question. In the film, when I am played by George Clooney in his first sexually ambivalent role, there will have to be mystical runes.'

'Runes.'

'*Always* runes, it is. Which George, as me, will read out in the original Runic, scattering dry ice before him. And lo, the air will sweeten, and there will be tranquillity, and little children and kittens and puppies will play here again.'

'After everything you've said, you're taking this with a pinch of salt?'

'Salt, yes, I forgot the salt. George would use lots of…' Cindy places his cup and saucer on the chess table. 'What I'm doing, lovely, is giving *you* a chance to take it with whatever mineral you find least offensive.'

'That's patronizing.'

'So it is.'

Two old pros, they are, hamming it up for the cameras.

'What I'm also trying to say is that it could be that absolutely nothing will happen. On Sunday we'll all assemble in here, crack a couple of bottles of Dom Pérignon or whatever fizz the producer thinks we're worth, and then Ashley and Rhys will proclaim a victory for common sense.'

'And then?'

'Then lives go on. Someone, presumably, will have to live here or supervise its opening to the public. And every so often there will be events of inexplicable misfortune, and people will mumble and move on. And Roger will write a chapter on it in his next book and tourists will point at the entrance, and say, isn't that the house where…?'

'So the runes don't work,' Helen says.

'In the films they do. Isn't that enough?'

He looks into the hearth, feels the vapours rising and wonders, worried now, how he can arrange for Helen to be evicted before the arrival of what his senses, all six of them, tell him is coming.

63

Borrowing a ghost

'SO WHAT ARE you doing here, Lisa?' Grayle says.

No more mystery. She's had it with mystery. She wants lights switched on, holes patched, grimy corners swept out. She pours coffee for Lisa, pushes brown sugar at her.

'Last winter, if you recall, you told me you couldn't even bring yourself to drive past the place.'

Lisa looks at her like she actually can't remember saying this.

'I talked to Poppy Stringer,' Grayle says.

'Mrs Stringer talked to you?'

'Yes, I think you can assume that if I talked to her, she talked to me also.'

'Oh.'

'Which means I'm now a little wiser. About what went on here. With the Ansells.'

Lisa looks down at the table.

'Oh... my... God.'

Grayle waits. Two Jamies and an Emily wander in from the fog, but there are people around to serve them. *No pressure, Lisa. 'Cept from me.*

'Broke up with my boyfriend,' Lisa says.

Grayle says nothing. These things happen.

'Well, he dumped me, to be honest. I was too... old-fashioned. That wasn't what he said, but you get the idea. I suppose I bored him, talking about Trinity and the times at Knap Hall. We had a big row, he's like, why don't you go and fucking squat there?'

461

'So when you told me you couldn't bear even to drive past…'

'I just couldn't bear not being here any more. Apart from the celebrities and parties, it was like where I really grew up. I was only a year or so out of school. Trinity, I think she thought I was more mature than maybe I was. We didn't all have her kind of life. I don't think she realized that.'

Lisa sits tinking a spoon on the rim of her coffee cup.

'My parents… they'd known Harry Ansell for years. The Ansells had stayed with us a couple of times, when they were looking for a house and they wanted to avoid the photographers. You wouldn't believe what some of these paparazzi guys are like.'

'Yeah, I would. So you got to know Trinity before she was your employer. Before they found Knap Hall.'

'Harry Ansell didn't like this place. Tried very hard to put her off. He said there were lots of stories about it being haunted and unlucky. Which *he* didn't believe, but he got my dad to tell Trinity what a bad reputation it had. My dad didn't know any of that. He'd barely heard of Knap Hall. Harry just wanted it to come from somebody else, somebody they trusted. Well, he got that wrong. Trinity didn't particularly connect with my parents. Harry's generation, not hers. When they were staying here she spent more time with me.'

'And what did you tell her?'

Lisa's suddenly close to tears.

'Couldn't tell her my dad was lying, could I? Cause a row between her and Harry? But like… naturally, I wanted them to buy it. I wanted a job with *her*. I wanted to be part of it. I mean, who wouldn't?'

She sniffs.

'When they had the re-enactment of Katherine Parr's funeral? At Sudeley? Trinity wasn't involved or anything, not in the funeral. We were just watching. But some scenes for *The King's Evening* had been shot there, so she felt quite at home, in a way.'

'Nobody recognized her?'

'Oh yeah, I'm sure everybody did, even if they didn't remember the movie, but nobody said anything. It was Sudeley's show, not hers. Moving, but a bit weird. Like Trinity was going to her own funeral.'

'I never thought of it like that.'

'When she walked away, it was like Katherine was walking away from her own tomb.' Lisa looks down into her coffee. 'And that was when I told her.'

'Told her what exactly?'

'I said maybe Katherine Parr was there already. I said the Knap Hall ghost was her.' Lisa squirms a little. 'I didn't make it up. There were stories... sort of. People saying Katherine had actually spent time at Knap Hall not long before she died. And there was maybe a romantic kind of...'

'A romantic aspect to Knap Hall? For Katherine Parr, former Queen of England? Are you kidding?'

'It didn't seem such an awful thing, at the time. Borrowing a ghost.'

The phone rings; Grayle ignores it.

Ashley's back in the house.

'You don't get rid of us sceptics that easily, folks.'

Her smile, once condescending, has been rendered endearingly lopsided by her injuries, Cindy notes. She looks tired. He's also detecting disquiet in the way she's looking around, at the dim panelling, the knobbly oak screen and the old, flaking fire. Sensing her subliminal response to an alteration in atmosphere, like a diver's reaction to the deep. If she's even conscious of it, how will she begin to explain it to herself?

'If you're feeling isolated, Ashley,' he says. 'I shall be happy to join you in questioning everything in the most brutally scientific fashion.'

'*Brutal*, Cindy?'

'I keep a pair of leather trousers in my room.'

Dear God, all this whimsy. He must be more nervous than he imagined.

Roger Herridge says, 'Your venture into the Outside, Ashley... has that given any indication where we might be? Soil colour or anything?'

'All I know, Roger, is that we're in a much bigger house than this seems, and some parts of it are more modern. And more comfortable. And no, I didn't meet either Ozzy or Rhys.'

'Did you observe the weather?' Cindy asks.

'It's not weather you can see. Fog. And dark now. Someone said it might freeze tonight. Never expected to feel I was in a better place than out there. Have I missed anything?'

'Nothing either you or I would have noticed,' Roger says.

Mournful, he is, now, all his schoolboy enthusiasm evaporated. His suit is creased as if, rather than hang it in the wardrobe, he's just let it fall on the floor of his room.

'Ashley...' Helen's stepping carefully away from the hearthstone, looking down. 'This is probably not an entirely sensible question, but were you aware of bringing anything in with you?'

Cindy turns quickly, bends to the heap in the hearth.

The tattered rook or crow or raven on the ashy stone, sooted wings spread, has evidently been dead some time.

Lisa says she's not sure where she heard about KP at Knap Hall. Maybe she got it wrong. Grayle reminds her of what she said about Jordan the gardener telling them ghost stories.

'Oh God, no, it didn't come from him. He didn't tell you ghost stories in a good way. Not the way people like to hear them. Not like sitting round the fire with mulled wine, like we did with the guests. Guests always asked about ghosts, especially the Americans.'

'And they were told about KP, right?'

'I suppose.'

How myths are made.

'When you say Jordan didn't tell stories in a good way...?'

'He just said we shouldn't talk about them and we shouldn't think about them. Don't let any of that stuff in, he used to say. We thought he was being... uncool.'

'And what do you think now?'

'I wish I hadn't started it. I don't think Katherine Parr was good for this place. Or for Trinity. Don't think I was either.'

'You were young. It was exciting.'

'Oh, yeah. Best years of my life. Best time was when I went with her to the dress designer. For the red dress. We had all these portraits of Katherine Parr?'

'You told her how much alike they looked?'

'I said she was even prettier.'

'And... on the night of the banquet you told me about. When she wore the dress. When she was incandescent. Like she was more than herself? Even more than Trinity Ansell?'

'Oh God, yeah.'

'She tell you what happened that night?'

'I was there.'

'No, Lisa, afterwards. You said that next day the light had gone out. Really gone out.'

'I'm... not sure.'

A pause. You can hear people moving sluggishly around outside in the foggy dark. Grayle decides to go for it.

'Did Harry rape her that night, Lisa? She ever tell you that?'

Lisa's face twists. Her elbow knocks over the coffee cup and the suddenness of it makes her cry, like little kids do, at something abrupt. It takes another ten minutes to get out of her what she was obliged to do after Trinity missed a period. At first, Grayle doesn't understand.

'Lisa, she could've... it's not like it's even complicated any more. She had friends in London and places who could organize it quietly.'

'She just didn't want to tell anyone. Why she wanted it, you know? Didn't want anyone trying to talk her out of it or asking her why. She was in a pretty bad way.'

'How?'

'Scared. I mean *really* scared. What was I supposed to do? She didn't even have a computer at Knap Hall. No access to the Net – she was like superstitious about it, letting the Internet into her world. All the bookings were made by post, if possible. So I ordered it from home. I was scared I'd get the wrong ones. Mifepristone. Horrible word.'

'I mean, I can see why she wouldn't want it on any of her credit cards or any gossip, but involving you to that extent… Where was Harry?'

'Not around much. If at all. Abroad or in London on *Cotsworld* business. He hardly ever came back to Knap Hall after that night. I think he was scared, too. Like of what he'd done. Or what he might do.'

'Talk of divorce?'

'Not really. Certainly not amongst the staff. It was the last thing any of us wanted.'

'How much did the staff know?'

'Enough to be unhappy. The atmosphere was awful. And then the place seemed to be getting well out of hand very quickly. The electricity kept going off. You'd turn on taps but no water came out. Came up between the stone flags instead. And I couldn't tell anybody what I'd done…'

'You didn't— Lisa, she died of heart complications. It's not exactly commonplace for that to happen in a home-abortion situation, but she wasn't the first.'

'But when Harry Ansell hanged himself—'

'Don't go there, either.'

Grayle's thinking, inevitably, of Harry Ansell wanting to watch. Poppy Stringer's take on it. *To see what it might do to other people. People who didn't matter.*

'But there is just one more thing I'd like to ask you about. This is likely to go back to the time when she was on her own. When she was depressed… paranoid… and having bad dreams. One of which may've been recurrent. Relates to the grotesques on Winchcombe church. You remember a night when she was in such a state you both went down to the kitchen and drank coffee with whisky?'

Lisa nods, like her head's gone very heavy.

'She tell you about that dream?'

'I tried to forget it.'

'Yeah, me, too. I saw her diary entry. She said the… this thing came down from the church and followed her through the town. Dancing like a puppet. Male… naked. What did she think it meant?'

'I don't know.'

'Did she see that and not Harry when she…?'

Oh God, there just is no way of asking this.

That's enough for now. This isn't going to end anyplace sane, and it's time for Defford's nightly briefing. Grayle picks up the cup, uses a napkin to mop up the coffee.

Lisa nods, starts to push back her chair and then stops.

'We… did one other thing, before she left for Dorset. The red dress. It was torn and not very… clean. We burned it. She'd put it in a drawer in one of the empty bedrooms, and when Harry was away, we locked ourselves in the… you know the main chamber, where the residents are? And we burned it on the fire.' Lisa stands up, unsteady. 'Never forget the way the fire went for it. The flames going… going blue.'

'Something in the fabric,' Grayle says. 'That's all. OK, one more thing. The bit you forgot to tell me about, but which you conveniently remembered for the camera. When you and Trinity tried to contact KP through a ouija board…?'

'Oh, look, it was just bits of paper and a glass! I only remember one bit that made any sense. All the rest was just jumbles of letters, so we stopped.'

'What was the bit that made sense?'

'Willing. I think that word kept coming up.' Lisa's edging away. 'Look, I have to get… Able and willing. Something like that.'

'Uh-huh.' Grayle nodding, keeping it casual. 'Able and willing. Normal spelling?'

'I suppose.'

'So like how was the word "able" spelt?'

'I don't remember.'

64

Bits of you

DEFFORD'S MADE AN executive decision. He tells the inner circle that for tonight's first hour, they won't go live; they'll have people talking and theorizing about Ahmed, and they'll run Grayle's interviews with Ashley and Rhys. It's about drawing a strategic line under the Ahmed incident, Defford says. They won't say Ozzy's walked away until they have to. They'll just unload him, move on.

And no one will be evicted tonight. They're already ahead on evictions, one by default, Defford says.

He's bullish. His white hair's been gelled into aggressive spikes which under the office lights look, to Grayle, worryingly like the effects of an unseasonal sweat. It's about moving the goalposts, he tells them. Seizing an initiative, stealing a march. Moving *on*.

It's this that worries her most. While the four remaining residents are dining, the mood of the big chamber will be altered, subtly and swiftly. Around eleven p.m., they'll emerge – *live* – into what is, Defford insists, the real world of Knap Hall, although nobody inside the house will know that and viewers will learn only gradually about the world of Trinity Ansell.

He's doing this, she guesses, because he's expecting imminent exposure by the national media. Twitter and Facebook are fizzing with speculation about which old house *Big Other* is using. The first accurate rumour to hit the Internet, and the invasion will be on.

But Trinity's world was never the real world of Knap Hall, and something didn't take to it, in a way that Harry Ansell came, too late, to understand.

Before the meeting, Jo Shepherd showed her the latest rushes, and that scared her. That scared everybody. Sure, birds and bats and other things are occasionally found in hearths, especially the hearths of old houses with wide, straight chimneys. It was dead, it may have been there a long time, caught in some crevice, disturbed by the resumption of firelighting.

Or, as she said to Jo, it may have been planted, just inside the chimney, when logs were brought in. Jo says Defford absolutely denies any knowledge of this. Defford loves that dead bird. In the absence of anything better, it will close tonight's programme. Grayle thinks she really needs to talk seriously to Jordan Aspenwall.

Meanwhile recognizing the pointlessness of raising a hand now and saying, Leo, you need to realize you could be refuelling something which led, however indirectly, to the death of both Ansells.

Because it's not unlikely that he *does* realize it. He's a TV producer, for Chrissakes, he needs serious momentum for the final days. He's going to back away from that in the face of madwoman whimsy? No. He needs more dead birds.

Grayle's first out of the executive office, speaking to nobody, pausing only to leave Sebold's cellphone on Kate's desk. During that uninterruptable session with Lisa, Rhiannon Littlewood came back, leaving a short message. She'll be in all night and will await a call.

Coming now…

Running through the village, all its lights furred by fog, and into her cabin, slamming the flimsy door behind her, locking it.

The TV's on, with no sound, and all she can hear as she slides down behind the desk is the night jackhammering, first in her head and then inside her chest, getting louder and louder and, oh God, what is this?

The silent screen has one of those flashing images they have to broadcast warnings about, for the sake of the epileptics out there. Flashing images and scenes some viewers may find disturbing. BIG OTHER in dazzling white on funeral black, the image serrating into stone flags by candlelight, a broken ouija board, the disturbed brown eyes of Ozzy Ahmed, an exploding mirror.

Grayle sags in her chair as the *Big Other* trail ends, replaced by serene summer pastures and a barn conversion, an invitation to create for yourself a new home in the country. All Grayle sees in her head is Leo Defford's wide smile opening up like a metal gate. She reaches for a bottle of Cotswold spring water. What is she *doing*? Why is this even important, for God's sake? It's a goddamn *job*. Just a well-paid job in an industry known for its lavish fees and occasional, short-lived creative satisfaction. Whatever they tell you, it is never, never NEVER life and death.

Believe that.

Unconvinced, she picks up the cellphone, itself an angry little planet.

'Mrs Littlewood? Rhiannon?'

'Who's that?'

'My name's Grayle Underhill. From HGTV?'

'Oh. Yes. Hello.'

'You may recall we've spoken before, when I was researching the programme.'

'About Rhys, yes.'

'You mailed us last night. And you tried to call Rhys.'

'Did he tell you that?'

Grayle just hurries on.

'I guess you know the format of the programme means the residents are... under house arrest, if you like, and we can't allow them to communicate with people outside. So they leave their phones with us on the understanding that if it's a seriously important personal call, we can make an exception.'

'It was.'

'Yeah, but unfortunately it also overlaps with material used in the programme. So we actually would rather you didn't get to talk to him until it's all over on Sunday.'

'It'll be too late, then.'

Her voice is calmer than Grayle was expecting from her text. She's older than her sister, Chloe, whose picture Grayle has seen online – dark and pretty in a tidy way, demure-looking. The first time they spoke, Rhiannon was describing herself as a second mother to Chloe, their parents both having died young.

'What I'm wondering,' Grayle says carefully, 'as we can't let you talk to Rhys, is if there's some way *I* might help.'

'So... are you the woman who asks the questions? In the chapel?'

'They're in the chapel, I'm not. But yeah.'

'I see.' Rhiannon pauses. 'I think... that I'd rather talk to you than Rhys. You come over on TV as if you know what you're talking about. And also quite sympathetic to... what some people think.'

'Well, it's not a script. For a time, I was a journalist specializing in, uh, mind- and spirit-related issues. I may've mentioned that the first time we—'

'Look, I'm not a crank.'

'I am,' Grayle says. 'Used to have windchimes in my car.'

Surprised laughter in the phone.

'And that isn't the worst of it,' Grayle says. 'However—'

'I'm not a practising spiritualist, Ms Underhill. I always thought a lot of it was rubbish. I just went along with a friend who thought it might help me. When your little sister's just died in a horrible way, life can seem very dark and pointless and you're open to anything.'

'Rhys reacted badly when you passed on a... a spirit message that said Chloe didn't want him to blame himself.'

'That's not quite what the message was, but I did want him to speak to me. He wouldn't, anyway. He just used me to savage spiritualism in the press.'

'Which, I guess, was how he wound up in the *Big Other* house. No producer wants a fence-sitter.'

'I understand he was very upset at the time, and I don't hold that against him. What I do hold against him is what happened yesterday. If I can explain, what so startled me the first time was when the medium got her name right.'

'Chloe?'

'Chloe's her second name, which she'd taken to using in her professional life because some people had difficulty pronouncing her first name. Our parents weren't Welsh – we're from Kent – but they spent all their holidays there and they gave their two daughters Welsh names. She and I were twelve years apart, but that was one of the things that seemed to hold us together. That and our parents' deaths in a motorway pile-up when she was very young. Motorways don't like us, Ms Underhill.'

'No. I'm sorry.'

'Rhys only knew her as Chloe when she was a researcher on his programme. Which suited her. She was uncomplicated. Just efficient and conscientious, although she got very starry-eyed when he started taking an interest in her. But they're not easy to live with, celebrities, even third-division ones like Rhys. They take away bits of you.'

The dumped partners of soap stars often talk like this, as Grayle knows from Three Counties days. Third-division, Rhys would love that.

'I'm sorry, did you tell me Chloe's first name?'

'Angharad.'

'Not the easiest to call across a crowded office.'

'But it begins with A…N…G.'

'I—'

'Same as Angela,' Rhiannon says.

'Holy shit.'

Grayle stiffens. Wasn't expecting this.

'And then someone rocked the table,' Rhiannon says.

'I hear what you're saying.'

She hears its echo, still. *Angharad*.

'Who around that table would've known that, Rhiannon? About her name.'

'Rhys, certainly, although he never used it. Look, I'm not stupid, I know it's not conclusive or anything, but he didn't say a word, did he? I know, he doesn't believe, why should he? But I wanted him to know *I'd* seen it. I'm not a lunatic, I'm a solicitor. And I think sometimes things do happen.'

'And what… how might we use this information, do you think?'

'Why don't you do it again? Get another ouija board.'

'Not my decision to make, but I'll certainly… Uh… Chloe, Angharad… did she own a long white raincoat?'

'Don't you know?'

'No.'

'She died in one.'

Grayle's mouth is too dry to form an easy reply.

'The night it happened,' Rhiannon says, 'it was August, very warm weather but there'd been thunderstorms that day.'

'Right. Listen. I'm gonna have to leave you now, I have… stuff to do. But I'm glad you told us this. I think it… I think it's something I need to look into.'

'As a crank,' Rhiannon says steadily.

A stupid, misguided woman, according to Sebold on the phone that day, so long ago.

She sits there shaking slightly. Who can she tell about this who might listen, might even think it worthwhile pursuing? Who has the authority to pursue it?

The clock tells her *Big Other* starts in half an hour.

So nobody.

She opens up her cellphone, looks down the stored numbers, finger hovering over Ozzy Ahmed's close friend and writing partner, Neil Gill, who hung up on her last time. This time he'll listen. Unless Ozzy's with him.

She puts in the number on the office phone. The line's busy.

As she's hanging up, the cellphone rings, the caller's name appears. Grayle sighs.

'Fred, there's nothing I can tell you right now, but if you're calling to say the *Daily Mail*'s asked you to check out Knap Hall as the *Big Other* house, I'll come straight back to you, soon as I alert Defford.'

Fred Potter makes an amused noise.

'No actually, Grayle, it's not that at all. It's *The Times*, and they do have an exclusive in tomorrow's paper, and they want some background from us. You ready for this?'

'I'm ready for anything, Fred,' Grayle says wearily.

'It's what you might call an historic sex allegation.'

'Please tell me it's not Defford.'

'No, it's… it's better than that. I mean, not better at all, but you know…'

'Yeah, yeah.'

'Woman called Karen Grant. I should know her, but I don't. Lives in Cheltenham.'

'OK.'

'She was Harry Ansell's personal secretary. She's saying he raped her.'

'Wh—?'

Two other women who worked in the *Cotsworld* office but who don't want to be named have made similar allegations. Not rape, but certainly serious sexual assault. You still there, Grayle?'

'Yeah.'

'When I say historic sex, it's actually not that historic. All in the period since he lost Trinity. Last one was the day before he hanged himself.'

'Why… why's this coming out now?'

'Because Karen Grant, it was more a date-rape thing, she went out for a drink with him because he seemed depressed and went back with him to his flat and made him some coffee, and then… She'd always had a lot of respect for him, and then when he hanged himself the following evening…'

'She thought it was a one-off.'

'What was she going to do, tell the inquest about it? She's married. And then, as the shock of his death wore off, the other stories started to come out from women in the office about sexual advances, and she began to feel guilty in case there were others out there who'd been damaged by Ansell and were afraid to talk about it. And her father works for *The Times*, some executive position. Look, I don't want anything from you, Grayle. I just thought you'd like to know. It's a kind of closure, in a way, isn't it? If Harry Ansell killed himself because he thought it was about to come out… and he'd be facing arrest, long court case, several years inside?'

'Or…' Grayle swallows some water, coughs. 'Because he couldn't face what he'd become. Or even understand it.'

'This could open the floodgates. Other women over the years. Blokes just don't *become* abusers. Do they?'

One answer is, not on their own, no. She keeps another to herself.

65

White sadness

THE CAMERAS MOVE playfully around a chamber reborn. There are new old chairs, new old tables. New old light. The wrought-iron candle hoop has gone, replaced by one the size of a carriage wheel, with more than twenty glistening tongues to probe the deep reds and ochres in the new wall hangings, bringing to surreal life the fantasy bestiary with lions and monkeys and unicorns.

But failing to animate the near-black eyes of the half-shadowed woman in the alcove. In the live gallery, Grayle grips her chair arms.

'*Oh* God, what is that?'

At first she thought it was Meg the actress, now she can see it isn't an alcove either.

'Ha,' Defford says. 'Even Grayle. Good-good.'

'Got me earlier,' Jo Shepherd says. 'Leo had it painted. It's an actual painting, on wooden panelling.'

'And here's me thinking Holbein retired.'

The woman is life-size in a dull wooden frame with scrolling around the top. The candles light the ruby necklace, the ruby pendant and the band of rubies in her French hood. But, no, the light doesn't touch the eyes.

Defford strolls away along the row of monitors, satisfied.

'Cost an unknowable amount,' Jo says to Grayle, behind a hand. 'Based on several of the existing portraits, but essentially…'

'Essentially a new portrait of Katherine Parr.'

'Done amazingly quickly. I was there when he was on the phone to the artist. He's going, Make it like one Henry VIII would've had on the wall opposite his bed to get him in the mood.'

'For what?'

'Yeah, I know. Wouldn't have it in my house, but then I'm not a sixteenth-century king.'

Or a TV producer who's decided a house should be haunted by two specific women. Grayle doesn't like this picture – too secretive, too heavy with hindsight. Holbein actually would not have portrayed her this way. It's too *good*. This is a woman pregnant with precognition, a Katherine Parr who knows she'll die too young. KP shadowed by Trinity Ansell.

'Jo,' Grayle says, 'I need to tell you—'

'Sssh.'

Defford's back, sitting down between them.

'So you like it.'

Grayle says nothing.

'We love it,' Jo says.

Cindy recognizes the choral music emanating from the walls: the *Agnus Dei*, from a mass written for Henry VIII by Thomas Tallis.

It settles upon him like a slow blossom-fall, a white sadness. Trinity played this same music. Trinity was having it played in this very room on the occasion of his unfruitful second visit to Knap Hall. As if God himself wandered amongst the guests.

The music fades as they walk in from the dining hall, Roger Herridge gazing around.

'This is all for us?'

'Just for you, Roger,' Ashley Palk says. 'They must've noted how badly your appreciation of the Tudor aesthetic was offended by the place as it was. Who is this, do we know?'

She stands before the portrait which is just a little taller than she is. Roger joins her.

'Anne Boleyn, possibly. Though not one I've seen before.'

'Now *she* haunts widely, doesn't she, Anne Boleyn? Hmmm…

don't suppose it's possible we're in some lesser-known wing of Hampton Court, or somewhere like that?'

'Almost certainly not. No, we could be anywhere. Henry and Anne travelled around quite a bit when they were first married. But, yes, someone does seem to be giving us a pointer here. A clue, perhaps, to the identity of Big Other. Cindy? Any thoughts?'

Oh dear. Is he permitted to recognize this woman? Perhaps not yet.

'Well now, fond as I am of Anne Boleyn, poor dab, I don't somehow think it's her.'

Helen Parrish looks at him, uncertain… but about what? Finding that bird in the hearth… it's affected her. Something has been dislodged. Confidence shaken, defences down. After they were locked in the dining room, Helen drank no wine at dinner, only water, listening to the movements from next door, like a poltergeist at work. The housekeepers doing more than taking away a dead bird.

The fire on the hearth, Cindy sees, has been enlivened by blazing birch and sycamore, inside the thighs of oak.

But, for all this and the extra candles, it seems, to him, no brighter. Not at all.

He knows what this is about. They're remaking Trinity's room, though not in a way obviously recognizable from the pictures in *Cotsworld*. Different hangings, different pictures. The false wall, of course, full of eyes.

And the new portrait, explicitly Katherine Parr.

A mistake. But what can he do?

Soon as tonight's programme starts consuming Defford and Jo, Grayle slips away, corners one of the Jamies and gets him to find her all the rushes from the ouija session. In a small viewing unit behind the reality gallery truck, she sits alone with the technology, scrolling through shots from three or four cameras.

This is new stuff, all these angles on it. She only saw the chosen pictures on TV, while dealing with Marcus on the phone, that queasy conversation about Abel Fishe and what he might have done to the dead KP. Now, she's getting a sequence on it, from when Helen says,

Someone's doing this.

What did she mean by that? Much of this got forgotten because of what happened afterwards, but it looks like Helen was the first to suspect the planchette was being deliberately pushed. And she didn't want to be a part of that?

Rhys Sebold's right in there with a put-down.

But it's a spirit, surely. Perhaps even Diana? *Anything's possible in a haunted house, Helen,* you *know that.*

Which is what makes Helen so mad she insists Sebold take her place at the table, and this is where it escalates. Grayle finds three different views of the spelling out of the letters A… N… G. Sebold, Ahmed, Herridge, Ashley and Cindy each with a finger on the moving triangle. It's impossible to judge from any of the shots if anyone in particular is pushing. You had to be there. You had to have a finger out there, and even then…

Herridge saying, 'A N G? Angela?'

OK, what's happening to the planchette now, in the split second before the table rocks? Where's it headed? Back to the centre, and then…

One shot was probably not used, because it doesn't cut easily to the best shot of the table rocking, the planchette launched into the air.

But it *is* the best one: a lovely angle, at ouija-level, from the bank of letters, so you can watch the planchette, five fingers still on board, as it makes its final journey, cruising along the surface of the board like it's returning to the G. But not quite… a touch to the left.

And left of the G from this angle, is H.

For ANGH…

Oh God, Oh God, this is far from conclusive, but…

For the fifth time, the table tips, and the board falls from under the planchette and even Ashley does a little scream.

*

From the temple of the live gallery, the house looks warm and opulent, just like in the old *Cotsworld* picture-spreads, as the residents listen, without comment, to a mystery man. A man unseen by viewers, a chaired silhouette, his back to the camera but speaking with Jeff Pruford's voice and telling the story of two women in a picture on another woman's phone.

Dead now, Grayle realizes. All three of these women. None named, all dead. No picture to see, except the one on the wall which seems to represent both Katherine Parr and Trinity Ansell and is, in Grayle's view, not a good idea, but what does she know?

Meanwhile, in the first hour of tonight's programme, the Ozzy story is getting dealt with, with several flashbacks to the upsetting of the ouija board and the hurling of the bottle, and Ashley Palk is still the fount of common sense.

Defford, watching, is looking as happy as you could expect.

For a man who doesn't know the half of it. Doesn't know that the Ozzy situation could be even more complex before tonight's programme is over. Doesn't know about Angharad. Doesn't know what he'll be reading in tomorrow's *Times* about Harry Ansell, who only wanted to watch.

Panic claws at Grayle's gut. She really needs to say something and throws a glance at Defford, who turns and frowns as her phone starts ringing, without permission, in the live gallery. She raises her hands in apology and takes the phone outside, where the aggressive fog hugs her thin sweatshirt with this almost carnivorous glee.

'Grayle Underhill?' Northern English accent, like Ozzy's. 'Neil Gill. Ahmed's writing buddy. Where is he?'

'I'm sorry…?'

'Ozzy. Where *is* the bugger? Everybody's talking about him on the box, but we haven't seen him onscreen, not personally since he threw his wobbly. Which we keep seeing, gratuitously, over and over again, and that Scottish woman being smug. But no Ahmed. Then, you ring me saying you're worried he might harm himself or something. And then he does that routine with the mirror. Which I figured you knew would happen, so that was all right, relatively speaking, but now I'm not sure.'

'Uh, no. No, we didn't know that was gonna happen.'

'So what's going on?'

'Yeah, well, I was gonna ask you that. Ozzy stopped, uh, talking to us a while back. You saw Ashley Palk stitch him up, and you saw him failing to respond to that in the way we and presumably you would've expected.'

'And then you let your biggest name walk out? Halfway through the week? That doesn't strike me as value for money. I keep trying to call him, never an answer.'

'We still have his phone.'

'Well give him his phone *back*, please.'

'We can't do that. Listen…' No way around this now. Grayle looks for privacy and shelter from the cold, finds none and starts walking, in the narrow alleyways between cabins. 'He left. He left us without a forwarding address, in the night. As a person, he's free to go; as a contracted professional, it wasn't what we expected. He didn't have a car here, but it's not a long walk to the nearest town.'

'You're saying… Ahmed did a runner? On foot?'

'That's how it looks, yeah. Our boss, Leo Defford, lives in hope he'll drive calmly in again before weekend. Personally, I'm less… let's say I have issues.'

'You haven't told the police?'

'Why would we? You really think he'd want us to do that?'

'I don't know.'

'Neil, uh, it's clear something's bothering you. Can I…?'

She can almost hear him thinking, tossing his options around.

'All right, go on.'

'You saw what happened before he smashed the mirror and demanded we take him out the house. That strike you as out of character?'

'It does now.'

'You'll know about the woman he kept claiming to have seen.'

'Will I?'

'White coat. Injuries. And the initials ANG. Rhys Sebold thinks he was on the edge of a nervous—'

'What the fuck does Rhys Sebold know?'

'His best friend?'

'I'm his best friend.'

'Yeah, well, I guess there are things I don't know either.'

'Oh, there are, darlin', bloody right there are. He's a clever lad, Ozzy. You offend him, he doesn't punch you in the face, he digs a hole around you that you can't see till you fall down it, and he doesn't care how long it takes. I need to call you back, all right? Somebody I need to talk to.'

'Who? Listen, I'm putting my ass on the line here.'

'I want to find out if he's talked to his agent. We have the same agent, and if he's pissed off he'll have called to check his legal position. He's funny but he's not daft.'

'No, listen we already…'

His agent. Defford said he'd be taking care of that. But Defford, like many reality-TV producers, doesn't like agents. Avoid them – one of the ground rules, next to always stay one step ahead. Agents, in general, don't like unscripted, open-ended reality TV; therefore it follows that Defford hasn't spoken to Ahmed's.

'What did you say?' Neil Gill's asking.

'Just talking to someone else. Sorry.'

'Let me get back to you.'

'Make it soon,' Grayle says.

The air smells acrid and hostile. Her throat tastes like she has a cold coming on.

She walks back between the furry lights. All this is nothing to her. She could just go back in the live gallery and sit and watch and let Defford do what he wants – like she can stop him anyway. And maybe nothing will happen, no one living will be hurt. So why, she's wondering, am I working for the dead?

66

Landmark

THEY ARE BEING introduced to their alleged unseen companions by a perfectly presentable, honest-looking fellow – ex-soldier,
he says – sitting in a tall-backed chair in front of the portrait of
Katherine Parr. The soldier is the first outsider to enter their
chamber. He tells them about a woman living here, a modern
woman, well-known, and another, even more famous woman
who lived nearby half a millennium ago. About the same age
when they died.

Are they supposed to guess at identities? Cindy wonders.

'How old?' Roger asks.

'Thirty-six, going on thirty-seven.'

'Like Diana,' Helen says, looking startled now in the wobbly
light. 'God almighty, why does all this seem so portentous?'

Ashley pushes her light blond hair behind her ears.

'You're saying this is not a good place to be thirty-six?'

Cindy thinks, *Oh dear.*

'Only, I actually turned thirty-six last week,' Ashley says,
'Didn't realise it was such a… psychic landmark.'

The absent Ahmed, no doubt, would have felt obliged, at this
point, to make some slick remark, but no one else does. Ashley
laughs lightly, as Ashley must. *You've changed, though, lovely,*
Cindy thinks. *Won't admit it, even to yourself, but you have.*

The soldier talks, guardedly, as some soldiers do, about what
he knows of the history of the unnamed house, about a banquet
so posh that photos of the hostess have to be secretly snatched,
and Cindy edges his chair inside the cloak of shadows in the
corner between the Gothic door and the screen of old-ship's

oak. It smells musty and oily and old as if the wood's seafaring years have seeped into its woody sinews. Cindy sits with his hands, palms down, on his knees, listens to his breathing, and sets up the steady pulse of an inner drum.

Normally, a real drum would be used, see, usually the Celtic hand-drum, the bodhrán. There would be preparation, perhaps fasting. Alas, no time. He pulls the shadows around him.

After a while there comes a quivering and a fluttering and here's his totem bird, Kelvyn Kite, taking flight. Freed from his stage-suit of fluffy wings and absurdly glaring pool-ball eyes, his inner raptor is released to seek out Belas Knap, the most ancient and aloof sacred centre, at the highest parts of the Cotswolds. Where all this, surely, begins.

Call me a coward, Trinity wrote, *but I stayed behind the wall. I felt sick… couldn't go any closer. I thought it would help me to touch it or something, but suddenly I knew it didn't want to help me, not at all.*

No, lovely, it wouldn't. You had no relevance to it. Its rules are old and stiff and primitive. It knows nothing of love.

The red kite circles, waiting for him. Eager. They haven't done this for a while. Patience, Kelvyn. Out of practice, see. Doesn't know any more if he's a man of psychic substance or a mere charlatan. But then, as Emrys Fychan always said, the uncertainty of it remains central to the experience. You must walk the horizon's rim in that indefinite place – *y plas amhenodol* – where past and present meet and the future might just, in some small way, respond to you.

In his cloak of shadows he's above the fog, above the hill. He can see the half moon, like a segment of apple. Down below, the remains of the hill fog trail a grey aura around the burial mound, the shape of a plump, ground-nesting bird, a pheasant perhaps, between trees and sheep-cropped fields. He starts his chant following the drum.

Old spirit, dead spirit,
Old spirit, dead spirit,

Arise, the deathless dead

He's standing now on the barrow, on Belas Knap, at the end above the false entrance, the enormous vagina, with the bulk of the mound behind him. He's waiting for the guardian. There's always a guardian, someone sacrificed in prehistory, willingly perhaps, in order to protect this place.

Old spirit, dead spirit,
Old spirit, dead spirit,
Arise, the deathless dead

Down in the valley, near the edge of the town, the faces on Winchcombe church gaze up. Some of them surely are memories of twisty, wind-formed faces seen at Belas Knap in the days when people were more aware of the spirits of place. The guardian's different faces later joined on the tower by stone caricatures of local despots and ne'er-do-wells, appointed sentries on the Church of St Peter, the town's gate-keeper. All this making perfect, lucid sense to Cindy on his shamanic journey.

He waits on the barrow's bristly coat of cold grass. Nothing comes. Maybe there's not much left of the guardian now, beyond a miasma of menace and misery. He moves away from the false entrance and stands on the lintel stone of one of the side chambers, looking down.

Ah...

In its entrance, old bones are laid out like toys from a toybox. Human bones – arms and legs, ribs and a pelvis. A child is squatting there, a child clothed in night-mist, thin arms outstretched like thorny twigs and, in each hand, a small skull. The skulls are grinning and the child is grinning, and a woman's voice comes to Cindy, faint and filmy as a chiffon scarf.

... dancing like an old-fashioned puppet, and it had a full body, a male body, and I saw that it was naked and...

'You saw the picture yourself?' Roger Herridge says.

'And I examined the phone, best I could,' the soldier says. 'No doubt it could have been fabricated, but not here.'

'We tend to react with surprise, even outrage,' Roger says, 'to the idea of a ghost manifesting through the most modern technology. In fact computers, tablets and mobile phones, digital signals, wi-fi... lend themselves far more readily to such manifestations than do...'

... I knew exactly what it wanted to do to me.

The breath, his own breath, is loud in Cindy's ears, shushing out Roger's voice as Belas Knap shrivels away beneath him, candlelight replacing moonwash, Kelvyn Kite finding his own way home.

'... energy, you see,' Roger says. 'It's all about energy. You want to ask any questions, Ashley?'

'I have no questions at all,' Ashley says. 'Ghostly pictures are, I'm afraid, ten a penny. I wish we had it to look at, but unfortunately it seems to be unavailable. I'm not saying our friend here made it up, but he certainly can't prove he didn't.'

'Cindy?' Roger Herridge asks. 'You must have some thoughts on this.'

'Yes, I... I have a question. The women in the picture. Did they seem content to be here?'

'I think I said that one of them, the...' the soldier glances almost furtively over his shoulder at the portrait, '... the ghost, if you like, was not content.'

The portrait indeed is sombre. Only the rubies around the French hood are aglow. *Little lights,* Trinity said that January afternoon. *There was a pattern of tiny red lights, like a constellation.*

Warning lights, Cindy thinks.

The soldier says, 'It seemed to me, pained, mortally offended... I don't know. She was very pale, like parts of her face had been eroded. Eaten.'

'Did she – either of them – seem perturbed? Afraid even?'

'Well, I—' The soldier looks fleetingly disconcerted. 'Aye... there were a sense of... let me put it this way, the woman, my boss, you'd expect her to have been very happy that night, but there was a sense of anxiety... trepidation. Agitation. Unrest.'

'And was there a male?' Cindy asks. 'A man or a boy?'

'Several men. It was a party.'

On his guard now, he is. And the very fact that he *is*...

'Thank you,' Cindy says.

'It's been very interesting,' Roger Herridge says. 'Thank you for telling us this. We're all— Oh. Helen. Sorry. Do you have any questions, any thoughts?'

Helen is apart from the others, on her usual cushion, though a little further away from the hearth tonight because of the ferocity of the fire. She's looking a little confused, plucks at the cowl neck of her smoky-blue jumper.

'Dead?' she says. 'Is he dead?'

Defford comes across to Grayle in the gallery, where directors are exchanging glances.

'What's she on about?'

'Leo, how would I know?'

Cindy comes into shot, sitting next to Helen Parrish on the stone. He looks concerned. He looks, momentarily, like a man in drag.

'Is who dead, Helen?'

'God,' Grayle says, 'Look at that.'

Helen's eyes are glistening with tears.

'Too clever for his own good,' she says. 'But he didn't deserve this.' She looks up. 'Sorry. Daydreaming again. No... I have no questions.'

'Daydreaming,' Defford says. 'She said that earlier. I mean, she fall asleep just then, or what?'

'I'm sure Helen would reject this,' Grayle says, 'but her eyes were... OK, I'm gonna say this, I'm thinking trance.'

'What?'

'I think we're inclined to take our eyes off the ball, Leo. In fact, we get so carried away with the dramatic stuff that we don't even see the ball. The ball's like very small and pale. Most of the time. We should be looking out for Helen. We know what this place is like, we should be looking out for all of them.'

'We *know*?' Defford stares at her. 'We don't *know* anything.'

'Leo,' Grayle says, 'do you have five minutes?'

To get into the live gallery, you walk through an area that still looks like the original stable. Part of it's been sectioned off, a cheap door installed, though the new room it accesses has never been used by HGTV, except, judging by the smell, as a smoking area.

A naked bulb throws jagged light over a bale of straw and a stack of metal hurdles. Defford rests his foot on one.

'You're telling me *you* saw… That's what you're saying?'

Defford shuts his eyes, shakes his head. He doesn't need this. This is not even the programme getting out of control, this is the staff. He does not expect to have to be one step ahead of the goddamn *employees*. Grayle sees all this in his face, and also an uncertainty.

'*Here?*'

'Up in the Ansells' old bedroom. You don't know whether to believe me, do you, Leo?'

'Grayle, it—'

'Same with the camerawoman, Jess. It's OK if the *residents* think they've seen something. That's what they're here for, and if they're crazy, what's that matter? But the guys *this* side of the camera, we're professionals, we're supposed to be above all this shit. Right?'

'Why are you telling me this now, if it happened days, weeks ago? Why now, Grayle?'

'Because it… seems to impact on what's happening now.'

'Harry Ansell?'

She's about to tell him what he's going to read in tomorrow's *Times*, and then stops herself, because that will immediately cancel out everything that went before. It's reality; this is not.

'I don't… I didn't even think of Harry Ansell at the time. I saw something hanging from a rope in what was left of the

490

Ansells' four-poster bed. And the air was full of this deep sadness, despair, regret… and something which I now feel was self-hatred. It was all over me. Never felt this desolate. Not even when my sister died. It was like being choked with someone else's misery. And yeah, maybe…' She sinks down on the bale of straw, and her head sinks into her hands. 'Maybe I should've told you earlier, but I didn't think it would actually improve my… standing.'

She looks up, and his face tells her she was dead right.

'You're saying this… experience… happened before you knew about Harry Ansell's death.'

'Several hours before. You must've known about Ansell before I did. I was in Devon.'

'You're saying it was the night that he…'

'And, conceivably, at the time it was happening. I don't know.'

The way he's looking at her, she knows he's thinking, *What the fuck use is this to me? You're not a resident, you don't matter.*

He pulls his glasses off.

'Ansell hanged himself in a wood. Not in his former bedroom.'

'In a wood, yeah. He died in a place he knew that nobody who knew him personally would find him, nobody who'd be personally affected by the sight of him. But in his mind… as he tightened the rope… we don't know where he was in his mind, do we?'

'Nor will we ever. I'm getting a headache, Grayle.'

'Yeah.'

Grayle stands up again, the cellphone throbbing in her pocket. This was going to be the opening to explaining what she now understands about Ansell's state of mind the night he died, his struggle against something in the house. The stuff that will sound even less convincing tomorrow after the paper comes out and the new Ansell sex story gets picked up by radio and TV.

'*Leo?*'

Jo's voice from the door of the live gallery.

'In here,' Defford shouts.

Sounding glad to be interrupted before he has to say something he might regret just to get rid of this unstable woman. Grayle's phone stops vibrating, as Jo comes in. She's wearing a heavyweight fleece over her fatigues, and she's out of breath.

'Leo, we have a problem.'

Defford leans back against the plywood wall.

'Just the one, Jo?'

'There's a barn on fire.'

Defford stares at her over his glasses, down his nose, like he doesn't get it. Jo maps it out with her hands.

'There's a barn full of old straw, apparently. I mean full. And... it's on fire. And old straw burns like...'

'And that started... how?'

'Nobody seems to know. We just had a call from security. But even if you just put your head out the door—'

'How far from the house?'

'Well, that's it. Not so far away we don't need to worry about it.'

'We have fire extinguishers, don't we?'

'I'm no expert, but I talked to one of the security men. He says, and I quote, using a fire extinguisher on a barn blaze is about as much use as pissing in a furnace. He was about to call the fire brigade, I said no, wait... it needed to come from you.'

'Fire engines? Sirens?' Defford lurches from the wall. 'Look, if it's only a barn, no animals or anything in there, and it's insured... it'll burn itself out eventually, won't it?'

'If it doesn't spread. Leo, we may have to evacuate the house?'

Defford is still for a moment. His eyes say they'll evacuate Knap Hall over his dead body.

'Go back in, Jo. I'll join you when I've sorted this. And get me a crew out there.'

He wants pictures of the fire? Well, of course he does. He leaves without looking at Grayle, who follows Jo back into the live gallery, where it's like nothing's happened, the residents in their candlelit time capsule, patched all over the walls, oblivious. She picks up her coat and her woolly hat and goes out into the fog, where the air's thickening and her phone's vibrating again.

It's Neil Gill.

'Is he back?'

'Ozzy? No, not that I know of.'

'You should call the police.'

'My boss—'

'Bugger your boss, you should call the police.'

Above the dull lights of the TV village, Grayle can see a billowing glow that turns the fog orange.

'Neil, I think you better tell me why.'

'I've been advised not to tell you anything, for legal reasons.'

'So you're saying I should call the cops and tell them a grown man apparently decided he wasn't gonna be availing himself of our accommodation any more and could they please organize a nationwide search?'

'You're a TV company.'

She pulls her woolly hat down over one ear and the phone and walks away from the stable and the noise of the diesel generator, towards the orange glow.

'Listen… I'm the researcher, on a short-term contract. One up the food chain from the caterers. I'm also probably the only person here who will make any kind of sense out of whatever you can tell me, and I'm not about to pass it on to anybody else. Even if I could guarantee they'd listen.'

'I don't know,' Neil Gill says. 'I'm his mate.'

'Neil—'

'We write together. We share our ideas. I tell him things, he tells me things. Things you know won't go any further because you're partners.'

'Angharad,' Grayle says. 'He tell you anything about a woman called Angharad?'

She keeps walking, as he talks, into something worse than fog.

67

Pig roast

WHILE THE SOLDIER is taking his leave, waiting for his escort out of the house, Cindy motions Helen Parrish into his corner, where the lighting isn't brilliant. Sits her in his chair, kneels beside it. He's prepared, if it comes to it, to disable her personal mic and take full responsibility, if it means she'll talk about this. Bigger than television, it is, but Helen isn't concerned.

She looks defeated.

'Cindy, I'm sure tonight's rushes are going to finish my career for good, but... I... genuinely do not remember what the bloody hell I said.' She leans her head against his shoulder. 'If I could give them back their contract in return for this never going out, and me being a hundred miles from wherever this is by tomorrow...'

He points to her mic, motions removing it. She shakes her head.

'Doesn't matter.'

'How long have you known?'

'I *didn't* know. Christ, odd things happen, they're just... odd things. Odd and useless. Maybe Diana, if I'd been on my own, without a crew and a budget to worry about... I don't know, I'm just a jobbing hack.'

He strokes her hair, says nothing.

'I'm buggered now, aren't I?'

He laughs.

She probably is.

*

The shaped bushes of the evergreen knot garden are black against the blaze, like a graveyard in front of a burning church.

That barn. The only barn it could be, and flames are already gobbling up the roof, alight almost end to end now, rafters burned through, blackened air sizzling with hot dust and chips of wood trailing fire like small comets.

Grayle watches roof tiles falling into the body of the barn. Her eyes are smarting. She's seen Eloise and Lisa Muir among groups of people watching and coughing, and Jordan on his own. Half the village must be out here. She can't see Defford.

'You in a bloody chest hospital?' Neil Gill says in her ear.

'We have a fire.'

'At the house? Are you serious?'

'In an outbuilding.'

But there's not much more than the knot garden between the barn and the oldest part of the house, where the main chamber is and all the bedrooms. They need the fire brigade, and fast. Defford must see that.

'Let me get away from here,' she croaks into the phone. 'I just needed to see how bad it was. Jeez—'

An interior explosion like a huge dragon-gasp has sent people backing off from the barn, hands and scarves clamped over their mouths. A cameraman drops to one knee, alongside a soundman with a fleeced-up boom mic, his hooded lens panning slowly across the ridge of fire which tonight is the horizon.

Neil Gill says, 'You want to call me back?'

'No, hell, Neil, I want you to keep right on talking. Go back to the word "Machiavellian".'

'Sounds daft when you say it, but that's the way he is. Too smart by half. When he's messed up emotionally, it's how he works his way through. Puts his broken heart into something. Didn't even start work on his mother-in-law till he found out Sophie was playing away.'

'His wife was…?'

Amidst the roaring and the crackling, Grayle's mentally replaying her tape of Ozzy's friendly Wiccan mother-in-law.

That lazy image – very misleading, luv. Austin has a steely determination, and he'll never give up on an idea... I could see him studying me... devising a persona for me that would sound realistic as well as being very funny... a very clever lad.

This was revenge? Recovery?

'Neil, did Ozzy actually tell you what he had in mind for *Big Other*?'

'Not directly. More a what if...? situation. He'd read this book about these people creating a ghost. The ghost of somebody imaginary, and he's going, What if you created the ghost of somebody who'd been alive and was now dead and shouldn't be? In a situation where it'd be believed without too many questions.'

'Rhys Sebold's dead girlfriend? His *friend*?'

She flounders through the murk of HGTV's amusement park, looking for a quiet place now. Passing the clock-towered stable, far enough away from the barn to keep on transmitting, as long as no cables are affected. Neil spells it out.

'Sebold has an ego the size of Greater London. He thinks everybody famous wants to be his mate and every woman wants to shag him, and a lot of the time he's not wrong. Women... he doesn't do equal. You listen to him on the radio, he's this big feminist. Away from the mic, what he likes, what he gets off on, is to be adored. Unconditionally.'

Under the sudden squawking of a fire truck in the lane, she can hear Rhiannon: *she got very starry-eyed when he started taking an interest in her.*

'Chloe... Angharad...'

'Little researcher. Did all the things for him that women are not supposed to at the ultra-feminist BBC. Rhys puts her in his pocket, takes her home. Life goes on as usual, drinking with his famous mates, one-nighters with women who adore him. You must've noticed him this week, turning it on with that Eloise before she got the elbow. And *she* thinks she hates him.'

'Angharad put up with all that.'

'Except for the drugs. It started to irritate him, her little England attitude to recreational narcotics. It was like, Oh, if you really loved me you'd at least give it a try. It's not addictive. Here's a list of Very Famous People who do it.'

'Sebold told him this?'

'Of course he didn't. Never said a word to anybody until after she was dead, and he was making a big deal about coming clean, getting his defence in first.'

The first fire engine comes howling past and she recalls Sebold on the phone.

I remember her turning round, shouting, 'It's a raid, it's a raid!' And we laughed. We laughed because some of the guys had been teasing her about being paranoid. We laughed, Grayle. We fucking laughed at her. We laughed because we thought she was winding us up.

'She walked out,' Grayle says, 'when she saw the cops, and Sebold and his pals ignored her. She walked out and she got into her car, in her white raincoat, and…'

'He wanted her to do it long before that.'

'Who did?'

'Ozzy. Leave him, Ozzy says. Leave the bastard…'

'Sebold was… listen, was there actual physical abuse?'

'Smacked her a few times, aye. Ozzy's like, Leave the bastard and…'

'What?'

'Come with me.'

'Oh, shit.'

'He met her when he was on Sebold's show. He liked her… as a person… a lot. Just friends for quite a while. Ozzy thought they were more than that, but I was never sure, to be honest. She liked the lad, he made her laugh, she confided in him. But she kept going back to Sebold. The way they do.'

'Sebold told me that Ozzy… that he'd've been at that party…'

… if he hadn't been touring Australia at the time – if I believed in something as ridiculous as astrology, I might say he'd been born under fortunate stars.

'He phoned her from Australia. On her mobile. He phoned her every night. She took her phone into the toilet, said they'd all been doing cocaine. He didn't get it. He said get out, go away somewhere. And then she saw the pigs coming and she did. She got out. Ozzy didn't know that she'd finally allowed Rhys to give her a line, just to keep the peace, or what effects that might have. She was probably feeling adventurous, thinking yeah, time to go… fuck them.'

'Oh my God.'

'Blamed himself. Ozzy. But, by Christ, not as much as he was blaming Sebold. And when he hears Sebold's about to get back in, full time, at the BBC and in the meantime he's collecting a hefty six figures from C4 for a week in a haunted house…'

Grayle stops, up against the back of the satellite van. Tonight, you can look up and barely see the white dish.

'Ahmed followed him into the house. With an agenda. His *friend.*'

'We're all friends in light entertainment. You rarely know who really hates you. How deep it goes. Everybody's an actor. He'll never be a great actor, Ozzy, but he can play himself to perfection. Whichever version you want.'

'He did that, all right. The confirmed atheist who hates ghost stories for very personal, convincing… *invented* reasons. Appalled at what's happening, refusing to accept he's psychic himself, thereby convincing everybody that he just might be.'

'You've got it.'

'He wants Sebold publicly exposed, disgraced?'

'Pilloried. Shafted. Hung out to dry in front of millions.'

'By the ghost of his girlfriend?'

'Clever, yeh? I'm thinking you'd know how that works better than me. People believe in them, don't they? Happen we all do a bit. Sometimes.'

'Estimates vary between a third and a half. In this country.'

'Chloe,' Gill says softly, close to the phone. 'Out there, still, and she's unhappy, she's distressed. And a *lot* of people knew her. And liked her. She was a researcher, they get about.'

'We do.'

'So how likely was it that some informed viewers wouldn't ring in, email, saying, Yeh, the ghost is right. And *this* is who she is. I mean people who know. Including Sebold. You could see him already covering his back, making out Ozzy was stressed out, losing his marbles, shouldn't be believed. Well, he can't say a wrong word to Ozzy – they're on TV… constantly. Where Ozzy knew he'd stay the distance. The comedian never gets evicted. He'd knew he'd get that name out before the end of the week. Angharad. Shit hits fan.'

'Sebold turned over the table before the name could be spelled out in full?'

'Really would be the end for him. Papers'd be all over him like flies.'

'But then Ashley, of all people…'

'What a bugger that was. Not expecting it from her. And being exposed as a phoney, that'd get him evicted for sure, if anything could.'

'So he gets himself out.'

'Buying himself some time.'

'Only then Sebold decides to follows him out,' Grayle says, breathing harder. 'Sebold does the one thing guaranteed to offend most viewers. He repeatedly insults Helen Parrish, who everybody likes. They… need to talk, don't they, Ahmed and Sebold. Without every word getting recorded.'

'Ozzy wouldn't want that. Not how he works. Doesn't lose his temper.'

'So you think he left when he heard Sebold was coming out?

To avoid confrontation. Maybe intending to come back for the reunion on Sunday.'

'And finish the job? I don't know. That's why I'm worried. It's a bloody time bomb, Grayle. Sebold has everything to lose. And Ozzy hasn't finished the job. Let's get him found, eh?'

The big oak door swings opens, and – how surreal – there's a man in a yellow suit and a helmet, a lamp in his hand and young Jo Shepherd at his shoulder.

'Sorry, sorry, sorry, people. Unscheduled intermission. The cameras have been turned off. I'm *really* sorry about this, but there's a fire in an outbuilding, and you're being evacuated.'

Cindy stands up. The man introduces himself as a senior officer from Winchcombe Community Fire and Rescue. A precautionary measure, he explains, but necessary. Jo tells them it won't affect tonight's programme and they won't be out long.

Nobody questions it. Institutionalized, they are, filing out, like children at the school fire-drill, up the few steps into the stone passage, where electric lights come on and even Ashley is momentarily blinded.

'Like moles, we are,' Cindy says.

He looks back at Helen Parrish, who shrugs, and they leave by the chapel yard and the walled garden, all of it smothered in a surprising fog, through which the fireman's lamp makes a solid corridor. It's bitter cold and the air stinks. The fireman tells him to keep close to the wall of the house which Cindy finds is warm to the touch and damp.

Around the side of the house, searchlights blast through steam and fog, into an open space where fat hoses intersect. A wasteland where bushes have been ripped up, flattened, gouged out of the ground, the whole area scattered with half-burned bales, burst and steaming. A fire engine has ploughed through one corner of this war zone which Cindy now recognizes, sorrowfully, as the remains of Trinity's knot garden.

The fire appears to have been subdued, but lumps of burning wood are widely scattered and there are small moments of erratic combustion.

'Don't stop to look,' the fireman warns. 'Just go round to the front of the house. Don't get separated.'

'There's a restaurant,' Jo says. 'Order whatever you like, but please don't talk to anyone or I'll lose my job.'

Bizarrely, even as she says the word 'restaurant', Cindy smells food – momentarily, through the smoke, the smell of a pig roast, and he sees their fireman being beckoned urgently by another.

'How did this start, Jo?'

'Cindy, we really don't know anything. Can we trust you not to speak to anyone? Even about the fire.'

'Of course you can trust us,' Helen says, irritated. 'You own us.'

Cindy follows behind the others, the only one of them who knows where he's going. Then he slows down and finally stops, watching the others vanish into the TV encampment, before turning and walking back into the wall of yellowy fog, silk scarf over his mouth, following his nose. Crossing the pools of water to where a wall of the barn has all but collapsed, he can see two firemen and a firewoman grouped inside, lamp beams pooled, and a fourth officer being noisily sick.

In this roofless shell, blackened bales lie around in the water.

Also something curled like a large, black, bloated embryo, knees bent, fists half-closed, all the hair gone from its charred and flaking head.

'You don't want to see this, madam.'

A fire officer taking his arm.

68

Presenter

THE ASH TREE is spectral against the obscured sky, all those upswung fog-softened boughs steady, like it's holding out its candles to be lit.

They won't be. Too far away from the fire and on higher ground, higher than the house, higher than the burning barn. Grayle's so glad to see the old sanctuary, a safe, known viewpoint beyond the village boundary, and she makes her way towards it, stepping carefully through the stiffening grass as the lights fall away behind her.

Still talking into the cellphone.

'Neither of them's a hero now, Neil. Not with all the collateral damage. The schoolteacher, Dave, who Ahmed made into a paedophile? All the people in the house who are either sincere in their beliefs, or their non-beliefs. All the people in the house… *most* of whom were sincere.'

'Oh, come on.' Neil Gill, scornful. 'They're all getting paid more than they're worth. End of the day, it's just television.'

'Makes us all look stupid. And Ahmed look obsessive, manipulative… and kind of cruel.'

'And Sebold? Have we forgotten what *he* did? What he is?'

'Power-crazed bully, desperate to save his career? What's *he* gonna do now? Go crawling to Ahmed, plead with him to stop all this? Beg his forgiveness for abusing the woman he loved? Really?'

Of all things that can possibly happen now, it's not gonna be that. They're way beyond forgiveness and redemption and into an area where control's out the window and reactions come fast and blind.

Grayle's shaking.

'One thing, Neil.'

'No, that's your lot. I'm finished, Grayle. Said too much already. Go and tell… thingy.'

'Defford.'

This time he'll be receptive. It's not rational, but at least nothing metaphysical is involved.

'Best thing,' Neil Gill says.

'Yeah, OK. Thank you, Neil. You cleared up a mystery. Not that it's gonna make anybody here feel good.'

'Be careful, eh?'

'You're thinking Ozzy's still here, right?'

'Could be.'

'There's a thick fog around the house. Big house. Could be in there. Could be standing right next to me, and I wouldn't know.'

'Try feeding him a line,' Neil Gill says. 'That nearly always works.'

'I might do that.'

From up here by the ash, HGTV is mostly buried under solid air. Even the orange glow of the burning barn is a tiny light at the end of a sulphurous tunnel, the blaze hosed down to a spark. Everything hosed down.

Killing the call, Grayle stares towards the fuzzy lights of the TV village, calls out in frustration.

'Ozzy?'

Thinking now about the night of the raid on Rhys Sebold's place. Chloe, who is really Angharad, taking a call from Ahmed in Australia, whispering to him about the cocaine. Him saying, 'Get out, go away somewhere'. And later blaming *himself*.

Why? No, really, why? Not like he told her to get into her car and head for the M25.

So who tipped off the cops in the first place? Must've been a hundred middle-class homes in that area where people were putting white powder into their nostrils that night.

Ozzy calling the British cops from Australia? Unlikely. But suppose Ozzy called Neil? Good old *said too much already* Neil.

God-*damn*. Grayle walks head down into the fog, climbing onto higher ground, clawing for enlightenment. Sensing movement behind her, she spins around.

'Ozzy?'

Hell, it's not very big, the village, and, if he's here, he's more likely to be at this end than watching the fire in full view of the people he crapped on.

'Listen, I know you're here, and I know *why* you're here. And about the woman in the white coat. The one who isn't called Angela?'

Is that breathing?

'And I'm truly sorry for your loss. And I see why you felt the need to hit back. But you… you didn't have to screw Defford and his programme with your… your own private production. That was just ego, your need to perform. To *out*-perform. Bottom line, you're an asshole, Ozzy.'

Can't even see the house, but she feels the rolling resentment. Whether he knew it or not, the house was helping Ozzy. Providing a mould for his fantasies. Maybe even letting him see what he wanted them all to believe he was seeing.

The house connives.

'Come on! Come outta there!'

She hears the words coming back at her, realises she's half screaming, hoarsely, into the polluted night. Damn place is taking her head apart. The air's like concrete, like stone, like the medium which formed the faces on Winchcombe church with their bulging eyes and howling mouths.

And he comes out.

'Something like this happens…'

The drawly voice is low and reflective and almost conversational, like they were already talking and got interrupted. He's wandering over, developing out of the fog.

'... it makes you realise how flimsy and inconsequential it all is.'

Wrong guy. She pushes both hands into her coat pockets, fists forming, one around her cellphone. How long has he been with her? How much has he heard?

She says, 'Something like what?'

'The fire. It's all too real, isn't it? While you're spending millions examining childish fantasies we all should've grown out of long, long ago.'

'Not me, Rhys. I'm just the hired help. Anyway, isn't that what most TV is? Fantasy?'

'*No*, actually,' he says, irritated. 'Good TV can be penetrating and informative.'

Oh yeah, wrong guy all right. Grayle takes the phone out of her pocket and puts it into flashlight mode, keeping it pointing down, away from him; there's enough light to see he's wearing an expensive black leather jacket and gloves.

'My money's on Eloise,' he says.

'Huh?'

'For the fire. Terrifying psychiatric issues, that woman. Buys a house that's been burned down with someone inside, claims it was started deliberately. Nobody believes her. Comes here looking for more publicity and she's the first to get evicted. Because *still* nobody believes her. So furious. Didn't you see that? She's thinking, how can I possibly draw attention to myself now?'

He's talking fast and excitedly like he sometimes did at the start of his radio programme. Like the show's already moving and he just swung into his seat. Grayle's shaking her head in disbelief.

'Start a fire? You truly think that?'

'Didn't say it made any logical sense, but it might to her. Retribution. She's flakey. Pity the fucking house didn't catch fire, too, don't you think?'

'I might agree with you there.'

'I couldn't stand any more of it. Worst kind of claustrophobia. Banged up with mad people. Eccentrics. People who can't handle real life, want to make their own worlds. Herridge – how did that man ever get elected to the Mother of Parliaments? Sad little man who wants to see a ghost. *Who*... has ever... seen a ghost? They see pale circles of fucking light on a fucking wall.' His hands are fixing shapes on the fog. '...and there's a cold draught... and that... *that* proves there's a *fucking God*?'

'Probably doesn't.'

Aw hell, the white powder went up there tonight all right, and not too long ago.

'Do you know where my phone is, by the way?'

'I'm sorry?'

'You had it in the restaurant, Grayle. You were talking to the waitress and you had my phone on the table.'

He was following her, *back then*? She shuts her eyes in dismay, fingers knotting on the hand that's in her pocket.

'As you know, we check phones, the residents' phones, for anything that might be important, so you don't get disturbed, but at the same time—'

'And *was* there? Something important?'

'I just called someone back and told her you weren't available right now.'

'And do you know where it is? My phone?'

'I—'

He holds up a leather-gloved hand.

'It's here.'

Her teeth set tight. So he saw her in the restaurant, maybe through the door. Followed her out under cover of fog. Waited for her to come out of Defford's meeting and saw her putting the phone on Kate's desk. From where he retrieved it. And it looks like he's been following her ever since. Not good. At all.

Sebold says, 'What did you tell her?'

'Who?'

'Rhiannon.'

'I told her we couldn't allow the residents to make or take calls that might identify the location. Which she understood.'

'And what did *she* tell *you*?'

Problem is, he may have called Rhiannon up himself. He might know all of this. Also, he could've heard her talking to the fog and, earlier, to Neil Gill.

She talks carefully.

'The initials that came out in the seance. Rhiannon told me it wasn't Angela. Told me what the letters ANG might've gone on to become if some asshole hadn't turned the table over.'

'I see.'

She's aware of him swinging his arms in the swirling air.

She says, 'You, uh, talked to Ozzy, since you both came out the house?'

'Why would I want to talk to Ozzy?'

'You and he… seem to have had issues. As they say.'

'Everyone has issues.' He pauses. 'I read about your sister.'

Grayle sighs. This is what he does.

'Because of whom,' she says, 'I am just a little famous.'

'You flatter yourself.'

'But, see, why would you bother to check me out, anyway, Rhys? Not like I'm ever gonna be on your show.'

'You were investigating me, I investigated you. Finding out that, while your sister was a respectable scientific scholar, you are as loopy as the rest of the losers in this dump, and Defford only hired you because you could talk their language.' Didn't he?' He shouts into her face. 'CORRECT?'

'This is… partly true. I do like to fool myself that there may be levels of awareness to which we can aspire.'

And other levels to which we can subside, deteriorate. Grayle doesn't move. They're not on his show now, they're on what's left of hers.

'So Rhys, when did you realise Ozzy wasn't your friend after all?'

Silence, then he says: 'You little bitch.'

'I guess. But then we're not supposed to be, are we?'

'What?'

'Friends. Celebrities and journalists. Not supposed to be friends.'

They have no common ground, her and Sebold. He's not even a real journalist, he's a *presenter*. She recalls from her research that he was a big supporter of the Hacked Off movement set up to handcuff the press after the big celebrity phone-hacking scandal. OK, hacking's bad, but some celebs were just grabbing a chance to hide sordid secrets.

These matters should not be hidden for ever, says Mary-Ann Rutter in Grayle's head. *Or if the stories are passed on as gossip they'll lose whatever truth they possessed and become legends.*

She watches Sebold's arms fanning the fog. A rural fog turned dark and urban by a fire, and he's an urban man and he doesn't look for the moon. She's in control here, this is her place, and she knows everything. She feels an unexpected exhilaration.

'So how're you and Ahmed gonna work this out? I mean about Chloe.'

'Chloe,' he says, 'is dead. GONE. OVER.'

'Gone over?'

'Don't you *dare* play with my words.'

'All I meant—'

His face bends to hers.

'Never fuck… with a power-crazed bully, desperate to save his career.'

Oh shit. Worst case scenario. She can only pretend she doesn't get the reference, that it means nothing to her.

Change the subject, just talk.

'You don't know' – she starts shifting quietly away towards where the distant orange fire has dulled to rust – 'that it was Ozzy pushing the planchette. Even Ozzy can't be sure. There's always that thin bar of… light.'

Lets her cellphone flashlight tilt a little, so she can see his face: narrow and strong-boned, wide-mouthed under side-razored hair, heavy on top. Aggressively inquisitive. It's how he sees himself. And the coke: you can almost hear the rapids in his brain. She lets the light shine directly into his eyes, and his head jerks away – another sign.

He's a big man, gym-fit and, as his head avoids the light, his shoulder and arm are bending away like they're powered by hydraulics. When they swing back, his leather-gloved hand is open and it's like a car-crash in her face.

'*Thin—*'

'Oh, G—'

Her head spins round so fast it feels like he's broken her neck, and she doesn't even see his other hand come round like the boom of a yacht in a gale, his voice hissing through it.

'*Bar of—*'

Her feet leaving the ground, and she's barely aware of the first hand swinging back and—

'—*light?*'

A distorting crack, agony exploding in an ear, and she's hurled away, feet sliding from under her, through thick air into a solid wall. The ash tree. She bounces off its bole, winded, and then she's curled up and retching. Her lips won't form words, not even a scream. Her necks twists, mouth dribbling too-thick saliva into the grass.

'*You hit me.*'

The words, so clear in her head, come out thick and muddy, with a salty slick.

Creak, creak. Flexing of fingers in leather gloves, and he snorts.

'Never laid a finger on you. Where are you? You must've walked into a low branch in the fog. Where are you?'

She throws up her hands, the phone still in one. Cowering against the tree, hurting so much. The pain is white, the fog around Rhys Sebold is blue, not the blue of a summer sky or the midnight blue of a fine night but the dirty blue of mouldy bread, and then the night… it's like the night yawns and, with her ears popping, she glimpses another figure, wire-thin, moving fitfully out of a hollow in the fog, bringing its own sour light. Half-seen, sporadic: here, gone, here, gone.

Through the slits of her wounded eyes she can still make out Sebold standing there, some distance away, the faint, woolly lights of the TV village behind him. His arms are swinging again, coke energy, and he's shouting something she can't hear. He's in a different place.

A trickle of cold is parting Grayle's coat. She chokes on the smell of earth and shit and leather, perceiving something sliding like a lizard inside a dull and oily glow, and then cold, old fingers are exploring her stiffening body, squeezing and pinching and probing, fast and feverish.

Aware of Sebold watching. The presenter. The presenter presenting. Breathing in someone else's warm, raw-meat breath, pulsing with revulsion, Grayle tries to squirm away.

Can't.

Sebold comes forward, and she can feel his excitement as he bends to her, and she can't move, as the presenter presents.

Greetings, greetings.

PART SEVEN

What you remember from the night

If your answer is that you are more than a biological accident whose ultimately meaningless life is bounded by the cradle and the grave, then I have to say I agree with you.

David Fontana
Is There An Afterlife? (2005)

69

Victims reunited

THE FOG HAS gone, like soiled sheets crumpled and thrown in the wash, leaving the sky pale and shocked, as they enter the walled garden at first light.

The stone is still in place. A loose stone that Cindy dragged from the wall to wedge open the electrically controlled door of the chapel.

'You did this last night?' Helen says. 'You came back? On your own?'

'No problem, with everyone watching the fire, cameras switched off.'

He holds open the door for her and follows her into the chapel where a liquid cherry light envelops them.

Helen says, 'What've you done?'

Cindy collects some of the broken wooden panels, puts them in a neat pile. Thinner than they looked while in place across the window, boxing in the stained glass. Easy enough, even in darkness, to splinter the wood, careful not to damage the two cameras.

Not that they'll be needed any more. *Big Other* is already history.

Helen stares up, above the scraped wall where the altar was.

'This… was always here? Directly behind us as we talked. Is it the Virgin Mary?'

'No, no.'

'It's a triptych,' Helen says. 'The same woman.'

'She used to live here.'

'Defford covered her up?'

'On the off chance she might be recognised. Doesn't matter now. Now that *Big Other* is history.'

He learned this a couple of hours ago from Defford himself, over a pot of coffee in the restaurant, after the bodies had been taken away and the more senior police had left. HGTV is now pulling together two long documentary programmes. Rescue programmes. Better than rescue, he'll sell them all over the world. They'll be *true crime* programmes. Neither of them will involve the paranormal. You could feel Defford's relief.

Cindy felt none. Cindy was in agony.

Too late. Too late again. He looks up into the exposed window, at the wide lips half smiling, the demurely lowered eyelids, the wine-dark cloak, the rubies. Close to weeping, he turns away to face another woman, more rubies glinting in the florid light projected through the stained glass to the back wall of the chapel.

Helen, following his eyes, flinches.

'Oh my God.'

Cindy sighs.

'Easier than I expected. The poor queen wasn't secured to the wall of the chamber. They probably didn't have time. And she wasn't all that heavy. And grateful to be out of there, aren't you, lovely?'

'She looks different. I mean less...'

'Heavy? Of course she does.'

'Bloody hell, Cindy...'

'Of course, it was too late.'

'You really think that if you'd got it out earlier... or if it had never been done in the first place...?'

'Helen, I don't know. How can any of us know?'

'The two women in the picture... that the guy told us about?'

'Both victims.'

'Reunited.'

'Not really. Just sharing a sanctuary.'

'I wonder if that picture ever existed.'

'Doesn't matter, does it?'

'I suppose not. Nothing gets believed in the end. All these bits of evidence for the unexplained.'

'Meaningless,' Cindy says. 'Just like Mr Defford's programme. It's an interior thing, it is. As you probably realize now.'

'God yeah.' Helen turns back to the stained glass. 'I don't think I'm the same person any more. I don't think I'll be the same person again.'

In the rosy light, she looks rather young. He watches her and tries not to think of the two bodies he saw before they were taken away. Helen looks up at the woman she hasn't yet recognized.

'Thank you, Mr Defford,' she says.

She doesn't know about Grayle.

70

Parameters

'WHAT DO YOU remember after that?'

This is Max.

'I remember him, you know, pulling at my clothes?'

'You just remember him doing that, not how he *came* to be doing it. How the – I'm sorry to ask stuff like this – how the sexual impetus took over from the plain violence.'

'Maybe I lost consciousness, I don't know.'

Max, the shrink, in the outsiders' interview lounge. Daylight, fogless. A digital recorder on his chair arm. She's on the sofa with the medieval bestiary, folding herself into gryphons and unicorns. Whichever way she's sitting, she gets some pain.

'This is...' Max leans towards her, hands together like he's praying. '...this is what you told the police, right?'

'That's what I said, yeah.'

The police took pictures of her face. Both eyes, swellings of red and purple and black. Later embossed with drying blood. She never wants to see those pictures, souvenirs of the rape suite, where no signs of rape were evident.

'How do you feel about it now, about what might have happened?'

'You mean do I need counselling?' She laughs, actually manages to laugh. 'Who you gonna find who could counsel me, Max? *Who?*'

Max doesn't reply. She leans back. Pain.

'I feel... fortunate. Like I came through something I was not supposed to come through. And I think of others who didn't.'

'You were afraid. Well, I mean, obviously…'

'I was more afraid than I've ever been in my life, and I'm afraid now just thinking about it. Afraid in ways I did not understand. And now I've told you more than I told the cops.'

Whole lot more. But still not the half of it.

'When you say others who didn't come through…'

'I don't just mean others who offended Rhys Sebold. When I say others, I might be going into areas where a guy like you would not, uh, want his professional colleagues to know he'd ever ventured.'

He nods.

'But Grayle… you do realize you're the only one who can tell us any of what happened. The only independent witness. Now that Sebold's dead.'

Max is responsible for overseeing the mental health of all of them, including staff, even though *Big Other* has been suspended for reasons apparent to anyone who reads papers or the Internet, or tunes into radio or TV news.

Or who knows Leo Defford, sole owner of those wonderful high-definition shots of Ozzy Ahmed's fire-crisped corpse still smoking in a burned-out barn. Of Rhys Sebold before the cops came.

And of the man who killed him.

'When were you first aware of the other man?' Max asks.

'Which other man?'

Shit. Mistake. Wrong to relax with Max.

He looks at her with curiosity, but if there was more than one other man, he doesn't need to know. He wouldn't understand any more than the cops would have. The second *other man*, if such he was or had ever been, is outside the parameters of his discipline, always will be.

'Jordan? He was just there. I didn't see where he came from. Didn't recognize him at first. He was just… like someone else pasted on the fog behind Sebold. But the spade…'

She recalls her cellphone lying in the grass in the flashlight mode. Its tiny LED bubble, uptilted, is reflected from a rectangular blade of stainless steel, worn thin. A bright star in the spade.

'Did he speak?'

'He shouted something out. I don't recall what it… I was pretty much out of it, in ways…'

In ways she won't be telling him about.

'Did you see what he did next?'

'Some of it. He saw what was happening. I'm assuming he'd also seen Ahmed's body in the barn. He knows the barn. And he saw the blood on my face. See, he couldn't have had much time to think. And Sebold's a bigger man than him. And visibility was not good. So when Sebold turned and went for him, he struck out blindly. That was how it looked to me. He didn't know if Sebold had a weapon. He just reacted.'

'You saw what happened. I'm sorry, Grayle, this must be awful for you. Very raw, still.'

'I heard it.' She swallows, her shoulders tightening. Pain. 'The spade made a kind of whine in the air. Or maybe it didn't. That's just how I hear it now. Or a keening. The blade is travelling very fast, like it's slicing through the fog. And then I heard something fall. Like when a coconut falls out of a tree? I never actually saw that happen, only on TV, where they kind of boost the sound of it landing. *Thunk*.' Her swollen lips shape what she guesses is a truly ghastly smile. 'You don't invariably get the truth on TV.'

'So I've heard,' Max says gravely. 'So Jordan…'

'He may have saved my life. That's what I told the police.'

'And what else?'

'Nothing else,' Grayle says, resolute.

This is what frightens her so very much.

She needs advice, though not from Max.

Is she right to keep quiet?

Has Abel's Rent been paid?

71

In the old and proper sense

'WHAT DO YOU remember after that?'

This is Cindy Mars-Lewis the next night.

Twinset and pearls, matching beret, under the ex-hospital Anglepoise in the bastard bungalow in Broadway. Marcus is behind his desk, making notes. A small sofa has been installed which Grayle shares with Malcolm, the white English bull-terrier with psychotic eyes.

'Just give me a couple minutes,' Grayle says. 'Let me go over it again in my head.'

Like she hasn't already done this, before she took the sleeping pill, after the sleeping pill wore off. And God knows how many times in between.

Before she left Knap Hall at dusk, she had a fortifying coffee in the restaurant with Roger Herridge.

'It's all right.' Herridge looking into her multi-coloured eyes. 'I'm not going to ask. I know how long you've spent with the police.'

He was wearing jeans and a sweatshirt with holes in the elbows. His hair was in slabs.

'It's been a travesty,' he said.

'Kind of.'

'Nothing happened for us, did it?'

'You think?'

'Oh, *a lot* happened. Two of us… two of us *died*.'

'But in the original *Big Other* context…'

'Quite.'

Grayle recalls feeling strangely relaxed.

'You know, it's weird, Roger. And yet it's not. There's this friend of mine who always tells you that it – *it* – is never gonna play to your rules. I look back over the last few days, and think who amongst the seven had an inexplicable experience. Cindy? Uh huh. Not what he expected. Maybe not what he was even used to. Ozzy – well who knows? He'd be in denial, anyway. Helen? Maybe. Maybe Helen – though she wouldn't admit it even to herself – came here to find out.'

'As did I.'

'Yeah, but you *wanted* it.'

'The time it'll actually happen is when I *don't* want it?'

'Count on that.'

Roger started stirring his big cup of coffee like it was a cauldron.

'I'd rather it happened to one of our party leaders, wipe away the inane smugness... or perhaps that prune-faced woman in the shadow cabinet who...' he began to laugh. 'I just wanted to know that the world was more than these people. The idiots whose company I once craved.'

'Ashley,' Grayle says. 'You thought about Ashley?'

'Really?'

'Worth keeping an eye on what Ashley's writing from now on, listening to what she's saying.'

Before she left the village, Grayle looked around for Ashley, but she seemed to have left.

A lot to think about.

Cindy, though serious tonight, seems happier, less absurd. She's watched him with Helen Parrish. He's spoken of a *spiritual dalliance.*

'Something else was there?'

'Oh yeah. I know there was.'

Cindy says, 'So the hands...'

'If hands they were... they weren't Sebold's. Least, not after he hit me.'

Hands that don't recognize clothing. *Trust terror, little else is safe*. She stares at Marcus, with his heavy glasses and his iron-grey hair. He and Cindy, these are guys – the only guys – she *could* tell, but not yet. She came here mainly so Andy Anderson could do some healing, work on the pain. Andy's good with pain on so many levels. She knows what Marcus wants to ask but nobody is ever going to be able to confirm to him if Abel Fishe wore leather or had fair hair. Or what he smelled of. Nobody.

Marcus says. 'I'm sorry, Underhill.'

Cindy says, 'Tell me this is hindsight, if you like, but when I saw the state of the knot garden after the fire I thought, this will not end well.'

Hearing the soft bump, seeing that the silhouette is shorter – these are the impressions the subconscious will store for nightmare material. And the thick rain. The thick rain on your face. And the spade, time-honed, earth-honed, wielded by a very strong man. A haunted man, a walking secret.

'Maybe I should've talked to Jordan more. Wasn't that he was unapproachable or unfriendly, just the kind of guy who if he doesn't want you to know something waterboarding wouldn't get it out of him.'

'He's still in custody?'

'No, Marcus, he's home. For now, anyway. I talked to Fred Potter. Fred has good cop contacts. They're guessing the CPS won't like Jordan for murder or manslaughter. Even though the edge of the spade hit Sebold's throat so hard that his head just…' Grayle laughs, too shrilly. 'Maybe there's a charge of like being in possession of an offensive horticultural implement.'

'Seems little doubt,' Marcus says, 'that Ahmed was murdered by Sebold.'

'Fred Potter figures that's down to forensics and the autopsy. Maybe a head injury before the straw got pulled over him. And lit.'

Maybe he wasn't dead then. Maybe they'll find that out, maybe not. No witnesses. Nobody saw them together. What Grayle keeps recalling is Sebold's radio interview with Eloise where she says the killers of Alison Cross got away with it on account of fire destroys DNA. And Sebold trying to tell her Eloise had to be in the frame for firing the barn.

She's concealed from the police none of what she's learned about Sebold and Ahmed and Angharad. All of it uncovered while she was doing her job, legitimate inquiries in the context of the programme. So far today, Kate Lyons has turned away over fifty journalists who want to talk to her about the best celebrity deaths for several years.

She won't be talking to anyone. At some stage, she and Marcus will tell this story. Marcus in his book, *In Defence of Mystery*, or whatever it gets to be called. And maybe she'll write about it, too, for whatever outlet is prepared to publish it in full. And she'll talk to Helen Parrish and the camerawoman, Jess Taylor. Even Ashley Palk. It all needs to come out, even if it's only to keep faith with Mary Ann Rutter.

With whom she talked on the phone today. This time about Jordan Aspenwall. Brought up by his grandparents in Winchcombe. His grandmother mainly, the old man was a wastrel. His grandmother took care of Jordan.

She wonders how close he actually came to talking about it, that day on the lawn in front of Knap Hall.

'*You remember the holiday home for bad kids?*'

'*Weren't the best idea. Boys didn't even get locked up at night.*'

'*The girl? Is she… still around?*'

'*Dead.*'

'*What… recently?*'

'*Year or so after it happened. Brutal. Nasty. Couldn't live with it. Took her own life.*'

This was the day Jordan, horticulturalist, man of science, advised her to talk to Mrs Rutter about Abel's Rent. Pretending he didn't know too much about it. '*All this spirits of the dead stuff, I got no patience with that, look. It's just an old house.'*

Everybody lies, especially at Knap Hall.

'The incident at the home for bad boys,' Mrs Rutter said today. *'Well, I learned all about that from Billy, my husband. Billy was the first policeman on the scene. Had the barn cordoned off. The boy had kept her in the barn all night, you see. He was fourteen and unbelievably brutal. When he was first questioned by Billy he said he thought he'd killed her. He said he thought she was dead, so it didn't really matter what he did to her. Diabolical was Billy's word. In the old and proper sense.'*

Grayle asked Mrs Rutter the name of the girl. It was Martha Worth. She was fifteen. Married quite soon afterwards, soon as she turned sixteen. The child was not her husband's.

A couple hours ago, Grayle forced herself to go up to the Ansells' apartment, the stabbing pains in her bones and sinews that made every stair an ordeal dulling any residual fear, twisting it into anger.

Someone had taken down the boards from the window so you could look down on the remains of the knot garden, view it the way it was meant to be viewed. Despite the damage, you could can still make out the shape of the two intersecting letters at its heart.

'You told me about the shrine,' Marcus says. 'In the barn.'

'Yeah.' Grayle nodding. 'Just a few religious items. I shouldn't think they're there all the time. Maybe a small, private – like *very* private – ceremony was enacted, to mark an anniversary.'

'I doubt,' Cindy says, 'that Trinity told him where to put the knot garden. She was always happy to take advice from an expert. Another memorial, perhaps?' He looks at Grayle, raising a neatly-plucked eyebrow. 'What *did* you hear Jordan say – that neither you nor he told the police?'

Here we go.

'He just…' Grayle gazes through the window at dim lights. 'He tossed the spade on Sebold's body and he said… *For my mother.*'

NOTES AND CREDITS

As usual, very little needed making up.

The second official funeral of Katherine Parr actually happened at Sudeley in 2012. Her body *was* found in the ruins of the chapel after the Civil War, in remarkable condition inside its lead packaging. And yes, it was interfered with. Much of this can be found in Emma Dent's *Annals of Winchcombe and Sudeley* (British Library General Historical Collections). In the 1830s, Lord Rivers sold the castle to members of the Dent family, who, through the generations, made it into the jewel it is today.

Mark Turner's *Mysterious Gloucestershire* (The History Press) reveals some of the nasty stuff.

Belas Knap is a steep walk, not easily found but well worth it, if you can't resist that kind of place. Paul Devereux's *Haunted Land* (Piatkus) looks at its reputation for strange phenomena, with a first-hand account of approaching monks. Julian Cope's *The Modern Antiquarian* (Thorsons) draws attention to one particular feature. Catherine Owers described an experience at Belas Knap scary enough to send her running from the mound.

Winchcombe Church features some of the most celebrated stone grotesques in the country and, while a few might be satirical, some are seriously scary and not sculpted at a time when there was much of a taste for spoof-horror.

Richard Wiseman's *Paranormality* (Pan) was well-thumbed by Ashley Palk, just as Diana Norman's *The Stately Ghosts of England* (Dorset Press) must surely have been consulted by Roger Herridge. Diana, who also wrote as Ariana Franklin, was a great, underacclaimed historical novelist who was spontaneously generous to me.

Many thanks, as always, to the tireless Mairead Reidy for uncovering some of the authentic history and coming up with Emma Dent's classic volume. Allan Watson for putting his immortal soul on the line.

And Cindy sends his thanks, for the journey, to John Matthews, working shaman, authority on all things Celtic and author of more books than you could fit on this page, notably Cindy's bible (though you'll never get him to admit it) *The Celtic Shaman* (Rider).

Thanks to Megan and Chris Stuart for putting me on to…

… Gavin Henderson, TV producer with serious *Big Brother* credentials, who was hugely helpful from the start and throughout the writing. Any technical implausibilities are entirely down to me and the demands of *Big Other*, as are the less-than-ethical methods employed by Leo Defford.

Many thanks to Sara O'Keefe and Maddie West at Corvus, who got the idea from the beginning, to Louise Cullen and Liz Hatherell for excellent fine-tuning. And, as ever, to my wife, Carol, who spent weeks editing the manuscript with her usual precision and (literary) scepticism and came up with the programme title *Big Other* before this book was even begun. After that, no going back.